A Note From The Author:

Dear Reader,

Stories about love and friendship are welcome additions to any season, and yet I think they are especially appropriate to inspire *Summer Dreams*.

These three stories are very special to me because they celebrate the warmth and joy of friendship in all its various forms—childhood friends, male buddies and friendship that brings generations closer together. In my opinion, friendship is the foundation on which other relationships are built.

I, too, am an avid reader, and I find myself writing about people and places that I like to read about. Being able to write for Silhouette Books has been one of the greatest joys of my life. It is my chance to share my dreams with you, dear reader.

Happy summer!

Sincerely,
Annette Broadrick

Books by Annette Broadrick

Silhouette Romance

Circumstantial Evidence #329
Provocative Peril #359
Sound of Summer #412
Unheavenly Angel #442
Strange Enchantment #501
Mystery Lover #533
That's What Friends Are For #544
Come Be My Love #609
A Love Remembered #676
Married?! #742
The Gemini Man #796

Silhouette Books

Silhouette Christmas Stories 1988
"Christmas Magic"

Silhouette Desire

Hunter's Prey #185
Bachelor Father #219
Hawk's Flight #242
Deceptions #272
Choices #283
Heat of the Night #314
Made in Heaven #336
Return to Yesterday #360
Adam's Story #367
Momentary Marriage #414
With All My Heart #433
A Touch of Spring #464
Irresistible #499
A Loving Spirit #552
Candlelight For Two #577
Lone Wolf #666

ANNETTE BROADRICK

lives on the shores of Lake of the Ozarks in Missouri, where she spends her time doing what she loves most—reading and writing romance fiction. Since 1984 when her first book was published, Annette has been delighting her readers with her imaginative and innovative style. In addition to being nominated by *Romantic Times* as one of the Best New Authors of that year, she has also won *Romantic Times* Reviewer's Choice Award for Best in its Series for *Heat of the Night*, *Mystery Lover* and *Irresistible*, *Romantic Times* WISH Award for her hero in *Strange Enchantment* and *Romantic Times* Lifetime Achievement Award for Series Romance.

Annette Broadrick

Summer Dreams

Silhouette Books®

Published by Silhouette Books New York

America's Publisher of Contemporary Romance

SILHOUETTE BOOKS
300 E. 42nd St., New York, N.Y. 10017

SUMMER DREAMS edition
Copyright © 1991 by Harlequin Enterprises Ltd.

ISBN: 0-373-15188-8

This edition printed in June 1991.

The publisher acknowledges the copyright holders of the individual works as follows:

THAT'S WHAT FRIENDS ARE FOR
Copyright © 1987 Annette Broadrick
First published as a Silhouette Romance.

COME BE MY LOVE
Copyright © 1988 Annette Broadrick
First published as a Silhouette Romance.

A LOVE REMEMBERED
Copyright © 1989 Annette Broadrick
First published as a Silhouette Romance.

Contents

That's What Friends Are For

★

ANNETTE BROADRICK

For Faye—
A new friend, an old soul.

IOWA

NEBRASKA

Payton

ILLINOIS

KANSAS

• Kansas City

Missouri River

St. Louis

MISSOURI

Underlined places are fictitious.

N

ARKANSAS

Chapter One

A soft summer breeze gently caressed Penny's bikini-clad body. The muted sound of water lapping against the dock where she lay provided a rhythmic accompaniment to the periodic melodies of the birds who made their homes near the shores of Tawakoni Lake.

Penny Blackwell had always enjoyed summer and the opportunity to do nothing more strenuous than work on her tan. Being indolent made a pleasant contrast to the hectic schedule she followed the rest of the year.

She smiled to herself. In another week her usual summer routine would be changing permanently. The tempo of her life would doubtless be increased to the point where days like today would be very rare.

"That's a very secretive smile you're wearing these days, Runt," a deep male voice said from somewhere close by. "I find it quite provocative."

Penny's eyes flew open in shock, not only because she'd thought she was alone but also because that voice from her past should have been two thousand miles away.

"Brad!"

She was suddenly conscious of what a small portion of her body her bathing suit covered. Penny grabbed her matching cover-up robe, and with strangely uncoordinated movements for someone normally graceful, she pulled it on jerkily.

"What are you doing here?" After her first glimpse at the man towering above her, she refused to look up again.

Penny knew very well what Brad Crawford looked like. In that quick glance she'd seen that the only item of clothing he wore was a pair of faded cutoffs that should have been discarded years ago. They hung perilously low on his hips.

"Is that any greeting for a friend and neighbor whom you haven't seen in three years?" he asked. Without making an obvious effort, Brad leaned over and picked her up, placing her on her feet in front of him. Even with Penny standing, Brad continued to tower over her, the top of her head coming only to his collarbone. No one else had the ability to make her as aware of her lack of inches as Brad Crawford.

He slid his hand under her chin and lifted her face until he looked directly into her eyes. "You're looking even more beautiful than I remembered," he said, the warmth in his gaze adding heat to her already sun-kissed body, "and I didn't think I had forgotten anything about you." He paused, as though relearning every feature on her face. "I've really looked forward to seeing you again."

Penny's mind seemed to lose all discipline as thoughts she'd assumed were buried years ago flew around in her head like fragments of a jigsaw puzzle—the scraps indecipherable, creating a confusing mélange. She searched desperately through the hodgepodge of disconnected thoughts for something casual to say in response.

She could hardly parrot his last comment. She certainly had not looked forward to ever seeing Brad Crawford again.

"You surprised me," she replied in a feeble attempt to sound natural. "When did you get home?"

He glanced back to the shoreline where the two homes that had sat side by side for three generations overlooked the lake. "Not too long ago. I've been here long enough to find something to wear that is more in keeping with this Missouri weather," he said with a grin that was as familiar to Penny as her own. "I visited with Mom for a few minutes, but she knew I was eager to come find you, so she sent me off."

Penny fought to ignore the implication in that remark. Pretending that she no longer wished to sunbathe, she gathered up her towel and tanning lotion and started toward her home. Brad kept pace with her.

"Why are you here?" she asked, dreading his answer.

He confirmed her fear by answering, "I received an invitation to your wedding. I decided to come home to meet the knight who stole my princess while I was busy slaying dragons."

Penny fully intended to discuss Brad's invitation with her mother at the very first opportunity. Brad Crawford had definitely not been on the guest list Penny had prepared.

Keeping her eyes on the path in front of her, she grumbled, "I don't know why you always make everything sound so dramatic."

"Don't you, Penny? That surprises me. Seems to me drama comes easily for both of us."

That was true, but she resented being reminded. Why now, of all times? One week, that was all she'd needed. Then her life would be safe and secure, just as she planned. Not that Brad could possibly make any difference to those plans, but he did have an annoying habit of creating confusion and uncertainty in her life.

When she didn't answer him, Brad continued talking, sounding relaxed and companionable. "So tell me about him. The name was unfamiliar. Obviously he's not from Payton."

Penny felt a measure of safety as they drew closer to her home. She had no desire to carry on an intimate conversation with Brad. Once they reached the house she could depend on her mother to bridge any uncomfortable silences.

"Actually, Gregory moved to Payton from St. Louis a couple of years ago."

"What does he do?"

"He's an attorney."

"Ah," Brad responded as though some mystery had been solved for him. "An attorney," he repeated with satisfaction, "a nice, safe, unexciting profession."

She glanced at him with annoyance. "Not all of us crave excitement, you know."

"There was a time when you enjoyed it, as I recall."

"I was only a child. 'When I was a child, I used to speak as a child, think as a child, reason as a child; when I became a woman, I did away with childish things.'"

"My! Reverend Wilder would certainly be proud of you, remembering your Bible verses that way. Let's see, that's from the thirteenth chapter of First Corinthians."

"Your early training still shows, too, you know, otherwise you wouldn't have recognized it," Penny replied in an even tone. She pushed open the screen door to the enclosed porch with relief. "Mom? You'll never guess who's here," she called in a bright voice.

"Oh, yes I would," Helen Blackwell said. Her face beamed a welcome as she stepped out of the kitchen carrying a tray filled with cookies and a frosted pitcher of lemonade. "Brad checked with me to find out where you were." She set the tray down and hugged him. "Oh, it's just so good to see you again after all this time. What a marvelous surprise to everyone, having you show up so unexpectedly."

Brad returned the hug with interest, his buoyant smile lighting up his face. "I'm glad to see that someone is happy to see me," he complained good-naturedly, glancing at Penny out of the corner of his eye. "For a moment there I thought Penny was going to shove me off the dock when she first saw me."

"Don't be silly. You just startled me, that's all." Forcing herself to sound casual, she said, "If you'll excuse me, I'm going to run upstairs and change."

"Not on my account, I hope," Brad offered with an innocent grin. "I'm thoroughly enjoying the view."

Helen laughed. She would, Penny thought crossly. Her mother had always found Brad amusing. As far as her parents were concerned, Brad could do no wrong. He was the son they had never had.

A small voice inside her told her that, to be fair, she needed to remember that she had been the daughter Brad's parents had never had as well. Penny wasn't in the mood for fairness at the moment. "If you'll excuse me," she said politely and left.

Helen poured lemonade in two of the glasses and said, "Sit down, Brad. She probably won't be long. Why don't you tell me how things are going for you. I'm so eager to hear about New York and your life there. Everyone in Payton is so proud of you—the small-town boy who made good."

Brad continued to stare at the door where Penny had disappeared.

"She's changed," he said in a flat voice.

Helen sighed. "Yes, she has," she admitted, "and in my opinion the change hasn't been an improvement."

Brad glanced at her in surprise.

Helen hastened to explain. "She seems to have lost some inner spark of enthusiasm, that enjoyment of life that always used to make her sparkle."

"I remember," Brad said with a smile.

"It could have been getting that teaching job as soon as she finished college. She wasn't all that much older than her high school students, which probably explains why she began to dress and act so much older than she really is."

"Does she like teaching?"

"Seems to. Of course, what she really enjoys is working with the drama club, directing their plays— she loves anything that has to do with acting."

"That isn't too surprising, since that's what she majored in at the university. She was one of the most talented students in our class. It's a shame she isn't using that talent now."

"I know. I suppose that's what bothers me about her. She seems to be settling for so much less than she's capable of."

"Such as Gregory Duncan?"

"Oh, heavens, no! Gregory is a brilliant man. Absolutely brilliant. He made quite a name for himself in the St. Louis area, I understand. Payton was extremely fortunate that a man like Gregory chose to move here and open a practice." Helen offered Brad the plate of cookies, pleased when he took a couple. "Of course, he's extremely busy. He still has a considerable caseload in St. Louis, so he's been dividing his time between here and there. Penny's hoping his schedule will let up some once they're married."

Brad took a bite of one of the cookies and moaned his pleasure. "Sitting here eating your homemade oatmeal-raisin cookies certainly takes me back, Helen." After swallowing some lemonade, Brad returned to the subject of their conversation. "If Duncan's so well-known and established, he must be considerably older than Penny."

Helen nodded. "Yes, he is. He's thirty-nine, fourteen years older than she is."

"And she doesn't mind?"

"Doesn't seem to bother her in the least. Like I said, she acts so much older—seems so settled and all. You'd think they were much closer in age than they are." Helen reached over and took a cookie. "She seems to have her life all planned out now. Penny intends to continue teaching for a couple of years, then start a family. Gregory does a lot of entertaining. Just playing hostess for him will probably be a full-time job. She seems to be content with everything."

Brad gazed out through the screen that enclosed the large porch and murmured, "I wonder."

As soon as Penny returned downstairs, she could hear the animation in her mother's voice. Brad had that effect on people. He seemed to generate excitement wherever he went.

"Everyone in town watches *Hope for Tomorrow*," she heard Helen say, "wanting to see what outrageous things Drew Derek is going to do next. He's a real corker, isn't he?"

Brad laughed. "That he is."

"Of course I know you're nothing like him, but you sure make him out to be a real ladies' man."

Penny could hear the amusement in Brad's voice at her mother's careful phrasing when he replied, "Yes, he's certainly a real threat to the virtue of every woman he meets, isn't he?"

They laughed companionably. Penny decided it was time to join them and change the subject when she heard her mother say, "Well, I think you're just fantastic in the role and very believable. Why, if I didn't know the real you, I wouldn't let you anywhere near my daughter, that's for sure. Speaking of Penny, I taped your program on the video recorder every day during the school term so Penny could watch it when she got home. She—"

"Is there any lemonade left?" Penny asked, stepping out on the porch as though unaware she'd interrupted her mother. She could tell by the expression on his face that Brad had not been fooled.

"Of course there is," Helen answered. "You know I always keep plenty on hand in the summertime. It's our staple drink around here during these warm months."

"So you watch *Hope for Tomorrow* every day, do you?" Brad asked Penny, a half smile on his face.

Brad looked very much at home. His head rested on the back of the well-padded patio chair, his legs stretched out in front of him, crossed at the ankle. He held his glass balanced on his lean, muscled stomach.

Penny stepped over his legs and sank down in the chair on his other side.

"When I have the time," she responded casually. "Which reminds me. How did you manage to get time off to come home? If you really are here for the wedding, that must mean you plan to stay at least a week."

"What do you mean, if I'm really here for the wedding? Don't you believe me?"

She shrugged. "I don't disbelieve you. I just find it unusual that you'd bother."

"Oh, I don't, Penny," Helen said. "Why, Brad is the closest thing to a brother you've ever had. It's only natural he'd want to be here."

"That's very true. So I asked the powers that be in our production for the time and eventually they decided that Drew really did need some R and R from all of his bedroom activities." He watched Penny's profile while he talked because she refused to look his way. Instead, she stared out at the lake. Of course, it was a very relaxing view, but she was studying it as if she'd never seen it before. Glancing at Helen, seated on his other side, he continued, "So they've put poor old Drew in a coma for a few days."

"Oh, really?" Helen said. "What caused it?"

Brad shrugged his shoulders. "Who knows? Too much sex, probably."

"Brad," Helen said, laughing. "That's awful."

"Sorry," he said in a teasing tone that said he wasn't sorry at all.

How many times over the years had Penny heard that exact inflection in his voice? Somehow it had always managed to get him off the hook. Perhaps because when he was in that mood he was practically irresistible.

"Besides," he went on, "I felt I had to meet the man who stole Penny away from me."

Penny stiffened at his words, but before she could come up with a caustic reply she heard her mother say, "Well, then you should plan to come back over for dinner tonight. Gregory is going to be here. It will give the two of you a chance to visit together, sort of get acquainted and all before the wedding."

Oh, Mother, how could you? Penny silently pleaded. No two men could be more unalike than Gregory and Brad. The evening would be a total disaster. What in the world would they find to talk about?

"Why, Helen, thank you," Penny heard Brad say, and a definite sinking sensation developed in her stomach. "That would be great." He glanced at his watch. "In that case, I'd better get home so I can visit with Dad when he arrives. I'm sure they'll understand why I'm over here my first night at home."

Damn him. Why did he keep making those little remarks, implying a great deal more than he had reason to? When Helen accepted his comment with an understanding smile, Penny could have thrown something.

Which was exactly why she didn't want Brad Crawford anywhere around her.

Penny considered herself to be a calm, even-tempered person. Everyone at school commented on how well she handled her adolescent students. She did not get upset. She did not lose her temper. She was in control at all times. Brad was the only person who had ever caused her to lose that control, and Penny hated his ability to upset her. Absolutely detested it.

The past three years had been wonderfully serene, and she was looking forward to a lifetime of similar peace and serenity. In other words, she intended to spend her life anywhere that Brad Crawford wasn't.

Penny waited while Brad and Helen made arrangements for his return that evening, smiled politely when Brad said goodbye and watched as he left her home and sauntered across the immense lawn that separated their two places. Then she turned to Helen.

"Do you know anything about how Brad received a wedding invitation, Mother?"

Helen had just picked up the tray to return to the kitchen. She looked puzzled by the question. "I sent him one. Why do you ask?"

"Because his name wasn't on the list."

Helen went into the kitchen; Penny followed. "I knew it was just an oversight. After all, you sent one to his folks. So I just stuck one in the mail to him as well."

"It was no oversight."

Helen set the tray on the kitchen counter and turned around. "Penny! Are you saying that—you mean that you didn't intend for Brad to come to your wedding?" Her shocked surprise could have been no less than if Helen had just heard that Penny was pregnant with triplets.

"That's exactly what I mean."

An expression of pain crossed Helen's face. "Oh, Penny. That's awful."

"What's awful about it, Mother? It's my wedding. I should be able to invite or not invite anyone I please."

"But to leave Brad out, after all you've meant to each other during these years."

"Mother, don't exaggerate. Brad and I grew up together because we lived next door to each other. Since we're almost five miles out of town, we didn't have too many choices as to whom we played with. And if you remember anything, you can certainly recall that we spent most of our time together fighting!"

Helen leaned against the counter, staring at her daughter as though she no longer knew her. "Why, Penny, that isn't true! Of course you squabbled at times—any kids who spent much time together would be likely to bicker. Besides, you're both extremely strong-willed and determined to get your own way. No one would expect that you'd always agree on everything."

Penny absently opened the pantry door and peered inside with absolutely no idea what she was looking for.

"But, Penny, the two of you were friends. Close friends. I don't understand your attitude toward him now."

Penny closed the door and turned around. "Well, I don't suppose it matters now, does it? He's here and he'll be here for dinner. I think I'll go on up and take a bath. I want to look calm and relaxed when Gregory gets here."

Helen stood and watched Penny as she went into the hallway and started up the stairs. There were times she didn't feel she understood her daughter at all.

* * *

Penny stared at her reflected image in the mirror. The pale peach of her dress showed off her darkening tan and brought out the red highlights in her russet-colored hair. She had pulled her hair smoothly away from her face into a cluster of curls at the nape of her neck. She looked poised, sophisticated and calm.

If only she felt that way! Her insides had been churning all afternoon, which was absolutely ridiculous. What possible difference could it make that Brad Crawford would be there for dinner? she asked herself.

Unfortunately she could come up with a half-dozen reasons before she had to draw breath. She knew him too well. Depending on his mood, he could be everything a hostess could want in a polite dinner guest. Or he could be perfectly outrageous. Funny, but outrageous. And he knew entirely too many things about her that he could bring up if he felt the urge. It wouldn't be the first time he'd embarrassed her in front of someone important.

"Oh, Mother," she lamented aloud, "If you'd only asked me, I would have told you that Brad's favorite pastime is ignoring the script and improvising in a situation." A reluctant smile played on her face when she thought of some of the things he'd done in the past. He really did have a wicked sense of humor.

She realized that she was being a coward, hovering upstairs when she'd heard him arrive at least fifteen minutes earlier. Penny had justified her delay to herself, knowing that her father would monopolize Brad for a while. Sooner or later she would have to face him. Glancing at her watch, she decided now was as good a time as any. Gregory should be arriving before much longer.

Sure enough, she found Brad and her father in animated conversation. They'd always gotten along well. Her dad had gone to all of Brad's Little League games and stood on the sidelines cheering during his high school football games.

The little voice inside her said, And don't forget, you were right there, cheering with the best of them.

Of course she was. She'd been proud of Brad. He was a natural athlete and she'd enjoyed seeing him play. But that was years ago, after all—just part of her childhood.

Brad stood up as soon as she walked into the room. "Wow!" he said in a reverent voice.

Penny couldn't help it. She began to laugh. "That's one of the things I've always liked about you, Brad," she said, grinning. "You were always so articulate, with such an artful turn of phrase."

He walked over to her and took both her hands, staring down at her. "And that laugh is one of the things I've always liked about you. I had almost given up hope that it was still around."

She could not ignore how well Brad looked in the navy blue blazer and gray slacks. The ensemble set off his blond good looks. Let's face it, she thought, he looked like every woman's dream of the man she hoped would appear in her life and take her away from daily drudgery. No doubt that was one of the reasons *Hope for Tomorrow* had become one of the most successful daily serials.

The doorbell served as a reprieve from Penny's runaway thoughts. "Oh, there's Gregory now," she said, unconsciously betraying her relief.

Brad frowned slightly as he watched her return to the hall. For just a moment he'd seen a glimpse of the Penny he'd known forever, but then she'd disappeared behind the polite, sedate facade of the woman he'd seen this afternoon.

He heard murmured voices in the hallway, and an intimate male chuckle that caused the hair on his neck to rise in protest. Brad determinedly ignored the fact that Penny's lipstick was definitely smudged when she returned to the room, leading a man who must have been Gregory Duncan.

Brad wasn't prepared for the shock he received when he saw Penny's fiancé. There was no denying that he was in his late thirties. The mark of time had added character to his face. What hit Brad like a doubled-up fist in his stomach was that Gregory Duncan looked enough like him to be a close relative.

They were both approximately the same height and build, and their hair was the same shade of blond. Brad felt as though he were looking into the future, at what he would look like in another thirteen years.

And this was the man Penny had chosen to marry.

After the introductions were made, Brad said, "I've looked forward to meeting you, Gregory. I've heard some very good things about you." He didn't miss the exchange of glances between Gregory and Penny.

"It's good to meet a friend of Penny's, Brad," Gregory replied in a deep, mellow voice that Brad was sure could be used to great effect in a courtroom.

"Unfortunately, I'm at a disadvantage. She's never mentioned you to me."

Brad glanced at Penny in surprise, and acknowledged to himself the pain Gregory's remark caused him. She had truly dismissed him from her life.

Penny couldn't meet Brad's eyes. She smiled at Gregory and said, "Oh, I'm sure I told you about Brad, Gregory. You've probably just forgotten. He lived next door for years."

"I'm sure you have, love," Gregory said, holding her possessively to his side. "It must have slipped my mind."

Brad was unprepared for the almost despairing rage that swept over him at the sight of Gregory holding Penny so intimately.

What had he expected, for God's sake? She was marrying the man, wasn't she? He found himself clenching his teeth in an effort to control his emotions. Helen earned his undying gratitude when she came into the room and announced that dinner was ready.

Dinner was almost as bad. Brad sat across the table from the engaged couple, a silent witness to their smiles and murmurs. Ralph and Helen kept the conversation going, and Brad determinedly joined them, knowing he would have to deal with his pain later.

Penny began to relax about midway through dinner. As usual, her mother had outdone herself with the meal, and the men were obviously enjoying it. She had just felt the tension in the muscles along her spine ease when Brad said, "Too bad you never learned to cook like your mom, Runt. Maybe she'll take pity on Gregory and have you two for dinner often.''

Gregory glanced up from his meal and looked at Brad in surprise. "What did you call her? Runt?"

Brad looked a little abashed. "Sorry. I guess that just slipped out. It was a nickname I gave her years ago."

Gregory's gaze fell on Penny. "I can think of many nicknames I might choose for her, but nothing so revolting as that."

"She was always small for her age, you know," Brad said lightly. "I think she always hoped she'd catch up with me, but by the time we were teenagers she knew she'd well and truly lost the race." He studied Penny for a moment, then smiled. "She's always looked younger than her years, anyway, don't you think so?"

Gregory smiled at her. "Oh, I don't know. I'd hardly confuse her with one of her students, despite her height. She's a very nicely endowed woman."

"Thank you kindly, sir," she said.

"As for her cooking," Gregory went on, "Penny doesn't have to do anything she doesn't want to. I'm not marrying her to gain a housekeeper."

"Of course not," Brad agreed. With a perfectly deadpan expression he went on, "I just hope you don't mind the fact that she snores."

The reaction of those around the table was a study of mixed emotions. Ralph looked as though he were trying not to laugh while Helen looked shocked. From the expression on her face, Penny looked as if she could have easily committed murder. Only Gregory showed little reaction—just a slight narrowing of his eyes.

"I had no idea you knew Penny quite that well."

"He's being obnoxious," Penny said heatedly. "Our families used to go camping together when we were children. Brad always used to accuse me of snoring, just to make me angry."

"And it usually worked," he replied with a grin.

She struggled with her anger now, unwilling to let him know that he had succeeded in riling her once again. She tried to laugh, but wasn't sure that anyone was fooled. "But not now. Your childish tricks no longer have any effect on me."

Brad leaned back in his chair. "That's good to know, Runt. That uncontrollable temper of yours used to get you into lots of trouble."

"Temper?" Gregory repeated, lifting a brow. "You must have Penny confused with someone else. A more even-tempered person I've yet to meet."

Brad began to laugh. "Oh, dear. Are you ever in for a surprise, Counselor." He leaned forward and rested his arms on the table in front of him. "How long have you and Penny known each other?"

"About a year, wouldn't you say?" Gregory answered, turning to Penny.

"Something like that," she muttered.

"And she's never lost her temper?"

"Not that I'm aware of."

"How very interesting," Brad mused.

"Only to you, Brad, dear," Penny said sarcastically. Then she stood and said with a smile, "I'll clear for you, Mother. Who would like some cherry-chocolate cake?'' She refused to look at Brad.

No one could pass up such a temptation, so Penny carried the dishes into the kitchen and began to slice the cake and place it on plates. She glanced up when she heard the swinging door open, then frowned.

''You don't need to help, Brad. I can manage.''

''I know. I just came in here to apologize.''

''It's too late.''

''Too late for what? Do you think he's going to beg off or something just because he's found out you have a temper, for God's sake?''

''I mean it's too late for you to think I'm going to always say, 'Oh, that's all right, Brad, it doesn't matter.' You think you can say anything you want, behave in the most outrageous manner, and all you have to do is smile that devastating, knee-weakening smile and I'll forgive you.''

''Knee-weakening?''

Trust Brad to pick up on her unfortunate choice of words.

''A figure of speech, Brad, nothing more.''

''Does my smile really affect you that way?''

''Would you get out of here?'' She picked up two plates filled with cake and shoved them into his hands. ''Make yourself useful.''

Penny watched as Brad laughingly returned to the other room, looking for all the world as if the two of them had been out in the kitchen laughing over old times.

Something told her that the next week might have a certain lack of peace and serenity. She would count the days until the wedding.

Surely after she and Gregory were married, Brad Crawford would no longer have the ability to disrupt her life.

Penny refused to ask herself why this would be so.

Chapter Two

"Good morning, Mr. Akin," Penny said the next morning. She placed the large package her mother wanted mailed in the window of the Payton post office and waited to have it weighed.

"Well, hello there, Penny," he replied. "Guess you're pretty busy these days, what with getting ready for your wedding and all."

She smiled at the elderly man who had worked at the post office as long as she could remember. "Yes, I have been."

"Did you know young Brad Crawford is back in town?" he asked, his intent gaze letting her know it was no idle question.

"Yes, I did. He had dinner with us last night, as a matter of fact."

"Did he now? That's right interesting, considering you're marrying somebody else."

"What difference does that make?"

"Well, folks around here kinda figured that sooner or later you and the Crawford boy would end up married to each other."

"I have no idea why they would think that, Mr. Akin, just because we were next-door neighbors for years."

"It's probably because the two of you were thicker than fleas on a hound's back, missy," he said in a no-nonsense voice. "Never saw one of you that the other one wasn't right there as well."

"That was a long time ago, Mr. Akin. We were just kids then."

"You weren't just kids when you went off to college together. Why, everybody knew that Brad spent his first year out of high school here in Payton, just waiting for you to graduate so you could go to school together."

"Mr. Akin, Brad worked at the textile mill for his dad the year after he graduated from high school. He was tired of school and wasn't sure what he wanted to do."

"Hmph. Figured that out quick enough when you decided to go up north to that big university to study acting, though, didn't he?"

Why was she debating the issue with a postal employee? People were going to think whatever they wanted to think, no matter how much she tried to explain. Penny managed a noncommittal response that seemed to appease him and watched as he weighed the package.

After paying him, Penny waved goodbye and went to the grocery store to pick up a few items her mother wanted. When she was ready to check out, she noticed Sonia Henderson had the shortest line of people waiting. She and Sonia had gone through school together, but instead of going to college, Sonia had married her high school sweetheart.

As soon as Penny began to unload her basket onto the moving belt, Sonia saw her.

"Penny! Did you hear that Brad Crawford is in town?"

Why did everyone want to tell her about Brad's visit, for Pete's sake? "As a matter of fact, I did, Sonia." Trying to forestall another interrogation, she asked, "So how are Timmy and Sarah?"

"Oh, they're fine. Timmy's glad to be out of school for the summer. Sarah's teething and she's been a little cranky, but Mom says that's only natural." Almost in the same breath she asked, "Have you seen him yet?"

"Seen who?"

"Brad! Have you seen him since he came back?"

"Uh, yes. I saw him yesterday."

"Does he look as good as he does on television?"

Better, Penny thought, but decided there was enough conjecture flitting around town without her adding to it. "About the same, I guess."

"Did he talk to you about what it's like, living in New York and being famous and everything?"

"Actually, no, he didn't."

"I think it's so exciting he's here. I hope I get to see him. Do you suppose his life is anything like Drew Derek's?"

"I have no idea."

Sonia giggled. "He probably wouldn't tell you if it was."

"Probably not," she agreed.

"Can't you just imagine what it's like, being famous and all, knowing all the women are dreaming about wanting to make love to you?"

Penny was saved from having to think up a reply when Sonia rang up the total for the groceries. Penny conscientiously concentrated on writing out her check. By the time she managed to get out of the grocery store, she was thankful her mother hadn't thought of any other errands for her to run. If one more person brought up Brad Crawford's name today...

"Good morning, Penny. I always thought that shade of yellow looked great on you."

Thank God she had a good grip on the two sacks of groceries. "Brad! Where did you come from?"

"Why, Penny, you never cease to amaze me. We had a discussion about the birds and the bees years ago. My, how quickly we forget."

"You're not funny, Brad. How long have you been lurking outside the grocery store?"

"I wasn't lurking. I happened to see your car parked out here when I drove by earlier and decided to see if you'd like to go get something cold and refreshing to drink with me."

"I need to get these groceries home," she explained with a certain amount of relief. Brad was looking every inch the virile male in his prime this morning, in faded jeans that fit him like a second skin and gave no doubt to his gender. The tan sport shirt he wore accented his well-developed shoulders and chest. His blond hair, worn much longer than most of the local men's, gleamed brightly in the morning sunlight.

"That's all right. I'll follow you home and we can go in my car."

She closed the trunk and came around to where he was casually leaning against her car. "Not today. I have too much to do."

"Such as?"

Penny quickly racked her brain, trying to think of something. What did she usually do on Saturdays? In the summertime? Not much. How about the Saturday before her wedding? Surely she had something urgent, something really vital, that could not be postponed another hour.

She couldn't think of a thing.

"Don't you want to have a drink with me?" he asked quietly.

Penny hadn't heard that note in his voice in a long time. It caught her totally off guard. She had heard pain, despite his attempt at lightness.

"It's not that, Brad," she began uncertainly.

"We haven't had a chance to talk since I got home, Penny," he reminded her, reaching out and touching a russet curl at her ear.

"Of course we have," she said, trying to defend herself. "We talked yesterday afternoon, then again last night."

"No, we didn't. You didn't say a half-dozen words around me yesterday, except for telling me off in the kitchen." He studied her in silence for a moment. "Are you still angry at me because of last night?"

Trying to ignore how close he was, she opened the car door and slid behind the steering wheel. After pulling the door shut, she looked up at him. That particular look in his eyes had always been able to sway her, even against her better judgment. And she was aware that she had overreacted to his teasing the night before. "All right," she said, giving up the struggle. "I'll see you at home, then."

His smile lit up his face, and for a moment she could only stare at him. He seemed to glow with it. No wonder he had been an instant hit on television. With that much charisma, he was lethal to a person's peace of mind. Or at least, to her's.

Brad followed her home and pulled into her parents' driveway directly behind her. He helped her carry the groceries into the house. "I'll be right back," he said as soon as he set one of the sacks down. "I'll meet you out front in a few minutes."

Penny hurriedly put the groceries away, found her mother working in the flower garden and told her that she was going out to have a drink with Brad.

"If Gregory should call, tell him I'll be home within the hour."

Helen glanced up at her absently. "I will, dear. Have a good time."

Have a good time. How often had her mother said that to her over the years? Probably every time she had taken off with Brad. Her mother had never seemed to worry about her as long as she and Brad were together.

Penny thought about her instructions to her mother for a moment. She didn't really expect Gregory to call. He'd been out of town all week and had told her last night he would probably have to work at the office all weekend. But they were going to have dinner together that night.

Penny smiled to herself as she walked through the house and out the front door, thinking about next week. They were going to take a week off for their honeymoon, although she had no idea where they were going. Gregory told her it was going to be a surprise. She really didn't care as long as she didn't have to compete for his attention with his law practice. For a few days, anyway, she would have him all to herself.

"There's that wicked smile again, Runt," Brad said, and she realized he'd already returned to his car and was waiting for her. "If I didn't know you better, I'd think the innocent Ms. Blackwell was thinking impure thoughts about something—or somebody."

She could feel the color mounting in her cheeks and cursed her fair complexion that let her reaction to his remark show. She knew from his grin that he hadn't missed her blush. "What makes you so sure I'm all that innocent, Brad?" she drawled. "After all, I'm twenty-five years old."

"Age has nothing to do with your innocence," he said with emphasis, holding the passenger door open for her.

He backed out of the driveway, and because she was so caught up in the conversation, Penny didn't notice that he had turned the opposite way from town when he got to the road.

"You don't know everything about me," she said emphatically. "After all, you haven't seen me in three years."

"So what? That doesn't mean I haven't kept up with what's been happening to you."

Penny turned so that she unconsciously fell into the familiar pose she'd always used whenever they went anywhere in the car together—she leaned against the door and pulled one knee up on the seat so that she was facing him.

He darted a lightning glance at her and immediately returned his gaze to the country road, a slight smile on his face.

"Your mother doesn't know everything I do," she said, irritated that she felt the need to defend herself.

"No, but yours does."

"Hah! Not likely." She was quiet for a moment, then asked, "Are you telling me that Mother has been writing to you?"

"Sometimes. Sometimes she just tells my mom, who passes along any relevant information."

"Which I'm sure you found very boring."

"You might be surprised."

They were quiet for a few minutes. Penny watched the passing countryside without registering that they were leaving Payton farther and farther behind. She was too busy trying to analyze what Brad was telling her.

"Then you knew all along when I started dating Gregory?"

"I knew," he agreed with a smile.

"If that's the case, then why did you ask last night?"

"Just being polite."

"That's a laugh," Penny said, although she didn't sound particularly amused. "You don't know the meaning of the word."

"Aah, Penny. I'm crushed. After I tried so hard."

"I know how hard you tried—to be irritating and aggravating."

"Did it work?"

"What do you mean?" she asked, straightening her back. "Do you think you bothered Gregory with your childish remarks? He's much too mature for that," she added, her tone sounding remarkably pleased.

"I'll say. He's almost old enough to be your father."

"He is not! He's only fourteen years older than I am," Penny responded heatedly, unaware that she and Brad had fallen once again into their age-old conversational pattern of baiting and fencing.

"Does he have any children?" Brad asked with polite interest.

"Since he's never been married, I rather doubt it," she replied with more than a little sarcasm.

"Or if he does, he probably doesn't talk about it," Brad added agreeably.

"Brad!"

"Sorry," he said with a grin, neither looking nor sounding particularly sorry. "So why is he getting married now?"

Penny could feel her temper getting the best of her, which only added to her irritation. How was it that Brad could set her off so quickly with his idiotic remarks? "You are really being insulting, you know that, don't you?" she said, her eyes frosty with disdain.

"Well, of course he loves you, Penny," Brad hastily assured her. "Who wouldn't? I just wonder what other reasons such a logical and analytical person might find to choose you for his mate, particularly since he's waited this long to marry."

Who wouldn't? Penny's mind repeated in surprise, losing much of what he had said after that. Was it possible that Brad had actually intended to pay her a compliment? If so, it was the first she could ever recall receiving from him.

"What other reasons could he have?" she asked, curious about his line of thinking.

"Oh, there are all kinds of reasons to get married. Maybe he's tired of living alone. Maybe he wants a family, a hostess. Maybe he's marrying you for your money...."

"That's a pretty vivid imagination you've got there, Brad. Do you write those stories on television as well as act in them?"

"There's nothing imaginative in any of that. It happens all the time."

"Not with me, it doesn't. I doubt that my teacher's salary attracts him. After all, he's a very successful lawyer."

"Then why did he move to Payton?"

Penny relaxed a little more against the door, watching Brad's profile. "Why not? It's a nice place to live, even though you found it dull."

"I never found it dull," he pointed out mildly. "I just wanted to become a professional actor, and Payton doesn't have that many job openings in that particular field." He glanced over at her and grinned when he saw that she was absently twisting a curl around one of her fingers. She only did that when she was agitated. Good. At least he had her thinking. "Besides," he went on blandly, "I wasn't talking about what you make. You're an only child and your family is very well off."

"So what? I'm certainly not apt to be inheriting anything for years to come, and you know it. Good grief. Mom and Dad are still in their forties."

"I know. They got married very young and they made it work but it was tough, which is why they're against teenage marriages."

Penny looked at him in surprise. "How do you know that?" she asked. "I've never heard them say anything about their early years."

"Never mind," he replied, deciding it was time to change the subject. "So if he isn't interested in your money, Gregory must want you to play hostess for him and preside over his home."

"What's wrong with that?" she asked, puzzled by his tone.

"Oh, Penny, that isn't you, and you know it. You've got too much vitality and sparkle for that kind of life. If you would just be honest with yourself, you'd admit that you're already bored with teaching school. How do you think you're going to feel playing helpful Harriet for a man who could pass as your father?''

''Would you stop with the stupid remarks about Gregory's age? In the first place, Gregory doesn't even look that old. As a matter of fact, you may have noticed that he looks a little like you—same hair coloring, similar build.''

He grinned. ''Is that why you fell for him? Because he reminded you of me?''

She stared at him in horror. ''Of course not! He's absolutely nothing like you, thank God.''

''You don't have to sound so thankful. I didn't turn out all that bad, did I?''

She heard the hint of pain in his voice again, and wondered about it. Brad Crawford was too self-confident to be easily offended. And yet twice today she had heard a slight hesitancy in his voice as though he were unsure of himself.

''You're living your life the way you want to, Brad. I can't fault you for that,'' she said quietly.

''But are you living your life the way you want to? That's my concern at the moment.''

She glanced at him, puzzled. ''That's the second time you've made a remark like that. I am not bored with teaching. I am very content with my life.'' She studied him for a moment in silence, then asked, ''And why should you care what I do or how I feel, anyway?''

''Come on, Penny, you know me better than that. I have always looked out for you and cared for you, ever since we were kids.'' He gave her a quick glance from the corner of his eye and smiled. "Why should I stop now?"

She wasn't going to let that statement go unchallenged. "Yet you could hardly wait to leave here once you finished college."

He was quiet for a moment. He heard the hurt in her voice and realized once again what a fine actress she truly was. Until now he had never really known that she had cared when he'd decided to go to New York. An interesting discovery, considering how he'd felt when she had blithely greeted his news three years ago by wishing him well.

"You could have gone with me," he said finally.

The interior of the car seemed to reverberate with sudden emotion. The silence that fell between them seemed to grow like a living thing, until Brad felt that he could almost reach out and touch it. Whatever she was feeling, it wasn't indifference. That he knew. He wished he'd had this conversation with her then, instead of now. He'd paid for his cowardice every day since.

When she did speak, her anger surprised him. "Of course I could have gone. We could have starved together! Why would I have wanted to go to New York, Brad? I was twenty-two years old. It was time for us to grow up, accept responsibility, make something of ourselves. Playtime was over…at least it was for me."

"Is that all that acting was to you, Penny? Playtime?"

She laughed, but she didn't sound in the least amused. "Well, it certainly isn't a way to make a living."

"I haven't done so badly at it."

Penny felt a sudden urge to hit something, she felt so frustrated. Who was she kidding, anyway? Why didn't she just admit the truth?

"Actually," she said, wishing her voice didn't sound quite so uneven, "the biggest reason I didn't go with you to New York was simple. You never asked me."

There. She'd finally said it, spoken the words out loud. In doing so, she finally faced them for the first time.

"Would you have gone?" he asked in a neutral tone.

Who knew the answer to that at this late date? The whole point was he *hadn't* asked. He hadn't even acted as though he'd given such an idea a thought. And Penny had been faced with the harsh reality of their shared life. At one time Brad Crawford had been everything in the world to her while he had considered her a friend—his buddy, a pal.

"It hardly matters at this point, does it?" she asked, staring unseeingly out the window.

"Have you ever thought about trying to make it as an actress?" he asked.

"Not for years, Brad. I'm content with my life."

"You keep saying that, but I'm not sure which one of us you're trying to convince. You were always such a natural on stage, you know. You seemed to come alive. It was a beautiful thing to see." He glanced at her, but she had her head down and he couldn't see her expression. "Don't you ever miss it?"

"Not really. I'm active with the local group... and I directed the high school play this year."

"When you could be starring on Broadway? Penny, that's a shameful waste of your talent and you know it!"

Once again she made no response.

Forcing a lighter tone, Brad asked, "What does Gregory think of your acting abilities?"

"He's never seen them," she muttered.

"But he knows about them, surely."

Penny rested her head against the window. "He knows I've had training in that area and assumes I minored in drama while I was getting my degree in education."

"Why haven't you told him? Showed him your clippings and reviews?"

She shrugged. "There's no reason to. That's just part of my past."

Brad wondered if he was too late. Was it even his place to attempt to save her? Obviously she didn't see herself as needing saving. She had chosen not only the man, but an entire way of life, and she was within days of cementing that relationship.

How could he let her do such a thing? Yet how could he, in good conscience, interfere if that was what she wanted?

He loved her. He had always loved her. He would always love her. And he wanted her to be happy. For years he had hoped that her happiness would lie with him. He'd listened to both sets of parents as they had urged him not to rush into a permanent relationship too early in their lives. They had insisted that each of them needed some space, a chance to mature separately, in order to recognize their own feelings.

So he had taken their advice. Because of it, he had lost Penny. He had wanted to be fair, and to do what was best for both of them. Instead, he had lost the only woman who had ever meant a damn to him.

But even in his worst nightmare it never occurred to him that Penny would turn into this subdued, quiet woman who was willing to accept so little in her life.

Now that Brad had brought up his move to New York, the past began to tumble into Penny's consciousness like a child's building blocks. They fell in colorful disarray around her. Mr. Akin at the post office had been right. She and Brad had been inseparable as far back as she could remember. Had anyone asked her back then, Penny would probably have explained that she and Brad would marry someday.

Strange how things had worked out.

She and Brad had never talked about their feelings for each other. There had been no reason to. They were so much a part of each other's life—until Brad announced his intention to go to New York.

Penny could still remember the day he told her. They had been home from college a week and had taken his family's boat out on the lake. The day had been warm and they had found a quiet spot to anchor and laze in the sun.

Penny had been almost asleep when Brad spoke.

"Have you decided what you want to do now that we're out of school, Runt?"

"I'm doing it," she replied in a sleepy voice.

"I mean, to earn a living?"

"I filled out an application to teach. I suppose I'll wait to hear from the school board. Why do you ask?"

He was silent so long that Penny eventually opened her eyes. He had turned so that he was facing her, and she found herself staring into his eyes. "I've decided to go to New York."

She smiled because they had talked about New York for the past year. "To become rich and famous?" she asked with a grin.

"I won't know until I try," he answered in a quiet tone.

Penny's smile slowly disappeared. "You're serious, aren't you?" she asked, and even now she could recall the sudden jolt to her system as the fear of losing him swept over her.

"Yes."

Penny never knew how she managed to get through that day. She'd fought hard to hide her reaction. Somehow it had been important for her not to let him know how devastated she felt. If he could so calmly plan his life apart from her, then she must not mean as much to him as he meant to her.

She determinedly hung on to her pride.

Penny had kept up the act of well-wishing friend until Brad left home. Only then did the true enormity of what had happened sweep over her.

Brad Crawford had blithely and without a care walked out of Penny's life. He didn't need her to make his life complete. Penny had never known such rejection, nor did she know how to deal with it.

As the months went by Penny mentally packed away all of their shared memories methodically and with grim determination. Obtaining the teaching position had been her salvation. She threw herself into the new experiences of teaching and interacting with students and co-workers. Penny learned to hide her thoughts and feelings from others, relieved to discover after a while that her highly charged emotions seemed to disappear.

When Gregory came into her life she was content. He filled a place in her daily routine. He offered companionship and conversation, all she really wanted anymore in a relationship.

Penny had overcome the pain and desolation she had felt when Brad had left. She'd forgotten, until now, what a hole he'd left in her life. Penny knew she could never allow anyone to become so important to her again.

As they continued following the country road, Penny slowly became aware of their surroundings. They had been steadily winding through the rolling hills for miles, she realized with dismay. Brad turned into the entrance of a state park and followed the road toward the bluffs where they had spent countless hours as children.

"What are we doing out here?" she demanded. "I thought we were going to get a drink?"

Brad began to laugh. "I wondered when you were going to notice."

"Brad, I don't have time to be out here. I've got to get home. I told Mother I'd be back by—" she glanced at her watch "—by now, darn you!"

"Okay, so you're late. Big deal. She knows you're with me. I thought it might be fun to come out here again. I haven't been to the park in years. I threw some snacks in a sack and brought some cold drinks. Why don't we wander around for a while, relax and enjoy the scenery? I'll take you back home whenever you say."

"Why is it I've never trusted you when you've used that tone of voice?"

"I have no idea. Everyone else always has."

"I know. But no one else knows you the way I do."

"Good point, Penny. You might want to think about just what that means to both of us. It could surprise you."

Chapter Three

Brad and Penny spent the next hour hiking along the bluffs, skipping rocks across the water and wading in the shallows—all activities they had shared during their years together.

Penny realized that, like Sonia, she really was interested in hearing how Brad had adjusted to suddenly being thrust into the limelight of the entertainment world. She plied him with countless questions—some serious, others teasing, and he patiently answered them, one by one.

When he grew tired of sitting quietly, Brad started a game of tag, and Penny seemed to forget her dignified years and chased him, convinced that he would be too out of shape to give her much trouble. She was wrong. Whatever he did in New York to keep in condition, it certainly worked.

Eventually they threw themselves on the grassy bank of the slow-moving river where they had left their food. Brad reached into the water and pulled out two soda cans dripping with water and handed her one. Penny was convinced that nothing had ever tasted so good.

"See? I told you I'd buy you a drink," he pointed out with a grin. He couldn't help but appreciate the fact that she no longer looked like the prim and proper Ms. Blackwell who was marrying the regal Mr. Duncan in a week. She'd lost the combs that had held her hair away from her face, so that the curls tumbled riotously around her cheeks and across her forehead.

Her face was flushed from running, and she was still breathing hard. The thin tank top did nothing to disguise the sauciness of her heaving breasts. Perspiration dotted her upper lip, and Brad had an almost uncontrollable urge to reach over and wipe it away with his thumb.

How could he possibly give up this woman? He had thought he would go out of his mind for the first several months he'd spent in New York. Only the remembered conversations with first her parents, then his, enabled him to recognize that before he asked her to marry him, Brad owed Penny a chance to have a life apart from him.

Their parents had known how to get him to give her time. They had pointed out that she would probably marry him out of habit, because she was used to following his lead. Did he really want a bride who accepted him for that reason? They had already known the only answer he could live with.

"What's the matter? Do I have dirt on my face?" Penny asked with a grin, looking totally relaxed and unconcerned with her appearance. She was stretched out on the grass on her side, propped up enough so that she could drink from the can without spilling it. In her shorts and skimpy top she reminded him of the young girl he'd known, free and uninhibited.

"Don't you always?" he teased. "I think you must bury your nose in the dirt every so often."

She broke off some blades of grass and tossed them at him, then laughed as they decorated his shirt. "You aren't much better, you know. Just look at your shoe."

They both gazed at his foot. His shoe and sock still dripped muddy water where he'd slipped off one of the rocks when they'd crossed the shallows. "What would your fans think of you now, Mr. Crawford?"

"I hope they would realize that I haven't enjoyed myself so much in years," he said with a smile. He gave up trying to resist temptation and reached over, running his thumb lightly across her upper lip.

Penny jerked her head, startled by his touch. His eyes were filled with golden sunshine, their toffee color warm and inviting.

"I'm not going to hurt you," he said softly.

"I didn't think you were," she admitted. "You just startled me, that's all."

Brad chose not to pursue her reactions to him. At the moment it was enough for him to see her looking so relaxed and at ease.

He rolled over onto his back and stared up at the trees above them. Sunlight dappled the ground around them, the leaves forming a canopy above. "We had some good times together, didn't we, Runt?" he asked.

She nodded.

"Do you remember the time you lost your glasses and accused me of hiding them from you?"

She laughed. "Yes."

"I almost got a beating for that. My folks believed you."

"I wonder why? You were always hiding something of mine—my baseball glove, my volleyball."

"Maybe so," he admitted, "but never your glasses. You couldn't see a thing without them."

"How well I remember."

"Contacts made a big difference for you, I know."

"You're right. A whole new world opened up. Particularly when I got the extended wear. Do you have any idea how wonderful it is to wake up at night and be able to see the clock without putting on my glasses?"

"Weren't you ashamed of accusing me of taking them and getting me in trouble?"

"Wel-l-l, maybe. But I'm sure you did a lot of things and never got caught, so it probably all evened out."

He reached over and touched her hand. "I've really missed you, Runt."

Penny looked at him a long time without speaking. "I missed you, too," she said, finally. "For the longest time I didn't think I'd ever be happy without you in my life." She began to smile. "Isn't that crazy? Now

I have a whole new life separate from yours, and everything in my life is just perfect.''

She looked over at him and idly noted that he had closed his eyes. His thick lashes rested on his high cheekbones. "Do you remember how we always used to argue? It drove our mothers nuts.''

"Yeah, but all they had to do was find something to get our minds off whatever we were arguing about.''

"Are you saying we argued out of boredom? Surely not.''

Without opening his eyes he said. "You were always such a tomboy, no bigger than a minute, convinced you could do anything anyone else could do, and you usually managed to prove it no matter how hard I argued against you.''

"I can remember a few times when you managed to help me in such a way that nobody else knew I hadn't done it all myself.''

He smiled to himself. "That's what friends are for.''

"Yes,'' she said with a hint of surprise. "I guess it is.''

The quietness of the park settled over them, and Penny laid her head on her folded arms. She was probably going to be sore tomorrow with all of her unaccustomed exercise today. Her eyes drifted closed. The park was so peaceful. She'd just rest her eyes for a few moments and . . .

"Penny? You'd better wake up. I'm afraid we both fell asleep.''

Penny sat up with a start. The sun had almost set, and she glanced at her watch in dismay. "Oh, no! Gregory was supposed to pick me up almost half an hour ago.'' She came to her feet and stared up at Brad and his rueful expression.

"I'm sorry, Runt. I didn't mean this to happen," he said softly.

The sincerity in his voice couldn't be mistaken. Quickly slipping her sandals on, Penny said, "It was just as much my fault as yours." She hoped Gregory would understand. She'd never been late for a date before. He was such a stickler for promptness.

Her life seemed to be falling into a shambles since Brad had appeared, although she couldn't really hold him responsible. He just seemed to have that effect on her. Life never seemed to be as serious when he was around. And it was a lot more fun.

They were quiet in the car going back. Penny tried to prepare herself for her coming meeting with Gregory. Surely he would understand. The time had seemed to slip away. Besides, she had needed that day. It was a day apart from her life, apart from time, separate and complete. She and Brad had returned to their childhood, the innocence of youth where time was meaningless because there was so much of it.

Surely Gregory would understand. If only she could think of a more logical explanation.

But she wasn't sorry for going to the park with Brad. At least she could be honest about that. She had enjoyed every minute, even the argument in the car with Brad earlier.

There was no reason to expect Brad to approve of the man she married. She was certain that Brad would never find a woman that was good enough for him in her estimation. The thought gave her quite a pang in the region of her heart.

Penny had been careful not to ask Brad about the women he had dated, many of whom he'd been photographed with. She hadn't wanted to know about them. She knew she was being silly, but she couldn't help it. Brad was very special to her and it was time she acknowledged that to herself.

He always would be.

As soon as they pulled up in the driveway, Gregory stepped out on the front porch of the Blackwell home. Penny took a quick inventory of what she and Brad looked like and almost groaned aloud. They both had grass stains on their clothes, and his shoe looked much the worse for a dip in the river. Her hair, from the glimpse she had gotten in the side mirror, looked as if she had styled it with an eggbeater.

She felt as though they had been caught skipping school as they walked up the sidewalk toward the well-dressed man who waited for them.

"I'm glad to see you two are all right. We'd begun to worry about you," he said calmly.

Penny smiled in relief. He didn't seem at all angry but showed a perfectly natural concern. Before she could say anything, Brad said, "I really am sorry about today, Gregory. But you see, after all that physical exertion we fell asleep and weren't aware of the hours passing." His tone and smile were friendly and nonchalant.

Penny saw Gregory's body stiffen and his expression freeze. Quickly reviewing what Brad had just said, her eyes widened with horror. Of course he'd told the truth, it was just that . . .

"How interesting," Gregory said. "Perhaps you'd like to go into a little more detail. Helen said you'd gone for a drink. I never considered that to be physically taxing, myself."

"Oh, Gregory, he didn't mean that the way—" Penny began, only to have Brad interrupt her.

"Why don't you run upstairs and get cleaned up, Runt? I'll be glad to make our explanations to your fiancé. After all, he has every right to want to know how you spend your time with me."

Penny glanced uncertainly at Brad, then at Gregory. Brad still sounded casually friendly, but there was a tautness in his stance as he stood facing Gregory that contradicted his tone.

"Good idea, Penny," Gregory agreed quietly. "We're running quite late as it is."

She glanced over her shoulder at the two men as she opened the screen door. Neither one of them had moved. They seemed to be waiting for her to leave before continuing the conversation.

Penny could have cheerfully wrung Brad's neck. There was absolutely no reason for the innuendos. What was he trying to do, give Gregory the wrong idea about their relationship?

The warm spray from the shower soothed her and Penny tried to relax. Brad had always had the ability to turn her world upside down. Why did she think anything had changed? However, she had complete faith in Gregory's ability to see through Brad's teasing and desire to cause mischief.

It would do no good for her to ask Brad to lay off. He would see that only as a challenge. So the next best thing would be to make sure she kept the two men apart. After all, it would be for only a few days, then Brad would be out of their lives once again.

When she returned downstairs Gregory was waiting alone in the living room.

She looked at him in surprise. "Where is everybody?"

"I convinced your parents to go to their dinner engagement earlier. If something had happened, I told them I'd get in touch."

Once again Penny felt guilty at her unusual and irresponsible behavior. How could she explain what she didn't understand herself?

"I really am sorry for making you wait," she said.

Gregory took her arm and escorted her outside. "Let's forget it, shall we?" he said, helping her into the car. "I managed to get our reservations changed, so there's no harm done."

Gregory was quiet on the way to the restaurant and Penny searched for something to say. Finally she asked, "Did Brad tell you we went to the park?"

He glanced at her with an enigmatic expression. "He did mention that, yes."

"It was so beautiful there. I'd forgotten how much I enjoyed being out of doors." She wondered when she had lost touch with nature. Her schedule didn't seem to include outdoor activities. Impulsively she turned to Gregory and said, "I wish you'd been with us."

Penny tried to picture Gregory hiking and wading but it was difficult. She couldn't see him laughing about his shoes getting wet or muddy. Gregory would have been out of place. She and Brad had been reliving their childhood, falling back into a familiar pattern, one in which Gregory did not fit.

"From the description that Crawford gave, I don't think I would have enjoyed the afternoon very much," Gregory said.

Even though Penny had just reached the same conclusion she was surprised to hear Gregory echo her thoughts. "Why not?"

"I generally get my exercise playing racquetball or tennis."

"Oh." Funny, they'd never discussed hobbies that much. Gregory had been so busy with his law practice since she had met him that she assumed he didn't have time for many activities. Everytime she felt that she knew him, Gregory revealed another facet of his personality. She wondered if he felt the same way about her.

Was it ever possible to find out everything about a person before you married? It wasn't that anyone deliberately omitted telling the other some things. There was just so much to learn about another person. Gregory had spent thirty-nine years doing things she knew nothing about. She'd spent twenty-five. How could you possibly catch up on everything? And how did you decide what was important to know before the wedding, rather than learning about it in the years after?

They had a quiet dinner at one of the nicer restaurants located near the interstate highway. Penny asked intelligent questions about some of Gregory's cases, drawing him out so that she could feel closer to him somehow.

One of the things that she admired most about him was his dignity in all situations. He always handled himself well. Tonight he could have justifiably shown anger and spoiled their time together. Instead, he seemed to have forgotten the less than auspicious beginning of their evening, relegating it to its rightful place of unimportance in their life.

Their life together would be one of consideration and understanding, of communication. There would be no arguments, such as she had with Brad. She and Gregory would calmly discuss then decide what needed to be faced in their shared existence. There would be no sudden bursts of emotion. Instead, they would share a sense of calmness and serenity.

After dinner Gregory suggested they move into the lounge for after-dinner drinks. A small combo played quiet music and Gregory asked her to dance. Penny willingly agreed. Gregory was an excellent dancer. Penny felt relaxed and totally at ease when they returned to their table after dancing a medley of slow numbers.

Gregory took her hand in his. He seemed to study it for some time before he looked up at her, his gray eyes serious.

"Why have you never mentioned Brad to me, Penny?"

She had been lulled into a relaxed state and his question dumped her out of the soft, fluffy cloud she'd been enjoying for the past hour or so. Penny stared at him with dismay. She had never seen quite that look on his face before. She wondered if that was the look he gave a witness just prior to cross-examination?

Not that it mattered, really. She had nothing to hide. "I don't really know, Gregory," she answered with a slight shrug. "I suppose it's because I never thought him important enough to mention."

His expression gave no indication of what he was thinking. "Not important enough, or too important to discuss?" he asked quietly.

How should she answer that? Penny had only begun to realize earlier that day that her feelings toward Brad were not as clear-cut as she had thought. "We're just friends," she offered tentatively, wondering what had prompted Gregory's line of questioning.

"I realize that. Since I've known you, I've met many of your friends, and you've talked of several others—some you knew here in Payton who later moved away, others you met at college with whom you continue to keep in touch. But you never mentioned Brad's name."

How could she not have been aware of the omission? she wondered. She shook her head. "I really can't explain it, Gregory. Is it important?"

"Not particularly. I find it a puzzle, that's all. And I've got the sort of mind that can't leave a puzzle alone until it's solved."

"I don't see much of a puzzle about it," she offered. "Brad's been gone for three years. He's no longer a part of my life."

"But he was."

"Yes. Do you have a problem with that?"

"Not necessarily. How does he feel about our getting married?"

Penny remembered Brad's earlier comments and knew she couldn't share what Brad had said with Gregory. "He wants me to be happy," she finally responded, realizing the truth of that statement.

"I'm surprised he doesn't think you'd be happier with him."

She grinned. "Brad? You mean you think Brad wants to marry me?" She laughed. "No way. He enjoys his freedom too much."

Gregory didn't respond. Instead, he took a sip of his drink and said, "I received a call today that means I have to go back to St. Louis. I'll be there all of next week."

Penny gave him a stricken look. "But I thought you had arranged to be here the week before the wedding."

"I had. I've had to rearrange my entire schedule. Unfortunately, it can't be helped. I doubt that I'll make it back much before the wedding rehearsal Friday night."

Penny felt the weight of her disappointment settle on her. Of course his law practice came first. She had always known that. At least he wasn't suggesting they postpone the wedding. After all the planning and hundreds of details, Penny shuddered to think of what it would take to change their plans now.

"I understand," she said quietly, accepting what she knew she couldn't change.

Gregory smiled. "Thank you for being so understanding. I appreciate your willingness to accommodate yourself to my schedule." He picked up his drink. "I'm glad we decided not to have the rehearsal dinner. I would have been pressed for time to have to arrange one."

"It's okay. My friends understand."

"I feel so fortunate to have found you. Nothing seems to upset you. You handle everything with such calmness."

Penny smiled. "It's taken a while for me to reach this point, let me tell you. I used to have a fiery temper."

"Well, I'm pleased that you are no longer bothered by it. The last thing I want to face at the end of one of my work days is a display of emotional fireworks." He reached over and patted her hand. "Your serenity is one of the first things that drew me to you. That, and your calm ability to handle people. Nothing ever seems to catch you off balance."

Penny thought of Brad's unexpected return and her reaction. Gregory had accurately described the person she thought she was, except when Brad was around. He seemed to trigger emotional depths in her that almost frightened her. She didn't like the emotional, out-of-control-person Brad seemed to bring forth in her with no apparent effort.

What a lucky escape she'd had, discovering what an adverse effect Brad had on her.

Later Gregory drove her home, walked her to the door and refused to come inside with her.

"It's late, love, and I have a full day's work on my desk tomorrow before I can even leave for St. Louis."

"Will I see you before you go?"

"I really don't think so, although there's nothing I'd like more than to spend tomorrow with you. However, I don't see how I can possibly get away, not when I'm going to be gone for a week on our honeymoon."

He leaned down and kissed her. Stepping back, he smiled and said, "If I don't stop that, I'll never get away from you tonight. Sleep well, my love." Gregory waited until she went inside and locked the door, then walked to his car. He glanced at the house next door.

Penny had brushed his questions aside regarding Brad Crawford. But there was something there and Gregory knew it. He'd sensed Brad's carefully concealed emotions the night before and earlier this evening. His light, casual air had been very well done.

Gregory hadn't been misled. He'd made a career studying human behavior. The man was in love with Penny.

The question was, how did Penny feel about Brad? And how would her feelings for Brad affect her marriage to Gregory?

Gregory drove back to town in deep thought.

Chapter Four

Penny slept restlessly that night. Her dreams were all mixed up. There seemed to be two men wandering through them—one calm and filled with authority, the other laughing and teasing her.

Scraps of conversation danced in her head. She heard Brad asking, "Come to New York with me... come with me... with me... me..."

Gregory appeared. He paced before her as she sat at the witness stand. He kept demanding, over and over, "What is your relationship to this man?" He would point to a cage in the corner of the room. When Penny looked inside the cage Brad sat there—a ten-year-old Brad with his baseball cap and ragged sneakers on.

No matter what she tried to say, Gregory continued to ask, "What is your relationship to this man?"

"Penny, you're going to be late for church if you don't get up soon, dear," Helen called through her closed door.

Penny groaned and pulled her pillow over her head, trying to drown out her mother's voice and the bright sunlight that streamed through her window.

What had happened to the night's rest she'd come to take for granted over the years? Penny felt as though she'd been up all night in some philosophical debate. Bits of her dreams came back to her, but they didn't make sense. Why would she have dreamed of a young Brad in a cage?

She forced herself up, trying to get her eyelids to stay open. Having Brad home was having a definite effect on her. She wished she could understand it. For the past three years she had built a life for herself, on her own, without Brad's influence.

Within a day of his return, she'd reverted to allowing him to influence her. Take yesterday, for example. They'd played in the park like a couple of kids. *You enjoyed it, though, didn't you,* the little voice inside of her said.

Of course I enjoyed it.

Then what are you complaining about?

She really wasn't sure. There seemed something rather childish about enjoying herself, but she couldn't quite decide what it was.

Penny wandered into her bathroom and turned on the shower. Her mother had been right. If she didn't hurry, she'd be late for church.

By the time she was dressed and grabbed some toast and coffee, Penny was late for the church service. She waited outside the sanctuary doors until after the opening prayer, then slipped into the pew where her family generally sat.

While she hastily thumbed through the hymnal for the first selection she glanced around her. Gregory had become a member of the church and, unless he was out of town, he usually attended Sunday services, but she didn't see him this morning.

The congregation was well into the second verse of the hymn when someone paused by the pew. Penny became aware that someone else was later than she was. She looked up, half expecting Gregory. Instead, Brad edged into the pew beside her and took one side of her hymnbook in a silent request to share.

He looked rested and well-groomed and when she met his eyes he gave her a smile that would have warmed the heart of the coldest critic.

Penny felt her own heart sink. She didn't want to see Brad Crawford. Not today. Not until she was able to get her life back into some sort of order. Whether she liked it or not, Brad was a definite distraction to her.

What would Gregory think if he saw them standing there together, after his questions last night? Why hadn't she ever mentioned Brad to Gregory before?

Could it be she was ashamed of their relationship? How absurd. That would be the same as saying she was ashamed of herself. Brad was so much a part of her he seemed to be an extension of herself. Funny she'd never really thought about that before this weekend.

She'd been so hurt when he went to New York. But it had been good for her. She'd gotten in touch with herself and her own views and goals. If Brad hadn't gone away she probably would have drifted into marriage with him, just because he was so familiar.

What would be wrong with that? that tiny voice asked.

I'm marrying Gregory! He's more my type, she responded sternly. *I don't want to hear any more of your irresponsible remarks.*

The pew where they stood was full. When the hymn was concluded and everyone sat down, Brad was pressed against her side, from shoulder to thigh. She tried to shift but it didn't seem to help. Finally, he placed his arm on the back of the pew, giving them a little extra space, but creating a visual intimacy between them that Penny could have easily done without.

Whenever she glanced at him, Brad responded with a look of smiling inquiry.

He certainly seemed pleased with himself this morning, she thought waspishly. Obviously nothing had disturbed *his* sleep last night.

Penny realized later that she hadn't heard a word the pastor had said during his sermon. It was only when he mentioned the announcements in the bulletin and she heard her name that Penny became aware that she'd missed most of the service.

"You will note that this coming Saturday Gregory Duncan and Penny Blackwell will be joined in Holy Matrimony before this altar," Reverend Wilder said with a smile. "The Blackwells have extended an invitation to each and every one of you to join them in celebrating their daughter's wedding and hope to see you there.''

Penny felt as though a spotlight had fallen on her and Brad as they sat there so closely. She forced herself to keep her eyes trained on Reverend Wilder, whose friendly smile served as a beacon of sanity in her sea of confusion. *This, too, shall pass.* The thought seemed to flow around her and she gained some comfort from it.

As soon as the final song was sung she was ready to bolt from the church and search for solitude.

Instead, it seemed as though everyone who attended church that morning wanted to stop and speak to her . . . and to Brad, who continued to stand beside her in the crowd.

"My, if it doesn't look natural to see the two of you together again," one woman said with a smile after she had greeted them.

"It's good to see you, Mrs. Fielding," Brad replied easily. Her husband owned the local hardware store and had been Brad's coach during his years of Little League.

"I don't suppose you came back in time to stop the wedding now, did you, young man?" she said archly and Penny suddenly prayed for a trap door that would allow her to drop out of sight.

Brad just laughed.

Mrs. Cantrell joined them. "Where is your young man this morning, Penny? When I first saw you standing there this morning, I thought Brad was your Mr. Duncan.''

"I'm not sure where Gregory is, Mrs. Cantrell. How's Mr. Cantrell's leg?"

"Oh, it's healing right nicely. He was just lucky he didn't lose it, being so careless around the farm machinery." Not to be led astray from her subject, she went on. "Guess Mr. Duncan can find better things to do with his time than to go to church on Sunday. Those big city people don't seem to consider it as important as some of us," she said with a sniff.

"Oh, I'm sure it's nothing like that, Mrs. Cantrell. But since we're going to be away for a week, Gregory's been putting in long hours trying to clear his calendar."

"Well, it's sure good to see you here, Brad," Mrs. Cantrell said without commenting on Penny's explanation. "Wish you were going to be back home all the time."

Brad grinned. "Well, if there's some way I could convince the production crew to film *Hope for Tomorrow* here in Payton, I'd move back in a flash."

Everyone laughed, except Penny, who had a sudden vision of what life would be like if Brad lived there full time. Her beautifully planned future would probably become a shambles! She edged her way around the group that had gathered just outside the church doors. She'd almost made it to her car when Brad caught up with her.

"Mind if I get a ride home with you?"

"What's wrong with your car?"

"As you know, I've been using Mom's car. It wouldn't start this morning, so I got a ride in with

Mom and Dad. They were on their way to visit friends for the day."

"I'm surprised you didn't go with them," Penny said, giving in to the inevitable and motioning for him to get in.

"I thought about it, but decided I'd rather spend the day with you."

"Why?" she asked baldly.

He looked at her in surprise, noticing for the first time the dark shadows under her eyes. "Why?" he repeated. "Do I have to have a reason to want to spend the day with you?"

She shrugged. "What if I've already made plans?"

"Have you?"

Good question. Gregory hadn't called before she left, but he'd made it clear today would be extremely busy for him. She'd be lucky to receive a phone call before he left for St. Louis.

She glanced over at Brad. "Not really," she admitted.

"Why don't we take the boat out on the lake?" he suggested. "It looks like a perfect day for it."

Penny thought about his suggestion for a moment. She enjoyed nothing more than being out on the water. The lake had been formed by a dam built over the river. When they were younger she and Brad had spent many a day following the river and exploring some of the coves that had formed when the water backed up.

The thought of a peaceful cove somewhere seemed to be an excellent idea. "All right," she agreed.

"Do you suppose you could find your way around your mom's kitchen enough to make us something to take along to eat?" Brad asked with a grin.

She refused to rise to the bait. "I'm sure I can. It would probably astound you how well I manage on my own these days."

He watched her in silence as they turned down the road that led to their homes. "Is something wrong, Penny?"

Funny he should ask. "What could possibly be wrong, Brad? I'm getting married in six days. Everything is perfect." She refused to look at him.

"You look tired."

"I've been keeping a busy schedule. School was just out and I've had a lot to do, getting ready for the wedding."

Brad said nothing more and Penny found some comfort in the ensuing silence.

Hours later, Penny knew she'd been right to accept Brad's invitation. This was just what she needed. Her sleek, one-piece suit was great to swim in. They had found a cove where they could swim without being afraid of being run over by a boat hauling water-skiers.

Brad and Penny had spent as much time in the water as they could all the years they'd lived at the lake. Consequently they were very much at home in it. They were like a pair of porpoises playing and they quickly returned to the pattern of their childhood. Once again, Penny forgot about Gregory and his promise to call her.

By the time they decided to eat, both of them were laughing and winded.

Penny had cheated. She had raided the refrigerator, knowing her mother wouldn't care. There had been leftover chicken, some ham, potato salad and fresh vegetables, all peeled and sliced. And for dessert, she had cut giant slices of her mother's cherry-chocolate cake.

By the time they finished eating, they felt too lazy to move.

"When do you have to get back?" Brad asked, squinting up at the sun as though trying to decide the time.

"No particular time, I suppose."

"Is Gregory coming over?"

Gregory. She hadn't given him a thought for several hours. A surge of guilt flooded through her. No doubt he'd spent the day working while she was out playing like some carefree teenager.

Brad seemed to have that effect on her. She didn't understand it. When she was with Gregory, she behaved as a mature adult would. Somehow Brad brought out the child in her.

"He didn't say," she finally said, in response to Brad's question.

"I suppose he's really busy."

"Yes."

"He appears to be very successful."

"Yes."

"Must put in some long hours."

"He has, ever since I've known him."

"Doesn't have much time to relax and enjoy himself, then," Brad offered.

Penny glanced over at him thoughtfully. "I think he enjoys himself. His practice is something he enjoys. Not only is it his vocation, it's his avocation as well."

"Do you think you're going to be happy with that sort of life, Penny?" Brad asked. His serious expression let her know he was really concerned.

She leaned back on the cushioned seat. "I won't mind it. I'm busy, too, not only with teaching but with the theater group. We each have our own lives, but we enjoy each other's company as well."

"It seems such a tepid existence for you, of all people."

She sat up and looked at him with a hint of indignation. "What do you mean me, 'of all people'?"

"Oh, you know, Runt. You're so full of life and vitality, your energy never seems to run down. I can't see all of that passion bottled into such a tame existence."

She laughed. "You're crazy. I'm not some wild, passionate creature who craves excitement."

"Maybe not. But you could be. The only time you let it loose is on stage. You've never allowed it to show, except when you lose your temper."

"Which I never do, except when you're around."

"Why do you suppose that is?"

"Besides the fact that you can be extremely aggravating at times and more than a little irritating at other times?" She widened her eyes in an innocent stare. "Why, I have no idea, Mr. Crawford. None at all."

He leaned back so that he was stretched full length across the rear of the boat. "I came home to break up your engagement," he said in a matter-of-fact tone.

His quiet statement caused her to come out of her seat. "You did what?"

"You heard me."

"How dare you even consider it!"

"I know. I finally came to the same conclusion."

She stared at him in disbelief. "But why would you even want to?"

He shrugged. "It doesn't really matter now. Since I've met him, and talked with you, I realize that if he's what you want I have no right to cause problems for you."

The idea that he had even thought of doing such a thing infuriated her. "Just who in the hell do you think you are—God?"

"No. But I am your friend. I care what happens to you. I didn't want you to make a mistake."

"And you think you know better than I do what's best for me?" she demanded to know.

"Obviously not, or I would have gone through with it."

"Fat chance, you egotistical, arrogant boob. I believe your new status and identity have gone to your head!"

"Aw, come on, Runt, you know better than that."

"And stop calling me that revolting name."

"You never used to mind it."

"Well, I certainly do now. It was all right when I was a child. It sounds perfectly ridiculous now."

Penny couldn't remember the last time she had felt such anger. Whenever it was, she was certain that it had been directed toward Brad then, as well. He was the most impossible, infuriating—she couldn't find enough names to call him.

"I want to go home," she said in carefully level tones. *Before I attempt bodily harm on you,* she added silently. To think that she had considered him a friend. But no friend would even consider doing to her what he had admitted planning.

Brad sat up. "Fine with me."

She turned the blower switch on, giving time for the fumes to clear before starting the boat. Without another word, they began to pack up the remains of their lunch. Then Penny, being the closest, started the boat and began to leave the cove.

As soon as they cleared the cove she moved the throttle to pick up speed. Out of the corner of her eye she caught a movement and glanced around in time to see another boat shooting around the point, coming directly at her. Pure reflex saved them from a nasty collision.

Penny yelled and jerked the steering wheel hard, cutting their speed at the same time. The combination of suddenly turning and losing speed caused quite a reaction on board and Penny heard a commotion of bumps and Brad's yell behind her.

The other boat went by. It was filled with a bunch of teenagers who were laughing and waving at her.

"Stupid jerks!" she yelled. "Don't you have any better sense? If you don't know water safety you should stay off the lake!" She doubted that they heard her words, but she felt better. Turning around she began to say, "I'm sorry, Brad, I hope you didn't—"

He was crumpled on the deck, the ice chest lying on top of him.

"Brad!" Penny scrambled over a loose oar, life jackets and other paraphernalia that had spilled out during the near-collision. She knelt by his side. Shoving the cooler aside she reached for him. His color seemed to be gone and he wasn't moving. "Brad?" There was a gash at his temple, and blood seemed to be everywhere. "Oh, God! Brad!"

He didn't respond.

Frantic, Penny looked around. They had come a few miles from home. There was nothing on shore that indicated people might be close by. Even in her panic she knew she had to get help. The closest she could think of was home.

Penny grabbed a towel and began to clean the blood from his face. She held pressure there until the flow eased up. Then she gently checked to see if she could find any other injuries.

He was out cold and she didn't know how badly he'd been hit. There was nothing more she could do now. She had to get him to the hospital as quickly as possible.

Penny didn't even realize she was crying until she had to keep blinking to see where she was going on the way home.

Brad was hurt and it was her fault. She'd been so mad at him. She'd even thought about doing him bodily harm! And look what had happened. "I didn't mean it, God! You know I didn't mean it. Don't let it be serious. Please. Please let him be all right."

She set new speed records getting home. As soon as she could tie up the boat at her dock she ran up the path. "Mom! Dad! Call the ambulance, Brad's been hurt!"

Penny burst into the house, gasping for breath. Gregory met her by the time she reached the kitchen, her parents right behind him. She absently noticed his casual dress but she had no time to question him.

"What's the matter!" he demanded.

"It's Brad! He fell. Hit his head. He's bleeding and I don't know how badly he's hurt."

He grabbed her by the shoulders. "All right, now. Calm down. You call an ambulance and we'll go check on him."

Quickly she nodded, reaching for the wall phone and glancing at the emergency number posted nearby.

Later, Penny couldn't seem to remember all of the events. She knew Gregory and her dad had gone down to the landing and had brought Brad up to the house. He was still unconscious.

She'd called his parents and they were all there when the ambulance arrived. Without thinking about it, Penny crawled into the ambulance with him, holding his hand and whispering to him. "I'm sorry, Brad. I never meant to hurt you. You know that. It was just a crazy accident. Please get better, Brad. Please don't be hurt bad."

The attendant handed her a tissue and she realized that tears still streamed down her face.

The doctor was waiting for them when they arrived and it was only when they'd taken him into the examining room that Penny realized she was standing barefoot in her bathing suit.

Both sets of parents and Gregory arrived within minutes. Her mother, bless her heart, had grabbed some clean, dry clothes for her and Penny excused herself and went into the ladies' restroom to change.

As soon as she came out she asked, "Have you heard anything?"

They all shook their heads. Gregory led her to a couch that looked as though it had been brought off the ark and sat down beside her. "Can you tell us what happened?"

As coherently as possible, she explained the sequence of events. When she was finished, Gregory asked, "Could you identify the other boat or any of the people in it?"

"I doubt it. It all happened so fast. They were just a bunch of kids out having a good time and not paying attention."

"Without your quick responses, it could have been much worse, you know. They need to be found and reprimanded."

Her eyes filled once again. "It was so awful, Gregory," she said in a choked voice. "We'd been fighting and I was so blasted mad at him, but I didn't want him to get hurt." She lay her head on his shoulder and cried, her sobs shaking her body.

"I know. He's very special to you. I'm beginning to understand that."

He held her until eventually the emotional shock began to abate and she had managed to gain some measure of control.

The doctor on call appeared in the doorway of the waiting room. He was new to the area and none of them knew him.

He smiled at the three couples waiting and said, "This young man was very lucky. He did receive a concussion, but it could have been much worse. Blows to the temple are very tricky things."

Brad's mother asked, "But he's going to be all right. You're sure?"

"Oh, yes. He came to for a few minutes. He's still groggy and we gave him something to ease the pain." He paused and glanced at the three women. "Which one of you is Penny?"

Penny came to her feet. The doctor's smile widened. "You might want to go in and see him for a few minutes. He's disoriented and seems to think something happened to you. He's been calling your name and fighting me, saying he had to find you."

Without a thought Penny joined the doctor in the doorway. "Where is he?"

He turned and started down the hallway. "We put him in this room," he said, opening the door and holding it for her.

Penny tiptoed into the room. The shades were drawn and it was dim. The doctor snapped on a night-light and she could see Brad lying there, his head swathed in white bandages. His eyes were closed and he looked so pale. Penny bit her lip to keep from crying out.

She glanced around and discovered the doctor had left the room. Hesitantly she approached the bed. Brad was in a hospital gown and the sheet was folded neatly over his chest. His hands rested on either side of him. She took his hand and slowly lifted it to her mouth, brushing her lips across his knuckles.

Brad's lashes fluttered, then he slowly opened his eyes. "Penny?" His lips moved but there was very little sound.

"I'm here, Brad."

"You okay?" he managed to say. He was having trouble moving his mouth.

"I'm fine. It's you we've been worried about."

"Wha' happened?"

"A boat almost rammed us. I dodged to miss them and threw you halfway across our boat." Tears began to stream down her face once more. "Oh, Brad. I'm so sorry."

"Wasn't your fault," he said drowsily.

"I'm sorry I got so mad at you. I was afraid you'd been killed and I would never be able to tell you how sorry I am."

"I'm...too hard-headed...to be hurt...by a blow...to my head," he said haltingly, trying to smile. She could see the pain in his eyes and she ached with shared pain. "Besides, you had a right...to get angry at me. Trying to break...engagement...was... childish thing to do."

She smiled. "I'm afraid I have to agree with you there, my friend."

"I'm sorry...forgive me?"

She stroked his cheek with her free hand. "You know me, Brad, I can never stay mad at you for long. I never could."

"Good thing," he replied, his voice slurred. "Or you'd...be angry...all...time."

"I'm sure the doctor wants you to rest," she said. "Your folks are waiting outside. I know they want to see you."

He smiled, a slow, sleepy smile that seemed to increase the ache in her heart.

She leaned over and kissed him. "I'll see you tomorrow, Brad." She laid his hand on his chest, but she didn't let go immediately.

He squeezed her hand but didn't say anything. She patted the hand she still held and slowly released him, suddenly feeling awkward.

Then Penny turned around and left the room.

Chapter Five

Gregory was quiet on the way home and Penny felt too drained to try to make conversation. He followed her into the house and she went to the kitchen to make coffee, motioning him into the living room.

Her parents had stayed at the hospital with the Crawfords. No one had expressed an opinion as to when they'd return.

When she brought the coffee into the living room Penny suddenly realized she had never asked Gregory why he'd been there that afternoon.

"I'm so glad you came today," she said, handing him his cup and settling beside him on the couch. "I'm just sorry I wasn't here. I thought you said you were going to spend the day working."

He looked at her and smiled, a wry smile that she found endearing. "Actually, I had no intention of leaving the office until I had made a dent in the pile of files and papers on my desk.'' Gregory settled back on the sofa with a sigh. ''After a few hours I noticed there was no appreciable difference in the amount of work in front of me.'' He took a sip of coffee. ''I kept thinking of you and how much I wanted to be with you.''

Gregory peered into his cup as though looking for an answer to a thorny question. ''As a matter of fact, I decided to forget about the work for a while and come get you. I thought we could spend some time together out on the lake.''

His eyes met hers. ''When I got here your parents mentioned that you and Brad had gone out a few hours earlier.''

Penny touched his cheek lightly with her hand. ''I wish I'd known. I could have waited.''

''Spending the day with you and Brad wasn't what I had in mind.''

''What I meant was that if I'd known, I would have waited and gone out with you. Brad would have found someone else to spend the day with.''

Gregory studied her face, enjoying the candid expression in her blue eyes, the way her flyaway curls clustered on her forehead. Most of all he enjoyed the unconscious innocence she projected, not so much a sexual innocence, although he was willing to bet that was the case. But Penny had a wholesomeness, such a trusting nature that he sometimes felt he was hundreds of years older than she. The ugliness of the world seemed to have passed her by, as though, like a princess in a fairy tale, she had been locked away and protected from some of the harsher realities of life.

"You mentioned earlier that you and Brad had been arguing," he said with a slight smile.

Penny felt her face flush. "Yes."

"About what?"

She stared at him in dismay. She had no idea what Gregory thought of Brad. He was an expert at keeping his thoughts and opinions to himself. For some reason she didn't want him to know about Brad's intention to break them up. The point was, he hadn't and he was sorry. There was no need to share the details with Gregory.

"I can't even remember," she said, not meeting his eyes. "Brad and I seem to argue every time we're around each other."

"I still find that surprising in you."

"I know. Some people have that effect on others."

He nodded thoughtfully. "Yes, that's true. Sparks fly."

She laughed. "They definitely fly whenever Brad and I get together." She hugged Gregory. "I'm so glad you and I don't react that way to each other. I much prefer our comfortable relationship." When he didn't reply she went on to say, "I never got around to thanking you for your help today. I don't know what I would have done without you."

He held her hard against his chest, unable to resist her lips so close to his. Gregory kissed her, feeling her warmth pressed against him.

When he finally released her he smiled at the picture she made—her cheeks flushed, her eyes sparkling, her mouth slightly swollen. "I was glad to help, but you would have done just fine without me. You handled yourself extremely well in the emergency, never losing your head."

"Oh, no. I almost drowned you in my tears at the hospital."

"Yes, after the crisis was over. But when you needed to be strong you managed to give Brad first aid, then got him home. I was very proud of you today. I want you to know that."

"Oh, Gregory. Your ability to understand me is one of the things I love about you," she said, her arms still around him.

He was quiet for a few moments, then said, "It's interesting, isn't it, the many different ways we can love. Some people seem to have a larger capacity for love than others. You seem to have grown up giving your love to people—your parents, Brad, his parents; later the people who live in Payton. Now me."

She smiled at him.

"I always had trouble understanding that emotion they called love. I've seen some of the tragedies that have occurred in the name of love, witnessed selfishness and possessiveness that have been given the label of love, but until I met you, I never truly experienced what it all meant—the generosity of love for its own sake, and what a difference it could make in life." He looked down at her, trying to memorize the beauty that was in her. "Thank you for showing me how unselfish love can be, how generous."

"It was my pleasure," she said with a mischievous grin. "You've shown me a great deal, too, you know."

"Have I? In what way?"

"You didn't treat me like some fragile doll sitting on a shelf. You've always treated me as an equal, with respect and admiration."

"Hasn't everyone?"

"It's hard to explain. But living in the same small town all my life has meant that everyone has preconceived ideas about me. Until you came along, nobody would even ask me out for a date!"

"Why do you suppose they didn't?"

She grinned. "Because all the eligible men already knew me too well, I guess."

"It couldn't have anything to do with Brad, could it?"

She frowned. "What does Brad have to do with my not being asked on a date?"

"Perhaps everyone thought you two were a pair," he suggested.

Penny rolled her eyes. "That's quite possible. I know everybody acted surprised when you and I announced our engagement. I just assumed they thought you'd been tricked into proposing to me."

Gregory threw his head back and laughed and she began to laugh with him. "Oh, Penny, what an innocent you are!" He studied her for a moment, the light of laughter gradually disappearing out of his eyes. "Then you admit that people saw you and Brad as a couple."

She shrugged. "I can't very well deny it. Since he's been home everyone I've seen has made some comment. But that's their problem. It doesn't really concern you and me. Once we're married, they'll get those silly ideas out of their heads."

"So you don't really wish that it were Brad you were marrying instead of me?"

"Brad and I don't have that sort of a relationship. We never did. You are the man I'm going to marry." She sounded very final.

Gregory smiled. "I'm glad to hear it." He carefully unwrapped her arms from around his neck. "However, at the moment I think I'd better let you get some rest. I've still got to pack and get ready to return to St. Louis."

Penny hated to see him leave. She enjoyed his companionship so much. She felt safe and secure whenever he was around. In particular, she needed his presence this final week before she married him, especially now that Brad was here. She couldn't explain it. She just knew it was true. But she knew she mustn't be selfish, so she walked him to the door in silence.

He paused at the door and looked down at her. "I'm going to be extremely busy, so don't worry if you don't hear from me. I'll be back in time for the rehearsal Friday night. You can count on it."

She nodded. "I'll just think about this time next week when we'll be on our honeymoon," she said with a grin. "That should help fill the next few days."

"I'm sure you'll want to spend some time with Brad while he's recuperating." Gregory waited for a denial, for some sign that, despite everything he had seen and heard, Penny wasn't as attached to Brad as Gregory was finally coming to accept.

"Yes, that's true," she said, unaware of what he was thinking. "You know his television character is supposed to be in a coma. He almost had a chance to find out what that was like firsthand." She shook her head. "I bet he's already regretting having come home for the wedding."

"Then again, it might have been a very crucial decision for his future. Who knows?" Gregory said, leaning over and kissing her softly on the mouth. "I suppose only time will tell."

I wonder what he meant by that? Penny asked herself when she went upstairs and began to prepare for bed. Gregory could certainly be enigmatic at times. No doubt that trait was one of the reasons he was such a brilliant attorney.

"Oh, how sweet," Brad cooed in a cloying falsetto voice, clasping his hands under his chin and giving her an idiotic smile. "You brought me some candy," he said as she walked into his hospital room the next morning carrying a gaily wrapped package.

Penny was relieved to see him looking so much better. His color had improved considerably since the day before. Today he looked almost rakish with his head bandaged, but there were still deep bruises under his eyes.

"What I have is much better for you than candy," she informed him, walking over to the bed and handing him the package. "I've brought you a coloring book and some crayons." It was worth the search she'd gone to that morning to see the expression on his face.

Without missing a beat he said, "Fantastic, what kind?"

"Only the best for you, my friend—a book immortalizing the characters from *Star Wars.*"

Brad started to chuckle, then gently touched his head. "Please don't make me laugh. My head feels like it's going to topple off my shoulders when I so much as move it. Laughter would destroy me."

She leaned over and kissed him on the cheek. "Poor baby. And here I thought you'd be so pleased."

"I am. I am. You're the only one who knows about my secret passion for the *Star Wars* trilogy."

"Oh, I don't think you managed to keep your deep, dark secret from your mom. Remember, she was the one who attempted to keep order in your room for years."

He smiled. "Yes, but I've learned that I can trust the two women in my life to keep my deeply-guarded secret."

"So how are you feeling?"

"Like I've spent a week wrapped around several bottles of booze and just surfaced."

"That bad, huh?"

"I knew there was a reason I never drank much. Can you imagine someone paying to feel this bad?"

"Who are you kidding? You never wanted to lose your wholesome kid image and you know it."

"Wholesome? Me? Don't let my producer hear you say that. He's convinced I look like the sort who'd start seducing maidens before breakfast and continue throughout the day without pause."

She grinned. "Are you sure that's the appeal? I always thought you looked like the sort women dreamed of being seduced by."

He eyed her speculatively. "Oh, yeah? Tell me more."

"Nothing doing. You're too vain as it is."

Brad patted the side of his bed and she perched on it. "I don't think I remembered to thank you for your help yesterday," he said.

"My help! That blow to the head must have really befuddled you, my friend. I'm afraid I was the one who caused it."

"That's not the way Dad explained it. You probably saved us both from a serious, perhaps even fatal, collision."

Penny couldn't think of anything to say. She glanced around the room, then back at him. "Has the doctor said when you're going to be able to get out of here?"

"Hopefully tomorrow. He said I would have to take it easy for a few days, but since that was the way I'd intended to spend the week anyway, I'm not going to have much trouble following the doctor's orders."

"Are you sorry you came back?" she asked quietly.

He waited until her eyes met his. They stared at each other for an indeterminable length of time. "No, I'm not sorry. My only regret is that I didn't come back sooner."

"Why do you say that?"

"It doesn't matter. Now you're deliriously in love with your handsome lawyer and soon you'll be a blushing bride and will live happily ever after.'' He took her hand and held it between both of his. "You know, Penny, that's all I ever wanted, for you to be happy. I've enjoyed our time together this week—the visit to the park, the fun we had yesterday.''

"Some fun.''

"It was, most of it. Sharing those things with you, one last time, helped me to say goodbye to our shared past. I needed the transition time, a chance to be with you before you become the oh, so proper wife of the esteemed and honorable Gregory Duncan.''

"Now you're making fun of us.''

"Not at all. I'm trying like hell not to envy what the two of you have.''

"You'll find it for yourself, someday.''

He nodded. "Of course I will.''

She made a face. "And I'll hate her on sight,'' she admitted with a slight smile.

His eyebrows arched slightly. "Without even knowing her?''

"Without a doubt. You always had such lousy taste in women, you know.''

"Oh, really?'' he said in a dangerous tone.

"Yes, really! Have you forgotten dating Diana during our second year at college?''

"How could I ever forget the lovely Diana? She was a knockout.''

"True. And she was also sleeping with every guy on the campus.''

"Yeah, well, no man's education is quite complete without a Diana in his life,'' he said with a grin.

"What about Beth?''

"What was wrong with Beth?" he asked with surprise. "I thought you liked her."

"Liked her? I felt sorry for her. How she ever managed to get out of grade school, much less find her way into college, always remained a mystery to me."

"So she wasn't the brightest person we've ever known. She was very sweet."

"Yes. And she adored you."

"Can't fault her taste."

"Only her intelligence."

They paused and grinned at each other.

Brad squeezed the hand he still held. "God, I've missed you. Nobody has ever given me such a bad time, or led me in such intricate circles as you."

"*Moi?*" she asked in mock surprise. "Surely not."

"Why didn't you ever come to New York to see me, like I wrote and asked you to?"

Penny gazed out the window, thinking back over the years. "Because I was still too angry with you."

"Angry! What had I done?"

"You left me here and went off to continue playing at life."

"Is that what it seemed to you?"

She nodded. "I guess I had always assumed you'd come back to Payton and go to work with your dad. It never occurred to me that your talk of New York was anything but the usual chatter we all had. About the time when we'd be discovered and cast in a starring role. Or being understudy one night, stopping the show as the lead the next."

"You could still do that, you know."

"Not me. I can't see Gregory content to have a wife living half a continent away."

"There is that."

Penny slipped from the bed and brushed the wrinkles from her skirt. "I don't want to keep you from your coloring, my dear. Maybe the nurse will help you if you get too tired to finish by yourself."

Brad didn't smile but continued to look at her. His hand still grasped hers and he slowly loosened his hold. "I love you, Penny," he said, his voice so low she almost didn't hear him. "Thank you for being a part of my life."

In all the years she had known him, he had never said those words to her before. Hearing them now did something strange to her. She wanted to laugh. She wanted to cry. She wanted to throw her arms around his neck. She wanted to go running down the hall.

"I love you, too, Brad," she finally replied.

"Now's a hell of a time to let me in on that little secret," he pointed out rather grimly.

"You haven't exactly been forthcoming yourself, you know."

"I know. Words of love are too special to use lightly. But then, you're a very special person in my life. You always will be."

Penny couldn't control the tears that suddenly flooded her eyes. "You are, too."

"Remember, if you ever need me, for anything, I'll always be there for you. That's what friends are for."

She couldn't say a word. Not one. For if she did, she would end up making a complete fool of herself. So she squeezed his hand, then turned away and walked out of the room.

When Gregory called her that night she was able to report that Brad was rapidly improving and due to come home the next day.

"That's good news, I'm sure."

"Yes," she said, a little abstracted. Penny had wandered around the house all day, like a lost soul trying to find its home. "How are things going for you?" she asked, determined to concentrate on Gregory.

He filled her in on some of the complications he'd run into and she found her thoughts wandering once again. She loved Gregory; there was no way to deny what she felt for him. But it was so different from the way she felt for Brad.

Would she ever be able to forget how she felt for those few moments when she thought Brad was dead? Penny never wanted to suffer through anything so traumatic again. She couldn't begin to picture what life would be like for her if she didn't know that Brad Crawford was somewhere in the world.

"Penny?"

"Oh, I'm sorry, Gregory, I was distracted for a moment."

There was a silence for a moment before Gregory responded. "I'm not surprised," he finally said. "You've had so much on your mind, lately."

"No more than you, I'm sure."

"Yes, well, different things affect us different ways. I've got to let you go for now. I'll see you Friday night."

"Fine. Take care now."

"You, too."

Penny hung up the phone, feeling oddly restless and discontent.

For a moment she wished she could lie down and go to sleep and wake up Saturday morning in time for her wedding. The prewedding jitters were getting completely out of hand.

Brad had been home for three days when his mother called him to the phone. He assumed it was Penny checking to see how he was feeling, although she generally came over. In fact, she had promised him a game of chess sometime that day before she had to go to the church for the wedding rehearsal.

"Hello?"

"Good morning, Brad. This is Gregory Duncan. How are you feeling these days?"

To say Brad was surprised to hear from Penny's fiancé would be a definite understatement. He had assumed that Penny was reporting his progress to Gregory whenever they spoke to each other. For some reason Brad didn't feel as though he had made Gregory's best friends' list.

"I'm feeling much better, thank you."

"I was wondering if you'd feel up to meeting me somewhere. There's something I would like to discuss with you."

"Today?"

"Yes, if at all possible. Penny may have told you I've been in St. Louis all week. I just got in."

"I see," Brad said, automatically. Actually, he didn't see at all. Why was Gregory calling him? More important, why would he want to meet with him?

"Brad? Are you there?"

"Oh, sorry. I was thinking. Yes, I suppose I could meet you at your office, if that would be convenient."

"Fine. I'll see you whenever you can get here."

Brad hung up the phone, still puzzled. Maybe Penny had told Gregory about their conversation at the hospital. Was Gregory going to tell him to keep away from his wife? That was a little dramatic, but then trial attorneys had been known to use a little drama to get a point across.

Brad absently touched his head, where a small bandage covered the blow he'd received.

Perhaps the blow to his head had caused him to feel all of this confusion. Maybe he was Drew Derek, recovering from his stay at the hospital. This visit home certainly had all the elements that could be found in a soap opera.

He could almost hear the strains of music in the background while the announcer intoned—"Tune in tomorrow to find out . . . What does Gregory want to say to Brad? Does Gregory know that Brad is in love with his fiancé and had hoped to break up their engagement? Will Gregory denounce Brad to Penny? Will Brad be barred from the church for fear he might try to stop the proceedings? Stay tuned . . ."

Brad shook his head. Obviously his vacation had been long overdue. He must be cracking up.

Brad had never seen the building where Gregory Duncan had his law practice. He was impressed. The office itself was even more impressive. A middle-aged woman sat at a secretarial desk in the reception area.

"May I help you?" she asked pleasantly.

"My name is Brad Crawford. I—"

"Oh, yes, Mr. Crawford. Mr. Duncan asked that you be shown in immediately." She came around her desk and led him down a hallway lined with law books. Tapping on the door at the end, she announced, "Mr. Crawford is here," and stepped back, allowing Brad to enter.

The office was a corner one, so two walls were almost entirely made up of glass. Since the building was located on the edge of town, the view from the windows was of meadows, rolling hills and a distant glimpse of the river.

"I'm impressed," Brad said quietly, standing in the doorway.

Gregory had stood when he walked in. Now he walked around his massive desk toward Brad. The room seemed large enough to hold a basketball court. All the furniture, furnishings and the well-dressed man coming toward him spoke of dignity and wealth. How could Brad have been so stupid as to suggest Gregory might be marrying Penny for her future prospects? He could probably buy and sell the Blackwells from his petty cash.

Gregory stuck out his hand. "I appreciate your coming in on such short notice, Brad." He motioned to the chairs that were arranged in front of his desk. "Won't you have a seat?"

"I don't mind. I haven't been all that booked up this week," Brad said casually.

"I'm sure that Penny has kept you company during your convalescence."

Brad tried to read something into that statement—sarcasm, anger, jealousy. He heard none of those things. It had been a simple statement. Brad looked at the older man who had seated himself behind the desk once more. "Yes, she has." He raised one brow slightly. "Does that bother you?"

"To the contrary," Gregory said with a brief smile. "I fully expected to hear it, which is why I called you. There's something I need to say to you."

Feeling as though he were in the middle of a play and had forgotten his lines, Brad waited for Gregory to continue.

Gregory leaned his arms on the desk blotter lying in front of him, clasped his hands and met Brad's gaze with his own. "You're in love with Penny, aren't you?"

He'd been right. Gregory was going to see that he was removed from Penny's life. Brad wished he found the situation a little more amusing. How could he convince the man that his love for Penny was the very thing that would prevent him from doing anything to hurt her marriage to Gregory? Searching for the right words, Brad finally shrugged and admitted, "Yes, I am, but you're the man she's marrying."

"No, I'm not," Gregory replied quietly.

Brad was convinced something was wrong with his hearing. Perhaps the blow to his head had... "I beg your pardon?"

"You heard me."

"Of course you're marrying Penny. The rehearsal is tonight and tomorrow—"

"Tomorrow I will be in California. I discovered earlier today where a key witness is located. I'm flying out tonight to take his deposition."

"But the wedding?"

Gregory leaned back. "Ah, yes, the wedding." He placed his hands behind his head. "An interesting situation, isn't it? Two men who love Penny, discussing a wedding that isn't going to come off."

"Couldn't you postpone your deposition or whatever? Surely Penny is more important than—"

"I understand your concern. Now you need to understand mine. I've had a great deal of time to think this week and I've come to the conclusion that Penny seriously misled me."

"What are you talking about? Penny doesn't lie!"

"Please don't put words in my mouth," Gregory responded.

Brad was now facing the courtroom lawyer and recognized he could be a formidable foe.

"When I met Penny I thought she was everything I wanted in a wife. Since then I've come to know her better, and I've had reason to revise that opinion."

"What's that supposed to mean?"

"I've decided that marrying Penny would be a mistake on my part."

"Why?" Brad demanded to know.

"For over a year I've spent time with the quiet, organized, unflappable woman I knew as Penny Blackwell. Yet in three days a volatile, passionate woman I never knew existed emerged as a result of your presence. I'm not comfortable with that person. I have no room for her in my life." He nodded to the younger man. "I believe I have you to thank for the transformation. As far as I'm concerned, I've had a very narrow escape."

Brad came to his feet. "That's a hell of a thing to say! You wait until the day before your wedding to decide you don't know the woman you intend to marry so you're backing out? How can you do this to Penny? When do you intend to tell her how you feel?"

"I don't."

Brad had never felt such a murderous rage in all of his life. Gregory was calmly explaining that he intended to destroy Penny's life without even bothering to warn her?

"You really are a no-good, son-of-a—"

"Yes, I probably am. However, I did not reach my age or gain the experience I presently possess by being quixotic and foolish. I don't believe Penny understands what it is she feels for me. Whatever she feels, I don't think it's what I want from my wife. It's better to make a clean break now."

Gregory watched the younger man as though evaluating his reaction to what he'd just been told.

He got an immediate response. "You really are cold-blooded, aren't you? You don't care what you do to Penny, how you hurt her. She didn't measure up to some ridiculous standards you seem to have, so you're going to abandon her at the church.''

"I don't intend to be that dramatic. I'll leave that sort of thing to you. You seem well-trained for it.''

"If you don't intend telling her you've changed your mind, how the hell is she going to know?''

Gregory met his gaze and deliberately smiled. "Why, you'll tell her, of course. Why do you suppose I asked you to come in today?''

"Me? Are you out of your mind? It isn't my place to—''

"You're her friend, aren't you?''

"You're damn right I'm her friend, but—''

"I'm sure she'd rather receive such news from you.''

"You're wrong! She'd rather hear it from you!''

"Somehow, I doubt that very much,'' Gregory said in a dry voice.

"Well, of course, you're right. Nobody wants to be told on the eve of their wedding that the other party has backed out.''

"I have to agree.''

"But it's none of my business. This is between you and Penny,'' Brad protested.

"Not any longer. I am here only long enough to pick up some papers I need. I'm leaving as soon as we're through here. How you want to handle everything from now on is up to you.''

"Well, thank you very much. For nothing. How in the hell can I help her face this?''

Gregory rubbed his chin thoughtfully. "You could always take my place at the church tomorrow.''

Chapter Six

By the time Brad reached home his head felt as though it were going to explode. He didn't even remember leaving Gregory Duncan's office or driving home. Only the intense pain in his head held his attention until he realized he was sitting in his room, staring at the wall.

He had to find Penny and tell her. But how was he going to break the news? Damn the man, anyway. How could anyone be so unfeeling as to walk out on someone the day before the wedding?

It would break Penny's heart.

Forcing himself to go in search of her, Brad started through the kitchen of his home.

"Your head must be really bothering you," his mother said when she saw his expression. "Why don't you lie down and rest awhile?"

He turned, wincing at the sudden movement. "I've got to talk to Penny."

"She should be over here before much longer. Why don't you rest until she gets here?"

Perhaps that was good advice. He would take some of the pain medication the doctor had given him when he left the hospital. He hadn't used it before, but at the moment he was willing to do whatever he could for some relief.

After swallowing the tablets he stretched out on the bed and waited for Penny to come.

Oh, God, Penny. If only you didn't have to go through all of this.

By the time Penny peeked in to see if he still wanted to play chess, she found him sound asleep. His mother had told her that he had gone out for a while and was concerned that he had tried to do too much, too soon. She mentioned that he wanted to see Penny, but they both agreed it would be better to leave him alone and let him rest.

Penny had enough on her mind. She hadn't talked with Gregory since Monday evening, which wasn't like him at all. And he hadn't called to let her know he was back today. What if he was late for the rehearsal, or even worse, unable to make it?

She wouldn't let herself think of that. If he was delayed too much, she was certain he would call. Gregory was an honorable man and dependable. If she hadn't been in such a turmoil all week she wouldn't have worked herself up to such a state now.

Everything was under control. She would see Gregory this evening and they could laugh at her silliness.

Her mother decided not to go to the rehearsal so Penny drove to the church alone. Her dad was coming directly from his office.

When everyone was there but Gregory, Reverend Wilder suggested they begin. "After all, the groom has very little to do. I think that's for a reason," he kidded. "Usually the groom is too nervous to think of much of anything."

They all laughed politely, then followed his instructions.

"Have you talked with Gregory today?" Penny's father asked while they waited their turn to go down the aisle.

"No, I haven't."

"I hope nothing is wrong."

"So do I. Perhaps he just got held up. He's probably on his way now."

"Well, he could have called to let you know."

She gave her father a sidelong glance. "You know, Dad, that thought *had* crossed my mind."

He chuckled and patted her arm. "I'm sorry. I suppose I'm more nervous about the groom's absence than you are."

"Not necessarily. But I don't want anyone to think I'm nervous. What you are presently witnessing is my superb acting ability."

At that moment Reverend Wilder motioned for them to start down the aisle. Penny and her father didn't have a chance to speak in private again.

* * *

When Brad woke up he noted with relief that his head felt considerably better. Then he noticed it was dark. "Oh, no!" His sudden effort to sit up on the bed reminded him that he was far from being cured, despite the rest.

By the time he got over to the Blackwells', he knew he'd missed Penny. Helen confirmed his guess. "If you want to see her, you're welcome to wait. I'm sure they'll be home soon."

Brad was too restless at the moment to sit and try to make conversation. What he had to tell Penny had to be said in private. What she chose to do after that was anybody's guess. But it wasn't up to him to inform her mother or anyone else.

Brad spent the next few hours rehearsing what he needed to say to Penny.

"You could always marry her yourself," Gregory had said. The refrain kept running over and over through Brad's head.

There was just one thing wrong with that idea. Penny had no desire to marry him. She was in love with Gregory Duncan. The louse. The no-good, rotten arrogant fool who didn't care that he was leaving her to face the embarrassment and humiliation of a church full of people and no bridegroom.

What was she going to do at this late date? How could she possibly call everyone and explain? What could she say? How could Gregory Duncan have done such a thing to her? If he had any feelings for her at all, he would have talked to her, either in person or even by telephone. At the very least, he could have written her.

Why the hell had he chosen Brad to break the news to her?

That's what friends are for. Was that it? Gregory knew that Brad would do his best to shield Penny as much as possible. He'd even marry her if it would help.

Brad thought about that for a long while. Would it help? It couldn't make things any worse. At least she could have the wedding as planned, the reception. He seriously doubted she'd be interested in a honeymoon. Not with him, anyway. Brad tried not to allow himself to think about a honeymoon where he and Penny would be together, alone, and legally married. That way of thinking led to insanity.

Perhaps he and Penny could work out something so that she wouldn't feel abandoned and forgotten. She would never have a need to feel that way as long as Brad was around.

Ralph and Penny got home at about the same time. Her mother said that Brad had been looking for her. There had been no message from Gregory.

She glanced at the time. It was almost eleven—too late to see what Brad wanted. Her parents went up to bed, knowing they would need their rest for the next day.

Penny almost called Brad anyway. She needed to talk to someone. Not just someone, she needed Brad, she realized. He was the only person she knew with whom she could share her fears and be sure he wouldn't laugh.

But his mother said he was still suffering from considerable pain. No doubt he was already asleep now, and he really needed his rest.

Oh, well. She'd see him at the reception tomorrow, and they could chat before she and Gregory left to go wherever it was that Gregory planned to take her. Once Brad returned to New York, Penny knew her life would resume its normal pace.

She knew that he wasn't to blame for all her restlessness this week, but he seemed to symbolize a certain freedom that she was willingly giving up by marrying Gregory. She knew she'd feel more at peace once Brad wasn't around to remind her.

Quietly climbing the stairs, Penny went into her room and without turning on the light grabbed her nightshirt and went into her bathroom. She went through her nightly ritual, showering and drying her hair. Tonight she needed to remember to soak her contacts. She wouldn't want to be bothered next week while they were traveling. Thank God she knew the way to bed blindfolded, she thought with a grin. It was amazing how dependent she'd become on her extended-wear lenses.

Flipping off the light she felt her way to the bed and had almost reached it when a hand touched her arm and a voice said, ''Don't let me scare—''

She was already beginning to scream when a hand clamped over her mouth in a firm grip.

''Oh, for God's sake, Penny. I'm not a rapist! What's the matter with you?''

As soon as she heard his voice, she recognized Brad but she hadn't been able to control her involuntary scream. She went limp in his arms and he released her mouth.

"Are you okay? I didn't hurt you, did I?" he asked in a low voice. Brad reached over to the bedside lamp and turned it on. They both blinked in the sudden light.

"How did you get in here?" she hissed.

"The same way I always got into your room—through the window, remember?" He motioned to the opened window and the oak tree that stood outside.

"What is so important that you have to scare me half out of my mind to tell me? Couldn't it have waited until tomorrow?" She wished she could focus on his face better. Penny couldn't see his expression at all. She sat down on the edge of the bed and glared at him.

"You're wearing my old football jersey," Brad said in a wondering tone.

"You mean you risked your neck climbing that old tree to crawl into my window to tell me that?" she asked incredulously.

"Of course not. I just didn't know you had kept it, that's all."

She sighed. "I kept every one you gave me. I find them very comfortable to sleep in. I've used them for years."

He couldn't help grinning but she didn't seem to notice. Now that he looked more closely, she didn't seem to be looking at him. At least, she was staring at him, but she didn't see him. She had that same vague, unfocused look she used to get when... "You don't have your contacts in, do you?" he asked, suddenly comprehending why she seemed somehow different.

Penny began to feel bewildered. Brad didn't seem to be his normal self at all, tonight. Then she remembered, but, of course; he was still recovering from his accident. That blow to the head might have caused more serious damage than anyone had realized.

Oh, how horrible! Maybe there had been some brain damage that was only now beginning to be apparent. Penny got up from the bed and walked over to him. Touching his arm she said in a calm, soothing voice. "That's right, Brad. I have to soak them once a week to keep them clean of protein buildup."

Leading him over to the bed, she coaxed him to sit down. She sat beside him and patted his hand.

"I'm really pleased that you came to see me tonight, Brad. I'm sorry I didn't get a chance to visit with you these past couple of days." She glanced up at him with concern. "I suppose your head still really bothers you."

Brad looked at her and had an almost uncontrollable urge to reach out and haul her into his arms. There she was, looking so concerned about him and his problems, unaware of what was happening in her life.

He loved her so much. She deserved better treatment, she really did. If he hadn't been so shocked when Gregory had informed him of his intentions, Brad would have loved to have laid him out. Let Mr. Duncan appear in California to take depositions with a lovely shiner! He deserved more than that.

Penny stroked his brow, subtly checking to see if he was feverish. "Why don't you go home now and get some rest. We're both tired.'' She smiled. ''It wouldn't do for the bride to be drawn and wan tomorrow, you know.''

He flinched at her words, grateful she couldn't see him any better. Otherwise she would read the distress that was obvious on his face.

''Yes, well, that's what I wanted to talk to you about, Penny,'' Brad finally managed to mumble.

His voice sounded so soft and hesitant, which only increased Penny's alarm. He didn't sound at all like himself. Oh, if only she'd taken the time to check on him during the past couple of days. But he'd seemed to be improving. His mother hadn't reported anything out of the ordinary. What could have happened to have brought on these dismaying symptoms?

''You want to talk about tomorrow, Brad?'' she questioned as casually as possible.

''Yes.''

She waited a moment, but he didn't say anything more. Finally, she said, ''Okay.''

Brad sat there, staring at her, remembering all of their shared time together. He'd lost track of how often he'd climbed the tree outside her window and sneaked into her room. She had been just as bad about using the tree as an escape to meet him somewhere.

The innocence of youth. It had not occurred to either of them that there was anything wrong with them shinnying in and out of each other's bedroom windows. It had been a game. Some of their greatest adventures had been planned while sitting on one of their beds cross-legged, letting their imaginations fly before them like kites in the sky.

Brad admitted to himself that he felt different now. He was well aware that they were no longer children. Even with her face freshly scrubbed and her hair brushed into submission, Penny could scarcely pass as a child. His old football jersey did not disguise her womanly form or hide her well-shaped legs. Brad felt such a strong surge of love for her that it set him trembling.

How dare Gregory Duncan hurt her—his wonderful, lovable, gentle Penny. She never harmed anyone; she only saw the good in everyone. Even now, Penny had complete trust and faith in the man who was too cowardly to tell her he wasn't going to marry her tomorrow.

"What about tomorrow?" Penny prodded gently, wondering if she should slip out and try to get one or the other sets of parents. Maybe they should take him to the emergency room tonight. Perhaps something suddenly had come loose inside his head, causing his rather strange and unusual behavior.

"The wedding," he managed to say, desperately seeking the right words to tell her.

"That's right, Brad," she said in the same soothing tone she'd been using for several minutes, "Tomorrow is the wedding. And I'm getting married."

"No, you're not," he said baldly.

Oh, dear. He was getting more and more irrational.

"I'm not?"

"No."

"I see. Why am I not getting married?"

She sounded so calm, as though she were humoring him. Of course she'd been under a great deal of strain this week, herself. "Because Gregory isn't going to marry you." There. He'd told her. He waited for her reaction. He knew the rest of the night was going to be hell. At first she'd try to deny it. That was only to be expected. Then she'd probably cry, and get angry—the anger would help, he decided. He would stay with her through all of it, and whatever she decided to do in the morning, he'd agree. If she wanted him to marry her, he would. That's what friends are for, after all, to help in a time of crisis.

What he hadn't expected was her calm acceptance. "Why isn't Gregory going to marry me?" she asked casually.

"Why?" he repeated, not knowing what to say.

"Um-hmm."

"Oh. Well. It has something to do with me, I think. I'm not sure."

"Brad, are you still feeling guilty because you intended to break up our engagement?" she asked with sudden inspiration and understanding. She put her arms around his waist and lovingly laid her head on his chest. "Oh, you poor darling. That's what we were discussing just before the accident. It must have been haunting you all week." She glanced up, unable to see the glazed look in his eyes. "Brad, love, I have forgiven you for that. Please try to understand. No one is going to hold your intentions against you. After all, you changed your mind. And you were even concerned enough to tell me, which I appreciated, very much." Placing her head back on his chest she continued, "Now I want you to go home and get some rest, okay? I appreciate your coming over tonight, I really do. But I don't want you worrying about anything, you hear me?"

She could feel his heart pounding in his chest, like a bird beating its wings against a cage. Penny felt like crying. There was no telling what was going through his poor, confused mind at the moment. Whatever it was, he was concerned about her. No matter what he was suffering, he was still thinking of her.

"Penny!" he said in a strangled voice, "You don't understand!"

She raised her head and kissed him lightly on the lips. Surely Gregory would understand why she would be kissing another man the night before her wedding. The kiss was meant only to comfort. She had to do whatever it took to calm Brad down until they could get some help for him.

His arms came around her convulsively and he hung on to her like a drowning man. During all the hours he had agonized over how to tell her, how much to tell her, never had Brad envisioned that she wouldn't believe him.

He couldn't understand why not. Was her faith in Gregory Duncan so strong that the only proof she would accept would be entering the church in the morning and finding no groom waiting?

She felt so small against him, and she was so vulnerable. Penny had no idea what she had to face tomorrow, unless he took Gregory's advice and became the substitute bridegroom.

Is that why Gregory had told him, instead of her? Was he giving Brad the option of marrying her, himself?

How could he explain to her? "Penny?"

"Hmm?"

"I love you."

She smiled, her head resting on his shoulder. "I'm so glad."

"No. I really mean it. I want to marry you."

Her head jerked up and she stared at him, truly concerned. "Oh, Brad, please don't talk that way."

"I mean it. Gregory won't marry you, but I will."

"Oh, Brad. Please don't do this to either one of us. Please. It's too late for us. Don't you understand that? Maybe if we'd had this discussion before you left for New York everything would have worked out differently." She pulled back slightly and placed her hands on his neck, cupping his jawline. "You can never go back, Brad, no matter what. Perhaps if I hadn't met Gregory, and I'd known how you feel about me..." She paused, wanting him to understand, not wanting to cause him any more grief. "It's too late for us," she finished softly.

"No, it isn't. Believe me, it isn't."

She just shook her head. "Oh, Brad. If only life weren't so complicated." She slipped off the bed and stood in front of him. "Go home, now, Brad. We'll meet tomorrow and pretend this conversation never took place. It's just between you and me, like so many other things that we've shared together."

Brad sat there staring at her. He'd tried to tell her. In fact, he had told her, but for whatever reason, she hadn't believed him. His options at this point were severely limited.

The question was, what would she do tomorrow when she discovered that Gregory wasn't there? Would she allow him to substitute for the missing groom?

Knowing Penny the way he did, he sincerely doubted it. In the first place, she would assume he was doing it out of pity for her because of the humiliation she would suffer. Pity had nothing to do with the feelings he had for this woman.

But he needed time to explain, time to make her understand. And from the looks of things tonight, she wasn't going to listen to what he had to say. She'd been under considerable strain all week. He knew that. Stress could have a strange effect on people.

Feeling a wealth of love for the woman who stood in front of him, Brad made up his mind. He would do whatever he had to do to protect her from a situation not of her own making.

Brad stood and smiled down at her. "Everything's going to be all right, love. I'll take care of it."

She nodded, glad to see that he appeared to be calming down.

He turned and pulled back the covers, helping her as though she were an invalid. Docilely she went along with him. There was no reason to upset him. He certainly wasn't dangerous to anyone—just a little irrational. Hopefully that would pass in a few hours. Surely it wouldn't take more than a few days to help him recover. Penny prayed his condition wouldn't be permanent.

"I'll get you a glass of water," he announced as though coming up with a brilliant idea. "That should help you sleep." He turned away and disappeared into her bathroom. She heard the water running, and he eventually reappeared.

"It will?" she asked, wondering if he had water confused with warm milk.

He carefully handed her a glass filled with water. Penny smiled and took it, dutifully taking a sip.

"Now don't worry about a thing, do you hear me?" Brad asked in an urgent tone. "Everything's going to work out just fine. You know I'll always take care of you."

"Yes," she agreed, nodding.

Brad leaned over and touched her lips softly with his. "I think I'll let myself out the back door rather than go down the tree, if that's all right," he suggested.

"Oh, yes! I wouldn't want you to slip and fall, for heaven's sake. You've had enough bumps to your head for one week!"

They smiled at each other, pleased that they had reached some sort of harmonious understanding.

Penny listened until she heard the faint sound of the back door closing, then sighed and turned out the light.

Now not only did she have to worry about whether or not the groom would show up for his wedding in the morning, she also had to live with the fear that her best friend might have received some sort of brain damage that had gone undetected until now.

Chapter Seven

"Good morning, darling," Helen said to her sleeping daughter. "I thought I'd bring you coffee in bed this morning, since it will be the last time you'll be here with us."

Penny rolled over onto her back and groggily looked up at her mother. She could see that her mother was trying not to cry at the thought that her daughter was leaving home at long last. Too bad she couldn't appreciate that very few women continued to live at home until they were twenty-five, Penny thought with amusement.

She pushed herself up, propping her pillow against the headboard. "Thanks, Mom," she said, sipping the coffee, then holding the cup between her hands.

Her mother sank onto the end of the bed. "I'm

being so ridiculous, acting like this, when I've known for months you were leaving."

Penny grinned. "That's true, but I understand. I suppose I feel a little weepy myself."

"However, I'm extremely happy for you, Penny. You know I was always a little concerned before. I'm so glad you decided to go ahead and follow your heart after all, no matter what," Helen said, her face radiant. "I want you to know how proud I am of you."

Penny stared at her mother in confusion. What in the world was she talking about? Follow her heart? She shook her head. It was too early in the morning to try to work out word games.

Helen stood, leaned over and kissed her. "Breakfast will be ready in a few minutes, dear. I know you're excited, but you'll need to eat something before we leave for the church."

"I know, Mom."

Her mother smiled at her from the doorway. "It's hard to believe it. My fondest wish is finally coming true."

Penny stared blankly at the door. Her fondest wish? Had her mother secretly coveted her room for some reason? Why else would she suddenly be so pleased while at the same time lamenting that Penny was leaving home today?

She shrugged. Maybe the excitement of the wedding was getting to her mother. She usually seemed very sane and sensible.

Penny discovered that her father wasn't making much sense, either. He came bounding into the kitchen while she was struggling to eat the breakfast her mother had prepared and gave her a big hug. "My God, Penny! You are simply wonderful. I still can't believe it. I'm so proud of you. I'm not losing a daughter, I'm finally gaining the son I've always wanted."

She watched as he poured himself a cup of coffee and joined her at the table.

"I still find it hard to believe," Ralph said with a wide grin. "The two of you are actually getting married this morning. Unbelievable!"

Perhaps her dad had been in some sort of time warp during the past few months. Otherwise he wouldn't find the idea of her wedding day quite so unbelievable. Although he had always been polite and cordial to Gregory, Penny had never heard her father express such a strong sentiment toward him before. She was pleased to see him warming to the idea.

Penny and her bridesmaids planned to change into their dresses at the church, so all she had to do before leaving home was her makeup and hair. After dutifully eating her breakfast, Penny took her time returning upstairs. She had plenty of time before they had to leave.

After a few moments in the bathroom, she hurried to her bedroom door, trying not to panic. "Mom!"

"Yes, dear," Helen responded from downstairs, a lilt to her voice.

"I hate to bother you, but I can't seem to find my contacts," she said, walking out into the hallway. Her mother came up the stairs and Penny went on, consciously working to stay calm. "I know they were here last night. I soaked them overnight but they aren't where I thought I left them." She turned back into her room.

Her mother followed her and walked over to the bathroom. "I'm not surprised. You were probably so caught up in all the excitement you didn't pay any attention to where you set them down."

"I wish I weren't so blind," Penny muttered. How many times had she said that, or thought it, over the years? She followed her mother into the smaller room, feeling frustrated and helpless. Her mother began to move items around on the countertop, then peeked into the cabinets above the sink.

"Find them?" Penny asked, hopefully.

Helen looked around, puzzled. "Are you sure you took them out? Because I don't see them anywhere."

"Of course I'm sure, Mom. I left them in their soaking solution. Believe me, I know when I've got them in or not."

Helen shook her head. "Well, they aren't here, Penny."

Penny could feel the surge of panic she'd been holding at bay sweep over her. "What do you mean they aren't there?" she cried. "They have to be! Maybe they got knocked off onto the floor." She immediately fell to her knees and began to feel around on the smooth surface. Helen joined her until they had covered every square inch of the bathroom floor.

"They aren't here, Penny," Helen said finally, stating the obvious. She and Penny stared at each other, nose to nose on the bathroom floor. The enormity of the missing contacts settled over them slowly.

"What am I going to do?" Penny asked in a pleading voice, begging for reassurance.

"I don't know." Helen pushed herself up and looked around the room, as if hoping the contacts would suddenly appear before her. "Perhaps you could wear your glasses?"

"Oh, Mother," Penny wailed, almost in tears, "I haven't had the prescription changed in years." She walked into her bedroom and glanced around wildly. "I don't even know where they are!" She sank down on the side of the bed, her face in her hands. "Oh, dear God. What am I going to do?"

Helen sat down beside her daughter. "Well, you're not going to panic, for starters. So what if you can't see very well?" she said briskly, making it sound as though Penny was worrying over a hangnail. "We'll call for another set to be made up for you and have them mailed to you. You'll probably only have to do without them for a few days."

"But what about today?"

Helen could see that her daughter was about to fall apart. Poor dear. So many things had been happening to her and she'd handled them all so well. Now here she was going to pieces over such a little thing. But not if Helen could help it.

"I'll do your face and hair and help you dress." She laughed and went on, "And your dad is going to walk you down the aisle. After that you can use your brand-new husband as a Seeing Eye dog for a day or two. I have a feeling he won't mind in the least!"

What a way to start a marriage. And why hadn't she ever ordered an extra set of contacts? Of all days to lose hers. And what in the world had she done with them? She couldn't imagine, but then, she'd been so distracted last night. For all she knew she might have put them in her cold cream or skin freshener!

Penny tried not to let the missing contacts cast a pall over her preparations. At least she could see shapes and wouldn't walk into any walls or doors. Her mother and dad seemed to be in high enough spirits to make up for any lack on her part. If she didn't know better, she would think they'd already gotten into the champagne.

Time seemed to speed up once they arrived at the church. There was a great deal of laughing and teasing among all of her friends while they dressed, and later, one or more would dash back in to report the swelling crowd. The church seemed to be filled to capacity.

Before she left home, Penny had slipped away long enough to call Gregory's house. There had been no answer. Of course he might have left early, even gone to the office for a final check. There was even the possibility that he had been held up in St. Louis and was even now driving back to be there on time.

But why hadn't he called her?

Penny knew that she could have her fears allayed by simply asking someone if Gregory had arrived, but after the teasing about the missing groom she'd received the night before, she wouldn't give them the satisfaction of knowing that she was worried.

Anyway, she would know soon enough. They certainly wouldn't be able to start without him.

So she waited, trying to be calm. This was her wedding day. The day she had looked forward to for months. The reason that Brad had—

Brad! She had forgotten to tell her parents about his strange behavior the night before! Oh, how could she have forgotten? She'd been so wrapped up in herself that his problems had completely slipped her mind. If his parents hadn't noticed, perhaps she was the only one who could sound a warning...

The door to the room where she waited swung open and Penny could hear the organ music. She heard a voice speaking to the congregation, then a burst of laughter and applause. What in the world?

Her father hurried through the door, a wide grin on his face. "You look beautiful, my darling daughter. Just beautiful. Are you ready to go?"

"Uh, yes. Is everything... I mean, are we all...?"

"Yes, everything's moving on schedule." He took her arm and gave it a squeeze as he escorted her into the foyer to wait their turn. "You have made me a very happy man, you know that, don't you?"

At least her father was making no effort to hide his elation at finally getting rid of his daughter, she decided with wry amusement. "I'm glad," she said softly.

"I just couldn't see you with— No. This isn't the place. I'm just happy that you made the right choice."

The right choice? More cryptic comments. Had it only now occurred to her father that she could have moved in with Gregory first, before the wedding? He needn't have worried. Her upbringing would have prevented her from even entertaining the idea and

Gregory had seemed content to wait for all the legalities before he claimed her.

She had no more time to think about her father's remark. Suddenly the music stopped and everyone in the church stood. The slow, stately march began, signaling that it was time for her entrance.

For the first time Penny was grateful she couldn't see more clearly. She was having an awful attack of stage fright, which was absolutely ridiculous. Crowds had never bothered her before. She'd found excitement on the stage. However, always before this she was playing someone else. Today she was Penelope Anne Blackwell and she wasn't at all sure she could make it down the aisle without tripping or in some way making a fool of herself.

She forced herself to take a calming breath, then began to take the slow, gliding steps they had rehearsed the night before.

The light from the stained glass window fell on Gregory's blond hair and Penny suddenly let go of the breath she unconsciously had been holding. He had come. He was here.

She began to smile. Everything was all right. All the last minute details had worked out. And the groom had managed to show up when he was needed. Penny began to plan some of the things she was going to say to him once they were alone. What a scare he'd given her!

When she got close enough Penny saw Reverend Wilder standing before her, smiling. At least she assumed it was he. The man appeared to be the right height and size for it. When she and her father paused she noticed that Gregory stepped beside her and faced the altar with her.

Reverend Wilder's melodious voice filled the sanctuary with the age-old ceremonial words of the wedding vows. Tears began to collect in her eyes at the beauty of the vows they were sharing.

Then the dream seemed to dissolve into a nightmare.

She heard Reverend Wilder say, "Do you, Bradley Aaron Crawford, take this woman—"

Bradley Aaron Crawford? *Bradley Aaron Crawford!* Penny turned her head and stared at the man standing beside her, the man she was in the process of marrying. There was a small white patch gleaming on his left temple.

Brad.

She never clearly remembered anything that happened during the rest of the ceremony. She must have made the right responses since no one seemed to find anything out of the ordinary in the situation. Perhaps it was only her; obviously she was suffering from some sort of delusion, she decided, dazed. Although she'd been convinced she was engaged to Gregory Duncan, she was marrying Brad Crawford.

"I now pronounce you man and wife," Reverend Wilder intoned. "You may kiss the bride."

Slowly Penny turned to the man she had just married. He carefully and tenderly lifted the veil from her face and folded it neatly back, then leaned down to kiss her.

"What are you doing here!" she whispered through barely moving lips.

He smiled and lightly kissed her on the mouth. "Marrying you," he replied as he straightened to his full height.

The triumphant music from the organ filled the large room and the entire audience stood and clapped their welcome to the new couple.

Penny wished she were the fainting type. What a wonderful way that would be to get out of an intolerable situation.

Brad swept her down the aisle, out into the foyer and into a private room. Closing the door, he reached into his pocket and pulled out something. "Here."

She blinked and peered into his hand. "What is it?"

"Your contact lenses."

"My contact lenses?" she repeated stupidly, wondering how he had known she hadn't been able to find them. And then the truth seemed to drop on her like a sudden resounding crash of boulders. "You?" she said, desperately trying to make some sense out of her whirling thoughts and emotions. A rage such as she had not felt in years took control of her. "You—Bradley Aaron Crawford—*you* took my contacts? You hid them from me, knowing I would be blind without them?"

He nodded. "I needed every advantage I could think of. You made it clear last night that if I gave you any warning, you'd refuse to allow me to help you, to save you from the embarrassment of having to call off the wedding."

"What are you talking about? Have you lost your mind?" she demanded. Then hearing her own words, things began to make a twisted sort of sense.

"Of course," she said, pacing, her long train trailing behind her, "That's it! You had that terrible blow to the head and now you've—"

She stopped suddenly and spun around, almost losing her balance in all the satin and lace material that wrapped around her when she turned. She gazed at him, her eyes widening with growing horror. "Gregory! You've done something to him. What did you do, Brad?" She fought the entangling folds of her dress and rushed over to him. Grabbing his arms and trying to shake him she yelled, "What have you done with Gregory, Brad? Answer me!"

"Penny, calm down! I haven't done anything to Gregory Duncan. Don't be so damned dramatic."

"Dramatic! Me? Why, I couldn't begin to compare with you, you no-good, rotten, egotistical louse. Just how much more dramatic did you intend to get? You managed to spirit away my fiancé in some way so you could take his place!"

Once again she began to pace, gathering her dress in both hands and bundling the folds in front of her, as though acting out a scene of a primitive washerwoman striding around the room with her load of clothes.

"Well, I won't stand for it, do you hear me?" Her voice continued to grow in volume. "I have had it with you, do you understand? I have taken all I intend to take from you and your stupid, idiotic pranks! You did your best to ruin my childhood by scaring me with snakes, putting frogs in my bed, hiding my glasses—"

"Damn it! I've told you and told you—I never did a thing to your stupid glasses. Even your mother believed me when I told her I had nothing to do with your losing them!''

She ignored the interruption. ''You'd invite me to play with you, then run off and hide so nobody knew where you were, and then you would laugh because I cried when I couldn't find you!''

''Come on, Penny,'' he said, ''be reasonable! That was twenty years ago, for God's sake!''

By now she was caught up in remembering all the many grievances she had against him. Ignoring his comment Penny continued going down her list. ''And what about that time when we were in high school, how mortified I was by your absolutely awful teasing in front of Frank Tyler when you knew I had a crush on him!''

''Hey, Runt, you held your own in that department and you know it! How many girls did you tell your ridiculous stories about me so they'd never take me seriously!''

''Take you seriously? You? The original good-time man-about-town? You've never taken anything seriously in your whole life! It's all been fun and games for you, all the times we were growing up, and even when we went away to college.''

She stopped pacing and stared at him from across the room, her face flushed and angry. ''I was never so glad when you moved to New York and out of my life, do you hear me? Every time you're around crazy things happen. Nothing ever works out the way I plan. It was only after you were gone that I finally managed to get some order in my life and find the man I loved and intended to marry and then you—'' The enormity of what had just taken place swept over her like a tidal wave and she began to cry, harsh sobs that shook her body. "No-w-w...yo-you've...com-completely...ruined...m-my life!"

Brad could only stand there and watch her. He had honestly thought he was helping her out. He certainly had no intention of ruining her life. He loved her. He had only wanted to help her...or so he had managed to convince himself when he decided to substitute himself for Gregory at the altar.

Who are you kidding, Crawford? he asked himself. *You've been eating your heart out every day since you learned she was marrying someone else.* When he'd seen his opportunity, he'd grabbed it, using Gregory's desertion to finally get what he wanted.

And Penny hated him for it.

Brad could feel the guilt churn in his stomach. He'd managed to make her his wife, but at what price? What could he possibly do or say that would ever help her forgive him?

Slowly he walked over to her and reached out his hand. She jerked away as if she found the mere thought of his touching her repulsive. He dropped his hand and just looked at her.

Penny fought for control, trying to get her breath. Through sobbing breaths she managed to grate out, "Where...is...Gregory?"

Brad sighed. He slid his hands into his pants pockets and turned away, gazing out the window.

"California."

"California? What's he doing out there?"

"Taking depositions."

She stared at him in disbelief. "You're making this up, aren't you? All of it? Gregory wouldn't have gone off like that, leaving me without some word."

Scrubbing at her face, Penny took a couple of breaths and forced herself into a semblance of calmness. "You warned me last Sunday," she said in a low voice that shook with the intensity of her hurt and rage. "You told me you had come back to break up the engagement! Too bad I didn't realize you were lying when you said you had changed your mind!"

"I wasn't lying, damn it!" he said, spinning on his heel to face her. "I've been telling you the truth!" Brad had finally been goaded beyond control.

"Well, if it wasn't a lie, what was it? You said you'd break us up. I'd say that substituting yourself for the groom certainly managed to do that! You don't care that Gregory and I already had our future planned together. You couldn't stand seeing me happy, could you? Well, Mr. Crawford, this time you managed to get caught in your own trap. Because you are just as married to me as I'm married to you. And I don't want to be married to you. I want Gregory!"

"You've made that good and clear. Believe me, there's nothing I'd rather see than you married to Gregory, damn it. Can't you understand that?"

She crossed her arms, her mutinous expression making it clear that she did not find his remarks appeasing.

"No, I can't understand it. Because you are here and he isn't."

"That isn't my fault."

"Isn't it?" she asked sarcastically.

"Listen to me, you hardheaded, obstinate shrew. If I hadn't married you, you would have been left here this morning having to explain to everybody who showed up why your groom begged off!"

His words were a verbal slap in the face and Penny flinched. "You mean that Gregory changed his mind?"

"That's exactly what I mean!"

"Why?"

"How the hell should I know?"

"He must have told you. Otherwise you wouldn't have known."

He nodded his head curtly. "He told me he had changed his mind. That he wasn't going to marry you. He said something about not really knowing you as well as he thought."

The look she gave him was filled with contempt. "And you really expect me to believe that? There's absolutely no way of knowing what horrible lies you must have told him to cause him to change his mind about marrying me!"

"Stop calling me a liar!"

"Stop behaving like one!"

They had made no attempt to keep their voices down. In truth, the volume of the argument was the last thing they had considered. The sudden silence as they stood glaring at each other seemed to bounce off the walls of the room.

A soft tapping on the door made them look in that direction. "Come in," Brad commanded.

Helen stuck her head around the door and looked from one to the other in shocked dismay. She stepped inside and firmly closed the door behind her, leaning on it.

"I absolutely can't believe the two of you! You haven't been married five minutes and you already sound the way you used to as small children when your mother and I had to drag you apart and make you spend the day at home by yourselves until you could play together without fighting! Do you realize that you can be heard for a city block? Are you aware that the recreation hall is full of people waiting to greet the loving bride and groom and watch them open presents and cut their wedding cake?"

They immediately burst into simultaneous explanations.

"Mother, you don't understand. Brad—"

"Helen, she's being totally unreasonable and won't even listen to me!"

She put up her hand like a policeman stopping traffic. "I don't want to hear it! Thank goodness I no longer have to play referee for the two of you. If you choose to kill each other, you no longer have to explain it to me. Now I want you both to go over to that hall with smiles on your faces and show all those people how happy you are. They expect to see some sort of love and joy in the occasion."

"Love!" Penny repeated contemptuously.

"Joy!" Brad said with a harsh laugh.

Helen opened the door with a decisive turn of her wrist. "Both of you studied acting for years. Surely you have something to show for all the money we invested in your education." She looked at her watch. "I'm going over there and explain that you've been delayed. I'll expect to see your happy, smiling faces in no more than fifteen minutes.''

Brad and Penny stared at the closed door for an unnoticed elapse of time after Helen left. Neither of them had any desire to look at the other.

Penny was the first one to break the silence. "What are we going to do?"

He glanced at her, then away, once again walking over to the window. "That's up to you, isn't it?"

"Why up to me?"

"You can go out there and tell everyone that you never intended to marry me."

"I don't understand why somebody didn't say something. I mean, everyone in the wedding party knew I was expecting Gregory to be here today."

"I told them that we talked it over late last night. You discovered that you couldn't marry Gregory after all . . . because you loved me."

"And they believed you?" she asked incredulously.

"Thanks a lot."

"You know what I mean. As Mother just pointed out, you and I fight as much as we're friends."

"Your parents didn't seem to be as surprised as they were pleased."

Remembering their rather strange behavior she asked, "When did you tell them?"

"Early this morning, just as I told my parents. You probably didn't notice, but Dad was my best man."

She shook her head and looked down at the small container she held in her hands. "As you well know, I couldn't see anyone."

"I'm sorry. I had no right to hide your contacts from you."

"At least you admit it!"

"I was only trying to help."

"Fine, Brad. How do you propose to help now, go out there and announce the whole thing was a joke?"

"Hardly. Our marriage was very legal. We have the license to prove it."

"And that's another thing. How did you manage to get a license?"

"Well, one of the benefits of having been raised in a small town is knowing everybody, including the county clerk. It's amazing what people will do when they think they're assisting true love. I explained everything to Reverend Wilder and he made the announcement before the ceremony began, with a few comments about love conquering all."

So that was what she had heard just before her father escorted her down the aisle.

Penny sat down, feeling as though she were a balloon and someone had suddenly let out all of her air. "So Gregory didn't love me, after all," she said slowly. "He certainly had me fooled."

Brad heard the pain in her voice and could think of nothing to say.

"I should have known," she said, not even aware she had spoken aloud.

"What do you mean?"

"I hadn't talked to him all week. That isn't like him. Not at all. I kept telling myself he was just busy, but something kept nagging at me, a little voice that refused to shut up." She glanced up, then quickly away.

"It's funny, really. I was just thinking last night that I wanted to discuss what I was feeling with you, knowing you'd understand." Looking down at her hands, she added, "Oh, you understood all right. I just wished you'd explained last night."

One corner of his mouth lifted in a half grin. "I tried, believe me. But you wouldn't accept what I said. I didn't want to go into all the details, about Gregory calling me and what he said. When I realized that you weren't going to accept what I was saying, I guess I used the situation to my own advantage."

Penny didn't seem to hear his explanation or apologetic tone of voice. She had dropped her face in her hands. When he stopped speaking she cried, "I can't face all those people out there. I just can't."

"I could take you home and tell them you aren't feeling well."

The thought of returning home and trying to explain to her parents what had taken place was just as bad an idea as pretending to be happily married.

She looked over at Brad. "I don't think I'll ever forgive you for this ridiculous situation, but since you got us into this mess, I don't see anything else to do but go out there and pretend we're happy newlyweds."

"Happy?" he repeated sarcastically. "I don't think I'm that good an actor."

"What about me? At least you had a choice."

"So sue me!"

"Don't worry. I intend to just as soon as I know how to go about it."

He looked at her incredulously. "You mean you'd actually take me to court? On what grounds?"

"Don't be ridiculous. I don't want any money from you. I just meant I was going to end the marriage as soon as I know what to do."

"Oh."

She stood and began to brush the wrinkles out of the skirt of her gown. "I'm going to go put my contacts in so I can at least see who's here."

"I'll wait out in the hall for you. We need to arrive together, looking properly blissful."

Every time she thought of Brad's audacity she wanted to throw something at him. How was she going to be able to look at him with a loving smile all afternoon? She shook her head. Acting ability, indeed. It would be the performance of her life.

Penny went into the ladies' restroom and replaced her lenses. Being able to see helped to boost her morale somewhat. She stared at herself in the mirror. Her face was white and strained, her eyes slightly puffy. It was not the face of a typically blushing bride.

Their delay in joining everyone at the reception did not go unnoticed. As soon as they walked into the room everyone started clapping and some of the comments held sly innuendos of Brad's impatience to get her alone.

Oh, no, Penny thought. She'd forgotten all the jokes and teasing that went along with a wedding. The only way she was going to get through the afternoon was by shutting her mind to the fact that she was with the wrong man.

Her mother hurried them over near the table where a three-tiered cake sat waiting for them.

"You can stand here and receive everyone. Then the photographer will start posing you for pictures."

The photographer! Something else Penny had forgotten. She glanced at Brad, and unconsciously did a double take.

She hadn't paid attention to him when she had come out of the ladies' room. It was only now that she saw what he looked like in his tuxedo.

He wore the traditional black and a ruffled shirt. The clothes fit him as if tailored for his tall body with its broad shoulders, lean hips, and long, muscular legs. He looked magnificent. The dark suit enhanced his tan and bright hair. The small bandage gave him a rakish look that made him very appealing.

"Well, if you aren't the sly one, young lady," Mrs. Fielding said, walking up and grabbing Penny's hand in a firm grip. "Letting us think you were marrying Mr. Duncan right up to the last minute. Of course you never fooled me a bit, you know." She winked at Brad. "But your engagement certainly served its purpose. It got Brad to come home so you two could work everything out."

Penny couldn't look at Brad. She couldn't believe the woman and she couldn't think of a thing to say in reply to the outrageous comment.

Brad spoke up, sounding relaxed and nauseatingly pleased with himself. "We're happy you and Mr. Fielding could come today."

"Oh, we wouldn't have missed it for the world, even before we knew of the dramatic denouement," she said archly. "It must have to do with your theatrical background and all."

Penny wondered how much longer she would be able to stand there and smile before she let out a scream.

"It was the most romantic thing I've ever seen," Mrs. Cantrell said when she reached them. "Why, when Reverend Wilder explained how you two suddenly realized how you felt about each other and that nice Mr. Duncan agreed to release you, I thought I would cry. It was better than anything I've ever seen on television!" She leaned over and whispered to Penny, "Even though he seemed a very nice man, I thought Mr. Duncan was too old for you anyway, dear. Isn't it nice how everything worked out so well?"

Penny wondered what all of these people would do if she suddenly started having hysterics? She felt very close to it at the moment. She had an absolutely insane urge to laugh and she knew the tears wouldn't be far behind. Already she could read the write-up in the local paper: "Bridegroom has to slap hysterical bride at wedding reception."

Somehow she managed to get through the next hour without breaking down. Then the photographer took over.

She would have been all right if she hadn't met Brad's eyes during one of the more soulful poses. The dancing light of amusement almost undid her. How many times had she seen the same expression on his face after they'd shared a joke?

Oh, Brad. No matter what, you manage to see the humor in every situation. Nothing in life ever really fazes you. How do you do it?

Then the photographer asked Brad to kiss her. This time the intent look in his eyes held a question. Taking a cue from him and determined not to treat what was happening like some gloomy Greek tragedy, Penny lifted her mouth and closed her eyes.

She felt his arms go around her and pull her tightly against him as his mouth found hers.

This kiss was nothing like the one he'd given her at the altar. As a matter of fact, it was like no other kiss he'd ever given her, and Brad had kissed her often over the years—friendly kisses, exuberant kisses, teasing kisses, hello kisses, goodbye kisses.

Penny couldn't compare this particular kiss with any of those. She felt a tingle in her body that started in her toes and shot up through her until she felt the top of her head seem to shoot off.

His lips felt firm yet they were also tender. He took his time, as though they had nothing better to do, as if there weren't a roomful of people watching and a photographer whose flash periodically added a fireworks display behind her closed eyelids.

Brad was kissing her the way he kissed the countless women Drew Derek pursued on television. No wonder they kept coming back for more!

Vaguely Penny became aware of the general laughter and a smattering of applause around them and she stiffened. They were making a spectacle of themselves.

She pushed herself away from him and glared up into his smiling face. "You're supposed to look happy," he said just under his breath, never breaking his smile.

Penny flashed him an equally brilliant smile. "You try that again and I will place my knee in the exact spot you instructed me to all those years ago to ward off unwanted advances!"

He flinched in mock horror. Then he laughed—he actually had the nerve to laugh. "To think that you would use my own teachings against me," he said, still too low for anyone to hear.

The photographer interrupted their murmured comments, convinced this was a couple who was counting the minutes until they could be alone. "Okay, now. How about some pictures with you both cutting the cake."

Why not? Penny thought. Maybe I can stuff enough cake into his mouth to choke him. "Bridegroom chokes to death on wedding cake." Then she remembered the previous Sunday's accident coming on the heels of her dire wishes for his early demise. Penny hurriedly explained to the Fates that she didn't really want him to die and to please ignore her last suggestion.

Opening the gifts brought back to her how differently this part of the afternoon would have gone if Gregory had been there instead. Brad seemed to be having a great deal of fun and the onlookers were relishing his reactions and comments.

She had to admit that his quick wit often caught her off guard and she found herself laughing at his hu-

˙mor and antics—until she picked up the envelope that must have fallen off one of the gifts. The envelope was addressed to Brad Crawford.

Very few people could have known that Brad would be there to open gifts. She handed the envelope to him in silence. When he opened it, Brad continued to stare down at the contents, his expression blank.

"Come on, Brad, don't hold out on us," someone yelled. "Somebody give you a million bucks?"

He glanced over at her and she noticed his color had faded.

"What is it?" she whispered.

Without a word he handed her two pieces of paper that looked like airline tickets. They were. She stared down at them in bewilderment. The tickets were for a round trip to Acapulco for Mr. and Mrs. Brad Crawford, leaving that afternoon from the airport nearest Payton, to return the following Saturday.

Penny looked up at Brad in dismay.

"Tell us! Tell us!" several people said, laughing.

Penny cleared her throat. "Well, it's, uh," she glanced at Brad helplessly. Brad looked at her and shrugged. She started again. "It's round-trip tickets to Acapulco, leaving in a few hours."

Her announcement created a great deal of excitement and speculation. "What a wonderful idea! Great wedding gift! Marvelous place for a honeymoon!"

Honeymoon? Penny's heart seemed to sink in her chest. She leaned over and whispered, "We can't use these. Who in the world gave them to us?"

"I don't think you want to know," he said, his expression deliberately noncommittal.

"What do you mean?"

He handed her a note that he had continued to hold. She stiffened when she saw the page with the name Gregory Duncan neatly imprinted at the top. His slashing handwriting read, "You might as well use these since they're paid for. The hotel reservations have been changed to your name." It was signed with Gregory's initials.

The realization of his betrayal seemed to flood over her and for a moment Penny thought she would double over with the pain. Brad must have recognized how she felt because he leaned over and said, "You know, Penny, it might not be a bad idea to take him up on the offer. It would give us time to get away and decide what to do. If we don't go, what then? All these people are just waiting to see us happily depart somewhere or another. Why not Acapulco?"

Acapulco. Gregory had remembered a conversation many months ago when she had commented that she had never been out of the United States. So that's where he'd planned to take her on their honeymoon.

What kind of man would leave his intended bride on the eve of her wedding, then provide the honeymoon trip as a wedding gift when she married someone else?

Penny realized that she didn't know Gregory Duncan at all. Perhaps she never had.

"What do you think?" Brad asked.

The problem was, she could no longer think. About anything. Everything had suddenly piled up on her and she felt that she couldn't deal with another decision. She looked at Brad and said, "I don't care at this point what we do or where we go. Just get me out of here."

Taking her at her word, Brad used the tickets as a reason for their hurried departure. But the well-wishers couldn't let them leave without the traditional spray of rice over them as they dashed for Brad's mother's car.

"My suitcases!" Penny gasped, hurrying down the sidewalk.

"Your dad said he put them into my car this morning."

They got into the car, waving at all the happy, smiling people who had helped them to celebrate their wedding day.

Brad took Penny's hand and squeezed it gently, then placed it on his thigh before driving away. "Well, Mrs. Crawford. We may have the shortest marriage in history, but it looks like we're going to have our honeymoon!"

Chapter Eight

Penny stood on the balcony of the luxury hotel and stared at the sun as it set over the Pacific. She had never seen the ocean before and knew that she should be experiencing all of the excitement of the unknown.

The view below had all the earmarks of a fantasy—white sands, gently swaying palm trees, and the variegated blues of the ocean—a virtual tropical paradise.

Penny felt no excitement, no anticipation, no pleasure. She felt numb.

From the room behind her she heard Brad's voice speaking to the bellhop, but she didn't turn around. She had nothing to say to Brad at the moment. Only questions that needed to be asked eventually, and decisions to discuss. But even the answers to those questions could do little to change the present situation.

Nothing could change the fact that she was now officially on her honeymoon—with the wrong man.

Staring out at the panorama spread far below her, Penny knew when Brad opened the wide sliding glass door and joined her on the balcony. She didn't turn around.

They had spoken very little since leaving the church. By the time they made their connections and were on the plane to Acapulco, Penny felt exhausted. She slept most of the way.

Penny recognized Brad's dispirited mood and no longer believed this was another one of his pranks. During the reception, fleeting memories of their conversation the night before had occurred to her.

Penny realized that the blow to his head hadn't affected him as she had thought at the time. He'd been trying to warn her that Gregory wasn't going to be at the church. One of her questions was how he had known. What could he have said or done to cause Gregory to risk ruining his reputation in Payton rather than marry her? Whatever it was, Penny knew she wasn't quite ready to face Brad's possible treachery.

And that was the cruelest blow of all. That Brad, her childhood friend, her most trusted companion, could be responsible for what had happened.

If that were true, she had not only lost her fiancé but her belief in the integrity of her best friend. How ironic that she was now married to him.

"The view is really something, isn't it?" Brad said quietly.

She could hear the tenseness in his voice. He wasn't feeling any better about the recent turn of events than she was. She supposed that was something they had in common at the moment.

"Yes."

When she didn't say anything more, he asked, "Are you hungry?"

"No."

"Neither am I." Brad pulled out one of the chairs tucked under a small table on the balcony and sat down. "At least we're away from the comments of all the well-wishers," he offered in a gentle voice. "Are you very tired?"

Penny continued to gaze out toward the beach. She hadn't looked at him since he'd joined her. Without turning she said, "Not really. I slept on the plane."

Brad was very aware of that. After she had fallen asleep he had pulled her into his arms so that she slept with her head on his shoulder. What had torn at his heart were the tears she had shed in her sleep.

Why had he ever thought that she would prefer to marry him than be abandoned at the church? Why had Gregory ever suggested it? Unconsciously he rubbed his head. Perhaps that was it—the blow to his head. His brains had been addled. Despite doing everything in his power to prevent it he had managed to hurt her, the very last thing he would ever have wanted.

Penny caught sight of the movement and turned slightly to see Brad massaging his forehead.

"Is your head bothering you?" she asked, suddenly remembering all that he had been through that week. She had been so wrapped up in her own misery she had forgotten what he was going through.

"A little."

"Why don't you take some pain medication and try to rest?"

He looked up at her and smiled ruefully. "Because the stuff is so strong, it puts me out for hours."

Penny found herself smiling for the first time since the wedding reception. "I don't find that such an unfavorable side effect. I wouldn't mind being unconscious for a while, myself."

His eyes met hers in total understanding. They had shared so much over the years. Today was one more experience that strengthened the bond between them. When the challenge of the reception confronted them, they had immediately united and faced the crisis together. Now that it was over, they could fall apart without fear of the other's ridicule.

Brad wondered if Penny had any idea how rare that bond was. Or if she cared.

"Good point," he said, answering her smile. "I may just take your advice." He glanced around, taking in the view from the balcony. "We certainly found a spectacular spot to hide and lick our wounds, wouldn't you say?"

She heard the underlying pain in his voice and she closed her eyes, almost wincing at the sound. Brad looked tired, as though he hadn't slept much in the past twenty-four hours.

His decision must have caused him a great deal of agony, and her accusations hadn't made the situation any easier. She had struck out at him in pain, perhaps unconsciously hoping to ease her own. Why had she placed all the blame on him?

Penny acknowledged that sometimes, when a person is so filled with hurt and the pain takes over, it's hard to recall who administered what particular jab of agony. She had struck out at Brad for some of the pain inflicted by Gregory.

"I'm sorry for all of those hateful things I said to you earlier," Penny said slowly, opening her eyes and meeting his gaze.

His gaze seemed to soften and grow warmer. "Thank you for that, Penny," he replied.

"I think everything will look a little better to us in a few days," Penny said, "once we've had a chance to get used to the idea of what has happened. We don't have to make any decisions today." She walked over to him and softly stroked his forehead. "Why don't you take something for that headache, okay?"

He studied the expression on her face for a long, silent moment. Apparently satisfied with what he saw, Brad nodded. "I think you're right. Without this throbbing in my head, I could probably think a lot more clearly."

Penny watched him walk back into their room. He took off his coat and tie, then opened his suitcase and took out the small bottle of tablets. After disappearing into the bathroom he soon reappeared, sat on the side of the bed and slipped off his shoes.

She could almost feel the groan of relief he gave when he stretched out on the bed and closed his eyes.

Poor Brad.

It was amazing how quickly her perspective changed as soon as she began to think of someone besides herself, Penny thought wryly. She had certainly been enjoying a pity party of her own all day—feeling misused, abused and totally duped.

She needed to look at what the nefarious Brad had done to her. Why, the dastardly fellow had sought her out the night before and attempted to explain that her fiancé had backed out of their engagement at the last minute. When she refused to take him seriously, Brad, being the blackguard he was, had filled in as bridegroom rather than leave her to face a crowded church alone.

Gregory was the one who needed to make explanations. Penny shook her head wearily. What difference did it make? It was much too late to search for answers, but she knew that her mind would busily work to solve the mystery of the disappearing bridegroom.

How well do we ever get to know a person? Penny wondered, leaning against the railing and looking toward the water. No matter how hard we try, there are too many depths to be plumbed in a person to hope that we can ever completely know him.

She probably knew Brad Crawford better than she knew any other living human being. He knew her equally well. He'd once mentioned to her that the knowledge they shared about each other was more significant than she had ever acknowledged.

One thing Penny knew with fierce certainty—Brad would never have done to her what Gregory had done. Never.

She sighed. Today had been the most traumatic day of her life. She was glad to see it end.

Penny slowly entered their room, unsurprised to find Brad asleep. A frown still creased his brow and without thought she reached over to smooth it away with her forefinger.

He muttered something and shifted restlessly on the bed. It sounded as though he had said "Penny." She felt an ache in her chest. It wouldn't be surprising if he were having nightmares with her in the starring role.

Poor Brad. When he had decided to go home to attend a friend's wedding, the last thing he'd expected was to find himself in a featured role.

Penny wandered into the bathroom, a little awed by the luxurious fixtures. "Well, Penny, old girl, it's your wedding night, so how do you intend to spend it?" She reached over and turned on the water in the large tub. A warm soak in the tub sounded like a good way to relax. Too bad she hadn't thought of bringing along a good book to read, she decided whimsically.

And then she'd probably be ready for bed. Bed. She was going to share her bed with Brad. Of course it wouldn't be the first time. But the last time they'd slept together was on a camping trip when the zipper wouldn't work on her sleeping bag and he had offered to share his. As she recalled, she was eight years old at the time.

Somehow she knew that sharing a bed with the adult Brad would be an entirely different experience.

Almost an hour passed before Penny decided that as enjoyable as the water was, there was only so much fun to be had soaking in a tub.

Why was she trying so hard not to think about what this night was supposed to have been? The sooner she came to grips with the reality of her life, and accepted it, the sooner she'd be able to put away her sorrow that the tapestry of dreams she'd woven over the past several months had come unraveled.

After drying herself, Penny remembered that her suitcase still waited to be unpacked. She wrapped the enormous towel around her and grinned. One advantage of being small was that it didn't take much to cover her. This particular towel hung below her knees.

Quietly opening the door she walked into the bedroom. Brad had rolled onto his side and his face had lost its grimness. He was well and truly asleep.

When Penny opened her suitcase she was forcibly reminded of her situation. Her bag was filled with the frothy lingerie and sleepwear she'd received from the numerous showers her friends had given for her. She remembered all the teasing and chuckles regarding the sheerness of the nightgowns and undergarments.

She suddenly yearned for one of her sturdy football jerseys that had kept her company for so many years. Too bad she hadn't had the foresight to pack at least one.

Eventually she found a peach satin gown that was more opaque than any of the others and took it back into the bathroom to put on. When she glanced into the mirror later she wondered why she had thought it would be less revealing.

The satin was cut on the bias and the gown was designed to look like an evening gown from the thirties. Thin straps widened to a well-cupped bodice. An insert of matching peach lace formed a diamond, with a point that nestled just below her breasts, widened at the waist, then made another point on her abdomen. When she moved, the satin slid over her body highlighting each curve and forming shadows at each indentation.

Glancing at her watch, Penny admitted to herself that she had stalled long enough. It was time to go to bed. Turning out the light in the bathroom, she entered the bedroom once again. Only one lamp was on and it was across the room from the bed. She hadn't wanted to wake Brad when she'd come in earlier to find something to sleep in.

She turned back the covers on one side of the bed, thankful of its extra width, then crossed the room and turned off the light. With the room darkened she was drawn to the lighter expanse of the glass door. She peered outside. The stars seemed so bright she felt she could almost reach up and touch one. Out at sea, she could spot an occasional flash of white where a wave had broken.

What a beautiful spot for a honeymoon.

She returned to the bed and carefully slid in. Oh, how wonderful to lie down at last, was her last conscious thought.

Moonlight pouring through the wide, uncurtained expanse of glass aroused Brad several hours later. He sat up, disoriented. Looking around him he suddenly remembered where he was. Damn! He'd done it again—fallen asleep for too many hours. Thoughtfully he touched his head. At least the headache was gone, he decided.

Penny was curled beside him, although she was underneath the covers. Gingerly he slid off the bed and stood while continuing to gaze at her. She looked so peaceful and serene.

Brad felt as if his heart would explode with the feeling that swelled up inside of him. He had never loved another person as much, and in so many ways, as he loved Penny Blackwell. Penny Crawford, he reminded himself. She was now his wife. His wife!

How many years had he dreamed about someday being married to Penny—making love to her, acting with her, raising children with her...teasing and laughing and enjoying life with her. When had that dream died?

He knew to the minute. The day he'd opened the mail in his New York apartment and found the invitation to her wedding.

He'd felt betrayed. How dare she! He'd been angry and hurt and felt deceived by those he'd most trusted.

All the time he'd been in New York he'd written to her, but Penny was the world's worst correspondent. Even when his mother had written that she was dating a lawyer, he hadn't been terribly concerned. He was dating, as well. Wasn't that the idea? For them to be sure how they felt?

He had been sure. He'd always known, from the time Penny had fallen out of a swing when she was four years old and he'd cried because she cried. He'd felt her pain. She was as much a part of him as his heart or lungs.

How could she possibly not love him in the same way? How could she not know how important they were to each other? The distance had never mattered to him because she had always been in his heart. He could call her up in his mind at will.

He'd studied the invitation and begun to plot. He would go home and put a stop to the whole thing—make her admit that she couldn't possibly love anyone else—that the two of them belonged together.

However, things hadn't quite worked out that way for him. In the first place, he was under contract and couldn't just take off. But he'd started talking to anyone who would listen. He needed some time off. There was a family crisis, one that needed his presence.

Eventually the powers that be had considered the possibility. Then they had needed to prepare new story lines, and that took time, and more time. Only time was quickly running out for Brad.

He'd ended up with a week. One lousy week to try to convince her she was marrying the wrong man. He'd realized as soon as he saw her that his task was going to be tougher than he'd expected.

Penny had changed from the woman he knew so well. That was when he had finally given up hope. He realized he could never do anything that would hurt her, and breaking up an engagement a week before the wedding was inexcusable. He loved her enough to let her go, knowing that nothing in his life would ever be quite so wonderful or joyous or sparkling again. Losing Penny was like losing all the sparkle in champagne. Life would be flat without her.

Somehow he should have known that life would never betray him in such a cold, calculating way. He'd been given another chance to win.

Looking down at her now, he realized he still had a considerable way to go to win her. But what better setting, or more romantic place, could there be to woo the woman that was already his wife?

Brad walked into the bathroom and shut the door. Turning on the shower he adjusted the heat of the water, stripped down and stepped under the invigorating spray.

Did Penny really love him enough to want to continue their marriage? She had told him she loved him, but what did she actually feel? How did a person ever know what another was feeling? Each person had his own conception of what love was, what it felt like, and how he responded to it.

Somehow he had to prove to Penny, as well as to himself, that she loved him and that marrying Brad, instead of Gregory, was the best thing that could have happened to her.

Brad was convinced he wouldn't be able to go back to sleep, not with all he had on his mind, and not with Penny lying so close beside him. He was unaware how quickly he fell asleep after he joined Penny in bed, this time under the covers.

Penny's dream carried her along on a wave of pleasure that she had never before experienced. She was on the boat, out on the lake, and she could feel the warm sunshine and a soft breeze. Brad was there, fussing because she hadn't put on more suntan lotion and insisting she would burn without it.

He was such a nag. She handed him the lotion and suggested that he put it on himself if he didn't like the way she did it. He grinned at her and she could no longer be irritated with him.

Brad began to spread the cream along her back with long, exploring strokes. She loved his touch. He was so gentle and yet his hands were strong, his long fingers sensitive. She could feel the pads of his fingertips softly moving over her.

No man had ever touched her so intimately. Only Brad. She loved Brad, so it was all right. Whatever Brad wanted to do, it was all right. She loved him. She loved...

Penny's eyes flew open. She was no longer asleep. No longer dreaming, and yet—she was in Brad's arms.

Her head lay on his shoulder, his arm holding her close to his side. And with his other hand, he was touching and caressing her. And she was letting him.

Brad shifted, pulling her tighter against him, lifting her chin as he lowered his head to hers. She barely had time to notice that his eyes were closed before his lips touched hers and she forgot everything else.

She could feel the heavy vibration of his heart pounding against her. His lungs seemed to be laboring for air but he continued to kiss her without pausing for breath.

"Oh, Penny," he managed to say when he finally broke away. His breathing was so ragged she could scarcely hear him. "I want you so much," he murmured. "So much."

She didn't need his explanation to know what was happening. Somehow everything that was occurring seemed so natural and right.

Both of them were still more than half-asleep, un-inhibitedly responding to their deep-seated, long-standing feelings for each other.

Vaguely Brad knew that he intended to make love to Penny. He loved her, they were married, and he knew of no better way to convince her that he wanted nothing more than to be her passionately loving husband.

Brad knew he could seduce her. From her reactions he realized she'd never been this aroused before. He knew she wouldn't stop him, if he took his time with her.

The question was, how was she going to feel afterward? There was so much that needed to be said between them. Even though they were legally married, the wedding had been a farce.

Did he really intend to use her sexual response to him to coax her into making a decision that would have lifelong ramifications for both of them?

Brad relaxed his hold on her and lay there, unmoving for a moment.

Penny felt swamped with all of the swirling, unfamiliar emotions she'd been experiencing since she'd awakened. Everything was happening so fast. Her lifelong friend had metamorphosed into a passionate, intriguing stranger whose very touch made her bones melt.

Before she could fully comprehend what was happening, Penny felt Brad move away from her. She watched with bewilderment as Brad tossed the covers back and, clad only in a pair of briefs, disappeared into the bathroom, closing the door behind him.

Chapter Nine

When the bathroom door opened sometime later Brad walked out and casually commented. "I'm sorry I took so long. I guess we'll have to flip a coin each morning to see who gets the use of the bathroom first."

This was the same Brad she'd always known, but Penny discovered she missed the passionate stranger who had shared her bed. She wondered what he would think if he knew how she felt. "That's all right," she said, following his example and entering the other room.

Brad quickly found some clean clothes and, dropping the towel he'd draped modestly around him, got dressed. She won't have any problem with the hot water, he thought wryly. I certainly didn't use much of it.

elt the need to deny the spontaneity that seemed to ubble inside of her?

Here was the woman who had loved Brad Crawford single-mindedly, had followed his lead throughout her childhood, and had played opposite him in most of the plays produced during their high school and college years.

"Where have you been?" she asked, amazed at the transformation.

From the moment she had awakened in Brad's arms to the feel of his touch and the taste of his lips, Penny felt like an entirely different person. She was reminded of one of her favorite stories as a child—the one about Sleeping Beauty, who was awakened by the prince with a kiss.

Her pulse accelerated at the thought that she could have married Gregory, convinced that she loved him, and never known the wonder of what Brad had already revealed to her. She had never been affected by Gregory in such a way. Penny had never known the difference . . . until now.

She laughed out loud, hurriedly finished applying her lipstick and flicked a comb through her hair. How could she explain what had happened to her when she didn't understand it herself? She cringed with embarrassment at the memory of all that she had accused Brad of the day before. He could have reacted so differently. Gregory would never have tolerated such an utburst from her. Subconsciously she had known hat her innermost personality must be kept submerged in order to be acceptable to him.

He was waiting for her when she came out, wrapped in a towel. "I'm sorry about what almost happened this morning," he said tersely. "I have no excuse for losing control like that. I hope you won't add this to the long list you seem to have kept over the years of my iniquities."

Brad stood by the opened door to their balcony, waiting for her reaction. She could think of nothing to say.

"We need to talk, Penny, the sooner the better. I've discovered I'm not nearly as noble as I thought I was."

After what she had just experienced with him, Penny wasn't at all sure she wanted his nobility. She'd made an astounding discovery since he'd disappeared into the bathroom earlier.

She very much wanted to make love to Brad Crawford. The thought shocked her right down to her toes. If that was what she was feeling for Brad, she'd had no business planning to marry Gregory Duncan.

Another revelation.

She was still reeling from these shocks when Brad greeted her with his apology in a no-nonsense tone of voice. Glancing down at her towel-draped body, she said, "I agree that we need to talk. I'd prefer to be dressed to do it, however."

Brad seemed to find her remark amusing. "I suppose I can understand that. Why don't you go ahead and get ready and I'll meet you downstairs for breakfast. Maybe later we can take a walk along the beach and enjoy some of the atmosphere around here."

"All right." Penny still felt bewildered by her responses to him earlier and her illuminating discovery regarding her feelings for Brad.

She wasted little time finding a sundress to put on, pleased that so much of what she had packed would be appropriate for a honeymoon in Acapulco.

Her honeymoon with Brad.

A conversation she'd had with her mother months ago suddenly flashed into her mind. She had told Helen that Gregory had proposed to her.

Helen had been working in the kitchen at the time so Penny had perched on the step stool nearby.

"Gregory wants to marry you!" Helen repeated in obvious surprise.

"That's what he said," Penny agreed.

"What did you tell him?"

Penny was quiet for a moment. "I told him that I needed time to consider it."

"I should think so!"

"However, I'm fairly sure that I want to marry him, Mom."

Helen turned around and faced her. "Are you, Penny?"

Penny met her mother's look and nodded. "Yes. Gregory offers the type of life I want. He's stable, successful and I know I can always depend on him."

"What about love?"

"That goes without saying, of course."

"Love should never go without being expressed, Penny. Don't mistake compatible and companionable with love. They're necessary to a good relationship, but love is what holds them together."

"I think we're well-suited."

Helen sighed. "I always thought you ￼ would end up together."

"Brad? You must be joking. That man ￼ know the first thing about making a comm￼ He'd run in the opposite direction."

The image of her mother's face dissolved and￼ again Penny realized where she was—on her h￼ moon with Brad.

He'd had every opportunity to run—from the￼ he'd learned that Gregory wasn't going to marry h￼ to the day of the wedding and afterward. But he￼ here. Despite the disruption a sudden marriage wo￼ cause in his life and career, Brad Crawford had ch￼ sen to commit himself to her and face whatever c￼ sequences his actions created.

When Penny returned to the bathroom to put on￼ makeup she was arrested by the sight of the woma￼ the mirror. She glowed. There was no other wo￼ describe the look of anticipation on her face. Sh￼ a woman in love, there was no denying that ex￼ sion, the sparkle in her eyes, the slight flush ￼ cheeks.

Penny couldn't remember the last time she'd ￼ that woman in a mirror. Gone was the sedate ￼ teacher, the level-headed, sensible woman G￼ Duncan had met and asked to marry. Instead ￼ the young girl she'd known years ago, her drea￼ fantasies shining like an aura around her.

"I had no idea you even existed," she wh￼ Why had she brushed aside this vibrant per￼ had patiently waited to be recognized? Why￼

With Brad, she'd always done and said exactly what she felt at the time. He was so much a part of her that she had never questioned that particular freedom. Nor had she fully appreciated it.

Now he waited for her downstairs, no doubt expecting another childish outburst. His list of iniquities? How about hers? To think that he loved her, despite all her faults. It was up to her to let him know that, for the first time, she fully realized how much he meant to her.

Penny rode the elevator down to the main floor of the hotel, unaware of the smile on her face. Brad noticed her expression as soon as she stepped into the lobby.

"I've seen that particular smile before," he said in a low voice, taking her arm and guiding her into the restaurant. "It bodes ill to someone."

She shook her head. "Not necessarily."

After they were seated and their coffee was poured, he leaned forward slightly and said, "For someone whose life was ruined yesterday, you seem to have made an amazing recovery."

She chuckled, amused by the wariness on his face, "What a difference a day makes, wouldn't you say?"

"That isn't something I find myself muttering very often, as a matter of fact. Actually, you're beginning to make me nervous."

"In what way?"

"I can recall several instances where that particular look in your eye meant trouble for me."

She shook her head with a grin.

"I've got it. You're leaving right after breakfast, flying back home."

"Nope."

"You've made arrangements to rendezvous with a local skin diver?"

She laughed outright. "Don't be silly."

He leaned back and studied her intently. "Oh. Now I understand. You've heard from Gregory."

She sobered. "Why would you say that?"

He shrugged. "Because you look so radiant. Somehow he must have let you know he's sorry and intends to make amends."

"Brad, I haven't heard from Gregory. It wouldn't matter if I had."

"What's that supposed to mean?"

She glanced up as the waiter delivered their breakfast. "Hmm. Doesn't that look wonderful? I can't remember when I've been so hungry, can you?"

For the rest of the meal Penny adroitly avoided anything resembling a serious conversation. She wanted to enjoy these new sensations she'd discovered and to come to terms with the insight she'd gained about herself.

She wondered if this was how a butterfly felt when it first opened its wings—astounded at the myriad of bright colors unfolding. Suddenly she felt free of the restrictions that she'd unknowingly placed on herself.

Today was a brand-new day for her to face the world and adjust to her new life and the person she'd just discovered.

Thank God Brad was a part of her new existence. He was a major part.

They had walked along the beach for some time in silence, watching the swimmers playing in the surf. Finally Brad said, "You're taking this much better than I expected."

"I've had time to think it over."

"And?"

"And what?"

"Have you come to any conclusions as to what you want to do?"

"About what?"

"Us. Our marriage."

He'd been quiet during most of their walk on the beach and she'd known he was thinking. "Some. What about you?" she asked.

"Well," he said after a moment, "I know that I really managed to mess up your life by trying to help out."

"Oh?"

"You might have gone through a few bad days, trying to face everyone when the wedding had to be called off, but then it would have been over, and you could have gone on with your life."

"Yes, I've thought of that."

"Instead, you're now going to have to..." He paused, as though unsure of what to say.

"I'm going to have to... what?"

"You're still going to have to explain why you ended your marriage so quickly."

"You do have a point there. How do we return home and tell everyone that we flunked our honeymoon?"

His head snapped around and he stared at her in surprise. She had an amused expression that added lightness to her teasing comment.

"I think we have our roles reversed here, don't you?" he finally muttered. "I'm the one you're always accusing of never taking anything seriously."

"Yes, that's true. I decided to see if I could become more like you. You've set such an example all these years."

"This isn't exactly the subject I'd use to practice my sense of humor, Penny."

"I don't see why not to use it. The fact is, we are married. To each other. I am very much aware that your vacation plans did not include acquiring a wife. But try to overlook that particular inconvenience and see if you can enjoy your time here," she said, waving her arms at the water, the palm trees and the carefully groomed sand.

Brad had never seen Penny in quite this mood before. Maybe the strain had been too much for her and her nerves had finally snapped. He'd find it difficult to convince anyone of that, however. She looked radiantly healthy and happy. And in love.

Whoa! Wait a minute. That line of thinking was going to get him in trouble. "Are you suggesting we postpone for a few days deciding what we're going to do when we return to the States?"

"Is there anything wrong with that?" she asked.

Brad thought of the long cold shower he'd endured that morning and almost shuddered. What she suggested wasn't unfair, just humanly impossible for him. Wasn't she affected by sharing a room with him, a bed with him? Hadn't their early morning kiss and caresses warned her of what could happen if they continued to ignore what was between them?

"I don't suppose there is," he finally answered.

"Good," she said, stopping and looking out at the water. "We've waited long enough after breakfast for a swim, don't you think?" she asked.

He glanced at his watch. "Yes."

"Then let's go change into our suits. I can hardly wait to find out what it's like to swim in sea water."

For the next several hours they kept busy, first swimming, then exploring the area, and finally spending a romantic evening watching the divers go off the cliff into the sea below.

Brad had forced himself not to dwell on the night ahead, but as the evening progressed, he had a hard time disciplining himself. He'd never seen Penny more beautiful, enticing, alluring, and yet so unobtainable.

This was his punishment for his sin of coveting her. She was his wife, but he was honor bound not to presume anything regarding their relationship.

By the time they returned to their room, he'd almost decided to fake another headache as an excuse to take more pain medication. At least he could seek oblivion for a few hours.

Penny gathered up her nightclothes and went into the bathroom. She smiled and said, "I won't be long."

"That's what I'm afraid of," he muttered to himself, wondering at his unusual ability to inflict pain upon himself. Wandering out on the balcony he studied the stars and tried to imagine where he would be if the wedding had gone as originally planned.

He felt a gut-wrenching pain at the thought of Penny here with anyone else but him. How could he possibly have borne it, knowing he'd never share this delightful intimacy with her? If that's the case, he thought, then you'd better convince her that the two of you belong together.

To his amazement Brad discovered a few minutes later that he needed to make very little effort.

He turned when he heard the door open and saw her standing there in a thin gown that left very little to the imagination, particularly as she was silhouetted against the bathroom light.

"Penny..." he said, trying to get his tongue unwrapped from around his teeth.

She walked over to him and casually put her hand on his chest. "Thank you for your patience."

There was something in her tone of voice that made him believe she was referring to something other than her use of the bathroom.

Brad could no more stand there and not touch her than he could leap from the balcony and fly. "That's okay. I, uh, think maybe that I'll..."

Penny went up on tiptoe and kissed him softly on the lips, her body relaxing fully against him. If his mind was attempting to resist what was happening, his body obviously did not suffer from similar scruples. It immediately responded to her closeness.

Instead of being repelled, Penny cuddled even closer, if that were possible.

The battle within Brad was intense but short-lived. He might hate himself in the morning, but there was no resisting what he felt tonight.

Penny knew exactly when Brad stopped fighting and gave free rein to what they both wanted to happen. His arms came around her in a grip so fierce she had a fleeting thought as to the safety of her ribs. But it was only a fleeting thought, after all. Having Brad hold her so fiercely was well worth any damage she might accidently suffer.

The kiss he gave her held all the longing that she could possibly want from him and when he paused a moment for them to get their breath she whispered, "Love me, Brad. Please love me."

"Oh, God, Penny. Don't you understand how much I love you?"

"Then show me."

He needed no further encouragment. Brad lifted her in his arms and strode over to the bed. Brushing the covers back, he lowered her onto the pillow.

Brad impatiently stripped out of his clothes, then came down onto the bed beside her. "Oh, love," he muttered as he gathered her in his arms. "Do you have any idea what you've put me through?"

"Not intentionally, Brad. I didn't know," she whispered. "How could I have known?"

Eventually he removed the gown she wore for the express purpose of getting his attention. Penny was more than satisfied with the results.

Brad took his time now that he had accepted the amazing fact that Penny wanted him and was willing to explore the physical side of their multi-faceted relationship.

She willingly followed his silent guidance, imitating each caress. Penny was delighted to see his immediate response to her touch.

By the time he was ready to claim her, she was almost pleading with him to show her the next step in their lovemaking. Yet nothing could have possibly described how wonderful she felt when Brad finally made her his own.

How could they have waited so long to experience something so beautiful, so fulfilling? If only she had known what she had been missing.

And later, just before she drifted off to sleep, Penny reminded herself to ask Brad where he'd learned to be such a gentle, sensitive, and obviously experienced lover!

They slept late the next morning, content to use the morning hours to catch up on sleep that had been abandoned willingly more than once during the night.

Penny quickly became adept at learning Brad's most vulnerable places. She discovered a great many advantages to knowing a person so well. Sharing a marriage bed became something of an adventure.

Until now, Penny had assumed she was not a particularly sensual individual. In a few short hours, she learned differently.

When she eventually awoke the next morning she saw that Brad was still sleeping. However, since he had an arm and a leg wrapped around her, she realized she wasn't going anywhere until he moved.

"Brad?" she whispered.

"Good grief, Penny," he mumbled. "You're insatiable." His mouth quirked into a mischievous grin.

"Would you kindly let go of me?"

His eyes flew open at her tone. "What's wrong?" he asked with a sinking feeling in the pit of his stomach.

She waited until he edged away from her, then she sat up with a grin. "Nothing. I just have to answer nature's call." Penny fled to the bathroom, laughing, the pillow that followed her barely missing its target.

He lay there for a moment, thinking about the previous night. If Penny intended to dissolve their marriage, she certainly couldn't ask for an annulment. Somehow he doubted her interest in pursuing such a course of action, if her response to him the night before was any indication.

When Brad heard the shower running, he decided to join her.

"What are you doing?" Her startled cry greeted him when he stepped into the shower with her.

"What does it look like?"

"I thought we were going to take turns," she said, suddenly shy with him.

He took the soap from her hand and began to apply it lavishly over her body. "But this is so much more economical, don't you think? We'll be able to get ready that much faster, and look at the water we're saving."

Penny could find nothing to say to refute his statement, so she smiled.

"We still need to talk, you know," he said quietly, after lovingly caressing her all over, then carefully rinsing her off.

"I know."

Penny felt much better prepared to discuss their future together after the night they had just spent. They belonged together, even if they had chosen a rather unorthodox way to achieve that goal. Or to be more precise, *he* had chosen.

They chose to order breakfast sent up so they could enjoy the view from their balcony and not have to dress any more than was necessary to greet the man who delivered their order.

"Are you coming back to New York with me?" Brad finally asked her over coffee.

"I suppose. I guess I haven't really thought about it."

"That's understandable, under the circumstances."

"I really have no desire to stay in Payton. I'm not ready to face Gregory just yet."

Brad could feel his stomach clench at the mention of the other man's name. He took another sip of coffee, not meeting her eyes. "I have to go back on Sunday to be ready to work Monday."

"It seems so strange to be planning to live in New York. Like another world. I'll need to resign my job..." Her voice trailed off.

"You know you don't need to work if you'd rather not," he offered.

"I'd go crazy sitting around all day."

"That's not what I meant. Since we don't need your income, you could take the opportunity to attend auditions and things . . . if you wanted to, of course."

"You mean, try to get a job acting?"

"You've certainly got the credentials for it."

"Oh, Brad, I don't know."

"About what?"

"I just never thought I'd try to act professionally."

He smiled. "Try it. You might decide you like it."

So many things were happening to her in a space of a few days, Penny felt as though a whirlwind had picked her up and swirled her away to another land. A land of endless possibilities.

She gazed at Brad across the table. He looked very relaxed and contented. She couldn't imagine Gregory sitting spinelessly in a chair, with nothing more on than a pair of swimming trunks. They were so different and yet she had been attracted to the one she had felt was more stable.

Her instincts had failed her. But Brad hadn't. She remembered the phrase he'd repeated to her—that's what friends are for.

"Thank you," Penny said with a tender look on her face.

Since Brad couldn't remember anything he'd done that deserved such a comment, he looked at her blankly.

She explained. "Thank you for loving me, for having faith in me, for pushing me until I had to face myself and learn who I really am. I realize now that I would have been miserably bored with Gregory.

Thank you for understanding that and doing what you could to save me from my own faulty decisions.''

Brad straightened in his chair and stared at her with a look that seemed to radiate happiness. "You mean you're forgiving me for ruining your wedding?"

"You didn't ruin it. You saved it and me."

"I know you still love Gregory, Penny. I can understand and live with that . . ."

She laughed. "I've never heard you sounding so humble, Brad. And it doesn't go with your personality at all. I'm not sure how I feel toward Gregory at the moment. What he did was brutal and inexcusable. Learning that he was capable of such behavior shocked me, because I realized how little I knew him. I'm immensely thankful I didn't marry him." She gazed out over the water. "It never would have worked for us."

"I was very much afraid you'd never see that," Brad said with relief.

Penny got up and trailed around to Brad's side of the table. She sat down on his lap and looked up at him. "There is one thing I have wanted to ask you, though."

Brad tensed. Things were going so well. They hadn't fought since their wedding day. Of course, that had only been two days ago, but he felt they'd made giant strides in learning to live together compatibly.

"What?" he asked warily.

"I've known you all your life," she began softly.

"That's right," he agreed.

"We were always very close, except for those three years you were in New York," she went on.

"Uh-huh."

"Then could you explain how you perfected your technique in bed? I seem to have missed something along the way."

Brad tilted his head back and laughed. Still laughing he picked her up and carried her back into the other room. Since she wore only a negligee that did little to cover her charms, he wasted no time in freeing her of her apparel.

As he lowered her to the bed and stretched out beside her, he said, "Honey, you haven't missed a thing. I intend to teach you all that I know. I told you that not all I learned in college was in the classroom."

There was that devastating grin again, the one that caused women all over America to turn on their television sets every afternoon.

The love in his eyes made it clear that there was only one woman who had his heart. She held him closely, thankful for the chance she'd had to discover just what friends are for.

Epilogue

"Hello," the young secretary said with a smile. "May I help you?"

"I would like to see Mr. Duncan, if possible."

"Do you have an appointment?"

"No, I'm afraid I don't."

The secretary nodded. "I'll see if he has time to see you. Your name, please?"

"Penny Crawford," she said quietly.

While the young woman spoke on the phone, Penny looked around the office. Not much had changed since the last time she'd been there. Everything had a stately, polished look that induced a sense of reassurance and stability.

She heard a door open behind her and she turned around. Gregory Duncan stood in the doorway, staring at her. "Penny! I thought she must have misunderstood—Come in," he said, stepping aside and motioning her into his office.

Penny walked past him, noticing the changes in him since she'd seen him last. He looked older, which she had expected, but much older than his years. Lines furrowed his brow and face. Up close she could see the gray in his blond hair. He looked just what he was—a successful, harried businessman. She wondered what she'd ever seen in him that she'd found attractive. The physical resemblance between Gregory and Brad was barely discernible.

"This is a surprise," he said from behind her. "Won't you have a seat?"

"I hope you don't mind my dropping in like this," she said, taking a seat and watching him as he walked behind his desk and sat down.

"Why, no. It's a pleasure to see you again. It's been a while."

Her eyes met his. "Yes, it has," she agreed quietly.

They sat there in silence, just looking at each other. Finally Gregory roused himself enough to say, "You're looking wonderful."

She nodded her head. "Thank you."

"Are you in town for long?"

"Just a few days, I'm afraid. We don't get much free time these days."

He smiled. "I suppose not. How does it feel to be working with your husband on stage?"

"It's been quite an experience. Surprisingly enough, Brad enjoys it. I was afraid television had spoiled him for the theater."

"Your reviews have been very good."

"Yes." She paused, searching for the right words. "I wanted to thank you for the beautiful bouquet you had delivered to me on opening night." Once more her eyes met his. "I was touched that you remembered me."

"I will always remember you, Penny," he said in a matter-of-fact tone. "As a matter of fact, I was in New York and caught your opening night."

"You were there?"

He nodded.

"Then why didn't you come backstage?"

"I had intended to. But somehow, when the time came, it seemed inappropriate." He smiled again. "However, I thought you did an outstanding job, for what it's worth. I had no idea you were so talented."

"There was a lot of luck involved there. A case of being in the right place at the right time." She shrugged. "I wish you'd let me know you were there."

"There was no need. Let's say I was appeasing my curiosity." He nodded slightly. "You and Brad work very well together, you know. You seem to be so in tune with each other that the audience can almost see the link."

"I know. We've often remarked on it ourselves."

Gregory picked up a letter opener and began to turn it over, end to end, in his hands. "I suppose your families are pleased to see you," he said.

"Yes. Brad's mother hasn't been well. We thought she might enjoy seeing Stacye, but to be on the safe side, we decided to stay at Mother's. Stacye's energy can wear anyone out. We didn't think Brad's mom needed the extra strain. This way we can let her visit in small doses."

"Do you have any pictures of her?" he asked casually.

Penny laughed. "Of course. I'm a typical doting mother." She dug around in her purse, then pulled out a folder and handed it to him.

Gregory studied the little girl carefully, noting the blond hair and the blue eyes. The smile was very familiar, as was the impish expression. It was her mother's smile, although he had never been exposed to the impish part of her personality.

"She looks a great deal like you, Penny," he said, handing the folder back to her.

"I suppose so. But she has her father's teasing temperament. Those two are a pair." She stopped suddenly, realizing what she was saying, and to whom.

"I don't need to ask if you're happy, Penny. It shows."

"I know, Gregory. That's why I came by to see you." His eyebrow lifted slightly in inquiry. "It took me a while," she went on to say, "but I finally understood what you did and why you did it."

He looked puzzled. "I'm afraid I don't follow you."

"I couldn't understand why you'd refuse to marry me without offering me any explanation, and yet present us with a honeymoon already paid for. On the one hand, one action was brutal, the other sensitive. The two actions didn't fit."

"I'm afraid you're being too generous in ascribing such kind motives to me, Penny," he said. "The truth is that when it came right down to it, I realized I'd been single too long, was too set in my ways to ever accommodate another person in my life. And you were right. I chose a brutal, cowardly way out.'' He looked down at the letter opener in his hand, as though wondering where it had come from. ''As for the honeymoon, I had paid for everything several weeks in advance and would not have gotten the full amount back, even if I'd canceled.'' His smile was a little forced. ''I'm afraid the tickets were a sop to my conscience. Nothing more.''

She could feel his embarrassment at being confronted by what he had done. Penny realized that she believed him. He hadn't particularly cared about her feelings, because emotions weren't very high on his list of desirable qualities in himself. He was a practical, pragmatic man. Had she married him, her own emotions would have eventually atrophied from lack of expression.

''Well,'' she said, coming to her feet, ''I wanted to stop by and thank you for the flowers and your good wishes, and to let you know that, just in case you've wondered, you did the right thing when you refused to marry me.''

He stood as well. ''I've never had any doubts about that,'' he said with a small smile. He walked around the desk and escorted her to the door. ''Thank you for coming in, Penny. I appreciate the gesture.''

''Yes, I'm sure by this time tomorrow everyone in town will know I came to see you,'' she replied with a grin.

His smile was more natural when he said, "I don't know what story you and Brad put about, but I was inundated with unspoken sympathy for weeks after the wedding. Totally undeserved, of course. I felt like something of a fraud."

She laughed. "Since Brad engineered the whole scenario, he was responsible for the story. I didn't know who I was marrying until mid-way through the ceremony."

For once Gregory's face registered emotion. "You mean you didn't know that I wasn't . . ." He couldn't seem to find the words.

"That's right," she said matter-of-factly. "Brad was convinced I would never have married him any other way."

"I had no idea."

She shrugged. "Well, that's Brad. Always being dramatic about something or other. Only the three of us know what actually happened. There was no reason for anyone else to know."

He stood there looking down at her for a long time in silence. Penny didn't feel as if she could turn and walk away from such an intent look.

"Brad must have known the best way to handle you," he said finally, still a little bemused.

"Yes, I guess he does. He's had enough practice." On impulse Penny went up on her toes and kissed his cheek. "Thank you for seeing me, Gregory. I always felt that our relationship had been left hanging, somehow. I needed to tie it off in my mind—to let you know that I've forgiven you for what you did. You did us both a real favor."

Penny's last sight of Gregory was his turning back to his office and his work—his real wife.

When Penny pulled into her parents' driveway, she saw Brad loping toward her from his parents' home. She got out and started toward him. He grabbed her around the waist, his momentum swinging her around.

"What are you doing, you crazy man?" she asked, laughing.

"I missed you. I was coming over to see if your Mother might have left a note that she had heard from you. Where have you been?"

They stood in the middle of the front lawn, their arms companionably wrapped around each other's waist. "I stopped in to see Gregory."

Brad's smile faded slowly. "Why?"

"It's hard to explain. Every once in a while I'd find myself thinking of him, what he was doing, if he'd ever married—that sort of thing."

"Wishing that things had turned out differently?" he asked with a smile. Penny was aware his eyes remained serious.

She went up on tiptoe and kissed him. "Hardly," she said with a grin, "I suppose I needed to see him again, in his own environment, to remind myself how close I came to making the biggest mistake of my life."

He held her close. "Was he surprised to see you?"

"Stunned is a better description. I don't think he ever thought he'd have to face me after what he did."

"So what did he say?"

"Not much. He saw the play the last time he was in New York. Seemed surprised that I could act."

Brad laughed. "He shouldn't have been surprised at all. You were giving him a great performance during your entire engagement."

Penny playfully poked him in the chest. "Not deliberately."

"I know, love," he said soothingly. Now his eyes were filled with mischief.

Brad turned toward the house and wrapped his arm around her shoulders. He glanced down at her with a grin. "Mom asked if Stacye could spend the afternoon with her. They're busy making cookies, so I said I thought it would be okay."

"Are you sure your mom's up to having such a little chatterbox around?"

He opened the door for them, then guided her up the stairs.

"Oh, I think so. She said the doctor thinks she's well on the road to recovery and that having her one and only granddaughter here was better than anything he could have prescribed." They reached the door to Penny's old room and Brad eased her inside, closing the door unobtrusively.

"Your mom went to town for her art class," he explained. "Said since she'd be late getting home we'd go out for dinner tonight." Brad casually began to unbutton Penny's dress.

"What are you doing?" she asked, suddenly aware of his preoccupation with her clothing.

He pushed her dress off her shoulders and eased it away from her breasts and rounded hips. "I'm rehearsing for a new role," he said with a grin, lifting her and placing her on the bed. Brad quickly discarded his clothes and joined her.

"A new role?" she asked, a little breathless at the sudden turn of events.

"Umm. Isn't this the way to play doctor?"

"I certainly hope not!" she said, looking at his unclothed body with feigned indignation.

"Oh, well. Maybe I just need some tender, loving care, after an afternoon away from you."

She smiled, pulling him closer. "Well, my dear, you certainly came to the right place for that."

"I know," Brad said with a satisfied smile.

* * * * *

Come Be My Love

★

ANNETTE BROADRICK

This book is dedicated to fellow writers Noreen Brownlie and Susan Naomi Horton whose long-distance encouragement and assistance in plotting and planning not only helped me to hang on to my sanity but also contributed to the increased revenues of the telephone companies for two nations!

Thank you both for your beautiful friendships. I have been doubly blessed.

IOWA

NEBRASKA

Payton

ILLINOIS

KANSAS • Kansas City

Missouri River

St. Louis

MISSOURI
Underlined places are fictitious.

N

ARKANSAS

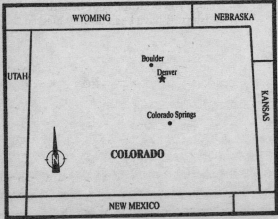

WYOMING

NEBRASKA

UTAH

Boulder
•

Denver
•
★

Colorado Springs
•

KANSAS

N

COLORADO

NEW MEXICO

Chapter One

The high beams of Gregory Duncan's headlights glimmered on the blanketing snow that weighted the branches of the evergreens surrounding Tim's A-frame chalet. The snow sparkled with a glitter that caused Greg to smile as he made the last sharp turn into the empty driveway.

He sat there for a moment, absorbing the night silence and the beauty of the heavy snow. He was looking forward to the next few days, to the solitude that he'd finally decided he needed. The long drive from eastern Missouri to the Rocky Mountains of southern Colorado had been worth the effort. Taking in the quiet serenity and beauty around him, he knew that he'd made the right decision—to escape from his busy world and enjoy the solitude of nature.

Greg climbed from the car and stretched, then reached for his bag. His skis could wait until morning. He had plenty of time now to do whatever he wanted. At the moment, sleep was his number one priority.

He felt in his pocket for the key his friend had given him years ago, right after Tim had purchased his hideaway. Thank God for a friend like Tim, Greg thought as he mounted the steps to the door. They went back a long way.

Greg had been unable to reach Tim at his Denver office when he had suddenly decided, after an unusually long jury trial, to get away for a while. Not that contacting Tim was mandatory before using the place. Tim had always insisted that Greg treat the place as his own and that he make free use of it.

Greg had half hoped that Tim might have had the same idea and be there ahead of him, but there were no other vehicles parked around the cabin.

Given Tim's business, he could be anywhere at the moment. He went to whatever part of the world he was needed in, whenever he was called. Greg was one of the few people who knew exactly what Tim did for a living and how valuable was his contribution to the safety and continued security of the country.

Tim was a very private person. Greg knew the same could be said about his own personality, which probably explained why he and Tim had been friends for so many years.

He also understood why Tim needed a place where he could retreat on occasion and why its location was a closely guarded secret from almost everyone who knew him. Greg appreciated the trust Tim had shown in him by sharing the retreat with him.

Greg let himself in by the kitchen door and flipped on a light. Everything looked ready for occupancy. Greg knew that Tim paid a couple who lived a few miles down the road to keep an eye on the place. Tim also kept it well stocked with food. Peeking into the refrigerator, Greg smiled at the plentiful supply of canned and bottled drinks.

At the moment, all Greg wanted was several hours of uninterrupted sleep. The very idea of being somewhere without a phone or an alarm clock seemed to be the height of luxury to him.

He turned out the light and made his way to the stairs by the reflection of light from the snow outside shining through the glass wall that made up the front of the A-frame home.

The place was small but fulfilled Tim's needs—as well as Greg's. The loft area was open, with a railing overlooking the main part of the house below. An oversize bed waited in the deep shadows of the room, and Greg sank onto the edge of the mattress, wearily pulling off his shoes, then unbuttoning his shirt. Within seconds he'd stripped down to his shorts, and with a sigh of anticipation he crawled under the covers.

Alone at last was his last conscious thought.

Brandi Martin slept heavily. Her exhaustion was as much emotional as physical. Yet even in her sleep she could not find any peace of mind—her subconscious filled her dreams with people who were after her. She had to get away. She had to hide, to hide before they succeeded in killing her.

A hand brushed her shoulder.

She screamed, waking herself up, and discovered that the hand touching her hadn't been part of her dream. The bedside lamp came on and a male voice said, "What the—"

Still half submerged in her dreams, Brandi found that she was in bed with a man she'd never seen before in her life.

She screamed again.

"Good God, lady! I heard you the first time. Your reaction is duly noted. Now, for hell's sake, who are you and what are you doing here?"

Brandi felt frozen with shock and fright. She watched as the tall, well-built blond man threw back the covers on his side of the bed and stood up, revealing a well-muscled physique with very little covering it. With economical movements, he pulled on a pair of jeans that were beside the bed. He turned around and stared at her, his hands resting on his hips.

All Brandi could think about was the horrible realization that somehow, someway, she had been traced to Tim's place.

"Who are you?" Her voice quavered, and she glanced quickly around the room, searching for a weapon, any weapon.

"I asked you first."

She glanced back at him nervously. If he'd come there to kill her, would he have taken off his clothes first? "What are you doing here?" she asked, trying to fight the horror of wondering who he might be.

"What the hell does it look like, lady?" Greg ran his hand through his hair. "If you were expecting Tim, I'm sorry to disappoint you." He glanced around the room. "Where is he, anyway?"

Hearing a name that she knew caused Brandi to draw her first deep breath since she'd been jolted awake. Her heart was pounding relentlessly in her chest, and she forced herself to try to calm down. Even though she didn't know who this man was, he obviously knew Tim, which meant that he couldn't be one of the faceless men who had been pursuing her for the past three nightmarish days and nights.

She spoke her relief out loud. "You must be a friend of Tim's," she murmured, trying to calm down.

Greg sighed and sank onto the edge of the bed. Whoever this woman was, he didn't give her much in the way of brainpower. Either that or she wasn't too swift when she first awoke.

Then again, having some strange female screech in his ear wasn't his idea of a great good-morning call, either. He glanced at his watch in disgust. He'd driven fourteen hours, hadn't gotten to sleep until two, and now it was barely five in the morning.

Greg studied the woman in the bed closely, wondering who she was and how she'd managed to get inside Tim's cabin. He knew he'd never seen her before. He would have remembered her. She was small, with short black curls that reminded him of a baby's fine hair falling over her forehead and feathering around her ears and the nape of her neck. Her eyes, a prominent feature in her elfin face, were so deeply blue they looked almost black in the lamplight, with lashes so thick that they appeared to be smudges that made her large eyes seem even larger. At the moment she was very pale, but Greg guessed that her skin was naturally fair.

She inched back against the headboard as though she were afraid of him when he sat down on the bed. Greg found her attitude ludicrous, but at the moment he could think of no way to reassure her that he didn't make a practice of attacking women—and particularly not at five o'clock in the morning.

He realized that they had been sitting there staring at each other in silence for several minutes, which wasn't getting them anywhere.

"All right," he said with a shrug. "I'll go first. My name is Greg Duncan. I'm a friend of Tim's from Missouri. Tim and I have been friends for more years than I can remember. He lets me use this place whenever it's available." He paused and, with a slight lift of his brow, added, "Obviously it wasn't as available as I thought. Now then, who are you?"

Brandi had had an opportunity to calm down a little. Her heart had finally slowed enough that she was fairly certain it wasn't going to leave her chest or go into cardiac arrest.

"I'm Brandi Martin."

As though they were meeting at a formal party, Greg nodded his head slightly and held out his hand. "How do you do, Brandi Martin?"

She stared at his hand blankly, feeling more than a little confused at the sudden polite turn to the conversation. When he continued to hold it out to her, she reluctantly placed her hand in his.

Greg smiled as she immediately withdrew her hand from his. "Rest assured that I have no intention of harming you in any way," he said in a quiet tone. "I apologize for startling you earlier, but quite frankly I had no idea you were in this bed with me."

"I had no idea you were here, either," she replied faintly.

"Yes, you did manage to convince me of that," he said solemnly. "I take it you're a friend of Tim's."

She nodded.

"Would you like to tell me what you're doing here?"

"Trying to sleep," she pointed out dryly.

He laughed. "Good point. Are you here to meet Tim? Are you expecting him soon?"

Greg noted that she appeared to be ill at ease with his questions, but he refused to withdraw them. He just waited patiently, knowing that most people were unnerved by silence, particularly when it came after a question directed toward them.

She dropped her gaze to the colorful quilt that covered the bed. "I was looking for Tim. I thought he might be here."

"Well, as you can see, he isn't."

Her eyes flashed as she met his inquiring gaze. "I know that now. But it was too late when I got here to go back, and I really didn't know where to go. I knew that Tim wouldn't mind— He once showed me where he kept an extra key, and I needed to—" She dropped her eyes and stared at her hands for a moment before continuing, "I needed a place to stay."

"So Tim doesn't know you're here; is that right?"

She shook her head, her gaze still on her hands folded in her lap.

"Where do you live, Brandi?"

"In northern Colorado."

That was vague enough, Greg decided. He decided to try a different tack. "Why did you need to find a place to stay?"

She met his intent gaze and knew that she couldn't tell him about the bizarre happenings of the past few days. Even if he believed her, telling him wouldn't change the danger she was running from.

When she let the silence grow, he sighed. "How old are you, Brandi?"

Startled by the personal question, she asked, "What difference does my age make?"

"It could make a great deal of difference," he said gently, "if you've run away from home and your family is worried about you."

The choked laugh she gave showed no sign of amusement. "I don't know who you are, Mr. Duncan, but you certainly aren't a very good judge of women's ages. How old do you think I am?"

She raised her chin and stared at him almost belligerently, and it was all he could do not to smile. He guessed she was sixteen—maybe—but he could tell that to suggest such a tender age would only incense her. So he chose blatant flattery. "Twenty?"

For the first time since he'd turned on the light, Greg saw honest amusement in her face. She glanced at him, then at the soft glow from the bedside lamp.

"Remind me to always stay in dimly lighted rooms. The light just took several years off my age."

Greg gave a start. Surely she must be lying. But why? And at the moment he had other, more important considerations to face, like trying to get caught up on some much-needed sleep.

"Look, I'm sorry, but I've been up for almost twenty-four hours and I'm dead on my feet. If it's all right with you, I'd like to postpone this meeting until sometime later in the morning."

He waited for a response. When she continued to watch him without saying anything, he shook his head. The chill of the room was making itself felt. With sudden decisiveness he stood and shucked off his pants, then yanked the covers up and crawled beneath them. He was still almost a foot away from her.

Glancing over his shoulder, he added, "Just do me a favor, okay? Try not to scream if I accidentally brush against you again. I promise to do my best to stay on my own side of the bed."

With that he turned off the light and pulled the covers over his broad shoulders, his back to her.

Brandi sat there stunned for a moment, startled by his attitude.

"But you can't sleep here—"

Without moving, he muttered, "Watch me."

"But I don't know you! I mean, you could be—"

"I'll sign an oath in blood not to touch your body if you'll just shut up and let me get some sleep now. We can spend all day tomorrow talking, okay?"

Brandi continued to sit there staring at his back with dismay mixed with a certain amount of admiration. Here was a man who could handle himself in an un-

usual situation. Her unexplained presence hadn't
fazed him.

Brandi slowly slid back down into the bed, making
sure the distance between them did not lessen. What
was she going to do? Obviously, her options were
limited. She could get up, get dressed and start hiking
down the side of the mountain.

And then what? She could call . . . who? Who could
she call if she couldn't find Tim? Who could she trust?
Who would believe her bizarre story, anyway? She had
no way of knowing why she was being pursued with
such single-minded zest.

If only she weren't so tired, perhaps she could think
straighter. Brandi knew that her behavior bordered on
paranoia, but how could she help it? In her case, there
really seemed to be an Indian behind every tree. And
she didn't know what guise he would be wearing.

At least she felt safer here at Tim's. Surely no one
had been able to follow her here.

She turned and stared at the blond head that seemed
to be buried in the pillow next to her. For now she
might as well follow his example and get some sleep.
Maybe everything would look better tomorrow. She
didn't know Greg Duncan or what he did, but he was
quick-witted enough to make her feel like a witness
being cross-examined. Perhaps she would tell him
what had happened to her tomorrow, when the sun
was shining and everything looked brighter.

Brandi slipped into sleep once again, unaware of
how she was drawn to the body heat nearby, unaware
of curling up to a broad back and feeling safe for the
first time in days.

Greg came awake instantly when he felt Brandi press closely against his back. He waited for her to say something, and when she didn't he realized that she was sound asleep. He smiled to himself without moving and drifted off to sleep once more.

The alluring aroma of freshly brewed coffee drifted into Brandi's dreams several hours later. Without opening her eyes, she stretched luxuriously, feeling rested, relaxed and more like her old self than she had in days.

When she awakened enough to register the smell, her eyes blinked open and she stared at the slanted roof over her head.

She wasn't at home, because there was no one there to prepare coffee and the ceiling of her bedroom was not formed by two of the bedroom walls coming together to meet overhead.

It was only then that she remembered the night before, and glanced at the other side of the bed. She had a certain sense of a good-news-bad-news situation. The good news was that she was alone. The bad news was that she was not on her side of the bed, or even in the middle. To be technically accurate, Brandi had awakened on the same side of the bed that had been occupied by Greg Duncan. She could only hope that she had moved restlessly after he had gotten up. Otherwise, she knew that she wouldn't be able to face him without her embarrassment showing.

Now that she was awake, she became aware of other sounds and scents drifting up from downstairs. The mouth-watering aroma of bacon wafted up to greet her, as well as the soft, homey sounds of someone working in the kitchen.

She also caught a distinct hum, as though whoever was in the kitchen were quite pleased with the world. Brandi lunged out of bed, quivering. Had she done something last night to put him in such a benign, even benevolent, mood?

She couldn't remember. She shook her head, then realized that it was too cold to stand there shivering beside the bed trying to remember what she might have done last night. She found her clothes where she had dropped them the night before and hastily pulled on her turtleneck undershirt, a bulky sweater, a long pair of thermal underpants and her jeans. Then she grabbed a pair of thick socks and pulled them on. Her fleece-lined leather boots followed.

Only then did she realize that she had to go to the bathroom, which was downstairs. But at least she felt protected now—against the cold and against the man waiting below.

Greg Duncan from Missouri. If she hadn't been so tired the night before she might have responded differently to his presence. However, once she had accepted that he was a friend of Tim's, she had relaxed, feeling safe—safe for the first time in days. The sleep that overcame her had been like a powerful narcotic, deadening her to everything else.

She grabbed the small zippered bag that contained the few toiletries she had hastily purchased the afternoon before and tiptoed down the stairs, hoping to avoid a confrontation until she was better prepared to meet the day.

"Good morning."

She'd just reached the bottom step of the stairway, and she knew that her luck had run out. Slowly turning toward the kitchen, Brandi smiled tentatively at the man who was leaning casually against the kitchen counter with his ankles crossed, his hands wrapped around a giant mug that contained enticing, steamy coffee.

Seen in the daylight, Greg Duncan was older than she had first guessed. He looked to be in his early forties, the dusting of silver in the blond hair showing only in the bright light. His eyes looked silver, glinting brightly as he studied her.

Brandi had to admit that he was very impressive, not only in his physical build but in the sense of alert intelligence that he seemed to radiate.

"Good morning," she replied in a voice that sounded disgustingly weak.

Greg studied the woman who hovered at the bottom of the stairs watching him with those unforgettable eyes. Now he could see the maturity in her figure and in her face that had been obscured the night before.

He could also see the wariness in her expression, and he felt that he understood it. He had a similar feeling hovering within him. If anyone had told him that he would find himself in bed with a strange young woman within hours of arriving at Tim's place, he would have blasted them all the way into the next county.

After ending his engagement a few years ago, Greg had faced the fact that he was not marriage material.

Other than a few casual friendships, he rarely spent any time with women. His work was his life, and he was content with that life.

His vacation was an opportunity to spend a few days away from his career and relax. It was not a time to be entertaining a curly-headed waif with large sapphire-blue eyes, and especially not one who looked at him as though he might attack her at any moment.

He smiled at the thought of her curling up to his back earlier. Did she remember that? He couldn't forget waking up this morning to find her head resting on his shoulder and his arm wrapped securely around her, holding her close to his side. His leg had been securely held down by her thigh, which had rested across him. Her fingers had rested trustingly on his chest, as though she were reassured by the steady rhythm of his heart beating beneath her palm.

Being the normal, healthy male that he was, Greg had had an immediate physical reaction to the provocative situation, and he had had to decide what to do about it. Despite his body's eager suggestions, Greg's mind had won the day.

Greg's mind took control of every situation in which he found himself, regardless of what he might be feeling.

So, although he had clearly registered how appealing she looked cuddled so snugly against him, Greg had eased away from her until he'd been out of bed. Then he had tucked the covers around her and left her sleeping soundly while he'd dressed.

By the time he'd showered, started a fire in the fireplace and had his coffee poured, Greg had a list of questions that he fully intended to have answered by his unexpected and impromptu roommate.

"Would you like some coffee?" he asked.

Brandi had noticed his smile as he had carefully studied her, and she knew that she must look a mess. Holding up the bag, she pointed to the bathroom. "Yes, as soon as I get presentable."

He nodded and straightened, reaching for another mug.

Greg watched her disappear into the bathroom and close the door, then slowly poured her coffee, wondering what tactic to use to get Brandi Martin to talk.

When she reappeared in the kitchen a few minutes later she had combed her hair and no doubt washed her face, but she was still pale, and he could count the tiny smattering of freckles across the bridge of her nose. She'd made no attempt to hide the slight shadows beneath her eyes.

"How do you like your eggs?" he asked, motioning for her to sit down. He had such an air of authority about him that she responded automatically, sinking onto one of the bench seats by the table.

"Over easy," she replied, vaguely surprised to see him place a skillet over one of the burners. Brandi hadn't realized she was hungry until the smell of the bacon had caused her stomach to growl earlier. She couldn't remember the last time she'd eaten.

Brandi picked up the cup he'd placed on the table and took a swallow of the revitalizing liquid. Her eyes were drawn back to the man before her. He made everything he did appear to be easy. There were no wasted moves, no unnecessary searching for things.

Everything had been laid out as though waiting for her to appear. He tapped an egg on the side of the pan, breaking it open with one hand and gently letting it slide into the pan.

"Are you a professional cook?" she found herself asking.

Greg glanced around, then back to what he was doing. "I'm a professional eater. I discovered a long time ago that if I didn't feed myself there was a strong possibility I'd starve."

"Oh." She continued to watch him for a few minutes in silence, then was appalled to hear herself ask, "Are you married?"

He laughed. "No. Why do you ask?"

She could feel herself blushing. "No reason."

"Are you?"

"Married?"

"That was the topic under discussion, I believe."

"No. No, I'm not."

"Then you aren't running away from a husband, either."

"What makes you keep thinking that I'm running away? I just needed a place to stay for a few days, that's all."

He slipped two eggs onto a warmed plate, put freshly buttered toast and crisp bacon beside it and set the dish in front of her. She stared at it until he said, "Eat before it gets cold." Picking up her cup, he refilled it and handed it back to her. Then he quickly prepared his plate and sat down across from her.

"Why were you looking for Tim?" he asked, ignoring her last question.

"What are you, a reporter?"

"No. I'm a lawyer. So why don't you answer my question?"

"Because it's none of your business."

"That's true. However, something seems to be bothering you, and if I knew what it was, perhaps I could help."

"Well, at least that explains your cross-examination style of conversation," she said, finishing the last bite of food on her plate and relaxing back in her seat with a sigh. She picked up her cup and sipped. "You serve a mean breakfast, Mr. Duncan. Thank you. I hadn't realized how hungry I was."

"You're welcome. I must say that you have a real knack for sidestepping my questions."

She grinned. "Being around Tim taught me how to do that, although I was never very successful at keeping things from him."

"How long have you known Tim?"

She shrugged. "All my life."

"Are you a relative of his?" he asked, knowing full well that Tim was an only child. But she might be a cousin.

"Not by blood, no. But in every way possible, Tim has been like a big brother to me. He's always been there when I needed him." Almost under her breath, she added, "and, boy, do I need him now."

Greg got up and refilled their cups, then sat down again. "Have you talked to him recently?"

She shook her head. "I tried calling his apartment, but all I could get was his recording machine. I left messages, but there's no way of knowing when he'll get them. I also tried another number he once gave me in case of an emergency, but that didn't get me anywhere."

"What do you mean?"

"Oh, I got some sort of answering service. They said they never heard of a Tim Walker. I must have gotten the number wrong or something."

"So you came here, hoping to find him."

"Yes."

"How did you get here?"

She was quiet for several minutes before she answered in a quiet voice. "I took a bus from Denver, then had a taxi bring me up here."

"A taxi! We're at least twenty miles out of town."

"I know."

"Don't you think you could tell me what's going on?" he asked. Not only was his curiosity stirred, but he was surprised to discover a feeling of compassion for this woman, who was obviously on edge.

Brandi replaced her cup on the table with a slight thump and stared at the insistent man across from her. "I'm trying to get away from some men who are trying to kill me."

Chapter Two

Greg recognized the distraught expression on Brandi's face. More than one client had come to him for help wearing a similar expression. He also recognized that she needed to talk. Speaking in a soothing tone, he slowly stood and said, "Why don't we take our coffee and sit in front of that gorgeous fire in there? We might as well enjoy it while we talk, don't you think?"

He picked up both cups and led the way, confident that she would follow him. He placed her cup on the end table by the long, comfortable sofa facing the fireplace. Then he gracefully folded his long legs and sank onto the rug.

Brandi felt as though she no longer had a will of her own. After a good night's sleep and a decent meal, she was beginning to feel as though she'd just awakened from a nightmare and that none of the strange happenings of the past few days were real. Only the man waiting so patiently for her in front of the fireplace seemed to have any meaning at the moment.

He wanted her to tell him why she was there. At this point, she hardly knew herself. She had been running away, but she wasn't sure from what. She had been looking for Tim, but she wasn't sure why.

"Ahhh," he said, watching her as she slowly followed him into the room. "This is my idea of living. No phones ringing, no demands being made on my time. Just a warm fire—" he waved toward the scene on the other side of the glass "—a picture-perfect scene outside, and someone to talk with."

Brandi sat down on the sofa and picked up her cup as though it were the only security she had to cling to at the moment.

"What happened, Brandi, that has frightened you so?" he asked, his voice soft and gentle. It seemed to flow over and around her, soothing her somehow.

"I live in a rural area, in the foothills," she began, staring down at the coffee in her cup. "I live alone, but it has never bothered me before, living alone. I like the quiet, the solitude, the opportunity to work long, uninterrupted hours."

"What do you do?"

Her eyes slowly lifted until they met his. "I make inlaid designs in wood—marquetry. Jewelry boxes, tabletops, room dividers, whatever I think might sell."

"Sounds interesting."

"I enjoy it. I spend a lot of time outdoors, looking for some of nature's designs that I can duplicate—"

she glanced out the window and nodded "—such as that limb that is almost touching the deck railing."

Greg glanced where she indicated and saw a branch weighted down with snow. Pine cones hung in a cluster at the end. He had never really noticed the symmetry of such an arrangement before.

"You must have a special eye for beauty," he admitted with a smile.

"I love nature. I enjoy each season, and I spend a great deal of my time exploring, snapping pictures, looking for ideas."

"You seem very content with your choice of a life."

"I am. At least I was, until I realized how vulnerable I am. I don't have any close neighbors." She turned her head until she was facing him once more. "I prefer to be independent."

Greg had so many questions, but he was hesitant to break into her story. Now that she was slowly opening up, he didn't want to distract her with interruptions.

She paused, as though thinking about what she wanted to say next. "We had snow last week, and that left everything so beautifully fresh and bright. I decided to take my cross-country skis up into the hills and explore. I've had plenty of time since then to regret the impulse."

"What happened?"

"I'm not sure exactly where I was in the hills. I know that there are some military installations up there, but I'm positive that I didn't accidentally go into a restricted area. After all, they're carefully marked." She took a quick sip of her coffee. "I was high up on the side of a hill, and as I rounded a crest, something below was detonated. I looked down and saw some sort of rough encampment. Men dressed in white and carrying some type of hand weapons were watching as something—I don't know how to describe it—began to climb into the sky, higher and higher. I stood there and stared. I didn't know what to think. Then I heard shouts, and when I glanced back down I saw men pointing at me and yelling. I started to wave back when I realized that they were angry, running in my direction and aiming their weapons at me!"

"What did you do?"

"I managed to turn and ski away as quickly as possible. Luckily, I had a long downhill slope ahead of me, and I was able to reach the shelter of trees before they spotted me." She shivered at the memory. "They began to fire into the trees."

Greg leaned forward. "They actually shot at you?"

She nodded.

"What did you do?"

"I kept going as fast as I could. I think the only thing that saved me was that my four-wheel-drive Blazer wasn't all that far away. I managed to get to the car, removed my skis and left."

"Did you see the men again?"

"Not right away, no. I really thought I'd managed to lose them. Then, several miles down the road, I happened to glance up and saw something following me."

"What was it?"

"I don't know. It was too big for a car. It looked like a camouflaged truck of some sort. You know the kind you see in army movies—big, with a heavy grill in front."

"What did you do?"

"I realized that I couldn't go home. I would really be isolated then. I didn't even slow down at the road where I live. Instead, I kept driving."

"Did they continue to follow you?"

"Yes. I was lucky to get into fairly busy traffic and managed to gain some distance on them. I was afraid to stop until I made it into town."

"You got to town, then?"

"Yes. I decided to go to the sheriff's office and report what I saw. I hid the Blazer on a back street and walked to the sheriff's office. Only when I got there—" She stopped and swallowed hard.

"When you got there—" he prompted.

"I had just turned the corner to the sheriff's office when I saw his door open and he came out—talking with two men dressed in white, wearing some kind of white military hats!"

"Did you recognize the men?"

"No. Only the way they were dressed. They wore the same type of clothing as the men I'd seen in the hills."

"What did you do?"

"I dodged back around the corner and waited. I could hear them talking and laughing. I heard the sheriff say he'd run a check on the license number right away and get back to them."

"Do you think they were talking about you?"

"I have no idea, but I was too scared to take a chance." She took a hasty sip of coffee. "That's when I decided to call Tim."

"Why Tim?"

"Because I know he's got some kind of connection with the government and I thought he might know what was going on."

"But he wasn't there."

"No. I filled the Blazer with gas and decided to drive to Denver, hoping to get lost in the larger city. After I got there, I knew I needed to hide the Blazer and get out of my ski clothes. So I parked in a parking garage and went to a local department store and bought these." She looked down at her sweater and pants. "I tried a couple more times to reach Tim, then decided to look for him here." She ran her hand through her short curls. "I was afraid to use the Blazer, so I came by bus."

Brandi took a deep breath, then slowly exhaled. Somehow, talking about it had helped. She was no closer to finding a solution, but sharing what she had gone through with another person had eased the tight band that seemed to have constricted her chest for days.

They sat before the fire in companionable silence for several minutes.

Greg recognized that Brandi believed she was being pursued. He was certain that what she had experienced had been very traumatic. It wasn't surprising that she had reacted so violently. However, he also knew that she could easily have misunderstood what she had seen and heard.

But he couldn't be sure. There was always the slim possibility that she might be in danger. That possibility gave him pause. Tim wasn't here. They didn't know when he'd return, but Greg knew him well enough to know he would respond as soon as he heard Brandi's messages.

"Did you tell Tim you were coming here?"

"Yes."

"Good," he said with some satisfaction. "Then I think you'd better wait until he shows up."

"Which could be in a day, a week, a month—or next summer sometime," she pointed out.

"Well, let's give it some time, okay? If he hasn't shown up in a few days, then I'll take you back home and see what we can find out, okay?"

She looked at him in surprise. "You'd do that for me?"

"Sure. Why not?"

"You don't know me."

"Any little sister of Tim's is a sister of mine," he said with a grin. "Of course, I was rather hoping to get some skiing in first. So if you don't mind waiting here a few days—" He paused, looking at her expectantly.

"I don't mind," she responded slowly. She looked around the room. "I can always sleep down here."

"I'm sure we can work out something." Greg got to his feet. "Now, then. Why don't we run into town and get you some ski equipment." He glanced at what she was wearing. "Did you bring your ski clothes?"

She nodded. "I have them in a bag upstairs, with another change of clothes."

"Great. Then let's run to town and find you some skis."

"You don't think they followed me?"

He allowed himself to smile slightly. "I think you were very clever eluding them. If anything, they are probably watching either your house or your car at the parking garage."

She stood up with a pleased smile. "You really think so?"

He nodded. "Yes. I'm impressed with your quick thinking."

"Then you don't think I overreacted?"

"I think you were playing it safe. I also think Tim will agree with me." He held out his hand. "Come on, let's go."

Hours later, Greg and Brandi were a fair distance from the cabin. Greg had quickly discovered that Brandi was quite adept at getting around on skis. She seemed to be enjoying herself, and he was hard-pressed to keep up with her.

During the past several hours, he'd gotten a glimpse of another side of her personality. She was quick to smile, and he discovered that he enjoyed provoking her smile. Although shadows sometimes lurked in the depths of her beautiful eyes, she seemed to be making an effort to relax.

He paused, looking around. Her bright red ski jacket should have been easy to spot, but at the moment he could see nothing but the snowy expanse around him, the dark brown and dull green of the pine trees.

"Brandi? Slow down, okay? I'm not in quite as good shape as I thought I was," he said.

Everything was quiet. She didn't answer. Greg had a slight sense of unease. He began to follow her tracks over the side of the hill.

A sudden avalanche of snow fell on his head and shoulders, and he yelped. The limb he'd paused under had just been shaken clear of its weight of snow. Greg heard delighted laughter behind him, and turned and saw Brandi peeking around the tree.

He slipped out of his skis and made a lunge for her, bringing her to the ground. Her squeal echoed in the clear air.

"That was unfair and uncalled-for," he said, pushing her so that she lost her balance and fell back into a snowbank. Greg began to laugh at her outraged expression. Every time she tried to get up, she lost her balance and fell back. Finally he walked over and offered her his hand, only to find himself jerked off balance. He fell face first into the snow beside her.

He came up sputtering, grabbed a handful of snow and mashed it into her face.

The afternoon's skiing was soon reduced to a snow fight deluxe.

Eventually Greg managed to subdue his opponent by the simple expedient of sitting on her and pinning both arms out away from her body with his hands.

"Do you give up?"

"Never! I never give up!" she managed to yell breathlessly.

"Even when you can't even move?" he asked, laughing.

"I can move! I can—" She kicked out with both legs but couldn't hit him. "Get off me, you big oaf! I can't breathe! Tim would never have—"

"I know. Tim, no doubt, always lets you win. That's why you're so spoiled."

"Spoiled! I'm not spoiled. I just—"

"You're just used to getting your own way, that's obvious." He grinned down at her. "Now, then. Do you give up?"

Brandi lay in the snow and looked up at the big man above her. He'd lost his cap in the tussle, and his blond hair fell rather endearingly across his forehead. His cheeks were red from exertion and he was wet, but for the first time Brandi saw a part of him that she hadn't guessed existed—a playful part. He looked years younger as he watched her warily, his smile gleaming brightly. His eyes, which had seemed so cold to her earlier, now sparkled with silver glints, and there were dancing imps in their depths.

Why, he's gorgeous! she suddenly realized. Gone was the implacable, pragmatic lawyer she had spent the day with. Here was a man who radiated a warmth and virility that caused her heart to set up an increased drumming in her chest.

She stared up at him, entranced by what she saw. Perhaps her expression gave her away, because Brandi noticed that Greg's smile slowly altered and the warmth in his eyes seemed to increase. He shifted so that his weight was no longer on her, but she didn't move. Not even when he lowered his head toward hers and placed his mouth on hers.

His lips felt warm as they tentatively touched hers. Brandi's eyes drifted closed, and she shyly returned his kiss.

Greg pulled her into his arms, holding her against his chest while he continued to explore the soft contours of her mouth. By the time he pulled away slightly, they were both warm and flushed.

Brandi didn't know what to say. She felt as though she had practically melted into his arms. She couldn't remember the last time she'd been so affected by a kiss. And this one had come from a man she hardly knew. *And you've agreed to stay with him,* she reminded herself. *What is he going to think about you now?*

Greg got to his feet and pulled her up beside him. He began to dust himself off without looking at her. "We'd better get back. It will be dark soon."

"Yes" was all she could think of to say.

They found their skis and put them on again. Then Greg took the lead and they followed their tracks back to the cabin.

Greg couldn't believe what he had done. He'd wanted Brandi to feel comfortable about staying there for a few days in case Tim showed up, but then he'd ruined it by doing something stupid like kiss her.

There was no telling what she was thinking at the moment. She was without transportation, totally at his mercy. The last thing he wanted her to think was that he would take advantage of the situation.

And yet that was just what he had done. And why?

He couldn't really explain his reaction to Brandi. She was young, too young for him. They were totally different in temperament. Now that she was no longer frightened, Greg could see that Brandi was normally friendly and outgoing. He, on the other hand, had trouble relating to people. He was good at what he did professionally, but he was a failure at relationships.

But he couldn't deny his attraction to Brandi. Perhaps it was because of her warm and friendly personality. He didn't know. All that he knew for sure was that he felt the same way around her as he felt after he'd built a brightly burning fire—as though he could warm himself and find comfort near that flame.

Somehow Brandi had become a flame to him. He had to be careful that he didn't singe himself.

By the time they reached the cabin, dark shadows surrounded the area. They had come around the side of the house so that they could enter through the kitchen door when Greg abruptly paused.

Brandi almost ran into him. She stopped and began to unfasten her skis.

"Stay here," he said in a low voice.

She glanced up, disturbed by the strange note in his voice. "What's wrong?"

He motioned for her to be quiet and stepped out of his skis. Stealthily he moved closer to the cabin, silently signaling that she should stay where she was.

Greg disappeared around the corner, only to reappear in a few minutes, motioning her to join him.

"What's wrong?"

"We had some company while we were gone." He pointed to two pairs of tracks leading up the driveway to the house.

"Maybe it was the people who check on the place for Tim."

"Maybe."

"Did they go inside?"

"If they did, nothing was disturbed. They aren't in there now. I checked."

When they got inside, Brandi shivered. She was feeling the effects of their snow fight.

"Why don't you get your shower while I build up the fire again?" he suggested.

She glanced around and saw the solemn stranger she had seen earlier in the day. Gone was the laughing, loving man who had kissed her earlier. Brandi discovered that she missed that man. She had a hunch that very few had ever seen him.

"All right. Then I'll find us something for dinner while you change."

Greg watched Brandi go into the bathroom and shut the door. Then he went over to the fireplace and began to blow on the coals. As soon as the new logs were burning, he straightened and looked around the room. As far as he could tell, nothing had been disturbed. The intruders had been professionals. He didn't like that, not at all. Having someone break in while they were gone gave more credence to Brandi's story.

Of course, he was going to let Brandi believe it was the couple who kept an eye on the place. There was no reason to make her more nervous. She was just now beginning to relax for the first time in days.

He was glad she hadn't looked at the door. Whoever had gotten in had not had a key, but they had managed to enter easily enough. Professionals.

Now Greg knew for certain that he couldn't leave Brandi until this whole mess was resolved. He just hoped that Tim got in touch soon. Brandi had been right. Tim had the contacts.

In the meantime, Greg had to make sure that Brandi was kept safe—from whoever was hunting her, and from himself.

Chapter Three

Dinner was over, and once again Brandi found herself sitting in front of the fireplace, alternately watching the flames and the man who sat on the rug nearby staring into the fire as though learning the secrets of the universe.

He'd been quiet during dinner, although he had complimented her on her imaginative casserole. However, Brandi had felt his distraction and wondered about it.

Was he thinking about the kiss they had shared earlier? She had found it a little disturbing herself, partly because the action seemed to be so out of character for this man. But then, she recognized that she really didn't know much about him. And she was discovering that she wanted to learn a great deal more about him.

"Greg—" she began, just as he turned.

"Brandi—" he murmured simultaneously.

They both smiled and said, "Go ahead." They began to laugh.

"What were you going to say?" she asked.

"I was just going to ask you about Tim. How you met, that sort of thing."

"Oh. Well, that's easy enough. We grew up next door to each other." She wondered why he seemed to withdraw a little at her words. "I was eight when my father died. Mom and I were taken care of financially, but I'm afraid we were both rather helpless. Tim's family adopted us, looking after things, seeing that repairs were made, inviting us to family gatherings, that sort of thing."

He nodded, as though waiting for her to continue.

"That's about it. Mom died in my second year of college. She'd appointed Tim the trustee of my financial estate." She laughed. "He's only a few years older than I am, but he's always been so responsible. She knew he would look after me, and he has."

"I'm surprised you haven't married him," he offered, looking into the flames rather than at her.

"Marry Tim?" she repeated, surprised at the idea. "It would have been like marrying my brother. I mean, we don't see each other in that light. Tim has always been there for me—" she paused, thinking about the past few days "—well, almost always, but he's not the least bit interested in me romantically, I assure you."

"I suppose I'm just surprised that someone like you is not already married," he said finally.

"Someone like me? What does that mean?"

"You have so much to offer a man."

"I do? I would hardly agree with that. I get too wrapped up in my work to pay attention to what is going on around me."

"You're a great cook."

"Thank you, kind sir. But then, I forced myself to concentrate. Besides, casseroles are easy—you dump the ingredients together, stick it in the oven and wait for the timer to go off." She grinned. "Of course, there have been times when I was concentrating so much on my work that I didn't hear the timer. The first thing I knew, the smoke alarm alerted me that dinner was slightly overdone."

They laughed at the verbal picture she painted.

"How about you? Why aren't you married?" she said after a few moments.

"I almost was, once."

She waited, but he didn't say anything more. "Don't tell me you're going to stop there, leaving my curiosity unrelieved?"

"It's a very boring story, really," he offered reluctantly.

"Nonsense. I can't believe you'd be involved in a romance that was boring." Her adamant remark surprised them both, and she found herself blushing.

Greg watched her discomfort with amusement. He was a little surprised by her comment. He knew himself very well and recognized that he was in fact more than a little boring. His surprise was that she hadn't already seen that.

Greg had never talked about his engagement to Penny Blackwell to anyone. It was a closed chapter in his life. Now, for some reason, he found himself wanting to look at it again, with another person. To be more precise, he wanted to share what had happened with Brandi Martin. More surprises.

He stood up and walked over to the small cabinet where Tim kept his liquor. Picking up a bottle, he said, "How about a snifter of brandy while I tell my tale of unrequited love?"

She wrinkled her nose. "Despite the name, I've never cared for the taste of the stuff. Does Tim stock any amaretto?"

He found the appropriate bottle and poured her a glass, then joined her in front of the fire once more. This time he sat down on the sofa beside her, handing her one of the glasses he held in his hands.

"I had a large law practise in St. Louis and decided to move to Payton, a small town that reminded me of the hometown where I'd grown up back east. Penny Blackwell taught high school in Payton. We were introduced. I noticed that she didn't seem to be dating anyone, so I began to ask her out. The more I was with her, the more I came to love her. After we'd dated for several months, I asked her to marry me. She accepted."

Greg had started off in a matter-of-fact tone of voice, as though he were explaining the facts of a case to a jury. However, Brandi heard a hesitancy toward the end, as though a slight note of pain had colored the timbre of his voice, when he'd mentioned his proposal and her acceptance.

For the first time, Brandi recognized that this strong, self-assured, almost arrogant man also had a vulnerability to him that was almost as appealing to her as the lightheartedness that had peeked out at her earlier in the day—just before he'd shared a kiss with her. She was fairly sure that few people had seen this side of him, either.

Now that he was talking, Greg discovered that it wasn't going to be as easy to relive the past as he had first thought. He took a sip of his drink and wondered how he could change the subject without being too obvious.

"What happened?" Brandi asked softly. Greg heard compassion and caring in her voice. He was touched. She didn't know him very well, and yet she recognized that what he was telling her was difficult.

"Well..." he said, pausing to clear his throat. "What I never realized during that time was that there was another man in her life—a man she'd grown up with who lived next door to her." He glanced over at Brandi. "Rather like you and Tim, from what you tell me." His gaze returned to the fire. "Only, in Penny's case, Brad had moved away and become a well-known television actor." He took a sip of his drink. "Have you ever heard of Brad Crawford?"

"Brad Crawford? You mean the hunk on *Hope for Tomorrow*?" she asked in surprise.

"That's Brad, all right. I found out a week before our wedding that Brad was Penny's childhood sweetheart."

"Then there's no parallel between Tim and me, that's for sure," she said with a chuckle. "What happened? Did Penny call off the wedding?"

"No."

She watched him for a moment in silence. "I'm afraid I don't understand."

"Neither did I, at first. It took me a few days to recognize the fact that Penny really did think she loved me and that she wanted to marry me. She didn't seem to realize how bonded she and Brad truly were. After spending hours analyzing the situation, I finally had to face the fact that what Penny wanted from me was the settled, comfortable, nonthreatening existence that I could provide for her."

"She was actually going to marry you, even though she was in love with someone else?"

"I don't think she understood her feelings toward Brad at the time. There was a lot of resentment and anger on her part. And yet—" he paused and absently ran his hand through his hair, mussing it in a way that Brandi found peculiarly attractive in this carefully ordered man "—it's tough to explain, but Penny came alive whenever Brad was around. She sparkled and glowed. He seemed to bring out all of her emotions, so that she practically vibrated with energy whenever he was around her."

He stood up and put another log on the fire. "Penny taught me so much. I had never felt so much love toward another person, not since I was a child. She brought my feelings to the surface, and I'll admit I was uncomfortable having to face them. But because she had taught me what love was all about, I recognized what was happening. I wasn't the man she needed to make her life complete. She was settling for less because she was afraid to reach out and grab what life was truly offering her."

"That must have been a very painful conclusion for you to come to."

He was surprised that she saw that so quickly. He nodded, unable for the moment to find the words to agree.

"You loved her. You loved her enough to understand that your loving her wasn't right for her. You loved her enough to let her go."

"I don't think I looked at it quite so unselfishly, I'm afraid. If I'd thought our relationship had a chance of working out, I'm sure I would have fought for what we had. But I knew it was only a question of time before Penny recognized what she had given up by not marrying Brad. I didn't want to stay around and watch her gradual disillusionment."

"So what happened? Did *you* call off the wedding?"

"I'm afraid I wasn't that honorable about it. I just didn't show up."

Brandi set her glass down abruptly and stared at Greg in shocked dismay. "What? You mean you let Penny show up at the church without telling her you'd changed your mind? How horrible!"

"Yes, Brad expressed similar sentiments to me the day before the wedding when I told him of my intentions."

She stared at the man sitting beside her, unable to comprehend anyone behaving in such a cold and callous manner. "Poor Penny."

"I was hoping you would give me a little credit for understanding human nature better than to think that Brad would allow her to be humiliated in front of everyone. By telling him my intentions ahead of time, I knew that I was giving him an opportunity to save the day. I deliberately made myself look like a heel. Otherwise, I was fairly sure that Penny would insist on going through with the marriage and ignoring how she felt toward Brad."

"But still—"

"I know. What I did was cowardly and reprehensible."

"And if you had it to do over again, you'd do it the same way."

"Yes."

"Because you didn't think you could face Penny and tell her."

"What makes you say that?"

"It was easier for you to play the cold-blooded reptile for Brad than to admit to Penny that you loved her enough to let her go."

"Now you're trying to make me a martyr. I'm far from that."

"And you're still in love with Penny."

"Of course not."

"How long ago did this happen?"

"Four or five years ago. Why?"

"And you've still not married?"

He laughed. "Not because I've been nursing a broken heart, I assure you. I enjoy my life the way it is. Instead of relinquishing my practice in St. Louis, I've managed to keep both offices open and busy. I don't have time for a personal life. Nor, to be honest, do I find the idea particularly appealing."

"Because you're afraid of being hurt."

"Now you're trying to romanticize me. Penny would have become bored with me very quickly. She quit teaching and moved to New York with Brad right after they married. As a matter of fact, they starred together in a Broadway play last spring."

"Oh, I remember that now. The character Brad plays—what's his name? Drew Derek?—disappeared and was missing for several months."

"I wouldn't know. I never watch the daily serials."

Brandi tilted her head and studied him. "So you were once engaged to marry Brad Crawford's wife."

"My one claim to fame."

She continued to study him. "You know, there's a definite resemblance between the two of you, now that you mention it."

"I didn't."

"Except that you don't smile as much."

"The courtroom doesn't encourage the practice."

"But you're as good at acting as he is."

He looked at her, startled by her comment. "But I'm not an actor."

"You've been putting on quite a performance right now, trying to convince me that your engagement and the ending of it hasn't had a profound effect on who you are and what you've become."

"Are you part witch or something?"

She laughed. "No, of course not. If I were, I would have conjured up a spell to have those men who are chasing me turned into tadpoles or something."

"And you could also figure out where Tim is at the moment."

She laughed. "I gave up trying to keep up with Tim years ago."

"A wise decision," he said quietly.

Brandi leaned forward, gazing into Greg's suddenly serious eyes. "I take it that you know what Tim does for a living."

Watching her warily, he said, "Maybe."

She shrugged. "I don't want to know. Not really. All I know is that it's dangerous and that he's very good at what he does."

"Yes. And yes."

"That's why I thought of him when I needed help. I think Tim has the contacts to find out what's going on up there in the hills."

"There's a strong possibility you're right."

Brandi stared into her glass, remembering her fright and wondering if she was safe even now. . . .

"Brandi?"

She glanced up. "Hmm?"

He took the empty glass from her hand and set it on the table nearby. "Try to put it out of your mind, okay?"

She nodded. "I'm trying."

"You're safe now. I'm not going to leave you until Tim shows up or we go back to Denver to try to get some answers without him." He recalled the unidentified footprints he'd seen earlier. "I'm not going to allow anyone to harm you."

She believed him. Here was a man who instinctively made her feel sheltered and protected. He might not be willing to share his innermost feelings, but he was willing to share his strength. At the moment, that was enough, but Brandi couldn't help wondering how it would feel to have this strong, polished, arrogant man in love with her. Would he allow her to see more than occasional glimpses of those other personalities hidden deep inside?

Brandi had never had a close relationship with a man in a romantic sense. She'd purposely avoided them because she was afraid. The loss of her father at an early age had been traumatic. Losing her mother while she was still in college hadn't helped her to come to terms with her fear of getting close to someone.

She had needed to learn how to be independent so that she would never be hurt like that again. Tim had understood her need for independence and had given her plenty of room. She'd never fully appreciated his understanding of her until now.

Looking at the man seated beside her, sipping his drink and watching her so intently, she knew that for the first time in years she was in danger of allowing someone to get too close to her. For some reason, she didn't find the thought as threatening as she would have in the past. Perhaps her feelings stemmed from the fact that she had finally met someone who was as shy of becoming involved as she was. Brandi felt as though she were coaxing him out of his protective shell, not the other way around.

"What are you thinking?" he asked, his hand cupping her face in a gentle caress.

"About you," she admitted in a husky voice.

"Very dull."

"Not at all. I was thinking about how little I know about men." She paused, searching for words. "And how much I would like to get to know you better."

"Really?"

"Really."

"That could be dangerous, considering the present situation."

"What do you mean?"

"We're alone in rather isolated circumstances."

She smiled. "I know."

"And you don't feel threatened?"

"Not by you. I feel very safe with you."

"Thank you. I think." He rubbed his thumb softly against her cheek. "I probably represent a father figure to you."

She burst into laughter. "Hardly."

"I feel old enough to be your father."

"I don't see you in that role at all, Greg. I find you very attractive..." She turned her head slightly and kissed his palm, which had been resting along her jawline. "...and very reliable..." She reached up and touched the strand of hair that had fallen across his forehead. "...and very, very sexy..." she whispered, pressing her lips against his.

She felt him tense at her words. Brandi rested her hand lightly against his sweater-covered chest and felt the heavy rhythm of his heart. Despite his lack of expression, he was not unaffected by her. She slid her arms around his neck, pulling him closer.

Greg clearly understood the dangers of this particular situation. A couple in front of a fireplace, relaxed from a large dinner and a glass of liqueur, miles away from any other human beings. They obviously found each other attractive, available and interested. Mother Nature couldn't have planned it better if she had tried.

So it was up to him to keep a grip on reality, to set the tone of the evening, to make sure that nothing happened between them because... because...

Greg's iron will seemed to shatter, and his arms wrapped around Brandi in a strong grip. For the moment, all he could think about was the woman in his arms.

Brandi quickly discovered that the kiss they had shared earlier in the snow had only been a playful sharing. What she was experiencing now was a man's desire for her, something she'd never known before.

Greg held her and kissed her as though he were starved for the taste and touch of her, as though he had waited for centuries to hold her close to him, as though he never intended to let her go.

Brandi reveled in the passionate intensity of the moment. Perhaps this man couldn't talk about his feelings. He might even verbally deny them, but he couldn't hide them completely.

She responded with wholehearted enthusiasm, enjoying the sensation of feeling the surge of power in his heavy shoulder and chest muscles as he held her against him so tightly. Her hands explored the contours of his shoulders and back, wordlessly encouraging him.

Greg pulled away slightly and looked at the small young woman in his arms. Had he lost his mind? What in the hell did he think he was doing? He'd always taken pride in his ability to control himself, and yet... and yet now he seemed to have lost all restraint, all the rational and reasoning processes inside him that he'd come to rely on all these years.

This tiny wisp of a woman seemed to have reduced all his thinking processes to a quivering mass of mush. She lay in his arms with a slight smile on her face, her eyes closed. Her lips were moist and rosy from his earlier possession of them. His mouth unconsciously sought hers once more.

The sudden crackling of the wood in the fireplace several minutes later jerked Greg's thoughts away from Brandi. The loud noise in the otherwise quiet room grabbed his attention. He looked around, forcing himself to regain his self-control.

Brandi was lost to the sensation of the moment. Never in her wildest dreams had she imagined that anyone could affect her in such a way. No wonder so many of her college friends had advocated sexual exploration with their enthusiastic boyfriends.

How could she have possibly missed such a marvelous experience before now?

Greg loosened his hold around her and carefully moved away from what he considered a dangerous and explosive situation. He got up and checked the fire, then walked over and looked out at the moonlit, snow-blanketed night.

"You'd better go on upstairs, Brandi," he said without turning around. "It's late."

"I'm going to sleep down here."

Still without turning around, he said, "No, you're not."

"But the sofa isn't long enough for you."

He finally glanced at her over his shoulder. "I'll be fine. I'll see you in the morning."

"But Greg—"

"Let's not debate the issue, Brandi. I'm afraid I'm not in the mood."

Gone was the passionate man who had held her so closely, kissed her so thoroughly and made her feel as though she were soaring high above the universe. In his place was the arrogant lawyer she had met the night before. Hadn't what they had just shared meant anything to him?

"If you're sure—" she began softly.

"I'm sure."

She walked over to the bottom of the stairs. "I'll get you some blankets and a pillow."

"Thank you."

"Good night, Greg."

"Good night, Brandi."

He waited without turning until he heard her moving overhead. Greg realized that he was shaking. He couldn't believe what had almost happened. He'd lost all control over the situation with a woman who obviously trusted him not to take advantage of their isolation from the rest of the world.

He'd never been affected so strongly by anyone before, not even Penny. How could that be? Penny had taught him everything he knew about loving and caring. So how could he feel such an intense need for Brandi that he was willing to forget all his scruples in his almost uncontrollable desire to make her his.

He'd only meant to hold and comfort her, to reassure her, but as soon as he'd been near her he'd wanted so much more. What a laugh. He, of all people, knew there was nothing more, nothing except disillusionment.

Greg turned and watched Brandi bring blankets and a pillow down the steps. He met her at the bottom of the stairs and took them from her.

"Thanks," he said in a cool tone.

Brandi's bewilderment at his sudden change of mood slowly turned to pain. "You're welcome," she managed to say before turning and slowly walking up the steps again.

What an inscrutable man, she thought. She was surprised by how quickly she'd allowed him to get close to her, both physically and emotionally.

She was determined not to allow it to happen again.

Chapter Four

Several hours later, Greg lay awake on the sofa, watching the trees swaying in the ever-increasing wind. A storm was brewing. He wasn't sure how he felt about that. On the one hand, he knew that anyone watching the cabin would be forced to seek shelter if the weather became severe. On the other hand, he had hoped to scout the area for further signs that the place was in fact under surveillance. Another snowfall would obliterate any clues he might otherwise be able to spot.

He wished to hell he knew how to contact Tim. If he was someplace where he could be contacted, Brandi's innocent call to the agency would be passed on to him. Greg was fairly certain that, despite convincing her that she had a wrong number, whoever had taken her call had managed to get her name. If the relationship between Tim and Brandi was as close as Greg suspected, Tim would waste no time in coming to her rescue.

Greg glanced over at the fire, which was going out. Throwing back the blanket that he'd tossed over himself, he got up, feeling the chill that had already invaded the room. Ignoring the fact that he had stripped down to his underwear, Greg built up the fire once more, making sure it was going before again seeking the comfort of his makeshift bed.

Despite Brandi's protestations, Greg felt certain that there was more than friendship between Tim and Brandi. He could well remember Penny's offhand remarks about Brad. If Tim had watched Brandi grow up, how could he possibly resist her?

Greg punched his pillow and turned over. How ironic that he continued to find himself in situations in which he was odd man out. He had long since recognized his wisdom in removing himself from Penny's life, even though the manner in which he'd done it didn't stand up very well under careful scrutiny.

Despite his love for Penny, he'd been able to distance himself enough from his emotions to make a clear, logical decision based on the facts of the matter.

Why was he having such a difficult time trying to deal with his emotions now?

One of the problems he was having was Brandi herself. He'd never known a woman like her before. She was such a mixture of warmth and impulsiveness, shyness and innocence. He had seen her truly frightened and was impressed by her ability to take care of herself under trying circumstances. He'd found himself eager to hear the peal of her infectious laughter and realized that no one had ever teased and played with him as she had that day in the snow.

Greg couldn't remember the last time he'd played in the snow with anyone, nor could he remember the last time he'd really laughed and enjoyed himself. Somehow, in his pursuit of a career, he'd lost sight of how to enjoy the little things in life.

Brandi had pointed out so many things today while they'd been out exploring: oddly shaped trees, a couple of squirrels, the sudden flash of color from a bird in flight. Even while skiing, he had a tendency to let his mind wander, more often than not trying to solve some knotty legal problem.

Brandi had shown him the fun of being fully conscious of the present. The first time he'd kissed her had been an impulse born out of the joy of sharing that moment with her. Her response had unnerved him, causing him to loosen his control for a few very precious moments.

The more he was around her, the more fascinating Greg found Brandi. He wasn't sure what he was going to do if his hunch was correct and there was more to Tim and Brandi's relationship than she was telling. He respected Tim more than he respected any other human being he knew. If Tim loved and wanted Brandi, Greg had to accept that. In the meantime, he had to get a firm grip on his emotions and not let them overpower him.

The situation at the moment was tense enough without his having to battle his sudden and totally unexplainable reaction to Brandi.

Turning onto his side, Greg determinedly closed his eyes. He had to get some sleep.

Brandi saw the men coming after her and tried to turn and get away, but one of her skis wouldn't move. She tugged and tugged, frantic to escape. She could hear them shouting and running toward her—big men dressed in white sheets with masks pulled down over their heads.

They were almost upon her. She broke out of her skis and tried to run through the snow, but it was so deep that she couldn't move. She tried to run...she struggled. They were gaining on her. She couldn't get away!

"Brandi? Honey, it's okay. It's just a dream. You're all right. I'm here. No one's going to hurt you."

The soft, soothing words managed to seep through her anguished mind, and Brandi opened her eyes. She'd been dreaming. The covers were wrapped around her so tightly that she couldn't move, which explained the sensation of being trapped in her dream. Tears wet her face, and she was breathing in sobbing gasps.

Greg hadn't turned on the lights, but she recognized his voice and his shadowy outline on the bed beside her.

"Greg?"

He smoothed her hair away from her forehead.

"I'm right here."

"Oh, Greg, it was so awful." Her shuddering breaths hurt her lungs.

"I know, love, I know," he murmured, gathering her into his arms and holding her close. He could feel the rapid beating of her heart against his chest. Her breathing was rapid and shallow.

Greg continued to hold her close, murmuring soothing phrases until she began to slowly relax in his arms. When he eventually loosened his hold, she stirred.

"Please don't leave me."

When Greg had heard her cry out earlier, his first thought had been to reach her side. He hadn't taken time to dress before racing up the stairs. She was still too caught up in her dream to realize that he was sitting there with very little on.

"Go to sleep, little one. Nothing's going to harm you."

"Stay with me," she whispered. "Please."

He could not resist the appeal in her voice. Knowing that he was putting a great deal of strain on his already weakened willpower, Greg mentally acknowledged this latest test of his character and crawled under the covers with her.

Brandi curled up against his chest like a kitten and sighed, arms draped around him. Despite the discomfort of having her so close and knowing he was not going to do anything about it, Greg found himself relaxing.

It felt good to hold Brandi in his arms again. He was reassured by her trust in him, even though he recognized that it might be no more than the fact that she had no one else to trust. He had learned something important that day—to take pleasure in the present moment.

He intended to do just that.

"What the hell is going on?"

Greg fought his way from a distant oblivion in order to make sense of the noise that seemed to be filling his head. He forced his eyes open and saw a dangerously irate redheaded man standing by the side of the bed. Greg's eyes drifted closed. He felt as though he'd just managed to fall asleep, and now there was someone—

He shot up in the bed. "Tim! When did you get here?" He glanced around and saw that Brandi was still sound asleep, although she had been curled up by his side before he'd moved.

The full picture of what Tim must have seen when he'd come up the stairs hit Greg. If Greg had any doubts about the conclusions that Tim had drawn, he had only to look at the ominously cold stare coming from his friend's normally smiling blue eyes.

Tim Walker was a few inches short of six feet tall, but no one meeting him ever thought of him as small. His wide shoulders, muscled arms and broad chest created the image of a man you wouldn't want to tangle with. Greg glanced down at his watch. It was five o'clock in the morning, certainly not a time he'd choose for a confrontation with Tim Walker when he was upset.

Greg hastily headed downstairs to where he'd left his clothes. "I can explain—"

"You're damn right you will," Tim growled, following closely on his heels. He stood with his hands hanging loosely at his sides while Greg dressed more quickly than he had since he'd left the military.

"This isn't what it looks like."

"It's exactly what it looks like, and you know it. My God! All the years I've known you, and I had no idea you could take advantage of someone as sheltered and protected as Brandi. I could tell by her messages that she was frightened, but I knew she'd be safe up here. Hah! That's a laugh, isn't it?"

"Lower your voice, will you, before you wake her up? I haven't hurt your precious Brandi. She's fine." He strode into the kitchen and began to make coffee. "What are you doing here at this hour, anyway?"

"Oh, so it's my fault for coming early enough to catch you in bed with her, is that it? What I don't know makes everything okay, is that the way your mind works? Good God, Greg, I knew you were ruthless, I knew you could annihilate an opponent in a courtroom, but I never thought you would take advantage of a man's hospitality and seduce an innocent woman!"

"She isn't some sixteen-year-old child, for God's sake! Brandi Martin is a grown woman, Tim, a consenting adult. It is none of your damned business what we did or did not do, might or might not do, and I resent your unfounded accusations and unsubstantiated claims regarding my character!"

If Tim wanted a fight, he was going to have one, Greg decided. Some of Tim's comments had hit extremely close to the mark, echoing some of Greg's earlier thoughts, which only made him angrier. He *hadn't* taken advantage of her, even though he'd had every opportunity. He *hadn't* abused his friend's hospitality or his trust, and he was furious that he should be judged so harshly on such flimsy and circumstantial evidence.

He faced Tim, waiting for him to make the first move.

Tim leaned against the counter and stared at Greg for several tense moments without moving. Then he straightened and took a step toward him.

"Has anyone ever told you how adorable you are when you're angry?"

Greg had been ready for anything but that. He stared at his friend in astonishment. Tim was grinning. Bewildered at the sudden change in Tim's mood, Greg just stood there looking at him.

Tim began to laugh at the expression on Greg's face. "You're right, Greg. It's none of my business what you and Brandi choose to do. I guess I've looked out for her for so long that I forgot that I can't live her life for her, or make her choices for her. As you said, she's a grown woman."

Tim walked over and poured two cups of coffee, handing one to Greg. "I'm sorry for making such a fool of myself. My only excuse is that I was really worried about Brandi, which is why I drove all night to get here. When I first saw your car outside I felt nothing but relief, knowing that if you were here she was all right. To say that I was surprised at your sleeping arrangements is putting it mildly."

"You may have noticed that I was sleeping downstairs earlier."

Tim sat down at the table with a soft sigh of pleasure. "I don't mind telling you I'm tired, which partially explains why I was less than my normally observant self. Instead of my continuing to make erroneous guesses, why don't you just tell me what's going on?"

Greg sat down across from him. "Brandi's had a real scare, and I think she's still dreaming about it. I heard her last night and went upstairs to check on her. Later, after she had calmed down a little, I started to leave. She asked me to stay with her. So I did."

"And that's it?"

"That's it."

"You mean I'm not going to get to give the bride away?"

Greg studied Tim closely. "Would it bother you to see Brandi get married?"

"Not if she decided to marry you, old buddy. I couldn't be happier."

"You're really serious, aren't you?"

"Of course I'm serious. Why? Are you thinking about marrying her?"

"Don't be absurd. I just met her. Besides, I'm old enough to be her father. We're too different. We have absolutely nothing in common. And we're—"

"Whoa, wait a minute," Tim said, laughingly interrupting. "Talk about an avalanche of ridiculous reasons for not marrying someone. All you had to say was that you weren't interested in her, you know."

Greg raised his cup to his mouth without meeting his friend's inquiring gaze. He carefully sipped from the cup and meticulously replaced it in the exact spot where it had been. "I didn't say that."

"Yeah, I noticed."

They sat there for a while in silence, drinking their coffee and watching as the sky gradually lightened to a dull, threatening gray. The wind had steadily increased, its whistling moan around the corners of the house sounding like the wail of some long-lost soul.

After a while, Tim began to speak in a musing tone. "Brandi's family moved next to mine when we were kids. I think Brandi was still in diapers. I know she hadn't started school. Her father was a good provider, loved his wife and daughter. They were a very happy family. Unfortunately, her father died unexpectedly a few years later. The change in Brandi and her mother was really sad. It got to me, somehow. Up until then I'd led a rather self-centered existence, like most kids."

Greg remained silent, so Tim continued. "I began to look in on them and offered to help with the chores. My folks took a more active interest in them and, over time, Brandi and her mother managed to pull out of the pain from their loss. By the time that happened, I'd already adopted my rather overprotective attitude toward both of them." He stopped and took a sip of his coffee. "I love Brandi, Greg, but I'm not *in* love with her. Not in the way you are."

Greg met his friend's gaze without hesitation. "I don't know what you're talking about."

"That's possible. You've never been one to stay in close touch with how you're feeling about things. I suppose your feelings for Brandi will hit you sooner or later." He stretched, got up and poured them some more coffee.

"I've already told you—"

"I know what you've already told me. You're too old, you have nothing in common. All of that's a bunch of hogwash, and you know it. Age doesn't mean a thing when you're both adults. Brandi is a warm, responsive person. She could teach you a lot about life if you'd allow her to get close enough. And you'd be good for her, as well. I think you have the ability to appreciate the subtleties in her character, even though you'd deny to your dying breath that you possess any sensitivities."

Greg's emotions tumbled inside him like a roiling sea. Meeting Brandi had unleashed previously hidden portions of him, and Greg was having difficulty knowing how to deal with these new sensations.

At the moment, all he could do was play for time like the good strategist he was.

"I think you'd better hear about what Brandi accidentally stumbled into. From every indication, these people mean business. I have reason to believe that they may have traced her here. If so, they are professionals who are determined to get whoever they're after."

Even though Tim recognized the suggested change of subject as the ploy it was, he knew that Greg was right. He needed to know what was happening.

By the time Greg had told him all that he knew, Tim's expression was as serious as Greg's. "I had no idea this mess was so threatening. I thought that Brandi might have had prowlers at her home or something. She's pretty isolated, and I could understand if she'd gotten frightened enough to leave. But this!"

Tim got up and began to pace.

Greg glanced out the kitchen window. "I think I'll go outside and look around before the weather gets any worse. I'll feel better, knowing that you're with Brandi. I didn't want to leave her here alone, but hesitated to suggest that she go with me. That damn red jacket of hers fairly screams for notice."

"Good idea," Tim responded, watching as Greg slipped into his gray ski pants and jacket. "I might try to get some sleep. I don't remember the last time I was horizontal."

However, Tim's sleep was postponed by Brandi's appearance downstairs within half an hour of Greg's leaving the cabin.

"Tim! I didn't hear you come in." She had found him stoking the fire and launched herself into his arms almost before he had time to straighten and turn.

"Hi, Mouse!" he replied, hugging her to him. "How do you manage to get yourself into such crazy situations?" he asked, shaking his head ruefully.

"So Greg told you what happened." She glanced around the room and over to the kitchen. "Where is he, by the way?"

"Oh, he said something about skiing before the weather closed in any more." He yawned. "I was too tired to even consider going with him."

"I'm surprised he would have much energy after spending the night on this sofa. I tried to get him to take the bed, but he insisted on staying down here. I know he must have been uncomfortable, but I gave up arguing with him. Somehow I get the impression that few people win in an argument with that man."

Tim watched her closely. It was obvious that she didn't remember Greg's going upstairs in response to her nightmare or her asking him to stay.

Brandi had been prone to nightmares for as long as he'd known her. One of the ways her mind dealt with them was to block them from conscious thought. No doubt she'd managed to block this most recent episode, as well.

"Have you eaten?" she asked.

"No. And I'm starved. Would you care to take pity on me, or will I have to make my own breakfast?"

"I'll be glad to feed you if you'll explain to me why those men would be so angry that they would shoot at me?"

Tim followed her into the kitchen. "You're sure they actually were shooting?"

"Believe me, I recognized the sounds when I heard them. And I didn't imagine the truck that followed me, nor the men I saw at the sheriff's office."

"What sort of clothes were they wearing?"

"Some sort of white camouflage. They looked military, but I could be wrong."

"Are you sure you didn't wander onto one of the military installations?"

"Come on, Tim," Brandi said, busily whisking eggs together, "those bases are well marked, with high fences and posted notices."

"That's true."

"So what do you think?" she asked, setting a plateful of eggs, bacon and toast in front of him.

"Looks good."

"No! I mean about those men. What were they doing?"

"I have no idea."

"Can you find out?"

"I can try. But first I'd like to eat and maybe get a few hours of sleep, if that's not asking too much."

She grinned. "For you, my friend, I'll allow it."

"That's big of you," he mumbled through a bite of toast.

Brandi laughed. She folded her arms on the table and leaned on them, watching him for a few moments in silence. Then, in a casual tone that didn't fool Tim in the least, she asked, "How long have you known Greg?"

Tim smiled but didn't comment on her interest. "We met overseas when we were in the service."

"Were you in the same unit or something?"

"No. Greg found me, badly injured, and helped me get medical attention. I doubt that I would have made it otherwise, but Greg gets irritated whenever I bring up the incident, so I've learned not to refer to his savior tendencies."

"You mean it was dangerous for him to have helped you?"

"Suicidal."

"And he did it anyway?"

"Yes."

"And he didn't even know you?"

"That's right."

"What sort of a man would do something like that?"

"A very unusual one." Tim stared out the window. "People are only now beginning to understand what it was like in Southeast Asia back then. We were just kids out of high school, raised on John Wayne war movies, raring to go fight for our country. Only we discovered when we got over there that it wasn't like the movies at all." He slowly turned to look at Brandi. "Most of us lost our youth over there. I did, and I know Greg did."

Tim was quiet for a long moment, remembering. Then he shook his head, and his gaze finally met hers. "I'll never forget the first time I saw him after we got back to the States. I'd lost track of him, and I wasn't going to let him disappear from my life. Whether he liked to hear it or not, the fact remained that I'm alive today only because of the risks he took to save me. You can never forget something like that."

Tim pushed his plate away. Brandi took it over to the sink and rinsed it, then poured him another cup of coffee. She didn't want to break into Tim's story. She could tell that thinking about those years caused him pain, but she felt that she needed to hear what he was going to say.

"The only address I had for him belonged to his parents in Virginia. So I went there. It was hard to believe that those two embittered people had produced the man I knew to be warm, compassionate and caring. They acted as though they barely remembered him. They didn't even know his address, just that he'd gone to Massachusetts to go to school."

Tim shook his head. "It took me a while to locate him, and when I did I almost didn't recognize him. He looked years older. He was cold and very distant. In fact, his attitude toward me was similar to the one I'd run into with his parents. As though he couldn't imagine why I'd bothered to look him up."

He sipped absently from the cup in front of him. "I wasn't accepting that sort of behavior from Greg. I'd gotten to know the man too well. Something was eating him alive, and I was determined to do what I could to help."

"He'd enrolled at the Harvard law school and had a small garage apartment. I deliberately got him to drinking until he loosened up enough to tell me what had happened. It was worse than I thought."

"What was it?" Brandi asked, watching Tim play with the handle of his cup.

"Greg explained to me that he was the youngest of three boys. He said he'd grown up knowing without understanding that he could never do anything to please his parents. He wasn't as smart as his oldest brother or as athletic as his other brother. His grades were never good enough, and neither were his achievements."

"How sad."

"The thing is, Greg never allowed their attitude toward him to stop him from trying to excel in order to win their approval."

When he didn't say anything more, Brandi finally prodded him. "So what happened?"

"Nam happened. Both his brothers were drafted, two years apart. When Greg's turn came before the draft board he was given a deferment because he was the only son left at home. When he told his parents about the deferment, his dad accused him of being a coward and hiding behind his brothers."

"Oh, no!"

"So Greg enlisted and ended up overseas."

Tim got up and poured himself another cup of coffee, but instead of returning to the table he began to pace in the small confines of the kitchen. "What he told me that night explained a lot of things to me, things about Greg that had puzzled me when I'd first gotten to know him. He'd been awarded several honors and medals for bravery, including the time he saved my life, but none of them seemed to mean anything to him. He brushed them off, and got irritated whenever anyone brought them up. It hit me that night that Greg had still been trying to prove that he wasn't a coward, which is ridiculous. Greg Duncan is one of the bravest, most courageous men I've met."

He paused in his pacing and picked up his cup.

"Surely his parents couldn't ignore all that he had done overseas," Brandi pointed out. "Didn't their attitudes toward him change at all?"

"His parents hadn't kept in touch with him while he was overseas, so Greg didn't find out until he returned home that both his brothers had been killed."

"How horrible! How awful for the whole family."

"Yes. Greg had loved both of them very much, even though, from what I could gather from his remarks about them over the months I was with him, they had been busy with their own lives while they were all growing up and showed only a casual interest in him. Losing them was devastating enough, but when his parents told him about his brothers' deaths they made it clear they resented the fact that he had survived while the two they had idolized had been killed."

"But that's really sick. How could they blame Greg for something over which he had no control?"

"Who knows, but obviously they did. By the time I managed to locate Greg he'd withdrawn behind a wall so thick I wasn't sure I'd ever get behind there and find the man I knew." He shook his head and sat down at the table once again. "But I couldn't walk away and leave him that way. He was my friend. He'd saved my life. Now it was time for me to do what I could to help him."

"So what did you do?"

Tim grinned. "Don't you remember? I ended up enrolling in school myself, moving in with him and spending hours over the following months in long philosophical discussions about the meaning of life and what we hoped to get out of it."

"It must have worked."

"Who knows? But we both got through the readjustment of returning to a country that was ashamed of what was happening in Asia and reflected those feelings onto those of us who had taken part in it."

They were both quiet for a while, thinking about the past. Finally Brandi shook her head. "It must have been terrible for someone as sensitive as Greg is to have to endure such callous treatments."

Tim glanced at her and smiled. "Does that mean you haven't been put off by his cold and aloof manner, Mouse? That you saw the man that hides behind that shield?"

"Well, just look at the situation now. He came to Colorado for a few days of peace and quiet. He obviously wanted to be alone, but instead he found me here. Greg could have been angry at my presence and irritated that I continued to stay. Every once in a while I've seen a glimpse of him that's intriguing, but he doesn't give much away about himself."

"I know."

"And yet he seems close to you."

"Because I broke through the barrier. I saw him when he had no defenses left against the world. I've watched as he rebuilt his life, set his goals and pursued them. I'm probably the closest friend he has. And yet we rarely see each other, except for an occasional visit here to ski or if I look him up in Missouri. We both keep heavy schedules, but we both know that we'd go to the wall for each other at any time."

"I know that feeling. You got me through some really rough periods in my life, Tim, and I'll never forget it. As you can see, you're the first person I turned to when I didn't know what to do."

He grinned. ''I'm always glad to assist a damsel in distress, Mouse. The problem is that I'm not sure how we're going to deal with this situation. But I'll think of something.''

Brandi's thoughts returned to Greg, and she wondered if he would ever allow her to get any closer to him. Their kiss of the night before continued to haunt her. She had been given a glimpse of the man hidden away from most of the world, the man she found so intriguing, the man she wanted to get to know better, to coax into sharing himself with another person— with her.

Chapter Five

Brandi and Tim heard a thump outside and looked around. Greg came in, stamping his feet to make sure he didn't bring in any snow.

Brandi felt her heart begin to race, and she forced herself to sit there quietly, watching him as he removed his outdoor clothes. The conversation she and Tim had been having seemed to ring in the room, and she was embarrassed at almost being caught discussing him, as though she had been spying.

Hearing Tim's story made her want to cry for the pain that Greg had endured with a great deal of stoicism for most of his life. He'd been trained from an early age to believe that he didn't deserve to be loved. For Brandi, the man was almost too easy to love. The feelings she was developing toward him were almost frightening in their intensity.

"Looks like you made it back none too soon," Tim observed, nodding toward the window.

For the first time, Brandi noticed the heavy flurry of snow swirling outside.

"I know," Greg said, pulling off his boots. He rubbed his hands together briskly. "I think I'm going to have a hot shower, then find something to eat."

Tim stood and followed him into the other room. "Did you see anything interesting while you were out?" He glanced over his shoulder at Brandi, then back to Greg.

Greg nodded his head. In a low voice he said, "I found where a four-wheel-drive vehicle had been parked up the road. Tracks led back this way."

"How many?"

"Two."

"I don't like the sound of that."

"Neither do I. However, I don't think we'll have any more company if this weather keeps up. As soon as it clears, I think we should get her out of here."

Brandi left the kitchen and joined them in the main room. "If you'd like, I could make you something to eat," she said, smiling at Greg.

The two men looked at each other in silence. Then Greg nodded. "That sounds great, Brandi. Thanks." Greg found some clothes in his bag and disappeared into the bathroom.

Tim began to pace. "I really should try to get back to Denver. There's no telling how long this might keep up."

Brandi looked at him as though he'd lost his mind. "But you just got here. You said yourself you needed some rest."

He ran his hand through his short, almost military-cut hair. "I know. But I'd like to get some queries started regarding the incident you witnessed."

"Maybe you could phone."

He thought about that for a moment. "Yeah, that might be the quickest way to go. Even so, I'll have to drive into town." He glanced at his watch. "That's what I'll do. I'll go into town, find a phone, then maybe get a room and wait this out. Are you going to feel comfortable staying up here with Greg until I can make it back up here?"

She smiled. Comfortable wasn't exactly the word that came to mind when she thought of Greg. "I'll feel perfectly safe, if that's what you mean," she said.

Tim studied her in silence for a few minutes. "What do you think of Greg?" he finally asked.

"I don't think I've ever met anyone quite like him, although there are times when he reminds me of you—in some ways."

Tim walked over and looked out at the falling snow. "That's not too surprising. We have several things in common."

Brandi wandered over to the fireplace and stood watching the flickering flames. "Now that you've shared with me some of his background, I can better understand why he's the way he is. I don't think he's ever learned how to play. I find myself wanting to teach him how."

Tim turned from the window. "Be careful, Mouse. I'd hate to see you hurt. Greg's had several years to erect a very sturdy wall between himself and the rest of the world."

"A couple of times I felt a deep loneliness in him that I really didn't understand at the time. I wanted to hold him close and to assure him that he wasn't alone," she said softly, not looking at Tim. "At other times, I felt that I must have imagined it. He appears so confident and self-assured."

"You're more perceptive than I gave you credit for, Mouse. Few people have seen the vulnerable side of him."

"Maybe it's because I can identify with the feeling. I consider myself strongly independent, and yet there are definitely times when I'm tired of fighting all of my own battles."

"Well, this is one time when you were right in looking for some assistance. It takes wisdom to realize that there's a certain strength in admitting when you need help. I'm glad you contacted me."

She went over and put her arms around his waist. "Me too. And I'm doubly glad you came."

Tim patted her awkwardly, then stepped back. "I'd better make tracks before it's too late to get off this mountain."

"And I want to make Greg something to eat. He must be starved." Brandi followed Tim into the kitchen area and watched as he bundled up for the weather. "Please be careful."

Tim grinned. "Always. I'll see you two as soon as I can, but I doubt that I'll brave the storm to get back up here today. Once I can get some inquiries going, I'll find a place to sleep and wait for some answers." He hugged her to him. "Take care. Tell Greg where I've gone."

Brandi waved and watched through the window as Tim carefully navigated the driveway out to the main road. The blowing snow drew a swift curtain between them and she turned away, going to the refrigerator and removing items. She'd never realized how much fun it could be to cook for someone. It was almost as though she and Greg were playing house.

Almost, but not quite, she reminded herself sternly.

A few moments later, she heard the bathroom door open and caught the scent of Greg's after-shave lotion. She would never smell that particular scent again without being reminded of him. Without turning around, she quickly filled a bowl with soup and sliced the sandwiches she'd made.

"Where's Tim?"

Brandi placed the food on the table before she looked up. Greg looked as good as she'd feared he would, the dark blue of his sweater emphasizing the blondness of his hair.

"He went to find a phone."

"In this weather?" Greg walked over to the window. "He must be crazy. He'll never make it back up here."

"I know. He said he'd find a place to stay in town and wait to get some answers to his inquiries." She didn't meet his eyes. "Sit down and eat while your soup is still hot."

When he didn't move, she glanced up at him. He looked grim.

"What's wrong?"

Greg wasn't about to tell her the truth—that he had counted on Tim's presence in the small cabin to help him get through the next couple of days without making a complete fool of himself.

"Nothing." He sat down and began to eat.

Brandi filled another bowl with soup and sat down opposite him. She noticed that he winced when he moved his right arm.

"What's wrong with your arm?"

"I don't know. I must have pulled a muscle in my shoulder or something."

"If you'd like, I could rub some cream on it after lunch."

He nodded, trying not to react to the thought of having her hands moving over his body. What the hell was wrong with him, anyway?

Brandi cleared the table and washed the dishes in record time, Greg decided later when she appeared in the living room while he tended the fire. She nodded matter-of-factly toward the rug and said, "Why don't you sit on the rug in front of the fire? You'll be warmer there without a shirt. I'll get the cream and be right back."

He heard her moving items in the bathroom medicine cabinet and almost hoped she wouldn't find anything, even though he knew that he needed some relief. The shoulder was steadily stiffening on him.

When she came back into the room, Brandi sat down on the sofa behind him and began to tug on his sweater. Reluctantly Greg helped her to remove the sweater, then his undershirt.

"My hands are probably going to feel cold to you," she said apologetically, rubbing them briskly together, then putting some cream on her palm.

Greg sat silently when she began to stroke his shoulder and down his arm. He forced himself to relax and tried to think of something else, anything but the fact that at the moment all he wanted to do was to turn and pull Brandi into his arms and kiss her senseless.

Eventually the heat from the cream began to seep into his muscles and he began to relax, luxuriating in the feel of her small hands touching him. After several moments of silence she paused and said, "How does that feel?"

"Much better," he answered gruffly, without looking at her. "Thanks." He reached for his shirt and sweater. He heard her move away from him.

"Would you like some coffee?" she asked from the kitchen area.

"Sounds good."

"The storm doesn't seem to show any signs of stopping."

He glanced out at the swirling white curtain on the other side of the glass and sighed. They were effectively marooned together, and Brandi didn't even appear to be bothered by that fact. She was treating him as though he were her brother.

He heartily wished he could share that attitude with her. Unfortunately, there was no way Greg could stir up any familial feelings toward Brandi!

When she brought the coffee in, Brandi sat down on the rug beside him. "Tell me more about what you do as a lawyer, Greg."

He accepted the cup from her and smiled briefly at the eager expression on her face. "It's rather boring, I'm afraid."

"I don't believe that. I'm sure you've had your share of interesting cases and intriguing trials."

He thought of an amusing incident that had happened a few weeks before and told her about it in precise and vivid detail, catching her off guard with his keen observational skills and his ability to capture and relate the incident with humor and compassion.

Before he fully realized what was happening, Brandi was drawing him out, asking gently probing questions about his life-style, his work and his personal life.

"You don't seem to have much time for anyone in your life with the schedule you keep, do you?" she finally asked after they had talked for several hours.

"You're right about that. Penny had a narrow escape."

"You still miss her, though, don't you?"

"I don't think so, no. I think of her occasionally, though, and wonder how my life might have changed if I had gone ahead and married."

"I think you're lonelier than you want to admit."

He shrugged. "Perhaps. I don't waste much time thinking about it."

"I'm surprised that you wanted to spend your leisure time alone. It seems to me that you would have preferred to go where there were people."

He grinned. "I'd be lying if I said I'm sorry that you've been here to share the cabin with me."

"You don't know how pleased I am to hear you say that. I've been feeling really guilty about crashing your party."

He lifted a cup. "Some party."

She smiled at him. "Well, when Tim returns I'll get out of your hair by catching a ride home with him."

"I could take you home when you're ready to go," he offered quietly.

She looked at him in surprise. "Why would you want to do that, Greg? You wouldn't get much skiing in around my place this late in the season."

"Because I want to get to know you better," he admitted, as though he were a little surprised at himself.

Brandi could feel herself growing warm. "There's really not much to know."

"Somehow I find that a little hard to believe, Brandi. For example, the field you've chosen to work in is most unusual. What made you decide to do marquetry?"

"When I was at school I became fascinated with the beautiful work done in woods during the Italian Renaissance, in the fifteenth and sixteenth centuries. At that time marquetry was regarded as a worthy art, equal to the finest paintings and sculptures of the time."

Brandi gazed into the fire as though searching for words to explain how she felt. "I was intrigued with the idea of pursuing this type of artistic expression. I wanted to see if I could help reclaim what was almost a lost art."

"I wish I could see some of your work."

She smiled. "I'll send you one of my more colorful boxes."

"That's one of the things that always puzzled me. How do you get the different colors in the wood?"

"Well, I buy wood in thin sheets. To get certain brilliant colors I dye the wood with a cloth dye by pressuring it in a pressure cooker. This causes the dye to penetrate the wood completely, which is necessary because I have to sand it."

Greg enjoyed watching the way the firelight highlighted the delicate bone structure of her face. Brandi obviously loved what she did. Her animation while describing it was proof of that.

"It must take a great deal of patience to work with the small pieces you'd need to form a picture," he commented.

"I suppose, but I really enjoy it. And there are special tools that help make it easier." Brandi smiled at him, her eyes dancing. "It probably doesn't make sense to a busy lawyer why someone would devote hours to forming in wood the variegated colors found in a flower's petal."

"On the contrary, I'm very much impressed. I noticed yesterday what a sharp eye you have for nature's beauty."

"I've always been fascinated by the shape and color of flowers…and limbs…grasses and shrubs…a bird's wing…" She paused, shaking her head. "It's not very profound, I'm afraid." Brandi was uncomfortable talking about herself, and she searched for something to say that would effectively turn the subject away from her. Without thinking about Greg's possible re-action, she said, "I'm so glad I've had this chance to meet you, Greg. Tim's right. You're a very special person."

His eyes narrowed slightly. "What sort of tales has Tim been spreading about me?"

Brandi shook her head. "Nothing that you need to feel ashamed of, I'm sure."

He frowned slightly, staring into the fire. "I should have known better than to leave him alone with you."

"He says you're a very private man."

Greg gave her comment some thought. "I suppose I am."

"And yet you've been very open with me," she pointed out.

"You have that effect on me. I don't understand it, nor can I explain it."

"I'm glad, Greg," she said softly. Leaning toward him, she kissed him softly on the cheek.

He turned and pulled her into his lap. Leaning back against the sofa, he looked down at her. "This is a dangerous situation, you know," he said slowly. "One of us needs to hang on to his sanity."

She smiled and stroked his cheek. "What a sensible idea. Should we draw straws and see who wins?"

He lowered his head slightly and touched his lips to hers. Raising his head a few inches, he asked, "And the winner hangs on to his sanity?"

She touched her lips to his for a brief instant and said, "No. The loser." Her arms circled his neck and she sighed, her mouth settling once more against his.

Brandi felt as though she had suffered through agonizing hours waiting to be kissed by Greg once again. She didn't understand the effect he had on her. She couldn't have begun to describe what was happening to her. All she knew was that she would be content to spend the rest of her life right where she was at this moment.

Greg felt as though he'd been fighting against the inexorable pull Brandi had on him ever since he'd awakened to find her presence a part of his vacation package. With her response, Brandi had inadvertently broken through all the barricades and restraints he'd placed between them.

A moan that was only barely audible registered Greg's capitulation to forces no longer in his control. The attraction he felt toward Brandi overrode every other consideration—of trust, of friendship, of the future. He knew that he would make love to her that night, regardless of what the morning would bring in the way of consequences.

Brandi sensed the change in his kiss. She felt possessed...claimed...branded—and never gave a thought to putting up a struggle. How could she, when this was what she wanted?

Greg eased her down onto the plush rug in front of the flickering flames. Pulling away slightly, he eased her sweater over her head, then removed the turtleneck shirt she wore for added warmth.

Her soft skin glowed with a rosy tint from the warmth and color of the fire. Brandi smiled, never taking her eyes off of Greg's face, not even when he unfastened her bra and carefully pulled it from her shoulders.

"I've never wanted to make love to anyone the way I want you," he whispered, planting tiny kisses at the base of her neck.

Brandi's hands came up, and she ran her fingers through the silkiness of his hair. "I know the feeling," she admitted.

"This is crazy," he muttered, unerringly finding the tip of her breast with his lips.

His hands lightly stroked across her back and down her spine, pressing her closer to him. Brandi slid her hands beneath his sweater and luxuriated in the feel of the taut muscles in his shoulders and arms.

His hand slid to the snap of her pants, and he hesitated. Raising his head, he listened for the sound he thought he had heard, a sound that did not blend with the others coming from outside.

Brandi slowly opened her eyes and gazed up at his flushed face. His profile was turned to her as he stared toward the front of the cabin. Gone was the lover. In his place was the instinctive animal, guarding its own.

"What is it?" she whispered.

"I'm not sure." He sat up.

Brandi hastily pulled her heavy sweater over her head, effectively covering her bare chest. Greg had tensed, ready to get to his feet, when Brandi heard something outside, as well. He moved swiftly into the kitchen on silent feet.

A sudden pounding started up at the door, and Brandi discovered that her heart was pounding erratically somewhere in the vicinity of her throat. Glancing around, she saw her bra and undershirt where Greg had tossed them earlier. She quickly gathered them up and stuffed them beneath the sofa cushion.

Brandi couldn't imagine who would be out on a night like this. Were they looking for her? What could she do? Where could she possibly hide? Then she relaxed slightly. Greg was there. He wouldn't let anyone harm her. She knew that with a certainty that needed no explanations.

She stood in front of the fireplace and watched as Greg walked over to the kitchen door and opened it.

When Greg saw the two snow-covered shapes standing on the deck, he stepped back and motioned them inside. They stumbled in. Whoever they were, the storm had gotten the best of them. Their ill-advised decision to be out had almost been the death of them.

They could barely move, and Greg began to pull their overcoats and gloves off. As soon as their coats were removed, he saw an insignia on one of their shoulders. They wore uniforms.

Glancing around at Brandi, he noted that she was still hovering by the fire. This was no accident, and he knew it. Something must have been very important for these two to have braved the elements. He only had a few minutes in which to decide how best to deal with the present situation.

"Not quite the night I would have chosen for a stroll, gentlemen," he said quietly, watching as the men sank down heavily on either side of the kitchen table.

"We got lost," one of the men finally said through wheezing breaths.

"I see." Greg saw a great deal more. They wore state police uniforms. These were not military men after all. He relaxed fractionally. "How about a cup of coffee? And you might find it warmer in by the fire."

"I need to thaw out a little before I get closer to any warmth," the other man said with a grimace. "My name is Pete Phillips and my partner is Jim Stanley. We're sorry to have disturbed you, Mr.—"

"Duncan. Gregory Duncan."

"Mr. Duncan. But believe me, seeing your light probably saved our lives."

The two men began to pull off their snow boots, then briskly rubbed their hands, trying to improve their circulation.

"What brought you men up into the mountains in weather like this?" Greg asked, placing a cup in front of each one.

After taking a welcome sip of coffee, Jim replied, "We got an urgent communication from Denver to be on the lookout for a dangerous suspect."

"Oh? And you thought he might be in this area?"

"She. We were told that she'd been traced to this area, yes."

Greg glanced across the counter that divided the main room from the kitchen and saw the apprehensive look on Brandi's face.

"Who are you looking for? And what has she done?"

"Her name is Brandi Martin. She's wanted for questioning. Once apprehended, she'll be returned to Denver."

"I see." Casually leaning against the counter, Greg said, "What does she look like?"

"We don't have much to go on at the moment—a description from a driver's license. Five-one, ninety-eight pounds, blue eyes, black hair. That could describe several people," Jim muttered. He glanced into the other room and saw Brandi standing in front of the fire. He froze.

"Oh, please forgive my lack of manners," Greg said, straightening, knowing that he was taking an irrevocable step. "This is my wife, Beth. We live in Payton, Missouri. We come here to ski whenever we can find the time." Greg reached into his pocket and pulled out his wallet and handed them a card.

Pete studied it carefully. "An attorney, are you?"

"That's right." Greg smiled.

"How long have you and your wife been here?"

He glanced over at Brandi. "I'm not sure. Are you, darling? Close to a week, I'd say." He shrugged. "I lose track of time when we're out like this. The days sort of run together."

Brandi felt frozen into immobility. These men were actually out searching for her, determined to take her back with them.

Greg's glib explanation had sounded so natural. He had poured himself a cup of coffee and seemed to be interested in what they had to say, though not unduly so. His acting skills amazed her. She wasn't certain she was going to be able to handle herself as well.

"You must be hungry. How long have you been out?"

"Since noon, but we have provisions with us," Pete explained. "The thing is, we turned onto a back road and got stuck. We radioed for help and were told that the roads were closed up this way. They also said that we'd find a few homes up here that would be able to provide some shelter until morning." He shook his head. "I was beginning to wonder. We haven't seen anything."

"You were fortunate that you saw our light," Greg said quietly.

Jim nodded. "No one is worth risking our lives over."

Greg glanced out at the storm. "Well, you're safe now. We've only got the one bed, but there are extra sleeping bags, and I'm sure you'll be comfortable down here in front of the fire."

He walked into the other room and put his arm around Brandi's shoulders. "Why don't you go ahead and get ready for bed, love? I'll be up shortly, after I've made sure that Pete and Jim are made comfortable."

Brandi forced herself to smile up at him. "That's a good idea. I am rather tired."

He squeezed her shoulder reassuringly. "We'll probably find the storm over by morning and will be able to get in some more skiing."

Greg watched as Brandi disappeared into the bathroom.

"We really appreciate your hospitality, Mr. Duncan," Pete said, padding into the living room in his heavy socks.

"Call me Greg. There's no problem, officer. Glad we were able to help." He went to the closet that had been built under the stairs and pulled out two down-filled sleeping bags. "Hope these will be all right for you."

"At this point, I think I could sleep on a bed of nails," Jim admitted. "That walk really took it out of me."

By the time Brandi came out of the bathroom, the men were settled in front of the fire, chatting. She paused uncertainly. Greg glanced at her and smiled. "I'll be up in a while, darling. Good night."

"Good night," she murmured softly, then climbed the stairs.

Once again she and Greg were going to share the bed upstairs. It was beginning to be a habit. Brandi couldn't help but remember what their visitors had interrupted. She had been in a wonderfully sensuous sea of sensation. Their sudden arrival and intentions felt like a load of ice being dumped on her. She was still shaking from the transition.

She wasn't an actress. Brandi had no idea how long she could pretend that their visit was nothing out of the ordinary. One slip and all her running would have been in vain.

Brandi hated to contemplate what she would have done if Greg hadn't been there. Would she have gone with Tim? Surely he wouldn't have let her stay there alone, even though all of them had figured that she would be safe at the cabin.

What in the world had she seen that could create a statewide hunt for her? Her only hope lay in Tim's ability to get to the bottom of it as rapidly as possible.

In the meantime, the only other danger she faced was the fear that she had lost her heart to Greg Duncan. Unfortunately, Brandi recognized, it was too late to worry about that.

Brandi crawled into bed and waited for Greg to come upstairs and join her.

Chapter Six

Greg felt as though he'd become two people in the past couple of hours—one who conversed with the two police officers and another who objectively monitored the scene. He was distantly aware of the fact that his heart was racing in his chest and that his adrenaline level had risen to unbelievable heights.

While the first part of him made sure his guests were comfortable, the other swiftly and inexorably catalogued the fact that for the first time in his adult life he had willfully and most deliberately stepped outside the law. He had lied to representatives of the very justice system that he had dedicated his life to supporting.

When he'd seen the possible threat to Brandi, he hadn't hesitated to protect her, regardless of the fact that in doing so he was compromising his integrity.

Of course, the whole thing was a mistake. Whatever she had stumbled into had political overtones, of that he was certain. She was no criminal. He was counting on the fact that if anyone could quickly get to the bottom of the situation, it was Tim. Brandi only had to wait for Tim to clear up the matter.

So why had Greg lied?

The answer astounded him. While inviting his guests to make themselves comfortable and bidding them good-night, Greg came face-to-face with the realization that in the space of two short days Brandi Martin had become more important to him than his own sense of right and wrong. The strong protective feelings sweeping over him were like nothing he'd ever felt before. But he recognized the strange feelings that had overcome him, changing his life.

He loved her.

He, Gregory Duncan, who took pride in the fact that he never made a decision without carefully analyzing all his options, had allowed his feelings to sweep away all thought of the possible consequences if these men discovered that he had lied to them and was at that very moment concealing the identity of a wanted suspect.

Given the same circumstances, he would do it again without hesitation.

Was this what love was all about—doing everything in his power to protect Brandi? Feeling the need to go to her side to hold her and reassure her that he would not allow anyone or anything to harm her?

What had happened to him in these few short days that he could ignore his training, his background, his way of life, in order to make sure that Brandi was all right? What mystical powers had transformed him in such a fashion?

As Greg said good-night to his guests and started up the stairway, he humbly and silently acknowledged a power he'd never been aware of—the power of love.

The overwhelming and astonishing power of love.

Acknowledging to himself how he felt about Brandi gave Greg a sense of freedom and joy that he'd never before experienced. He felt such a wealth of emotion wash over him that he wasn't sure he could contain his reaction. Yet he knew he must.

When he reached the loft area, Greg noted that Brandi had left on the bedside lamp for him. He also noted with a grin that she was lying as far on her side of the bed as she could get without falling off, with her back turned to him.

Without saying anything, he quickly shed his clothes and crawled beneath the covers to her side. Then he reached over and turned off the light, absorbing the silent darkness while he carefully sorted through his suddenly inadequate vocabulary to find the words to tell Brandi about his recent and amazing discovery.

"Brandi?" he said softly. "Are you awake?"

A slight glow of light from downstairs enabled him to watch her as she slowly rolled over onto her back, turning her head to look at him. The faint light revealed that she had been crying, and he felt a pang in the region of his heart.

"Did you really think I could drift off to sleep without a worry?" she asked in a low voice.

"They're nice guys. You don't have to worry about them."

"I'm sure they're nice enough, to the vacationing lawyer and his wife. I have a hunch their attitudes would change if they were to learn the truth."

"They won't," he said emphatically.

She noted the grim expression around his mouth and decided that she much preferred having Greg Duncan on her side. He would make a formidable adversary. No doubt there were many attorneys in the St. Louis and Payton areas who had discovered that fact.

"Try to get some rest," he said, studying her.

She smiled. "This is becoming a habit, sharing a bed with you."

Without returning her smile, he replied, "What would you think about the idea of making it permanent?"

Her eyes widened slightly. "Making what permanent?"

"Our sleeping together."

"I'm not at all sure that I understand what—"

"I want to marry you."

His calm statement did nothing to help her comprehend what was happening between them. She knew that they had both been under considerable tension these past few days, but she could think of nothing that had happened that would cause him to suddenly make such a statement.

"Greg, you can't be serious," she said, conscious of the need to keep her voice down. The one thing neither of them wanted was to be overheard discussing marriage by the men downstairs.

"I am."

"But you can't be. You don't know me. I don't know you. A few days together isn't enough time to make a decision of that importance."

"I'm well aware of all the logical reasons, Brandi. I'm telling you how I feel. I don't want you walking out of my life. I want to marry you. I want to take you back to Payton with me. I want to know that you're safe and protected from anything life might throw your way."

Brandi could not control the trembling that overtook her at his words. The thought had never occurred to her that Greg would offer her marriage. They were both wary of getting close to anyone—of that she was certain.

As far back as Brandi could remember, she had felt that she would never marry. She wasn't sure when she had first made up her mind about that. Perhaps when her father had died and she'd seen the devastation his loss had caused to her mother and, to a lesser degree, herself.

She felt as though she had learned a valuable lesson at a very young age—it was not healthy to be dependent on another person. Brandi had accepted that belief and learned to live with it, and that had helped her later to survive the loss of her mother.

She had learned to live alone, to take care of herself—most of the time, at least. Recent events had certainly caused her to question her ability to take care of herself.

For some reason she had thought that Greg understood and even agreed with her philosophy of life. He had seemed to be content with his solitary existence.

She placed her hand on his cheek and stroked it softly, enjoying the feel of his slightly rough skin. "That's very kind of you," she said quietly. "But it isn't necessary. And it certainly isn't wise."

Her loving touch and soft tones were in contradiction to her words, and Greg stared at her in bewilderment.

"I didn't propose because I was being kind, Brandi," he pointed out dryly. "I proposed because I love you and want to marry you."

"Not really," she contradicted in a reasonable tone of voice. "You're feeling this way because we've been alone together here. Once you return home you'll wonder what you ever saw in me."

Greg could feel his irritation at her matter-of-fact explanation of his feelings. "Brandi, I'm old enough to know myself, what I want, and how I feel. I love you. I want to marry you." As if to prove a point, he pulled her into his arms and kissed her.

His kiss was filled with a possessive fervor, as though he were determined to prove to her that his feelings were authentic.

Brandi discovered that no matter how logically she viewed their situation, as soon as Gregory began to kiss her, all thoughts flew out the window. The only thing she was aware of was how he made her feel.

Greg knew by her response to him that she was far from indifferent to him. Why didn't she know that? How could she possibly ignore what they experienced together? Every time he touched her, spontaneous combustion occurred.

Didn't that count for something?

He pulled away slightly and gazed down at her. "I want you to marry me," he said fiercely in a low voice.

"No."

"You can't mean that."

"Take my word for it. I mean it."

"Do you realize that if I wanted to I could make love to you right this minute?"

"Isn't that what you've been doing?"

"Honey, I haven't begun to show you what I intend to do when we make love."

"Just for the record, counselor, I'd like to point out that the evidence shows I am putting up absolutely no struggle. There's been no force used in this seduction."

He jerked away from her and sat up in bed, running his hand through his hair. "Damn it, Brandi. You're making fun of me. And I've never been more serious in my life."

She obligingly sat up beside him and said, "I believe that's one of the problems here. You take everything seriously, Greg. Where's your sense of humor?"

"What are you talking about?"

"Well, here we are having a debate—whispering, of course, so those two downstairs won't discover that I'm the woman they're searching for—on the possible merits of a marriage that you've already told them took place."

"You find that humorous?"

"I'd rather laugh about it than cry."

Greg realized that Brandi was unaware that he'd seen her slightly swollen eyes and tearstained cheeks when he'd first come to bed. Obviously she wasn't going to admit to giving in to tears. She wasn't even going to admit that she needed him—or anybody else, with the exception of Tim.

He should feel ashamed of himself for taking advantage of the situation. He should; but he didn't.

"Brandi, we both know that eventually we'll get to the bottom of whatever's going on in the hills near your home. As soon as Tim comes back he'll know what actions will be the most sensible for you to take. I'm not trying to rescue you, for God's sake. I want to marry you."

She was quiet for several minutes. "I really believe that you believe that statement."

"Damn it!" He paused, then consciously lowered his voice. "You can be very irritating. Has anyone ever pointed that out to you before?"

She smiled. "Oh, yes."

"Good. Then it probably doesn't come as a complete shock to you that I've mentioned it."

"No. That's just one of the reasons I'd never consider getting married. You see," she explained in a confidential tone, "I don't want to ever have to worry that my being irritating is going to create a problem in someone's life. Now they can get away from me until they get over it."

"This may come as a real blow to your theory, my love, but finding you irritating does not make me want to marry you any less."

"It doesn't?"

"No."

"Oh."

"You see, you have all sorts of personality quirks that I find endearing—lovable, actually. Irritating I can live with."

"You just don't understand, Greg. It isn't as though I don't like you. I do. Very much. And I'm very attracted to you."

"Well, thank God for small blessings."

"But that isn't enough on which to base a good marriage."

"It's a damn good start."

"What I mean is, I'm not marriageable material."

"What's that supposed to mean?"

"Some women grow up knowing that they will eventually become wives. I've always known I wouldn't. Therefore, I've never made any effort to find out what it would take to be a good wife. Take my word for it, Greg. You're going to look back on this night as one of the narrowest escapes you ever had." She stretched out on the bed once more and sighed. "I hadn't realized how tense I was. Thanks for talking to me. It's really helped me to relax." She plumped her pillow and turned over. "Good night, Greg."

He stared at her, dumbfounded. She was through talking. She had found their discussion relaxing, for God's sake. She had turned down his proposal of marriage as though he'd offered a second helping of dessert, and she'd refused in the same manner as she would have dessert, explaining it wasn't good for her.

What kind of woman was she, anyway?

Greg lowered himself to the bed and stared at her back. Was she right? Had he just had a narrow escape? After all, what sort of life would he have with a woman like that? Didn't she understand what he was offering her—a stable home life, a devoted husband, a *wealthy*, devoted husband . . . a boring, workaholic husband?

She knew. A couple of days in his company had shown her what a narrow existence he led. He didn't really blame her. He'd made no effort these past few years to do more than work.

Greg lay there for hours and faced the kind of person he had become. He didn't like what he saw. He didn't like it at all.

When had he become so set in his ways? So inflexible? So pompous? Why had he thought that a proposal of marriage from him would be immediately and gratefully accepted? He didn't have the foggiest idea how to be a part of a relationship. Perhaps that was why he spent so much of his time working. He was comfortable practicing law. He knew what to do and he was good at what he did. There was a sense of accomplishment and purpose, tangible evidence that he was a success at something.

He didn't know how to relate to another person.

When he'd met Penny he'd been drawn to her warmth and her even disposition. He had visualized them establishing a companionable marriage—with no unexpected scenes or surprises. When her childhood sweetheart had turned up just before their wedding, Greg had been given the opportunity to see a whole new side of Penny, one that he hadn't known existed.

Rather than deal with his discovery, he had walked away from the situation.

Walking away from emotional situations had always been his way of handling them. Now he didn't want to walk away. He wanted to explore these new emotions, to come to terms with them, to incorporate them into his world.

Greg felt as though his life had gone from black-and-white photography to living color. The color was dazzling, almost blinding in its intensity. He needed help in coming to terms with the full spectrum before him.

He felt as though meeting Brandi had snapped him out of that colorless, emotionless world. Even his irritation had been surprising. As a rule, he was adept at not letting his feelings surface. He'd always had the ability to present his case effectively.

Now he'd tried to win the most important victory of his life, and he'd blown it completely.

He forced himself to relax, closing his eyes. All right, so he'd blown it. He'd asked and she'd turned him down. She hadn't really believed he was serious—and if he was, she wasn't interested.

He couldn't blame her. He didn't have much to offer in the way of companionship...love...excitement. But he intended to learn as quickly as possible. He certainly wasn't going to give up. Now that his goal was within sight, Greg knew that he was going to do whatever it took to win Brandi Martin.

As he was dozing off to sleep he felt her curl up to the warmth of his back, her arm curving around his waist. He smiled to himself. Awake, Brandi might not think they had a future together, but asleep she was already making it clear that she was comfortable having him nearby.

When Brandi opened her eyes the next morning she was dazzled by the brilliant light coming from outside. She raised up on her elbow and gazed out the bedroom window. New snow lay everywhere in drifts, the sunlight catching glints of sparkle in the pristine white mounds.

The storm was over.

She could see small animal tracks crisscrossing the hillside, and she smiled. It would be a perfect day to go out and explore.

Then she remembered.

The two police officers had spent the night. Greg had once again shared her bed. He had proposed to her. She sank back under the covers and pulled them up to her ears. Perhaps she wasn't as ready to face the new day as she'd first thought.

Brandi listened for voices from downstairs, but she could hear nothing. She could only smell the tantalizing aroma of fresh coffee, which was enough to give her courage to crawl out of bed.

She felt rested, which surprised her. For some reason she seemed to sleep better when Greg was there in bed with her than when she slept alone. She couldn't understand it. She certainly wasn't used to sleeping with anyone else. How was it possible that she could sleep so deeply, without dreaming, and not be disturbed by his presence?

Brandi shrugged and crawled out of bed. She found the heavy velour robe she'd purchased during their last trip to town, slid her bare feet into her warm fleece-lined house slippers and made her way downstairs.

She paused at the bottom of the stairs. There was no sign of their previous night's guests. The room looked neat and clean, and there was a fire dancing merrily in the fireplace. The coffee was warming in an empty kitchen. She poured herself a cup and sat down at the table.

Glancing out the window, she could see that Greg had been busy since he'd gotten up. The porch and stairs had been shoveled clean and a path had been dug to the car. Squinting slightly against the glare, Brandi spotted Greg clearing the drive to the cabin.

On sudden impulse, she decided to join him. She finished her coffee quickly, then, after dressing into her ski clothes, let herself outside.

What a glorious day. It was crisp and clear, with no sign of wind. She didn't feel the cold through her warm clothing. Brandi wanted to laugh out loud with the sheer joy of being alive and able to experience this latest miracle of nature.

Greg glanced up, and she waved. He waved back and began to walk toward her. His proposal from the night before popped into her head, and all at once she wondered how she was supposed to treat him now. She'd never had anyone propose to her before, and she wasn't certain of the proper etiquette in such a situation.

She hadn't wanted to hurt him. In some uncon-scious way she knew that she was actually protecting herself by refusing to even consider the idea. What she had said the night before was true. She'd never considered the possibility that someday she might meet someone who would change her mind about marriage.

It wasn't the institution of marriage she was avoiding as much as it was the long-term intimacy that marriage suggested. Greg had implied that she had been willing to make love to him, and he'd been correct, even though she still couldn't explain her reaction to him.

Brandi had never been tempted to make love with anyone before. She'd never allowed anyone the opportunity to get through her defenses. Somehow Greg had. No doubt the frightening situation she'd run from had already shaken her so that she hadn't been able to rebuild her defenses by the time she'd awakened and discovered him in bed with her.

Whatever the cause, she had allowed Greg more liberties than she'd ever allowed another man—and she'd thoroughly enjoyed every minute of it.

But that didn't mean that she could be a wife to him, or that she had the foggiest understanding of what he might expect from her as a wife.

"Good morning."

Brandi realized that the man had an unfair advantage. The combination of his flashing smile, dancing eyes and seductively low voice played havoc with all her good intentions to spare him a future with her.

"Hi."

Brandi couldn't think of anything else to say. She just stood there and looked up at him, enjoying the sight of him along with the rest of nature's miracles.

"Did you sleep well?"

She nodded. "What happened to the police officers?"

He glanced back to the road, which curved out of sight around the hillside. "They heard the snowplow out early this morning and went to catch up with it. They've had time to get their car unstuck and back to town by now." He dropped his arm companionably around her shoulders, the snow shovel in his other hand, and started walking back up to the cabin. "I don't know about you, but I'm starving."

Greg didn't want to tell her that when he'd awakened that morning, just past dawn, he'd had the worst struggle of his life not to make love to her. She had felt so natural there in his arms, and he'd wanted her so badly that he still ached with it. But making love wasn't going to settle the questions between them.

He'd gotten up and made coffee for himself and Pete and Jim, seen them off and decided to start clearing the driveway. Greg could only hope Tim would make it back that day. His sense of honor and his willpower had never before been so tested.

Greg had spent the intervening hours looking at himself, his life and his goals. He had realized that if he didn't like what he saw, he could change it. He was in control of his life. He accepted full responsibility for the restricted, shallow existence he'd chosen up until the time he had met Brandi.

With firm resolve, he was determined to change... not because of her but because of what he wanted out of life. He wanted a full, substantial, loving relationship. He wanted a family. He wanted sons and daughters with curly black hair and big blue eyes in elfin faces. He wanted to be there for them, to watch them grow, to listen to their stories, to share in their triumphs and their disappointments.

No longer was he willing to settle for the tepid companionship that he had thought he wanted with Penny. With Brandi he knew that he could have a Technicolor spectacular of a marriage—filled with fireworks, crashing cymbals and rooms filled with love and laughter.

All he had to do was to convince her of that.

A piece of cake.

Chapter Seven

Breakfast became a hilarious affair. Brandi wasn't sure what had caused the difference, but Greg seemed to be lighthearted, teasing her unmercifully with outrageous suggestions for breakfast.

She ended up preparing *huevos rancheros*, a Mexican dish of scrambled eggs and chopped beef wrapped in a flour tortilla and covered with a hot sauce. Brandi was determined to show him that despite his ridiculous suggestions she could turn out a breakfast that was neither dull nor boring.

"My God, my tongue is on fire," he said after a few bites. He grabbed his glass of orange juice.

"I told you not to be so liberal with the hot sauce," she pointed out calmly, continuing to eat.

"You also said it wasn't all that hot."

"I told you the bottle was labeled Medium Spicy. But if you aren't used to it, the sauce can seem rather hot."

"You can say that again." He tentatively took another bite. "Great flavor, though."

"But not what you'd expect a lawyer to have for breakfast on a daily basis."

He grinned, wiping his mouth with a napkin. "Oh, I don't know. I have a hunch it might give me an unusual amount of energy to meet the demands of a busy schedule."

Brandi unobtrusively tried to study him at odd moments, wondering why he seemed so different today. He was dressed in a heavy sweater and winter pants, his usual attire since she'd known him. The morning exercise had given him a ruddy color that was in attractive contrast to his light hair.

The change seemed to be from within. It was as though he glowed with an inner light. He seemed more relaxed, somehow. There were no distractions today. He was totally and completely focused on her. She found the attention a little unnerving. It was almost as though he were a missile locked in on a target. Brandi had an uneasy suspicion that she was the target.

She hadn't brought up his proposal of the night before. Neither had he. Brandi supposed she was relieved that he wasn't going to try to debate the issue with her. She reminded herself once again that he would be a formidable foe. She had no desire to cross swords with him.

If you lost this battle, you'd probably find yourself married to him, she reminded herself. A shiver ran down her backbone at the thought.

"Are you cold?" he asked, getting up and pouring them some more coffee.

"No."

"Good. I was hoping I could talk you into going skiing after we give our breakfast a chance to settle."

She grinned. "I'd love it. I just wish I'd brought my camera. Today looks like a winter wonderland."

Greg sat down across from her again and picked up his cup. "I can't help wondering if we'll hear from Tim today."

"He said he'd get back to us as soon as he learned anything."

"I know you'll be glad to have this nightmare behind you."

She nodded.

"I've been thinking. Why don't you come back to Payton with me? No one would question your presence there. You'd be safe while you wait until this mess is resolved."

She was quiet for a few minutes, thinking over his suggestion. He'd been casual enough in his offer, in much the same way she imagined he'd have made such an offer to Tim.

Now that she knew she had been traced to this area, Brandi knew she couldn't stay there.

But would she feel any safer with Greg at his home? He had an unusual effect on her. All her lifelong convictions seemed to waver and wilt whenever he was around.

"I might consider it, on one condition," she finally said.

"Name it."

"There will be no discussion of marriage between us."

"Whatever you say," he replied immediately.

"Because you know how I feel about the idea."

"Not really. All I know is that you don't consider me ideal marriage material."

"I never said that!"

"That's the impression I got."

"Well, I never even implied that. I'm sure you'll make someone a fine husband, if that's what you really want. I'm just saying that you don't know me well enough to want to marry me."

His grin widened. "Then I find it very accommodating of you, Ms. Martin, to allow me the opportunity to get to know you better."

"Wait a minute. That's not what I meant." Why was she having so much trouble explaining something so simple? "I don't mind getting better acquainted with you. I would like to be your friend, Greg. I just don't want more than that."

"I see."

"Somehow I doubt it."

"What you're saying is that you will come and stay with me for a few days until Tim lets us know you can go home safely only if I treat you as a friend and not as a potential mate."

"That's it. You've got it."

"I can live with that."

"Good."

"Can you?"

"What do you mean by that?"

"I suppose that only time will tell. Why don't we get some skiing in while we're waiting to hear from Tim? Who knows? He may be able to get to the bottom of it immediately and we can go our separate ways, content to mail Christmas cards to each other annually."

She looked at him through narrowed eyes. "Are you making fun of me?"

"Of course not! Why do you ask?"

"Because you're smiling."

He immediately stopped smiling. Looking at her sternly, he asked, "Is that better?"

"Your eyes are smiling."

He grinned, "You're adorable. Has anyone ever told you that?"

She shook her head. "Mostly I'm told that I'm irritating, stubborn, opinionated, too independent and a pain in the posterior."

He stood and pulled her up with him. "Then I've got a great deal to look forward to, haven't I? Just think, by the time I see all those sides of your personality I'll be eternally grateful that you refused to marry me."

As she pulled on her outdoor clothes once again, Brandi couldn't help but realize that she rather resented his cheerful assessment of their present relationship.

Hours later they returned to the cabin, happily exhausted, and saw Tim's car. Brandi breathlessly shed her skis and stumbled up the stairs and across the deck to the door.

"Tim?" she called, throwing open the door. "What did you find out?" She bent over and started unlacing her boots.

She heard a noise from the couch, and Tim's frowning face appeared over the back of it. "I found out that I might as well forget about catching up on my sleep if you're anywhere in the vicinity," he grumbled, running his hand through his hair.

Brandi stepped out of her boots and padded over to where he sat stretching.

"Well? What did you find out?" she demanded.

Tim glanced around. "Where's Greg?"

"Oh, he's coming. We were out skiing. Isn't it a gorgeous day?"

He narrowed his eyes when he looked toward the bright expanse of snow and sky. "Yeah. Gorgeous."

"C'mon, Tim. Tell me."

"I only want to explain once, and I need Greg's opinion on a couple of things." He stood and dropped his arm around her shoulder. "So, Mouse, have you been behaving yourself while I've been gone?" He began to walk toward the kitchen.

"Of course."

"And Greg has been the perfect gentleman, has he, chivalrously giving up the bed to you?"

"Well, not exactly. You see, we had some unexpected company last night."

Tim stopped in the kitchen and looked down at her. "Last night? In that storm? Who in the hell was out in that?"

"Two state police officers, looking for a dangerous suspect for questioning—Brandi Martin."

Tim sat down rather abruptly at the table and muttered several unprintable phrases just as Greg walked through the door.

"I resent that last remark. I know for a fact that my parents were married for several years before I was born," he said calmly, unzipping his jacket.

"I wasn't talking about you, counselor."

"Well, that certainly relieves my mind, let me tell you. Whose ancestry are you discussing?"

"I want to hear about your visitors last night."

"Oh, them," Greg said nonchalantly, pulling off his boots and walking over to the counter, where he poured himself a cup of coffee. "I don't know about you guys, but I could use something to eat. How does soup and sandwiches sound?"

"Greg, I'm serious," Tim said in an irritated tone.

"So am I. I really burn up energy when I'm skiing. Anyone else hungry?"

Brandi tried to hide her smile as she got up and began to help Greg with the meal. She'd never known anyone to give Tim Walker a hard time before—besides herself, of course. She was enjoying it immensely.

Greg glanced over his shoulder. "We could make a deal, Walker. Fill us in on any information you picked up and I'll do the same."

"Damn. I forgot about you and your negotiating skills, Duncan," Tim said with a grin. They looked at each other and burst out laughing.

Brandi felt left out of the male camaraderie for the moment and yet felt a warmth pervade her at the obvious closeness of the two men. She had a tremendous respect for Tim Walker and his judgment. There was no denying the close bond between these two men.

Within minutes they were seated and in front of them were steaming bowls of soup and a platter piled high with sandwiches. Without thinking about it, Brandi had sat next to Greg, across from Tim.

Greg nodded toward Tim. "Any information?"

"Some, but nothing conclusive. Whatever is going on up there is either supersecret or without sanction by the government. My guess is that it's both. I had to put my reputation on the line to convince some high-ranking people that what I described had actually happened."

"So what's next?" Greg asked.

Tim paused long enough to take a couple of bites of his sandwich. "Well, that's what I was going to discuss with you before I heard about your visitors," he said to Greg. "I don't want to take Brandi back to Denver with me. I thought she'd be safer staying here with you, if you would be willing to spend some extra time. Now I'm not too sure about that idea, either."

Greg smiled at Brandi. "We've been discussing that this morning. The two men who were here last night had not seen a picture of Brandi, so I introduced her as my wife, Beth."

Tim raised one brow slightly. "Your wife, Duncan? Couldn't you have been more original than that? What about your daughter?"

"Very funny." He glanced around at Brandi, who was studiously eating her soup without looking up. "Although you're probably right, I could pass as her father just as well."

Brandi choked and looked up at the two men.

"I asked her to marry me last night, but she was too polite to point out the difference in our ages."

Tim stared at his friend in disbelief. Brandi wished she could hide under the table. She couldn't remember ever having been so embarrassed. How dare he bring up his proposal so casually, and in front of Tim?

"You want to marry Brandi?" Tim said in a surprised voice.

"Well, I thought I did, but after she carefully enumerated all of her many faults, she's almost convinced me that I had a rather lucky escape." He winked at Tim.

Tim's gaze fell on Brandi's crimson face. "You turned him down?"

"He was just being polite," she managed to get out.

"That's funny, I've never thought of Gregory Duncan as particularly polite before. Must be a side of him I've never seen."

"Well, it was the third night I was going to be sleeping with her, so I thought I should at least offer—"

"Third night!" Brandi interrupted indignantly. "It was only the second night. You slept downstairs—"

"'Fraid not, Mouse," Tim interjected. "The morning I got here I found the two of you all snuggled up together."

Brandi stared at each man with dismay.

"Don't you remember the nightmare you had?" Greg asked in a low voice.

Brandi paused, thinking back. "Vaguely. I've been dreaming a lot lately."

"I heard you cry out and went upstairs to check on you. You asked me to stay."

"And I demanded that he do the proper thing and make you an honest woman. Obviously he took my advice."

Brandi threw her napkin down. "This is the most ridiculous conversation I've ever been involved in." She glared at Tim. "It's none of your business who I sleep with!"

Tim smiled and took a sip of his coffee. Over the rim of the cup he eyed her and said, "So Greg reminded me."

"Good." She turned to Greg. "And as for you, it would have served you right if I'd said yes! Then where would you be?"

Greg's mouth twitched slightly, but he said in a solemn tone, "The possible consequences of my reckless behavior bring horror to my innermost being, Brandi. All I can say is I had the narrowest escape of my life. Thank you for your mercy." He picked up his sandwich and took a bite.

Brandi jumped up from the bench. "I hope both of you are having a marvelous time at my expense," she said in an injured tone.

Two pairs of innocent eyes turned and stared at her in puzzlement. "What did we do?" they said in unison, for all the world as though they'd practiced for hours to perfect their response.

"I'm going upstairs to take a nap," she announced, walking away.

"Try not to have any nightmares," Tim called out with a grin. "Otherwise, Greg will be upstairs forcing another proposal on you." Greg bit his lower lip to keep from laughing.

The two men were silent for a few moments after she left. Finally Greg said in an entirely different tone from the one he'd been using to tease Brandi, "What's the word?"

"I don't like it. Not at all. I was able to get in touch with the people who should know if something of that nature was going on. They were totally unaware."

"Do you believe them?"

"In this case, yes. They're men I've worked with before. They wouldn't lie to me."

"So where does all of this leave Brandi?"

"In a very vulnerable position at the moment. I was told to bring her in—for questioning."

"What?"

"Yeah. They believe *me*, all right, but they're hoping that maybe she only imagined part of what she saw."

"And I suppose she imagined the men chasing her, even to having an all points bulletin out for her arrest?"

"Calm down. I'm not turning her over to them." He studied the man across the table from him. "Care to explain what's going on with you and Brandi?"

"Obviously nothing, as far as she's concerned. But I'm not ready to give up."

"You mean you sincerely want to marry her?"

"Come on, Walker. You've known me a long time. I don't go around proposing to women out of motives of chivalry. I fully intend to marry her. But it may take a little time."

"It will take more than a little, let me warn you. Brandi's petrified of commitment. The only reason she's allowed me in her life is because she feels safe with me. I give her plenty of space, don't try to become a part of her daily existence."

"I love her, Tim."

Tim grinned. "I had a hunch that might be the case, particularly after I walked in on you the other morning."

"My overreaction was strictly due to a guilty conscience, believe me."

"Well, it sounds to me as though marriage might be the safest thing if you're going to continue sleeping with her every night."

"I haven't made love to her, Tim."

Tim leaned back and studied his friend in silence. "Why not?"

"For several reasons. One of the biggest is the fact that I didn't come prepared for such an eventuality and I have a hunch she isn't protected. I don't want to take a chance at this stage in our relationship that Brandi would feel forced into marriage with me due to an unplanned pregnancy."

"Good point."

"Well, I just wanted you to know I'm not totally without principles, old man."

"To be honest, I'd breathe a lot easier at night if I knew she was with you. I'm not sure what to do now. As soon as I get to Denver, they're going to be watching me, hoping I'll lead them to her."

"What about now? Do they know she's here?"

"No. That's why I was so surprised to hear the police had been here."

Greg threw up his hands. "Great. So now not only do we have to keep her hidden from the characters who've been chasing after her, but also from our own government officials."

"That's about the size of it."

"She's agreed to go back to Payton with me."

Tim leaned back. "That's a thought. Nobody would connect her with you."

"I don't care if they do. I still intend to marry her."

"Even after the list she gave you of all her undesirable traits?"

"Well, I'm not going to give her a list of mine, that's for sure. She can find them out on her own."

Tim grinned. "Oh, I don't know. You're not so bad. It's a shame you're not my type—I'd marry you myself."

"Has anyone ever told you what a rotten sense of humor you have, Tim?"

"It may have been mentioned once or twice. Why?"

"Never mind."

"When are you planning to leave?"

"I'd like to get on the road as soon as possible. We were waiting to hear from you before taking off." Greg glanced at his watch. "We wouldn't get too far before dark. Maybe we should wait until morning."

Tim stood. "That's up to you, but personally I feel that the sooner we get Brandi away from here, the better off she's going to be. Not too many people know about this place, but if someone was determined to find me, they could. I'd sleep better knowing she wasn't anywhere around me."

Greg stood, too. "Good point." He walked into the main room, and Tim followed. "I think I'll load up the car so Brandi can rest as long as possible."

"Has she already agreed to go with you?"

"Yes, if I don't discuss marriage with her."

Tim looked startled for a moment, then burst out laughing. "My only regret," he said when he paused for breath, "is that I won't be able to witness your courtship. Maybe you could videotape it for me."

Greg grinned. "Go to hell."

In a more sober tone, Tim replied, "No, thanks. I've already been there... and so have you." The two men looked wordlessly at each other, nodded and turned away.

When Greg went upstairs to awaken Brandi, he found her contentedly curled up under one of the heavy quilts.

"Brandi?" he said softly, sitting down beside her. She looked so peaceful, so innocent of the many undercurrents that were swirling around her. "Honey, I hate to wake you..." His voice trailed off. Leaning over, he braced his arms on either side of her and kissed her softly on the lips. Without opening her eyes, Brandi raised her arms and curled them around his neck, holding him close.

Once again, she'd been dreaming. This time, however, her dreams were far from nightmarish. She was with Greg. She knew she was safe... knew that she would always be safe... because of Greg. His kiss seemed so natural, and she pulled him closer to her, loving the feel of his body against hers.

Why had she fought her feelings for him? She loved him. She never wanted to lose him from her life. She couldn't lose him, not now. She needed him so much. She needed—

Her eyes flew open, and she realized that Greg was actually kissing her and that she was encouraging him. She stiffened, pulling away and staring up at him in alarm. What had she been thinking of? Of course she didn't need him. She didn't need anyone.

"I'm sorry to wake you," he said, "but Tim and I both feel we need to get you out of here. Are you still willing to go with me to Payton?"

She glanced toward the window. "Now?"

He nodded. "The sooner the better."

"Why?" She struggled to sit up, and he moved away from her. "What's happened?"

"Nothing new. This is just a preventive measure. There's no reason to take any chances when we don't have to."

Brandi threw back the covers and stood, then swayed, almost losing her balance. Greg reached out and braced her shoulder with his hand. "You okay?"

"I got up too quick, that's all." She started downstairs. "Is Tim still here?"

"Yes. We've been loading the car."

Brandi found that everything she'd managed to accumulate in the few days she'd been at the cabin was now packed in the car.

Tim grabbed her and held her close to him. "Take care of yourself, Mouse. I'll be in touch."

She hugged him back. "Then you think this is the best thing to do?"

"Yes." He leaned down and whispered, "I also think you should consider making an honest man out of this fellow. You've already ruined his reputation, staying with him like this. What are all of his neighbors going to think when he shows up in Payton with you as a houseguest?"

Brandi pulled away. "My God! I hadn't thought of that."

"I was only kidding."

"Maybe so, but you're right. I can't go over there and stay with Greg. Payton's a small town. What are the townspeople going to think?"

Tim grinned. "You know very well what they'll think, Mouse."

"I can't go."

"Yes, you can. But you might want to seriously consider his proposal."

"Don't be silly. He wasn't serious." She glanced around to make sure that Greg hadn't heard her. He was in the kitchen pulling out cans of drink and putting them into a Styrofoam carrying case.

"You think not? Greg doesn't joke around about things like that."

"But I can't marry him! I don't intend to marry anyone. You know that!"

"I know that has been your opinion of things for several years now, Mouse. I'd like to leave you with a thought—if you haven't changed your opinions in the past ten years, you might want to check your pulse. You may be dead."

"But, Tim, I'd make a lousy wife. I don't know the first thing about it."

"Funny you should say that. Greg feels his qualifications as a husband are equally nil. Personally, I think that's a great foundation. You don't have any preconceived notions to unlearn."

He gave her a brief hug and a kiss on the cheek. "Think about it, Mouse. Don't let your fear of the unknown stop you from fully enjoying all that life has to offer. Life is too short to deny yourself."

"Brandi, are you ready?" Greg called from the kitchen.

She looked up at Tim. "No," she whispered for his ears only. "I'm not. But I'm going anyway."

Tim grinned. "That's my girl. You can do it."

Brandi joined Greg in the kitchen. While she was pulling on her coat, the two men discussed the weather conditions and driving time, and Greg told Tim the approximate time he hoped to arrive home.

"Don't call me," Tim cautioned. "I'll call you when I have any news."

Greg nodded, understanding what Tim didn't want to put into words in front of Brandi—that his own employers would be monitoring his calls and looking for answers.

The car was running and warm inside when Brandi and Greg got in. Brandi glanced back at Tim, who stood on the deck and waved as they drove away. She didn't know what she would have done without Tim in her life. His support and encouragement carried a great deal of weight with her.

But could she take his advice? Glancing out of the corner of her eyes, Brandi took in the competent picture that Greg made driving down the narrow, winding road to the main highway.

She trusted this man with her life. Could she possibly learn to trust him with her heart?

Chapter Eight

"I think I'm going to stop at the next town, Brandi," Greg said several hours later.

Brandi glanced at her watch, surprised to see how long they had been on the road.

"I'm sorry. I should have offered to drive. I was so involved in our discussion I didn't realize the time."

During the hours on the road they had covered a multitude of subjects and had discovered how many times their views coincided. Greg had been greatly encouraged to find how similar their perspectives and values were, although he doubted that Brandi had given much thought to what was happening between them.

She had debated several times with considerable spirit while Greg had played devil's advocate. He'd enjoyed her keen insight and incisive mind as she'd made her points. Whether or not she realized it, Brandi could have put her logic and eloquence to good use in a courtroom.

"If we stop now we should get into Payton tomorrow afternoon, which will give you an opportunity to see it during the daylight."

Brandi suddenly remembered what they were doing. Greg was taking her to his home in a small town.

"How are you going to explain my presence in your home?" Brandi asked after a few moments of silence.

"I didn't intend to make explanations to anyone. Why do you ask?"

"Surely your reputation is important to you."

He grinned. "My reputation can only be enhanced by showing up with an attractive woman."

"You know what I mean. Perhaps I should stay in a motel or something."

"Nothing doing. You're going to stay with me, including tonight. I intend to register as Mr. and Mrs. Duncan. I don't want to take any chances with you."

"Surely that's not necessary."

"Tim and I feel it is. Since you've allowed us to help you, I think you should follow our advice."

He pulled into a driveway near the famous logo of a national motel chain. Driving up to the front door, he stopped and looked at her. "I'll be back in a few minutes."

"Are you certain you should leave me alone that long?" she asked, a little waspishly.

He leaned over and kissed her on the nose. "You're right. You do get a little cranky when you're tired. Don't worry. You'll be in bed within a half hour."

Brandi was still sputtering her response when he closed the door and went inside.

Cranky, indeed. I've been the soul of tact and diplomacy, allowing the two of them to play macho saviors.

Admit it, Brandi, you needed their help.

Maybe so, but he doesn't have to be so complacent about it.

Look, he didn't complain about your crashing his vacation, or the fact that you're now going to be his unexpected houseguest. So what's your complaint?

I don't know. I just don't like this feeling of not being in control of my life. I like to make my own decisions, do what I think best. I don't need a keeper.

Maybe not. But he certainly hasn't been overbearing or shown any dictatorial tendencies, now has he?

No. Not really. He's been very kind . . . and thoughtful . . . and caring.

Watch it. You might realize there's a great deal in the man to admire, which wouldn't do at all, now would it?

What do you mean by that crack?

Think about it.

"Oh-oh. The frown's increased even more since I left. Remind me never to keep you up past your bedtime again," Greg said, sliding under the steering wheel once again.

"I'm sorry. I was just thinking."

"In that case, spare me your thoughts. I'm not sure I could handle them this late at night."

Greg drove to the back of the motel, helped her out of the car and carried their bags inside through one of the doors. She followed him down the hallway. When he found the correct room number, he shifted the bags to one hand, inserted the key and opened the door. Then he stood back and waited for her to enter.

Brandi was surprised to find a spacious room with two queen-size beds. She walked over to the window and pulled back one of the drapes.

"I didn't ask for a room with a view. I didn't figure we'd spend much time admiring the scenery."

Brandi turned around and looked at him. He'd placed the bags on the floor and was over at the wall, adjusting the thermostat.

"I'll be a gentleman and let you have the shower first, unless you need help scrubbing your back." His gaze met hers, an expression of innocence on his face.

Brandi grabbed her bag and headed to the bathroom. "I think I can manage on my own, thank you."

"I was afraid of that," Greg said with a grin.

As soon as the bathroom door closed, Greg sat down on the side of the bed and sighed, his smile forgotten. He was trying his best not to think about the provocative situation they were in. Even though they had been alone at the cabin, this bedroom seemed to emphasize their present intimacy.

If Brandi had deliberately devised a way to torture him, she could not possibly have come up with a better method than this. However, he'd made his own decision. He had to know that she was safe. He'd rather be unable to sleep because she was only a few feet away from him than because he was concerned about her being alone.

When she came out of the bathroom, he almost groaned aloud. The soft scent she used seemed to waft around him, taunting and teasing him. He took a deep breath and stood. "Sleep well. We shouldn't be disturbed tonight."

She nodded and crossed over to the other bed, pulling back the covers without looking at him.

When she heard the door close behind him, Brandi sighed. Did Greg have any idea how difficult it was for her to continue to be this close to him night after night? She wasn't some saint without feelings. He had caused her to get in touch with emotions that she'd never known she had. Never before had she been tempted to make love.

The truth was that she knew she wanted to make love with Greg. What shocked her was the realization that she *wasn't* shocked at the thought.

She had a scary feeling that what she felt for Greg Duncan wasn't going to go away, at least not anytime soon. She kept getting sudden mental flashes of what their life together could have been like if she hadn't been so quick to turn down his proposal.

Would he want children? Brandi had never thought about having a child before, since she had never considered the possibility that she might decide to marry. Thinking about a child now seemed different, somehow. There was nothing abstract about thinking of having Greg's child—a blond-headed little girl with smoky gray eyes, or maybe a towheaded little boy with her dark blue eyes.

She shook her head, trying to dispel the images. What was the matter with her? Brandi was no longer certain that Greg had been serious, anyway. Hadn't he made a joke of his proposal with Tim? Surely he wouldn't have done that if he'd been serious.

The bathroom door opened, and she quickly closed her eyes. She'd left the bedroom lamp on so that he could find his way to his bed. Peeking beneath her lashes, Brandi discovered that Greg had tied one towel around his waist and was using another one to briskly dry his hair.

He had such a beautiful body. Her fingers itched with the longing to touch him. She must be losing her mind. How could she be wanting to touch and love this man after she'd made it clear to him that she didn't want any kind of permanent commitment with him?

The light went off, and she opened her eyes. She watched his shadowy figure crawl into bed and settle under a mound of covers.

"Good night, Greg," she whispered.

"Good night, love."

Brandi knew at that moment that there was nothing she would rather be than this man's love, if only she weren't too much of a coward to accept the challenge that he offered.

They were on their way early the next morning after having breakfast at the motel coffee shop. The weather had warmed considerably, and Brandi began to think about springtime and her plans for the craft shows.

Greg noted Brandi's absorption in her own thoughts, which suited him, since he had several things to think about. He wondered how long she would be staying with him.

He recalled that he had a trial coming up the week after next in St. Louis that he would have to prepare for.

Very seldom did he get involved in domestic-relations matters. In this case, the sister of the president of one of his corporate clients had come to him for help in getting a divorce. After hearing what she had been going through, he had decided that he could not turn her away. It was going to be a messy suit. The woman's husband was a powerful figure in the city and had strongly resisted the idea that his wife wanted a divorce. According to his wife, he had a history of being abusive to her and had a definite drinking problem. The man denied all his wife's accusations, insisting that she was hoping to blacken his reputation.

The case was going to take a great deal of preparation during the coming week, and Greg would have to go to St. Louis to try it the following week.

Would Brandi want to go with him or stay in Payton? He didn't like the idea of her staying alone, but he knew that she was chafing at the restrictions he wanted to place around her.

Greg recognized that he was at a definite disadvantage because he couldn't tell her all that Tim had related to him. As long as Tim didn't tell his colleagues

Brandi's name or where she was, no government agency people would be looking for her. But what if the men now searching for her—the military—continued their search? If those men had found her in southern Colorado, they might be able to find her in Missouri.

He smiled as he thought about kidnapping her and forcing her to marry him, surprised that he could be so cavalier about the matter. As a rule, he wasn't much for fantasies, but somehow he could see him whisking Brandi away to some forgotten island, coaxing her to come be his love and share with him all the treasures that life had to offer.

Greg never noticed that the divorce case looming on his calendar had been erased from his mind and pleasurable fantasies of Brandi had taken over.

When they pulled into Greg's driveway the next afternoon, Brandi could scarcely believe her eyes. Somehow she had thought that Greg either lived in a luxury condominium or a modern, high-tech type of home. What she saw instead was a large Victorian-style house, the last thing she would have expected to find.

"What a beautiful place," she said as he helped her out of the car.

He grinned. "I'm glad you approve."

"I wasn't expecting something this large."

"I have to admit that it was an impulse buy on my part. I happened to see the For Sale sign the first time I drove the streets of Payton, not long after I had decided to move my practice here. I looked at other

places, but kept returning to this house. There was
such a sense of peace and permanence, as though I
were a part of a family who had spent generations in
the town.''

They walked up the sidewalk, climbed the steps and
stood on the wide porch. A swing hung at the far end,
and a couple of chairs were grouped around a small
round table. It looked homey and very comfortable.

The house gave Brandi an insight into Greg's character that touched her very deeply. When he opened
the front door, Brandi was greeted by a wide staircase
that curved to the second floor.

''I feel as though I've gone back in time. This is so
beautiful. I love old homes. They have so much character.''

''Yes. I feel the same way.''

Brandi turned at the husky sound of his voice. The
afternoon sun shone through the doorway, placing a
soft glow around him and causing his light hair to
shine. The casual clothes he wore in no way detracted
from his appearance. Rather, they enhanced his rug-
ged good looks.

She turned away, trying to get control of her reactions. ''When do I get a tour?''

''Anytime you wish. I'll get our bags from the car.''

Brandi glanced at him. ''You do realize that I'm
going to have to get some more clothes. I can't keep
wearing these,'' she said, looking down at her heavy
woolen pants.

''There are several shops here in town, or you can
wait until next week and go with me to St. Louis.''

''I didn't know you were going.''

"No. I haven't mentioned it. I have a trial coming up."

"Of course. I forgot that you were a busy lawyer."

He could no longer resist the temptation. He walked over and put his arms around her. "Quite frankly, so did I. It's going to be rough getting up tomorrow and leaving you for the day."

"Greg—" She paused, uncertain of what to say. Whatever this was between them was growing stronger with every hour that passed. It scared her because she couldn't seem to hang on to any sort of control.

"I know," he said softly. "All of this is very strange to me, too. I've never felt like this about anyone. Not ever."

He leaned down and kissed her, loving the feel of her in his arms, enjoying the scent and taste of her, refusing to consider the possibility that she might not continue to be a part of his life.

"I didn't hear you come in, Mr. Duncan. I wasn't expecting you back until tonight. I told Harry this morning that—"

Brandi pulled away from Greg and peered around him. The woman who stood in the wide doorway of what appeared to be the dining room stood staring at her in shock.

"I—I'm sorry, Mr. Duncan. I thought you were alone, or I would never have—"

"That's all right, Mrs. Beasley. I'd like to introduce you to Brandi Martin. Brandi, Mrs. Beasley is kind enough to look after the place for me." He could hardly keep from laughing at the look of astonishment and curiosity on Sarah Beasley's face. "Everything looks fine, Mrs. Beasley. I really appreciate your keeping an eye on everything while I was gone.''

Sarah continued to stare at him, then realized what she was doing. Her face turned a splotchy red. ''Oh, that's all right. Glad to do it. I would have knocked if I'd known you were here. I just came in the back way, like I normally do. I wanted everything to be ready for you when you got in.''

Her eyes kept straying to Brandi. Then she'd force her gaze back to Greg. Brandi could tell that Sarah was not used to finding Greg standing in his hallway kissing anyone. She carefully avoided meeting Greg's eyes.

''Do you live in Payton, Miss Martin?'' Sarah asked.

''No. I'm just visiting.''

''Yes. She'll be staying here with me.''

If possible, Sarah's eyes widened even more than they had when she'd discovered Brandi's presence. Brandi almost felt sorry for the woman. She refused to make any explanations. If Greg felt it necessary, then he could make them.

He obviously didn't find it necessary, because he excused himself and went outside to get their luggage, leaving the two women standing there in the hallway.

''Well,'' Sarah said uncomfortably, ''It's a pleasure to meet you, Miss Martin. I'm sure I'll be seeing you again.''

''Probably,'' Brandi replied with a smile.

Sarah gave a quick nod and left the way she had come in.

When Greg returned to the house, Brandi met him at the door. "That poor woman. Couldn't you have said something to ease her curiosity?"

He laughed. "What? And attempt to curb her rampant imagination? I wouldn't think of being so cruel. I told you that this will do my reputation a world of good. The kind folk of Payton have been treating me like someone with an incurable disease ever since Penny and Brad were married. They're convinced I've been slowly pining away with a broken heart."

"I take it you don't date anyone from around here."

"No. I'm too busy to do much socializing, either here or in St. Louis."

"So my meeting you and having a chance to spend time with you was unusual."

"To be honest, I can't remember the last time I spent this much time away from work, so I suppose you're right."

"Are you going to tell Mrs. Beasley how we met?"

"Of course not. She'll have so much more fun speculating with all of her friends."

She shook her head. "You should be ashamed."

He took her by the hand and began to lead her up the stairway. "Perhaps. But I'm discovering that I rather enjoy doing the unexpected. I've lived by rules and regulations for so long that such an existence has become a habit. You showed up just in time to save me from my rut, you know. I'll be eternally grateful."

Brandi didn't know what to say. Greg paused on the landing and said, "Now you get the superdeluxe tour of my home. If you have any questions, please do not hesitate to interrupt my elaborate narrative. Refreshments will be served in the parlor directly after the tour.''

His heartwarming smile enveloped her in its glow. The man was rapidly becoming irresistible. Brandi could feel her resistance to him becoming weaker and weaker.

And she didn't even care.

Chapter Nine

A week later, Brandi sat before the mirror in the guest bedroom and carefully applied makeup. Greg would be home within the hour, and he was taking her out to dinner.

Not for the first time, Brandi wondered if what she had experienced this past week was anything like marriage. If so, she could well understand why so many people were drawn to the idea.

She had come to look forward to the time when Greg would arrive home. They had fallen into a pleasant routine of sharing their experiences of the day. Brandi discovered that her days took on new meaning when she was able to report them to another person in order to once again examine what she had learned that day, either about herself or about others.

The more she was around Greg, the more she was impressed by his keen intellect. He seemed to understand her when she sometimes had trouble finding the words to describe her feelings. It was as though he were in tune with her thought patterns and able to comprehend what she was thinking.

She was also impressed by his intuitive knowledge of her, and how she must feel, having been so abruptly uprooted from her own routine and environment. He had made several suggestions that indicated he had given considerable thought to how she might wish to spend her time during the day.

There was never a doubt that she played a very large role in his thoughts even when they were apart, and she was encouraged by that fact.

One major difference between the week she had just spent and one spent married was the fact that Brandi no longer shared Greg's bed. The guest room was comfortable and she could not complain, but Brandi had discovered that sleeping with Greg had become a very pleasant habit, one that she was having trouble breaking.

She knew that she was safe and that she had only to cry out for Greg to be there by her side, checking on her. However, he never gave her any indication that he wished the relationship to progress any farther.

Had he forgotten his proposal, or was it simply that she had convinced him it was unnecessary? During this time together, neither of them had brought up any subject that could not have been discussed at a public meeting.

What Brandi had discovered was that she missed the man she'd first met, the one she'd played with in the snow, the one who couldn't seem to resist holding her . . . kissing her . . . making love to her.

She also discovered that she missed him during the day while he was gone, although she had bought a pad and pencil and had kept herself busy sketching future designs for her marquetry work. Another rather startling discovery for Brandi was that when left with no guiding thought, her pencil invariably sketched Greg in various poses. Sometimes he looked intent and serious; at other times he was laughing, his eyes filled with mischief.

She felt as though her whole body had absorbed and memorized his impression.

During the past week she had gotten into the habit of having a meal prepared and waiting for him when he got home. At first he'd explained that she didn't need to do that, but when she had insisted on trying her newfound skills in the kitchen Greg had begun to tease her about her culinary creations, which bore little resemblance to the pictures in the cookbooks.

Brandi couldn't remember a time in her life when she had enjoyed life quite so much, when she had laughed so hard, when she had so wanted to throw herself into a man's arms and plead with him to love her.

She restrained herself, of course, but she was finding it more and more difficult. As much as he teased her, and as often as she saw the softened expression he sometimes wore when he looked at her, Greg treated her with an aloof courtesy that prevented her from attempting to draw closer to him.

Not that she blamed him. His life functioned very smoothly as it was. He put in long hours at the office, Mrs. Beasley came in on a regular basis to keep his home clean, and he either made his own meals or went out to eat. Whatever he'd had in mind when he'd proposed, he wasn't looking for a housekeeper.

Brandi knew that the longer she was around him the harder it would be to adjust to being alone once again. For the first time in her life she'd discovered a person she preferred being with to being alone. What a revelation that had been.

If only she would hear something from Tim. Greg had stressed that she was not to call Tim for any reason. Tim would be in touch as soon as he knew something definite.

Tonight she had decided to do everything in her power to show Greg how much she appreciated him, how much she wanted him, how much her thinking had changed since they had first met.

The week spent in Payton had been an eye-opener. Just as Greg had predicted, by the time she had decided to go shopping everyone in town had seemed to know that she was the young woman visiting Gregory Duncan.

Brandi found the townspeople friendly and filled with carefully disguised curiosity. After several conversations with various neighbors and shopkeepers, Brandi recognized that the townspeople were proud of the fact that Greg made his home in Payton. They respected him; some revered him. To Brandi's amusement, she discovered that they all felt it their duty to warn her not to take him for granted in any way and to appreciate the sterling qualities he possessed.

Perhaps it wasn't fair to accuse the friendly folk of Payton of matchmaking. In their minds, the fact that she was actually living in Greg's home made a romance a foregone conclusion.

Brandi smiled at her image in the mirror as she put the finishing touches on her makeup. Perhaps she could prove the townspeople right in one respect, anyway. At least she was going to do her very best to remind Greg that she was a desirable woman who found him fascinating.

The phone's sudden jangling near his elbow startled Greg out of his deep concentration on the deposition he was reading. He was preparing for the Sherman dissolution hearing, which was scheduled for Monday. Otherwise he wouldn't have spent all day Saturday at the office. But he'd had no choice.

The phone rang a second time before he grabbed it. His secretary had left at noon. It was past four now.

"Hello?"

"I figured I'd find you at the office on a Saturday afternoon, even with Brandi there to keep your attention off your law books."

"Tim! It's about time you called. It's been over a week. What's taking so long?"

"I was just behaving myself, being the loyal employee whose life—and phone calls—were all legitimate and aboveboard."

"I'm impressed. What's the word?"

"Officially, nothing ever happened. Unofficially, there are a bunch of red faces in Washington, and a colonel who is getting the tail-wrenching of his life."

"You mean the colonel was working on his own?"

"You got it. What I find a little amusing—or would if Brandi hadn't been seriously threatened—is the fact that the colonel is now claiming that the men in his charge overstepped *their* authority in pursuing and threatening a witness. He denies all knowledge of the attempts on her life and swears he never extended any such authority to his men."

Greg leaned back in his chair and smiled. "How interesting. Perhaps he has some idea how his superiors must feel about him at the moment."

"He probably hasn't given a thought to anything else. He's career military, and this may send him right out the door. He feels that what he was doing was justified and that eventually he will be proven right, that it's all been a misunderstanding."

Greg leaned back in his chair. "So where does that leave Brandi?"

"Now that the truth has come out, I admitted that I only heard about the incident through rumor. That I didn't know the person who had actually witnessed the incident."

"And they believed that?"

Tim laughed. "Of course they do," he said, his irony apparent. "They know me so well. They also know that I don't intend to tell them anything else, and we've all agreed to drop it."

"So Brandi's safe to return home."

"If you want her to go, yes."

"It isn't a case of what I want. I want Brandi to be happy, and I'm not at all sure I know how to accomplish that. She was right. I was trying to help her out of a tight situation. Now everything can return to normal."

"Maybe you can get Brandi to accept that sort of an explanation, pal, but don't try it on me."

Greg straightened in his chair, leaning his elbows on the desk in front of him. "All right, so I'm a coward. I know all about fighting to win a lawsuit. I don't know how to fight to win the woman I love."

"At least you admit that."

"Of course I do. How could anyone not love Brandi? She's so full of life, she's so unpredictable, she's so—"

"I know, I know. Then I suggest you put some of your most persuasive powers to work and win her, counselor."

Greg laughed. "I just might take your advice. I'm taking her out to dinner tonight. Do you think I should do the whole thing—candlelight dinner, romantic music and another proposal?"

"Don't ask me. That's not my line of work at all. I can save her from subversives, but not from romance."

"The only thing is, I've got a case in court in St. Louis on Monday that may take all of next week."

"So? Let her get used to seeing you in action. Take her with you."

"Are you crazy? She'll be bored out of her mind."

"I doubt that very much. I think you should give her the opportunity, anyway."

"I'll think about it."

"You do that. I've got to go. Keep in touch."

"You, too. Bye."

Greg replaced the phone slowly, his mind already reviewing all that Tim had told him.

The best news was that Brandi's life was no longer threatened. However, he'd still feel better if she agreed to marry him and move to Payton immediately. He didn't like the idea of her living all alone in such an isolated area.

He looked at the file in front of him. He needed to finish it before leaving today. Within minutes, his concentration was once again on the papers in front of him.

By the time he finished, he was determined to have his client gain her freedom from the man she'd married. She had tried several avenues to get help, but none of them had worked. The man had many problems, and it was obvious that he was refusing to face them. Instead, he was blaming everyone around him, most especially his wife.

Locking the door to his office, Greg strode to his car. He was looking forward to the evening with Brandi. Although he'd been concentrating on the case, another part of his mind had been mentally reviewing all that Tim had said.

The past week had been torture for Greg. As his guest Brandi deserved his respect. He hadn't wanted to take advantage of the situation. He hadn't wanted her to feel trapped, with no place to go. So he had given her plenty of space.

Each night he kissed her, then went to his own bed-room. He wasn't sure where he found the self-discipline to keep his hands off her. He loved her and he wanted her, and knowing she was asleep nearby was an agony that he wasn't sure he could handle much longer.

Tim's news changed things; Brandi now had a choice. She could go home, or she could stay with him, but this time the conditions would be different. He had honored her terms and treated her as a friend. Now he wanted to convince her that he wanted to add another dimension to their friendship.

When he got home, he let himself in quietly and went upstairs to shower and change. He was pleased at the way he'd managed his time since Brandi had been with him. No longer did he spend most of his waking hours at the office. Instead, he left by six each evening. If it hadn't been for this trial coming up, he wouldn't have worked today.

Greg had already started delegating some of the work in his St. Louis office by phone, knowing that he wanted to be spending more and more time in Pay-ton. With Brandi.

Now all he had to do was to convince her to stay.

When Greg went back downstairs, Brandi was waiting.

In the time that he'd known her, he'd only seen her dressed in casual clothes. The stunning beauty wait-ing for him near the fireplace of his large living room stunned him.

She wore a filmy red Grecian style dress, tied at the shoulders and crisscrossed over her breasts. The skirt was full and ended at her knees. Scarlet high-heeled sandals completed the look. The bright hue played up the creaminess of her complexion and the ebony sheen of her hair.

"You look gorgeous, Brandi," he said in a husky voice.

"So do you," she managed to reply.

And he did. The black suit he had chosen to wear that night was the perfect foil for his tall, wide-shouldered figure and his bright hair. He looked commanding, arrogant and utterly luscious. Brandi swallowed, trying to rid herself of the lump that had suddenly appeared in her throat. This was the man she intended to seduce, to reduce to quivering jelly? *Her* knees felt as though they were weakening.

"Are you ready to go?" he asked.

She nodded, unable to find her voice.

He held her new coat for her, approving of the weight and length for the climate. He had teased her all week about making a career out of shopping for a new wardrobe. He'd enjoyed her showing off her latest acquisitions each day, pleased as a child who'd just discovered a new game.

She'd explained that shopping *was* new to her, that she'd never particularly cared about clothes, preferring to be casually dressed to work at home.

"I don't believe I've seen this coat or dress before, have I?" he asked, rubbing his index finger against the downy softness of her cheek.

"No. I just bought them today."

"You look lovely in them."

She smiled up at him. "I'm glad you think so."

Brandi saw such a look of warmth and caring in Greg's eyes that from that moment on the evening seemed to possess a magical quality. He made her feel beautiful and cherished and wonderful. He made her feel witty and interesting and charming.

The restaurant contributed to the mood of the evening. The tables were secluded from each other in the darkened room. A candle on each table gave additional light that seemed to leave everyone else round them in shadowy darkness—distant and unimportant to this time in Greg and Brandi's life.

Except for the occasional visit of their waiter and the wine steward, they were left alone to enjoy each other.

The music that played softly in the background called to them, and after dinner they danced to several songs. It was the first time they had ever danced together.

"Brandi?"

"Hmmmm."

"I have some news for you," Greg said, slowly circling the dance floor.

"That's nice," she murmured, enjoying being so close to him after almost a week of no more than brief good-night kisses.

"Do you want to know what it is?"

"I suppose."

"Tim called today."

That got her attention. She raised her head from where she'd been resting it on his shoulder. "What did he say?"

"That everything's been cleared up. You can go home anytime you wish."

"What was it I saw?"

"I have no idea. I doubt that you'll ever know. It's just better to forget about it and go on with your life, with one suggested change."

"What's that?"

He gazed down at her with a smile and a very vulnerable expression. "That you spend your life with me. I don't want you to go back to Colorado. Stay here and marry me."

He'd really meant it. He did want to marry her. Those were the thoughts that circled in Brandi's head.

"Oh, Greg."

He was quiet for a moment as they continued to dance to the slow music. "Is that a yes or a no?"

"I don't know what to say."

"I like that better than a no. I'll wait."

"I love you more than I've ever loved anyone in my life. It's not that—"

She couldn't say any more. His arm had tightened around her waist. She thought she heard his murmur, "Thank God," but she wasn't certain.

"Let's get out of here."

Those words were distinct and understandable. He walked her back to the table, placed money on the tray and helped her with her coat, and then they left.

The night air was crisp and clear. Hundreds of stars lighted up the sky, and Brandi lifted her face. "What a beautiful night."

"You aren't going to get off that lightly. No changing the subject." After making sure she was safely inside the car, he closed the door and walked around to the driver's side. After closing the door, he reached for her the way a hungry man reaches for a long-awaited meal.

"I love you so much," he muttered, pulling her to him. His kiss reinforced his words.

Brandi felt as though the world had suddenly exploded into a kaleidoscope of color. This kiss was not the friendly kiss he had given her each night before leaving her for the night. This kiss made leaving a sacrilege. This kiss could go on for eternity with very little effort.

When Greg finally raised his head, his face was flushed and his hair had been disarranged by Brandi's fingers.

"Let's go home," he suggested quietly.

She nodded.

When they walked into the house, neither one of them spoke. Greg slipped her coat off and hung it in the hall closet. "Would you like some coffee or something?" he asked, like a gracious host.

Brandi shook her head.

Greg led her into the living room and guided her to the sofa. As soon as she was seated he sat down beside her, taking her hands in his. "Brandi, if you aren't willing to marry me, tell me now. I have to know— Did you mean what you said earlier?"

She nodded. "I think I must have fallen in love with you the first time you kissed me, in the snow, even if I didn't realize it at the time."

"Oh, Brandi," he whispered.

Brandi felt his arms enfold her, and she felt that she was surrounded by the wonderful haven of his love. His kiss was so tender it brought tears to her eyes. How could she possibly resist this kind and sensitive man? Buried deep inside him was that young child who had never experienced unconditional love. Brandi's heart seemed to expand with a surge of feeling for him.

When he finally pulled away from her, they were both trembling. Greg's voice broke when he started to speak. He cleared his throat and in a husky tone said, "I know I'm rushing you, but I'm so afraid of losing you. I don't want to take that chance."

"I don't feel rushed at all," she admitted with a smile.

"You have no idea how badly I want to make love to you, Brandi. But I want you to be mine when I do. Can you understand that? I want our first night together to be perfect. I want to know that you want and love me as much as I want and love you. I couldn't bear to make love to you, then lose you."

Brandi placed her hand along his jaw. "You aren't going to lose me, Greg. I promise."

"I've got to go to St. Louis for a trial next week. I know I'm rushing you, but would you go with me? We could have the judge marry us. I don't want to wait any longer than I have already."

Brandi was aware of the tight rein he was holding on his emotions. She knew this was important to Greg. She didn't need the public vows and the signed document. Her commitment had already been made to him.

However, she could better understand him since Tim had explained about his background. His first engagement also played an important role in how he felt now. He didn't want a long engagement, a large wedding, a reminder of his past.

Brandi knew that she loved him enough to agree to whatever he wanted.

"I'll marry you, Greg. Whenever and wherever you want."

Chapter Ten

Brandi stood in the judge's chambers and glanced around as though she were in a dream. She was becoming used to the sensation. In the past four days she had often felt as though she would wake up any minute and find herself at home, would discover that everything that had been happening to her was the result of her vivid imagination and too much rich food.

She looked across the room at the man she had met a few short weeks ago, the man she had just married. He was deep in discussion with the judge who had performed the ceremony.

Brandi focused her attention on the rings that nestled on the third finger of her left hand. The engagement ring had been placed there three days ago, the day they had arrived in St. Louis. Greg had wasted no time in starting the paperwork, arranging the blood tests and purchasing her rings.

The trial that they had come to St. Louis for had been postponed because the judge was in the midst of another trial that had run over from the week before. In fact, that trial was the topic of discussion between Greg and the judge at the moment.

Brandi almost laughed at the situation. Somehow Greg had managed to sandwich the wedding ceremony between his other appointments. How like him! If she hadn't loved him so much, she would have wanted to point out that his distracted interest in their union was not the most romantic attitude she could wish for in her groom.

But she did love him, and she wanted to be a part of his life, regardless of how much or how little of his time she shared. She knew he loved her. She also knew he had a well-organized, fully established life that had nothing to do with her. She couldn't expect him to change. She could only love him just the way he was.

Greg nodded at something the judge said, shook hands with him, then strode across the room to Brandi. He smiled as he took her arm and started toward the doorway. "Ready to go?" he asked, opening the door.

Brandi looked over her shoulder at the judge, who was already donning his robe to return to the courtroom. "Yes. Where are we going?"

He grinned. "You're asking a brand-new bridegroom where he's taking his bride? I thought I'd been too obvious to leave any doubt in your mind."

She could feel her face flush at the obvious look of desire in his face. "What about the trial?"

They came out of the courthouse and headed toward Greg's car. "The judge expects this one to be over this afternoon. Therefore ours will begin at nine in the morning."

"Don't you have to get ready for it?"

He helped her in the car. "Honey, that's all I've been doing since we got back from Colorado. I'm ready for the trial." He paused and touched her cheek lightly with his finger. "I'm also more than ready to get this marriage started."

Brandi watched as he walked around the car and got in. One thing she could say about Greg was that he had great powers of concentration. Now that he was concentrating on her, she felt that she was vibrating from the intensity of his attention.

They drove to the condominium where he stayed while in St. Louis. It was located high above the downtown area, with a view of the Mississippi River and St. Louis's famous arch.

Since they'd been in town, Greg had shown her the sights, and had taken her for a marvelous dinner at one of the restaurants located in the Union Station mall. She'd been fascinated by the artwork displayed there.

"Did you get in touch with Tim?" she asked in hopes of diffusing some of the tension that seemed to fill the car.

"I tried, but couldn't reach him."

"Then he doesn't know we're married?"

"He isn't going to be surprised. I told him when he called on Saturday that this was what I wanted."

She smiled. "And he didn't try to talk you out of it?"

"He knew better." Greg reached over and took her hand, rubbing his thumb across the rings he had placed there. "I've rushed you, haven't I?"

"I don't mind."

"But you deserved so much more—a big wedding, a white gown...."

"I'm not Penny, Greg. No matter how we would have planned it, you are the only man I've ever loved, ever wanted to marry."

He took her hand in his. "I didn't realize I was being so obvious."

"I'm sorry about the past, Greg, but I'm glad you weren't married when we met."

"So am I. It scares me to think about not having you as part of my life."

They pulled into the underground parking lot of his building, got out of the car and walked over to the elevator. Brandi glanced at her watch. "It's only two o'clock. It seems strange to have you here in the middle of the day. Are you sure there isn't something you're supposed to be doing at your office?"

He grinned. "Positive. Why do I get the feeling that you're trying to get rid of me?" They stepped into the elevator, and Greg punched the number to his floor.

She shook her head and watched the numbers of the floors they passed flash by. "I suppose I'm just nervous. I'm not really very experienced at this sort of thing."

"Neither am I. I've never been married before."

She shook her head. "I just don't want to disappoint you."

The doors opened slowly, and they stepped into the hallway. Greg already had his key out. They walked to the door in silence. After unlocking it, he motioned for her to precede him into the foyer.

They had been staying here for the last few nights. Once again, Brandi had been occupying the guest bedroom. Now she had no reason to continue to sleep alone. She turned to Greg.

"I'm being silly, I know."

"You're being adorable, as usual," he said, sliding his arms around her waist. "I apologize for my Neanderthal behavior, love. I'll admit it. All I could think about was being alone with you . . . without interruption. I didn't mean to frighten you."

Her arms crept around his neck. "I could never be frightened of you, Greg. I love you. I want to learn how to express that love. Show me how."

Never in his life had anyone looked at Greg with so much love and trust. He could feel a trembling deep within himself that he could only pray wouldn't reveal itself to her. Surely it wasn't traditionally the bridegroom who trembled.

He loved her so much. He wanted everything between them to be perfect from this day forward. Greg picked her up and carried her into his bedroom. At long last, she was where she belonged, where he had wanted her to be since the first day they had met.

Slowly he allowed her feet to touch the floor so that she was standing only a few inches from him. Then, for the first time since the wedding ceremony, Greg leaned down and kissed her.

Brandi felt as though she had been waiting for days for his kiss. Not since Saturday night had he kissed her with so much feeling, so much passion and fervor. Since coming to St. Louis he'd reverted to the chaste good-night kisses that had almost driven her out of her mind.

Now he showed no reserve whatsoever. The heat they were generating at the moment raised the temperature of the room several degrees. By the time he reluctantly raised his head, Brandi knew her knees were not going to hold her weight.

She sat down on the side of the bed and looked up at him helplessly. He knelt beside her.

"You okay?"

She nodded. His face was flushed, and his eyes glittered in the afternoon light. Without thinking, she brushed her fingers through his thick hair. Then she reached for his tie and began to loosen it.

He looked gorgeous today, the well-fitted suit contrasting beautifully with his shirt and tie. And yet all Brandi could think about at the moment was how good he looked without them. Following her instincts, she quickly unbuttoned his shirt so that she could touch his bare chest.

When her fingers touched him, she felt his reaction and her eyes met his.

Greg felt as though his heart were going to explode from its rapid beating. Brandi's touch seemed to bring his body to a quivering awareness. Quickly he shrugged out of his jacket and shirt, giving her more room to explore.

He found the zipper to her dress, slowly moving it from her neck, down her spine and to her hips. The dress fell away as though its presence were no longer necessary, the warm woolen material giving way to his masculine warmth.

In less than a minute he had Brandi totally disrobed and under the covers. After removing his shoes, socks and suit pants, Greg joined her.

"This does have a certain sense of familiarity to it, doesn't it?" he asked, pulling her into his arms.

He was right. Their bodies adjusted to each other as though from years of habit.

"Only this time we're not asleep," Brandi managed to say, a little breathlessly.

"Were you thinking about taking a nap?" he asked, tracing the gentle curves beneath his fingers.

"The thought never crossed my mind," she responded honestly.

"Good," he murmured with a great deal of satisfaction. Then there were no more words, unless their soft murmurs of pleasure could be considered as such.

Greg took his time experiencing the fantasies that had filled his head about Brandi since he'd first met her. He kissed and caressed each and every part of her body, coming to know her and enjoy her, revealing to her the wonderful secrets her body had harbored while she'd waited for the right man to come along, the man with the right touch and the right timing to share with her all that she needed to learn about her own sexuality.

By the time Greg had moved above her, Brandi had lost all of her self-consciousness. She had imitated his explorations, learning his body and its responses to her touch. Her body had taken over, eagerly awaiting each step on the journey to fulfillment.

Greg's patience with her was rewarded. As he took careful possession of her she relaxed and absorbed him, accepting the natural culmination of all that they felt and shared.

Brandi marveled in the sensations she continued to experience as Greg showed her how beautiful an experience their coming together could be. He made love to her gently, but with an intensity that left no doubt that she was more important to him than anyone or anything else in his life.

Brandi felt the tension continue to mount within her as she followed his lead. Never had she experienced anything like the wonderful sensations he was evoking. She felt as though the two of them had been lifted up high above the universe to experience all that was there for two lovers to enjoy.

She let out a soft cry as her body seemed to contract and then expand, and she felt as though she were melting and becoming a part of him. Her cry seemed to be a signal to Greg, for as she held him tightly, he groaned, making one last convulsive lunge before rolling to her side and collapsing against the pillow.

So that was what lovemaking was all about, Brandi thought with a small sigh of pleasure. The complete giving of oneself to another. That intimate sharing in which hearts, minds and bodies intermingled. How could she possibly have thought that she didn't need such a sharing in her life?

Within moments they were asleep.

Streams of sunlight shone through the drapes the next morning. One fell across Brandi's face, causing her to open her eyes.

For a moment she had no idea where she was. Then she became aware of the solid warmth at her back and across her waist. Greg.

Memories of the previous day came tumbling back into her mind with clarity. They had gotten married the day before. Since then, they had spent most of their time in bed.

She glanced at the clock. It was still early. Greg had to be in court that morning, but he had plenty of time. She smiled. He needed his rest. Although they had gotten up later in the afternoon to eat, their impromptu meal had been interrupted more than once by a kiss or a caress, and they had soon found themselves back in bed.

Brandi stretched, feeling a sense of well-being that she had never before experienced. Not even her imagination had prepared her for the wonderful sense of beauty that resulted when she willingly shared herself with the person she loved.

"Good morning."

His lips touched the nape of her neck, causing her to shiver.

She shifted so that she could see his face. "Yes, it is," she said with a shy smile.

"Are you happy?"

"Extremely."

"Not sorry that I rushed you into marrying me?"

"How could I possibly be sorry about that?" She kissed him lightly, enjoying the intimacy of holding him close without the urgency of lovemaking. "What more could I possibly want in life than this?"

He glanced at his watch. "This wasn't exactly what I had in mind for a honeymoon, however."

"It doesn't matter."

"Once this trial is over, I'll clear my calendar and we'll take off, go somewhere. Wherever you want."

"I need to go home, you know. I left in such a rush. There's so much to do…pack, talk to a realtor, get my car."

"We'll do all of that. We've got all the time in the world to take care of whatever needs to be done. We're together now. That's the important thing."

"Yes," she murmured, kissing him once again.

Greg deepened the kiss and began to show her the many pleasurable sensations that could occur during lovemaking, even when there was not the urgency that had once controlled them.

Hours later, Brandi sat in the unfamiliar atmosphere of the courtroom and looked around. This was part of Greg's world, a place where he felt at home and at ease. The hushed tones of the attorneys sitting at the tables in front of the judge's bench speaking to their clients were the only sounds she heard.

There were only a couple of people sitting in the spectators' seats. Brandi smiled. She'd seen too many movies and television shows, she guessed, in which the courtroom had been filled to overflowing. The reality was much less dramatic.

She sat quietly during the morning session, not understanding any of the various motions and exhibits offered. For some reason she had thought there would be a jury, but Greg had told her that very few divorce hearings, even contested ones, had a jury.

Brandi enjoyed watching Greg at work. Now that she had seen his informal side—and his passionate side—she could better appreciate the professional who was emerging before her. She'd seen glimpses of him since they had met, but now the full force of his personality and his quiet strength seemed to take over.

She was still having trouble remembering that this man, this marvelously skilled and analytical professional, was in love with her, was married to her, was her husband.

As the days went by, she was more and more enthralled, not only by the intricacies of the law but also by the man who took her home each evening and continued showing her all the many ways a man and woman could express their love for each other.

Even now she had trouble concentrating on the case he was trying. When she watched him move between the table where his client sat and the witness chair she was reminded of the sleek muscles that were hidden beneath the suit coat he wore. When he leaned over and picked up a document she could almost feel the strength of his arms as they pulled her hard against his long, lean body.

Brandi shook her head, embarrassed that her imagination could be so active. She found the case engrossing and was determined to pay attention, and she prayed that the outcome would be all that Greg wanted.

The tension in the courtroom had steadily increased as each day had passed. Brandi felt a real compassion for Greg's client. She had been married to her husband for almost twenty years. The evidence had shown that although he was a successful businessman, his behavior at home and in private had been shocking and atrocious.

Greg glanced around the courtroom, his eye catching Brandi sitting quietly in the rear. He was pleased with the progress of the trial. The thorough investigation and careful preparation he had done on the case had given him a decided edge, one he intended to use to his client's advantage. He had managed to introduce enough damaging evidence against Clyde Sherman, his client's husband, to cause the man to become obviously agitated.

Greg had hoped to show the judge the more unstable side of Sherman's nature by having the man lose some of his composure in court.

So far, his strategy appeared to be working. During Greg's cross-examination of Sherman, the man became increasingly flustered and irate. Although Greg carefully kept his questions low-key, the man continued to respond in a loud and insulting manner.

After a particularly abusive outburst on Sherman's part, the judge reprimanded him and suggested a recess until Sherman could gain some control of himself.

Greg turned and walked away from the witness stand. He glanced at his watch. It was a little after eleven, close enough to noon that they probably wouldn't reconvene until after lunch. He'd take Brandi over to the little café where he liked to eat during a trial. He was amazed that she had insisted on coming with him each day, but pleased, too. She was taking an active interest in his life, all phases of it. For some reason that surprised him. But then, so much about Brandi continued to surprise him.

Once more he glanced toward the rear of the courtroom. This time she smiled, and he returned her smile.

There was a commotion behind him, and he spun around. Sherman had left the stand, but not quietly. He was shouting obscenities and shaking his fist at Greg and at Greg's client, Carol Sherman. The bailiff was trying to quiet the man when a woman's scream rang out.

Carol Sherman shouted, "Oh, my God! He's got a gun!"

By the time Greg understood what she was screaming, he could see what the man held in his hand.

Everything seemed to move slow motion around him. Sound seemed to echo from all sides. Greg saw the man struggling with the bailiff and, for a brief moment, breaking free.

Clyde aimed the gun at the table where Greg and Carol Sherman stood and fired the pistol. Before Greg could register the events around him, he felt a heavy blow to his body, and at the same time he heard the exploding sound of the gunshot reverberating in the courtroom.

He felt no pain, just a sense of faint surprise before he lost consciousness.

Chapter Eleven

Everything happened so fast that Brandi didn't understand what was going on until she saw Greg double over and fall to the floor. Then the loud noise, the yells and the scuffling across the room began to make a horrible kind of sense.

Greg had been shot by his client's husband.

Brandi ran to the front of the courtroom, not even realizing that she was screaming Greg's name. One of the court officials caught her by the arm. "Don't crowd him, miss. We're sending for the paramedics. They should be here in a moment."

"But I've got to see him. He's got to be all right. I can't lose him now. Not now!"

She knew she wasn't making sense. Nothing in her world made sense at the moment. What was it about her that caused people to die? Was Greg going to die because he loved her? Was that why she had lost her father? And later her mother? Did she carry some sort of curse that caused the deaths of those she loved?

They wouldn't let her get near him, but one of Greg's associates, who had been sitting in on the proceedings, came over to her and guided her away when the ambulance attendants arrived.

"Mrs. Duncan? Let me drive you to the hospital. We can follow the ambulance."

She looked at him blankly.

"I'm Jack Stern, Mrs. Duncan. We met when Greg brought you to the office. Remember?"

She nodded uncertainly.

"Will you come with me?"

"I want to see Greg."

"I know you do. We'll get there as soon as we can, all right?"

The rest of the day was a blur to Brandi. People were talking all around her. Flashbulbs were going off everywhere. She vaguely remembered watching the traffic on the way to the hospital and hearing the soothing voice of Greg's associate talking to her, trying to calm her.

She felt calm. She felt numb—cut off from the world. It was her fault. She knew it was her fault. She had done this to him. She had known better. If she hadn't fallen in love with him, he would be safe.

Later she remembered them saying that he had been rushed into surgery to remove the bullet. A doctor had taken one look at her and treated her for shock. People kept asking her questions, but she didn't know how to respond. She didn't know what had happened.

When she tried to find out how badly Greg was hurt, she got only guarded replies.

Someone finally asked if she wanted anyone notified and she remembered Tim. Frantically she searched through her purse until she found his number.

She lost track of time. The doctor must have given her a sedative, because she woke up at one point and found herself lying in a quiet, shadowy room. She sat up, staring around wildly. "Greg? Where is Greg? Greg!"

A darker shadow rose from a chair beside her bed. "Try to stay calm, Mouse. I'm here."

"Tim? Oh, thank God you're here! Where is Greg? How is he? What is going on?"

"They've had Greg in surgery for several hours, love. You're going to have to be brave and hang in there."

"Oh, my God! He's going to die, isn't he? And it will all be my fault!"

Tim sat down on the bed beside her and held her close. "Your fault! What are you talking about?"

"I should never have married him. I should have known better. Don't you see? People around me die. I can't love anybody. Why didn't I remember that?"

"Brandi, get hold of yourself. You're not thinking rationally. You are not to blame for what happened today, do you hear me?" He stroked her hair. "It never occurred to anyone to search the man. So he walked right into the courtroom carrying a pistol."

"What did they do to him?"

"What they should have done before now—put him behind bars and ordered psychiatric testing. He's mad."

"That's what Greg thought, too. But he was always able to control himself around most people."

"Until now."

"But why did he shoot Greg?"

"Who knows? I personally think he was aiming for his wife. He was shouting at her, from what I can gather from the eyewitness accounts. I think Greg just happened to get in the way."

"How bad is he, Tim? Please tell me."

"I would, Mouse, if I could. I don't know anything except they've been in surgery for several hours."

"When did you get here?"

"A couple of hours ago. I chartered a jet as soon as I got the call."

She glanced around. "How long have I been in here?"

"I'm not sure. You were sound asleep when I arrived. The doctor admitted to giving you a fairly strong sedative. He said you were taking the shooting hard."

"Hard? Is that what I was doing? They wouldn't let me see him, they wouldn't tell me anything about him, I couldn't find out anything."

"I know, Mouse, I know. But I'm here now. I won't let them give you a bad time."

She felt herself relaxing against him. Thank God for Tim. What would she do without him?

They sat there quietly for a long time. Eventually Brandi stirred and said, "We've only been married a few days." She looked up at him. "Greg tried to let you know, Tim, but he couldn't reach you." She rested her head against him once again. "Neither of us wanted to wait."

Tim glanced down at her as she continued to lean against his chest. "And here I thought I was going to be part of the ceremony. Now I won't even get to be the maid of honor or the flower girl. I'm crushed."

"We'll do it again if you want. I'd be willing to do anything, if only he was going to be all right."

"Then do me a favor, will you?"

"What?"

"Stop blaming yourself because you lost your dad so young. He had a bad heart, Mouse. He knew that and he pushed himself anyway."

"But Mother always said he worked too hard to provide for us and that's what killed him."

"Brandi, your dad knew what he was doing and the chances he was taking. It was his choice. He did what he thought was best. Whether you or I agree with him is beside the point. Neither you nor your mother had anything to do with the choice he made. He loved you very much, and I know he would have hated to know that you have insisted on blaming yourself for his death all these years."

"I loved him so much, Tim." She began to cry.

"I know you did. It's all right to love him. It's even all right to miss him. But it isn't all right to limit your life because of something that happened in the past.

You couldn't change it then. You can't change it now.''

"And if I lose Greg, too?''

"You're brave enough and have courage enough to accept that loss without taking the blame for it, as well. Don't try to shoulder the problems of the world, Brandi. You can love Greg without feeling responsible for him. What happened today was a freakish, totally unpredictable accident. We can't change it. We can only deal with our reaction to what has happened.''

Tim was quiet for several minutes. "Greg has a real fighting spirit, Mouse. If there's any way he can, I know he'll pull through. He has so much to live for. I could see the change in him after he met you. You knocked him right off his feet, kid. He never knew what hit him. And I think you're the best thing that could ever have happened to him.''

"I'm scared, Tim.''

"So am I, Mouse. So am I. We've just got to leave it in God's hands now, and trust in the belief that He knows what He's doing.''

There was a tap on the door, and then it opened to reveal one of the nurses.

"Mrs. Duncan?''

"Yes.''

"Dr. Graham ordered a dinner tray for you. May I bring it in?''

Tim stood and answered for her. "That sounds like a great idea.''

Brandi shook her head. "Oh, I don't think so. The thought of food right now—''

"Is just what you need. We can't have you in one bed and Greg laid up in another, now can we?"

Before the nurse knew what had hit her, Tim had charmed an additional tray from her. He made their meal lighthearted, keeping Brandi's mind on a multitude of subjects until she had eaten everything that had been brought to her.

Then he excused himself and left the room, promising to be back in a few minutes.

Brandi acknowledged to herself that Tim had been right. She felt better now that she had finally eaten something. She got off the bed and searched for her shoes, then went into the adjoining bathroom.

When she came back, Tim was waiting for her.

"They have Greg in Recovery. There was extensive damage that needed repair, but they feel that they did what was necessary, and he held up very well during surgery."

"Oh, thank God." Brandi burst into tears of relief. "He's going to be all right, isn't he?"

"I hope so. They said that he'll be in Recovery until morning, and they won't allow any visitors until sometime tomorrow. So how about you and me breaking out of this joint, kid, and going somewhere to get some sleep?"

Brandi was torn. She wanted to be close just in case Greg should awaken and ask for her, but Tim was no doubt right. They wouldn't allow her to see him for several hours. Despite the sleep she had gotten earlier, she knew that she needed rest. Once Greg was conscious, she wanted to spend every minute with him. She needed to prepare herself for that.

"I've got a key to the condominium. That's where we've been staying this week. We can go there." She smiled at Tim. "You'll like his place. He has a beautiful view of the river."

Tim took her arm and guided her out into the hallway. "About all I'm going to do is sleep for the next several hours, Mouse. I don't know what it is about you, but whenever I'm around you I lose sleep."

She glanced up at him and smiled. "You know, Greg was making the very same complaint this morning, over breakfast."

Tim began to laugh at the color that rose in her cheeks as she spoke. "Oh, really?" He ruffled her hair. "No doubt that's been good for him."

Her thoughts returned to the present situation, and her color faded. "He's taught me so much about loving a person." Her eyes filled with tears as they stepped into the elevator. "I can't lose him now. Not now, when I've finally found him."

Tim squeezed her hand. "Greg's not going to let anything happen to him, not if he can help it. He'll make it. Just wait and see."

Greg wasn't sure where he was. He seemed to be surrounded by a swirling gray mist. He couldn't remember why he was there. The mist seemed lighter in one direction, and he began to move toward the light.

He felt strange. Something was different, but he couldn't quite put a finger on what it was. He felt lighter, somehow, as though his body were buoyant.

Then the cloudy mist seemed to dissipate and he found himself standing in the strangest room he'd ever seen. The entire room—walls, floor and ceiling—appeared to be made up of Plexiglas. He looked down at his feet, and he could see right through the floor. The room appeared to be suspended in air. Everywhere he looked was the vast expanse of stars and the total blackness of space.

Then he saw a large round table in the center of the room. As he continued to look, a group of people appeared around the table. They glowed as though they were individually illuminated. Greg stared, trying to see their faces, but the light they projected was too bright.

"Where am I?" he asked faintly, *"And who are you?"*

One of the figures beckoned to him and said, *"Join us. It is time that you meet with the council."*

"What council? What are you talking about?"

"We are a part of your guidance group, Gregory Duncan. We have worked with you and have been with you since you were born."

"I don't understand."

"Yes, we know. Your conscious mind is unaware of our existence. It is only at night—through your dreams—that we are able to communicate with you."

"Is that what this is? A dream?"

"If you wish to view it as such. We need to confer with you to see if you are prepared to get on with your mission in life."

"My mission? I don't know what you mean."

"You have a specific lesson that you chose to work on during your lifetime, Gregory Duncan, but you have lost sight of what you wished to learn. You have

been busy working in your profession and neglecting other parts of your life.''

''I don't understand.''

''It is oftentimes easier to hide behind the duties and responsibilities of one's job rather than face the unpleasantness of growth.''

''What do you mean?''

''You have been generous with your time and your money, Gregory Duncan. It is time for you to learn to give of yourself. You talk of commitment, but you have not understood the meaning of the word. You must be willing to open up, to become vulnerable, to allow others access to your innermost feelings. You must learn to share those feelings. There is much to be done in this area.''

''I realize that. I never understood that before. Not until I met Brandi.''

''This is true. That is why we sent Brandi to you. It was time for each of you to get on with your lives, to join together and establish the family you both have secretly yearned for. It is time.''

''You mean meeting Brandi was no accident?''

''There are never any accidents, Gregory Duncan. Not even this latest one, you see. You had already grown accustomed to the idea that Brandi would fit into your life-style and that you would continue living as before. We could not have this. We understand the way your mind works, you see. Once Brandi agreed to stay with you permanently, you were already forgetting the things you had decided in Colorado to change about your life-style. This was a

reminder for you to think about these things and never to forget them.''

''What are you talking about? What has happened?''

''Don't you remember?''

''Remember what? What am I doing here?''

''You were shot, Gregory Duncan. You were shot while you were in the midst of a trial.''

"I was shot. . . ."

Brandi heard the murmured words, the first coherent thing she'd heard from Greg since she'd been there. Quickly coming to her feet, she leaned over and said, "I know, darling. But you're going to be fine. The doctors all say you're recovering beautifully—"

Her voice broke on the last words, and she hastily wiped away the film of moisture that clouded her sight.

Brandi had lost track of time since Greg's shooting. She had stayed at the hospital with him as much as the doctor and nurses would allow, waiting for him to regain consciousness. Tim had gotten an emergency call that demanded his return to Denver, but he had promised to keep in as close touch as possible.

"Brandi?" Greg's voice was so faint that she could scarcely hear him.

"Yes, darling?"

"Don't leave me."

"I would never do that, believe me."

"I love you."

"I love you, too."

"I really need you in my life."

Tears poured down her cheeks, but it didn't matter. Greg had still not opened his eyes. "I need you, too."

Slowly his eyes opened. He seemed to have trouble focusing on her face. He blinked several times.

"I was shot," he repeated in a wondering tone.

"Yes."

"I had no idea they would go to such lengths to get my attention."

"Who are *they*, darling? Your client's husband was the one who shot you."

"Never mind," he murmured. "It doesn't matter." He gently stroked her hand, which lay beside his on the bed. "It worked," he said with a rueful smile. "It worked."

Two weeks later Brandi arrived at Greg's hospital room, as soon as he was allowed visitors, just as she had done each day since he'd been admitted. This time, however, he was not in bed. Instead, she found him sitting in the chair by the window.

His color was so much better. He looked more like the man she had first met. She could barely speak past the lump in her throat at the sight of him.

"Greetings, counselor," she managed to say. "You look like you're ready to practice law. All you need is a desk in front of you." She leaned over and gave him a loving, lingering kiss.

When she drew away, he grinned and said, "It's a good thing I'm no longer hooked up to those machines that monitor my heartbeat. After a kiss like that the nurses would be racing in here to see what had created such a change in my pulse."

Brandi sat down in a nearby chair and smiled at him. "Has the doctor mentioned when you might be able to leave?"

"Not exactly. He suggested we see how I do for a couple of days of limited exercise. I can now walk up and down the hallway in addition to sitting here."

Brandi shook her head. "I can't believe how differently you have reacted to your hospital stay than either Tim or I predicted."

"What do you mean?"

"We were taking bets on how long it would be before you had your secretary bringing you files and taking your dictation. Tim said he knew you'd be giving the doctor fits, demanding to be allowed to return to work."

"And you said?"

"I wouldn't take his bet. Yet here you sit without a file in sight. I'm truly amazed."

"Well, to be honest, I have been doing some business this morning. My three partners came in at my request for a short meeting."

"Oh?"

"Yes. I wanted to tell them all that I'm resigning from the firm."

Brandi stared at him in astonishment. He sat there, looking relaxed and at ease, as though he hadn't just dropped a bombshell into the conversation.

"I don't understand. Is there something about your health you haven't told me?"

"Nope. The doctor assures me there should be no lingering aftereffects of my injury and surgery. I was really very lucky."

"Then why would you resign?"

"Well, an interesting thing happened to me while I was laid up here. I discovered that I wasn't indispensable. The world is perfectly capable of running along on its own without my help."

He took her hand and cradled it between his. "When I first moved to Payton I fully intended to relinquish my practice here in St. Louis and enjoy the laid-back life-style of a small-town lawyer." He looked out the window for a moment, then returned his gaze to her. "I suppose I enjoyed being in demand, having clients insist that I handle their cases, and I allowed my work load to continue, even though I was building a practice in Payton, as well."

Studying her hand as though searching for a message, he went on. "I've had time to ask myself, 'What is the point of all of this?' and I wasn't really sure of the answer. I have all the money I need, but somehow, in the making of it, I found it easy to always want more than I had, no matter what amount that was."

Brandi knelt beside him, but she didn't say anything.

"I suppose what I'm trying to say is that I want some things in my life that money can't buy—the sound of a small child's delighted giggle, an opportunity to walk along a sandy beach with you and watch the sunset. I've had time to do a great deal of uninterrupted thinking during these past few weeks. I've been reflecting back on my childhood and teen years."

Brandi could see the shadows in his eyes when he mentioned that time in his past, but she didn't interrupt him. She knew how painful that area of his life was, even though she had never discussed it with him. Perhaps it was time for him to face that pain.

"I was thinking about what a vulnerable time in a person's life his early years are, when the need for healthy regard for yourself and your talents can make a real difference in how you turn out as an adult." His gaze met hers. "I've decided that I'd like to do something, maybe spend some time with young teenagers who might need someone to talk to once in a while, someone who remembers what it feels like to be that age. Someone who understands."

"I think that sounds wonderful, Greg. I'm sure you'll find a way to get in touch with boys in that age group once you're spending all of your time in Payton."

"I hope so." He brushed his palm across her cheek. "I also want to spend the rest of my life with you. I want us to establish a family, a warm, loving family that will provide the strong foundation for any children we might someday have."

Tears sprang to Brandi's eyes. "I can think of nothing that would please me more."

"Then you want to have children?"

"Very much, as long as they're yours."

He smiled. "Almost losing my life gave me the opportunity to see how precious and largely unappreciated my life is. Each of us is given equal amounts of time to do with as we wish. I want to enjoy my time—with you, with my family, with others that I feel an affinity for." He smiled. "Does all of this sound as though I've lost touch with my sanity?"

She shook her head. "On the contrary. It sounds extremely sane and sensible to me. And wonderful. I'm so glad you want me to be a part of it."

"A part? You are the whole of it. I would never have understood any of this if you hadn't appeared in my life. I love you so much, Brandi. It scares me to think that we might have missed meeting each other."

Brandi leaned over and hugged him. "It was only a question of time, love. I don't know how we managed not to meet before now, but we would have found each other somehow, someway. You are the other half of me. Didn't you know?"

Greg kissed her and reluctantly pulled away. "I'll be glad when I can get out of here. I seemed to have been laid up during my honeymoon. When I thought about spending the time in bed, I didn't plan on being alone!"

"We might have a slight problem, love. Tim feels that we should have another ceremony."

"Why?"

"Well, it seems that Tim was incensed that we went through a ceremony without him. He said this was the only occasion he'd ever have the opportunity in some wedding not only to give the bride away but to be the best man, as well." She grinned. "He also said that you owed the town of Payton a splashy wedding, and he for one was going to insist that you pay up."

"And how do you feel about it?"

"I don't care, so long as I'm with you. I'd repeat my vows every day of my life if necessary."

"It would be nice to have a church wedding, don't you think?"

She smiled. "I'd like that."

"So once again, Tim gets his own way." Greg shook his head and began to laugh. A less likely-looking guardian angel he'd never seen, but he had a hunch that Tim had recently earned his wings.

Epilogue

"Daddy, Daddy, he's here!" Becky cried, racing into the house and letting the screen door slam behind her. "Uncle Tim's here!"

Greg had just walked into the kitchen to see if Brandi needed any help with the lemonade and cookies she was preparing for the boys who had been helping Greg in the woodworking shop.

They turned around and looked at their five-year-old daughter, whose flyaway hair was the same color as her father's.

Greg knelt beside his oldest daughter and drew her into his arms. "Well, honey, did you invite him in, or is he still standing out on the porch?"

Becky giggled. "No. I saw his car coming, so I came to tell you."

Greg stood and took Becky's hand. "How very wise of you. Why don't we go meet him?" He glanced over his shoulder at Brandi. "He made good time, didn't he?"

Brandi grinned. "I'm not surprised. He loves my chocolate-chip cookies. I bet he locked in on them from a hundred miles out of town." She finished removing the last batch of cookies from the oven and turned. "Come on, let's go say hello, okay?"

So when Tim stepped out of his late-model sports car, he saw Greg, Brandi and Becky waiting for him at the top of the steps.

"Uncle Tim!" Becky cried, and hurled herself into his arms.

"I can't believe it," he said, catching her and hugging her to his chest. "I think you must grow an inch a week and add a pound a month! Where's the baby girl I used to bounce on my knee?"

Becky chuckled. "I'm almost ready for school now, Uncle Tim. But you can bounce Cindy if you want. She likes it, too. And she isn't so heavy."

Tim grinned at Greg and Brandi, who waited patiently for him to join them on the porch.

"I see. How heavy is she?"

Becky shrugged. "I dunno. She's still little," she said, and she held out her hands to show him.

He put her down on the porch and took Brandi in his arms. "I'm sorry I couldn't get here sooner, Mouse. But it sounds like you handled everything just fine without me."

Brandi hugged him back. "I'm just glad you made it to see us, Tim. You're looking good."

Greg threw his arm around Tim's shoulders as soon as Tim released Brandi. "Whatever you've been doing certainly seems to agree with you. I've never seen you look so rested."

They all walked into the house and, by unspoken agreement, headed for the warm, country-style kitchen.

"I decided to learn from your example, counselor. After my last assignment I decided to take some time off and just rest." He slanted a glance at Brandi. "Of course, I didn't know that Mrs. Duncan was going to get in a hurry and have the latest edition early. I wanted to be around in case you needed help with the other two." Sinking onto one of the kitchen chairs, he asked, "By the way, where are the other two members of the family?"

"Derek's taking his nap," Becky told him. "He has to take a nap because he's only three. When he's big like me he won't have to."

"I see," Tim replied with a solemn nod.

"Cindy's asleep, too. She sleeps all of the time," Becky added.

"Don't we wish," Greg said with a laughing glance at Brandi. "I'm afraid that Miss Cindy has her days and nights turned around. After her two-o'clock feeding each morning she thinks it's her place to entertain her very sleepy parents."

Tim studied Greg for a moment, then grinned. "I don't know. Fatherhood certainly does something for you. You look ten years younger than you did ten years ago."

Greg laughed. "If anyone would have told me ten years ago that I'd have three preschoolers to keep me occupied at home I would have laughed in his face."

Brandi set glasses of lemonade in front of each of them and looked at Greg. "Why don't you have Tom and Larry join us?"

Tim's brow lifted. "Tom and Larry? How did you manage to produce two more that I didn't know about?"

"They aren't ours," Brandi explained. "Well, not full-time, anyway." She looked over at Greg.

"Tom and Larry belong to my gang here in town," Greg said with a smile.

"Your gang? Like in motorcycle?"

"We're not quite that mobile, but we have a club-house and a charter, sweatshirts and jackets with our emblem emblazoned on the back."

"Aren't you a little old for that sort of thing, Greg?" Tim asked quizzically.

"I guess not. You see, it was my idea, and I found some young teenagers who wanted to become a part of a group. They allow me to participate because I keep the adults off their backs. In other words, I'm their token adult." He rumpled Becky's already-tousled hair and said, "And Becky's our mascot."

Greg stood and added, "I don't think the guys will want to take the time to come in right now. They've got a woodworking project they're trying to finish before the craft show next week." He picked up the second pitcher of lemonade and a plate of cookies. "I'll deliver this and be back in a minute. I'm eager to catch up on all your news, Tim."

Becky followed her father out the door, carefully carrying two glasses to hold the lemonade for Tom and Larry. Tim looked around the kitchen with a sense of satisfaction, then smiled at Brandi.

"The place feels like home, doesn't it, Mouse?"

"It should, Tim. There's so much love in this place, I'm surprised the walls haven't burst their seams."

"I wasn't kidding earlier. Greg looks so much younger, I'm amazed."

"I know. Do you know how wonderful it is to see him so happy, so content with his life?"

"How's his law practice?"

"Busy, but he's hired two associates to help with the work load. He keeps very set hours. He has the other men do the legwork, the depositions and any investigative research that's necessary. Greg is doing more consultation work, outlining the areas that need to be dealt with and allowing the others to handle the time-consuming details."

"I don't have to ask if you're happy. You're positively glowing. I can't believe you had your third child just a few weeks ago."

She grinned. "I'm afraid I'm not glowing much in the middle of the night. I don't know what I'd do without Greg. He's so good about getting up and checking on Cindy. Once I've fed her and she's in the mood to visit, he lets me go back to sleep. He's such a loving father, Tim. It's beautiful to watch him."

"I know. There's very little resemblance to the cold and aloof man I met overseas all those years ago. Whatever the demons he was fighting, he's successfully overcome them."

Brandi heard a sound at the doorway and looked around to see Derek staring at her out of his wide silver-gray eyes.

"Where's Daddy?"

"He's out in the shop with Tom and Larry, darling. Would you like a cookie and some lemonade?"

Derek nodded and wandered into the room.

"Do you remember Uncle Tim?"

Derek's smile reminded Tim so much of Brandi's that a lump suddenly formed in his throat. He was looking at the same hair color and shape of eyes. Only the color of the eyes was different.

"Come here, sport," Tim offered, holding out his arms. Derek immediately clambered into his lap and settled there contentedly.

"You look rather natural with a child in your arms yourself, you know," Brandi pointed out with a mischievous grin.

Greg walked back into the house and paused in the doorway. Tim and Brandi had not seen him, so he had a chance to observe the scene without being noticed.

The love and affection between Tim and Brandi was apparent. Tim looked contented sitting there with Brandi's son on his lap. For a flickering of time, Greg was reminded of his fears from the past. He'd learned something very important: he didn't need to be concerned about the long-term relationship these two shared.

They had each come into his life and touched it in a very special, meaningful way. They had shown him what love was all about—how to share and become even more than who he had thought he was.

Greg remembered the years he had spent watching Brandi with their children, watching as her loving patience had spilled over to include him. They had both been so afraid at first, trying to create a marriage that would be long-lasting.

Tim had encouraged them every step of the way. And Brandi's belief in Greg when he had doubted himself at times had kept him going, even through the uncharted areas of sharing with her all that he was feeling—about himself as a man, as a father, as a guide to the young boys with whom he came into contact, as a person worthy of being loved.

Brandi had steadfastly reflected to him that he was indeed worthy.

She glanced up and saw him standing there. "Come on in, darling. We were just talking about you."

Greg forgot about the years he'd spent alone and allowed himself to rejoin their circle of love.

*   *   *   *   *

A Love Remembered

★

ANNETTE BROADRICK

To my one and only sister,
Derralee...
who insisted that I tell
Tim's story.

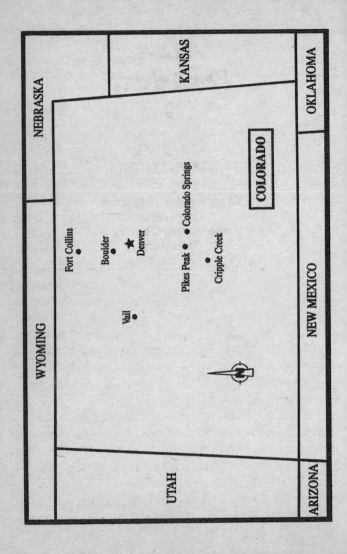

Chapter One

The first thing Tim Walker noticed when he woke up was the ferocious pounding in his head. It echoed like a steady drumbeat and created a pulsing pain that could not be ignored.

No hangover had ever felt so rough. He'd never been one to do much drinking, but he must have really tied one on this time.

He groaned, groping for his head in a useless attempt to stop the ceaseless drumbeat.

Tim received his first shock when a soft voice spoke from somewhere nearby. He froze, his hand halfway to his head.

"Are you in pain? Let me get your medication for you."

His eyes flew open. A light came on, and he used his hand to shield his eyes from the glare. He watched warily as a woman slipped from beside him in the bed and disappeared through a doorway nearby.

What the hell? he wondered, forcing his eyes to stay open despite the light. Who was she, and what was she doing in his bed?

Tim's second shock came when he discovered that he was not, in fact, in his room at all. He looked around, his sense of bewilderment growing. Was he dreaming? Or had something in the universe slipped a cog and had he somehow awakened in another time?

The room could have come from the nineteenth century or before. The bed in which he lay was a four-poster with a canopy. Draperies hung at each corner. Across the room was a massive fireplace, and grouped in front of it were two wing chairs and a table. Heavy drapes framed windows that were tall and narrow, ending only a few inches from the floor.

He closed his eyes deliberately, deciding that he was dreaming, even though he couldn't understand the significance of the dream.

Being single, he certainly wasn't used to waking up to find a woman in bed with him. At the moment he wasn't even dating anyone. Perhaps his lack of a love life had prompted him to dream about a woman, but why the room?

Slowly Tim opened his eyes. The room hadn't changed.

Where the hell was he?

He heard a sound and looked around. The woman was back.

''Here, these should help.'' Her voice was a rich contralto that caused a tingling in his spine as though she had run her fingers lightly across it.

She sat on the bed beside him and held out two white tablets and a glass filled with water. Now that the lamplight fell across her features he could see her more clearly.

He had never seen this woman before in his life. Without a doubt, he would have remembered.

Her silver-blond hair shone in the soft light, falling around her shoulders and down her back in a profusion of waves. Green eyes, slightly tilted like a cat's, stared at him from behind a fringe of impossibly long dark lashes, their color a stark contrast to her hair.

High cheekbones created a classically shaped face, and yet it was her mouth that drew his attention. Her upper lip curved enticingly above a full lower lip that gave her mouth a slightly pouty look.

His gaze slowly lowered to take in the powder-blue silk and lace of her gown, lingering at the V between her breasts and finally coming to a stop at her hands, which held the glass and pills.

Tim stared at the pills with suspicion. ''What are they?''

Her brows lifted slightly. ''The pain medication Dr. Madison prescribed. Don't you remember?''

Of course he didn't remember, damn it! He didn't remember much of anything at the moment, except the pain in his head. Tim decided that he wasn't going to admit his memory lapse. Not at the moment, at least. No doubt it was temporary, and he'd wake up in the morning and they would laugh about it.

He hoped.

At the moment he didn't really care about much of anything. The pain seemed to be intensifying, and his head felt as though it was going to explode momentarily.

He held out his hand, and she dropped the tablets into his palm. Quickly tossing them into his mouth, he drank the water and slowly returned his head to the pillow, laying his arm across his eyes to shade them.

"Thanks," he muttered.

"You're welcome." Her voice held a faint trace of amusement, as though their formality in the middle of the night and in such an intimate situation teased her sense of humor.

If his head wasn't pounding so, no doubt he could better enjoy the joke. At the moment, Tim found nothing amusing.

He heard the small click of the light switch and allowed his arm to fall away from his head. Inky darkness greeted him. The mattress shifted, and he knew that the unknown woman was once again sharing his bed.

Tim continued to lie there staring into the darkness as he waited for relief from the pain. He let his mind wander in hopes of finding a stray answer or two to the situation. He didn't know where he was or why, nor did he know the lady who so calmly and intimately shared his bed.

What did he know?

His name was Timothy Joseph Walker. He lived in Denver, Colorado, and worked wherever he happened to be sent.

His work for the government was never defined. His name was not on any payroll, nor was his job description printed in any manual. Only a handful of people knew who he was and what he did. He thought of himself as a person who gathered information and at times utilized his negotiating skills.

Tim knew that he was good at what he did. He also knew that he was tired of his life-style, the lack of permanence and the danger inherent in what he did.

What was his last memory?

His mind seemed to blank out at the question.

He could come up with no explanation for what he was doing in a strange bedroom nursing a violent headache with a beautiful woman he'd never seen before playing nurturing angel. Whimsically he wondered if he had offered his headache as an excuse to the woman earlier in the evening.

Waking up in a stranger's bedroom was not typical behavior for him. So what was going on?

The pounding in his head began to ease, and he took a deep breath, allowing the air in his lungs to escape in a soft sigh.

The woman spoke in her soft, husky voice. "Is the pain easing any?"

She must be tuned to every sound he made, he decided with a sense of strain. "Some."

"You'll probably feel much better by tomorrow. I hope the doctor knew what he was talking about when he called your concussion a mild one."

Cloudlike fog seemed to roll through his head, causing him to drift away from the sound of her voice. He could smell the light floral perfume she wore.

Searching through the whirling fog within his head, he finally found words to respond.

"I appreciate your concern."

Her hand brushed his shoulder, then slid along his cheekbone. Once again he heard the slight sound of amusement in her voice. "Try to rest," she whispered.

He smiled, warmed by her touch. His last waking thought was to reflect that if this was a dream he certainly had great taste in fantasy women!

The next time Tim awakened, sunlight poured through the windows across the room. He blinked from the light and took careful inventory of the pain in his head before he did something foolish—like moving. He noted that the pain had lost some of its urgency but he was fairly certain that he would be well advised not to leap out of bed and start touching his toes.

Shifting slowly, he rolled onto his back and found himself staring into the top of the canopied bed. He hadn't dreamed the place after all.

Now that his head was clearer, Tim tried to search for answers. What had the woman said last night? Something about a concussion. Was that why he couldn't remember anything?

What could have happened to him?

He felt the bed shift, and he turned his head faster than he wished he had. Forcing himself to move more cautiously, Tim came up on his elbow and stared at the woman who slept beside him, curled up on her side, facing him.

Her long hair was draped across her shoulders and curled around her hand, which rested on the pillow. Her dark lashes brushed against softly tinted cheeks that looked like satin. The covers rested around her hips, showing him the curving line from her shoulders down to a narrow waist and widening slightly down to the covers.

Tim decided that he must have awakened in the middle of a fairy tale. He had found Sleeping Beauty.

He watched with a great deal of interest as she stirred once again, realizing that she must have moved earlier thereby awakening him. She rolled onto her back, her eyelids slowly opening to reveal her sleepy green gaze.

She blinked uncertainly when their eyes met.

Tim could feel himself responding to her deliciously disheveled appearance. He became aware of the heavy beat of his heart as his blood began to surge throughout his body.

"I must have done something right in my life," he mused aloud, "to be rewarded in such a manner. I just wish I knew what it was, and I would concentrate on continuing to do it."

"What are you talking about?" she managed to say, despite a rather delicate—almost kittenlike—yawn.

"Who are you and what are you doing in my bed?" was his warm response.

Her startled reaction removed much of the sultry, sleepy look about her eyes. They rounded in surprise.

"You don't know?"

He shook his head. "Nope. I haven't a clue."

She raised her head slightly, staring into his eyes intently. "Oh, no." She closed her eyes and shook her head, a rather pained expression on her face.

"Not that I'm complaining, you understand." He immediately sought to reassure her. "I feel honored. More than honored, actually. I feel—"

"Never mind what you feel, Tim," she interrupted, her eyes scanning his taut body and heated gaze. "I'm afraid you're getting the wrong idea."

He glanced around the room as though searching for some explanation from the drapes or furniture, then looked at her with a grin. "How could I possibly misunderstand? What is there to misunderstand? You are here. I am here. You are a beautiful woman. I am very appreciative of all your charms. In fact, I'm—"

She sat up, inching away from him. "Yes, I'm very aware of what you are. You are concussed. You're not yourself." She imitated his all-encompassing glance around the room and added, almost to herself, "And I'm in trouble."

He reached out and cupped her bare shoulder soothingly. "Not at all. I'm perfectly harmless, you know. I wouldn't take advantage of you, not unless you encouraged me, of course." He peered at her hopefully. "You *are* encouraging me, aren't you?"

Despite her obvious effort to control it, she laughed. "If I didn't know better, I'd swear you were drunk," she admitted ruefully.

"Drunk on your charms," he agreed with a grin.

"What is my name?" she asked in a stern voice.

Tim blinked. He thought for a moment, then shrugged. "What's in a name, after all? A rose by any other name would still smell as sweet."

She touched her forehead lightly with the tips of her fingers where a slight frown was forming. "Isn't it a little early in the day for quoting poetry?"

Tim glanced at her in surprise. "Is that what I'm doing? You mean that wasn't original?"

She shook her head.

"But it was sincere," he pointed out.

"Do you remember anything?" She could not quite hide the concern in her voice.

"About what?" A reasonable enough request, he thought, for clarification this early in the day.

"Do you know who you are?"

"Of course I do."

"Tell me."

He looked at her suspiciously. "You mean you don't know? Are you in the habit of sleeping with strange men? I should warn you that such a habit could be quite lethal."

"Of course I know who you are! Don't be ridiculous. You're the one that received the blow to the head!" She pushed her hair over her shoulder in exasperation and glared at him.

One long strand of hair continued to lie across the upper curve of her breast. With delicate precision Tim lifted the curl with his index finger and carefully moved his hand until the curl slid behind her shoulder. He glanced at her and smiled, feeling pleased with his helpful assistance.

She sighed and looked away from him.

He studied her profile, intrigued with the view of her small, patrician nose and the way her short upper lip revealed the pouting curve of her lower one. There was a great deal of determination exhibited in the lift of her small chin. He found himself itching to trace the line of her jaw, the slender arch of her neck, the slope of her shoulders, the—

"Tim Walker," he finally said out loud in an effort to distract his thoughts.

She looked around at him, her eyes registering her relief. "Oh, thank God!"

"For what?"

"You remember something."

He shrugged modestly.

"Do you know where you are?"

He smiled. "In bed with you," he pointed out. "I would just like to add that I can think of nowhere else I would prefer to be at the moment. Now, then," he went on, slipping his arm around her and tugging her toward him, "if that's all your questions, we can—"

He had caught her off balance, and she fell across him, causing him to land flat on his back once more. He winced and absently rubbed his head. Obviously he wasn't in as good shape as he could hope to be given the circumstances.

She pushed against his shoulders a little more forcefully than he considered necessary and drew away from him.

"Do you always come across so aggressively to women whose names you don't even know?" she asked sweetly.

His last move definitely had been a mistake. The sleeping drummers in his head had come awake with a vengeance, and the cadence of their beat pounded rhythmically along the lining of his skull.

"Only when I find them in my bed," he managed to reply, wishing she would lower her voice. He closed his eyes.

She was silent as though aware of his unvoiced wish.

Tim wished to hell he knew what was going on. Whatever had happened to him had certainly managed to incapacitate him on several levels, only one of which had to do with his memory.

"So who are you?" he finally repeated after the silence had stretched between them for several minutes.

"My name is Elisabeth Barringer—"

"Barringer?" He opened his eyes in surprise. "Are you any kin to Charles Winston Barringer?"

Her eyebrows lifted slightly. "So. At least you remember my grandfather." She nodded, looking almost relieved.

Tim felt anything but relieved. "I just spent the night with Charlie's granddaughter? Dear God, he's going to kill me." *If my head doesn't explode and wipe me out first,* he added silently.

As though she were talking to a child, Tim decided resentfully, Elisabeth continued. "What do you remember about my grandfather?"

Tim forced himself to concentrate, willing the pain to subside. "I met Charlie several years ago, when he was still in Washington, D.C. We became friends. After he retired we stayed in touch. We both had homes in Colorado . . . we had several things in common...." Tim opened his eyes. "I don't remember his ever mentioning having a granddaughter."

"Was there any reason he should?"

Tim considered the question for a few minutes, feeling as though his brain was made up of several cogs of machinery that had been drenched in molasses and refused to move with any degree of briskness.

"No," he finally admitted. "I suppose not."

"Do you remember my grandfather's letter?"

Letter? Tim tried to think. He remembered the pile of mail that generally awaited him at the post office when he returned home after weeks away. What could he recall? A letter from Charlie? When? About what?

In disgust he shook his head, then wished he hadn't. He groaned.

"Your head is bothering you, isn't it?"

He opened his eyes, absently noting that the light seemed to create even more pain. He squinted, looking at her. "You must be psychic."

She rolled her eyes. "And you are definitely being sarcastic."

Elisabeth tossed the covers back and climbed out of bed. In the daylight Tim could see that the bed was on some sort of platform. What the hell? Did Charlie treat his granddaughter like some damned princess? What was Charlie going to do when he discovered that the princess hadn't slept alone? It was one thing to find her sleeping. It was another to be spending the night sleeping beside her.

Maybe Charlie would listen to reason. Tim would explain about his hangover—no, she had called it a concussion. Even better. A concussion was not something one did to oneself, after all. He was concussed. He wasn't of sound mind. He'd be honest and explain that he didn't know how the hell he'd wound up in Princess Elisabeth's bed but it was all very innocent. He was in no condition for it to be anything else but innocent.

Perhaps he needn't go quite *that* far in his explanation. Now that he knew who she was, Tim would certainly make sure that he kept his hands off her.

Charlie had written him a letter? Why? Tim couldn't remember the last time he had visited Cripple Creek. He'd been in the habit of dropping in on his old friend when he had a free moment, but there never seemed much spare time in Tim's life.

Was that where they were now? It made sense, even though he'd never been through all the rooms of the hundred-year-old mansion that was Charlie's pride and joy. Certainly the downstairs area had been furnished in keeping with its period. Or perhaps Elisabeth had chosen to decorate her room in such a manner. He had a sinking hunch that he was, in fact, in Elisabeth Barringer's bedroom.

"Here." Her voice, although as low and vibrant as ever, had a distinctly schoolmarmish tone. He forced his eyes open. Gone was the blue-gowned nymph he had seen earlier. In her place stood a young woman dressed in a lightweight pink sweater and well-worn jeans. A single thick braid was draped over one shoulder. She held out a glass to him, and two white tablets.

He had no trouble remembering her doing this sometime during the night. He looked at the tablets with suspicion.

"Go on, take them. They'll help your headache."

"They knock me out," he pointed out.

"Not really. What they do is ease the pain and you relax, which causes you to sleep better."

"From the looks of things, I seem to be the one who slept for a hundred years."

"What are you talking about?"

He forced himself to sit up. "I need to know what's going on. I need some answers."

"There's nothing you can do at the moment, anyway, Tim," she pointed out. "You should rest and give your head time to heal. Perhaps then you'll be able to think a little more clearly."

"That's easy for you to say. You're not the one with a memory problem."

"Yes, I know. At the moment I remember a great deal more than I wish I did!"

Reluctantly he reached out and took the tablets and the glass of water from her.

"What do you mean by that remark?"

She shook her head.

Tim knew that whether or not he liked the idea, he needed relief from the pain that seemed to be steadily growing in his head. Although he needed answers, at the moment he wouldn't be able to do much with them. After swallowing the tablets he drained the glass and handed it to her.

"Is your grandfather here?"

Her calm expression wavered as a flash of pain swept over her face. "No."

"Where is he?"

"He's in the hospital."

"My God! What's wrong with him?"

She shook her head, looking through the windows without speaking. She swallowed as though she found the simple action difficult. Tim caught a brief sign of moisture in the corner of her eye, but when she turned and faced him, her expression was calm once more.

"He's dying."

Chapter Two

"Dying? What happened?"

Elisabeth moved away from the side of the bed, starting down the steps of the platform. "His heart is tired."

Tim lowered himself to his pillow once again. Charlie Barringer dying? It didn't seem possible. Charlie had always appeared to be ageless, his strength and stamina such an integral part of him that Tim couldn't imagine Charlie ever succumbing to old age.

"Is that why he wrote me?"

Elisabeth continued across the room toward the door. "Among other things." She didn't sound pleased with whatever other things might have caused her grandfather to write.

"I need to see him," Tim muttered.

"You're in no shape to go anywhere," she replied in a reasonable tone of voice that Tim found more than a little irritating. He hated it when someone pointed out the obvious to him.

What wasn't obvious was why he was sleeping with her. What wasn't obvious was the reason Charlie had written to him. What wasn't obvious was how he'd come to be recovering from a concussion.

He noticed that she wasn't rushing to answer any of those questions.

Tim could feel the soothing relief from pain reaching into his head like cool fingers caressing the ache away. He had no choice but to allow the blissful fog of oblivion to overtake him one more time.

But he would have his answers. Oh, yes, indeed. He was used to being in control . . . of his life and his environment. He liked having his own way.

No doubt that was why he had never married. Marriage was made up of compromise. He'd been on his own for too many years. Besides, he had never met any woman who had tempted him to consider settling down . . . no one at all.

He carried the steady green-eyed gaze of the woman who had shared his bed into sleep with him.

From the position of the sun when he awakened, he knew several hours had passed. However, his head felt considerably more clear and Tim's first thought was of Charlie. He had to see him. Somehow he knew that Charlie was the key to at least some of the mystery that surrounded Tim at the moment.

With grim determination Tim crawled out of bed, descending the ridiculous steps and searching for the bathroom. After a long, hot shower he felt even better. The only thing that unnerved him was to find his shaving gear in the bathroom cabinet. He had certainly made himself at home, he decided, cringing at the thought. Whatever could he have been thinking of?

After shaving he returned to the bedroom, looking for his clothes. As soon as he opened the closet door he spotted one of his shirts hanging there. He shook his head and reached for it. A pair of his slacks hung nearby.

Glancing around, he spotted a chest of drawers and decided to see if he would find any of his socks and underwear. Why wasn't he more surprised to discover both in the second drawer?

Somehow he had a hunch that his moving in with Charlie's granddaughter had not been Charlie's idea, and Tim had trouble believing he, himself, would have suggested it.

That left the princess.

As soon as he was dressed Tim opened the door that led into the hallway. Spotting the top of the stairs, he headed toward them. By the time he was halfway down he saw a familiar face—Charlie's housekeeper.

"Hello, Mrs. Brodie." He paused at the bottom of the stairs.

The short, middle-aged woman had been crossing the wide foyer when he spoke, and she glanced up, obviously surprised at the unexpected voice.

"Mr. Walker! You shouldn't be out of bed!"

Wonderful. Did everyone know where he'd been sleeping?

"I'm feeling much better, actually. I was hoping I could find something to eat."

Her face lit up. "Now, that I can help you with. I have everything ready on a tray for you. If you'd like to follow me into the kitchen."

He dropped his arm around her shoulders and hugged her. "With your skill in the kitchen, my dear lady, I would follow you anywhere."

She laughed, her cheeks glowing a fiery hue.

"Where's Elisabeth?" he asked, watching her bustling around heating something in the microwave and pouring him a cup of coffee.

"She's at the hospital. She hoped to get back before you woke up."

"Is there any word on Charlie's condition?"

Mrs. Brodie motioned for him to have a seat, and he followed her silent instructions. "At the moment the doctors say he's holding his own." She shook her head. "There's just so little they can do for him."

"Elisabeth said it's his heart."

"Yes. It's just a question of time, I'm afraid."

"How long has he been in the hospital?"

"But don't you remember? You arrived a few days after he was admitted."

Tim shook his head. "I'm afraid not. That knock on the head seems to have completely wiped away my recent memories."

Her eyes rounded. "You don't say!"

"Yes. Unfortunately."

"Does Elisabeth know?"

"I suppose." He remembered their early morning discussion. "Yes, I'm sure she does."

"Oh, that's awful, really awful. Do you think the doctors will be able to do something for you?"

"I don't think anyone will be able to do anything about it. Head injuries are tricky. I've been around more of them than I would have liked. Fortunately, even those that have caused amnesia have generally not been permanent."

Tim was pleased to hear himself sound so casual, so unconcerned. He only wished he believed all that he was saying.

There was no guarantee that his memory would return. None whatsoever. Even if there was, he didn't want to sit around and wait for it to happen. Patience had never been one of his virtues. He wanted some answers. He wanted them now.

As soon as he finished eating, he announced, "I'm going in to town to see Charlie."

Mrs. Brodie had been busy chopping vegetables and preparing a roast for dinner. She glanced up at him in surprise. "Oh, but, Mr. Walker, do you think you should be doing so much?"

"It won't hurt me. I feel much better than I did when I first woke up this morning."

Tim left the kitchen and let himself out the front door, glad he had worn his sport jacket. Even in May, the late afternoon felt cool to him, and he knew the night would be even cooler.

Okay, so perhaps he was rushing things a little. He had to admit that he had felt considerably better at other times in his life than he did right then, but he wasn't going to curl up into a fetal position and suck his thumb. Maybe later, he decided with a grin, climbing into his car.

Strange that he couldn't remember driving here, although he'd visited Charlie at the house several times. He knew his way into town without thought. He watched for the sign along the highway that signaled the correct exit for the local hospital.

The last hospital he'd been in was in St. Louis when his friend Gregory Duncan had been recuperating from a gunshot wound. That had been several years ago, right after Greg and Brandi were married.

That was one relationship that gave Tim reason to believe that with some people, marriage was the best thing that could happen. He had known both of them for years before they had met each other. He felt a special closeness with each of them. As for their children, he couldn't feel closer to his own than he did to the Duncan tots.

He loved those kids, partly because he knew they were the closest he would ever come to having a family of his own. He had accepted that idea years ago. In his business there was no way a man could plan a future of any sort.

He followed the street signs to the hospital and pulled into the designated parking area. Tim wondered if Elisabeth would still be there or whether they had passed on the highway. He had no idea what sort of car she drove.

He knew nothing about her, but for some reason he couldn't keep his mind off her.

After stopping at the front desk to find out Charlie's room number, Tim followed the arrows until he saw the door, which was ajar. He pushed on it until he could step inside the room.

Elisabeth stood beside the hospital bed, her hand engulfed by the larger one of the man who was lying propped up in the bed. He was a big man, with a mane of white hair and bushy white brows that he could use to good advantage when he felt it necessary to intimidate someone. He turned his head at the sound of the door opening, a look of surprise on his face.

Tim felt the shock of seeing Charlie. His color was poor, his cheeks appeared sunken, but his eyes still glittered with sharp intelligence. No one had to tell Tim how Charlie was doing. Not now.

"What the hell are you doing here, boy? You're supposed to be in bed."

"Says who?" Tim's mild manner hid his concern.

"The doctors, that's who!" Although the delivery was in keeping with the man Tim knew, his voice was weak.

"Do you do everything the doctors tell you?" Tim asked with amused interest.

"We're not talking about me."

Tim glanced over at Elisabeth and noticed that she would not meet his eyes. He wondered why. Could it be that she was afraid he might tell Charlie where he had spent the night?

"Good evening, Elisabeth," he said, smiling politely.

She glanced at Charlie, then looked slightly past Tim.

"Good evening."

"Elisabeth tells me you're suffering from a memory lapse," Charlie said after a rather awkward silence.

Tim shrugged. "I'm afraid so."

"You don't have any idea what you're doing here in Cripple Creek, then, do you?"

"Not a clue. I was hoping you could fill me in. I have a hunch it has something to do with a letter you wrote."

"Ah. So you remember that."

Tim shook his head. "Elisabeth mentioned it. Unfortunately, I can't recall it at all."

"I see," the older man said, looking at the woman who still held his hand.

She met his gaze with a level one of her own, but Tim noticed that her chin was raised and her jaw was tense.

Charlie looked at Tim. "I suppose it's only natural that you might have some questions."

Elisabeth spoke up. "But you aren't the one to give him the answers, Granddad. You need your rest."

"Nonsense. I've got all of eternity waiting with nothing to do but rest. I'm not going to my grave without trying to take care of this situation."

Elisabeth looked at him. "If you would just follow the doctors' directions, you'd probably be able to go home in a few days."

"Like hell," the old man muttered.

"Elisabeth's right, Charlie. Why don't you try to rest? I can come back tomorrow. We'll visit then."

"You're here now. I may not be here tomorrow." Charlie patted Elisabeth's hand. "I want you to go home now, honey. You've been here all afternoon. Tim and I need to talk."

"But, Granddad—"

"Don't argue with me. You know it will just upset me."

She choked on a laugh. "You're disgraceful, you know that, don't you? Using your health as a weapon against me."

"Never against you, love. Just using whatever tools I have at my disposal to get my own way. What's wrong with that?"

Elisabeth shook her head, knowing she was defeated. She looked at Tim with a silent plea, meeting his gaze for the first time since he'd walked in.

Tim found himself reassuring her. "I'll only stay a few minutes."

She leaned over and kissed Charlie's cheek. "I love you, Granddad."

"I love you, too, darlin'. Never forget that. Everything I've done has always been with your best interests in mind."

"I know that. It's just that you and I have different ideas about what my best interests are."

"I know it's not going to be easy for you, girl. I wish I could be there to make it easier. I've done everything I can."

Elisabeth blinked away the moisture that seemed to fill her eyes. "Take care of yourself. I'll see you in the morning."

She turned away and walked out of the room without looking at Tim.

He watched the man on the bed carefully, wondering if he should, in fact, postpone their discussion.

"See this little box?" Charlie asked, pointing to what looked like a small tape recorder on his chest. "Know what it is?"

Tim shook his head.

"It's hooked up to the nurses' station down the hall. If my heart starts doing the two-step, or do-si-doin' around, they all come running—doctors, nurses—you never saw such a crowd."

"I'm sorry about your health, Charlie. You've had me convinced that nothing would ever stop you."

Charlie's smile was amused. "Yeah, well. Things happen. And life has to go on. I can't really complain. I've always enjoyed life. I've been determined to live it to the fullest. I don't have regrets. Just remember that, son." He paused, his gaze slowly taking in the room. "I insisted they leave me here because I know that my old ticker isn't going to work much longer. I didn't want Elisabeth wearing herself out looking after me."

"From what I've observed since I woke up this morning, she's been too busy looking after me."

Charlie grinned. "And you don't have any idea why. She's been mighty upset over that, let me tell you."

"Because I can't remember anything?"

"Partly. Partly because she didn't care about all the arrangements you and I have made these past few weeks. The only way I could get her to agree to them was to play on her sympathy."

There was so much said that Tim didn't understand, that he didn't know where to start. "I've been here weeks?"

"Something like a month, maybe."

It was worse than he thought. How could a whole month be missing from his life, possibly more? "You'd better fill me in, Charlie."

"Yes. It feels a little strange, going through all of it with you once more. It was tough enough the first time. Sometimes I wonder why God ever intended us to have family."

"You mean Elisabeth?"

"Hell, no, I don't mean Elisabeth. She's the only thing that's been worth anything to me. Has been for years."

"How come you never told me about her?"

Charlie sighed. "Don't really know, Tim. For one thing, she's only moved in with me these last couple of years, and you and I have been out of touch lately." He frowned. "Besides, I have to admit that I've been ashamed of the way she's been treated by all of us . . . like some orphaned stepchild."

Tim didn't want to interrupt Charlie, but he hated to see him wear himself out. And Tim needed some answers.

"Why did you write me, Charlie?"

The older man's eyes closed for a moment, as though gathering strength. "I wrote when I got the verdict about my heart. I managed to pull through a massive heart attack, but there's not much they can do for me without surgery. And I'm too old for surgery.

Hell, I'll be eighty-two if I live to see my next birthday.''

Tim shook his head. "I had no idea. I thought you were in your sixties."

"Humph. I've got grandsons pushing forty— Jason's thirty-eight and Marcus is a couple of years younger. Elisabeth's brothers," he muttered with evident distaste.

"She doesn't look that old."

"Of course she doesn't. She's not quite thirty. And she's nothing like them, thank God. Maybe that's because they have different mothers."

"I see."

"The hell you do. I know I'm not making much sense. My son, Chuck, never got around to divorcing his first wife before he moved in with Elisabeth's mother. He was killed overseas before he ever knew she was pregnant with Elisabeth. I never met Cathy. I have a feeling I would have enjoyed her. I always hoped that she made the last couple years of Chuck's life happy."

Tim had heard the story of Charlie's only child, had sat with him one night as he'd relived the loss of his son, but had never discussed the children the son had left behind.

"How did you find out about Elisabeth?"

"Her mother had left a letter with her lawyer, to be mailed to me only in the event something happened to her before Elisabeth was grown. So I didn't meet Elisabeth until she was a teenager. But I knew she was mine. There was no denying her. She's the feminine version of Chuck, all right, right down to her damned stubbornness and her willfulness.''

Tim grinned. "She couldn't have gotten any of that from you, of course."

"Damn right. I've still got all of mine."

The two men smiled at each other.

Charlie sighed. "I did what I could. She was so damned full of pride. Didn't want anyone's help. Was convinced she could do everything on her own. But she was only fourteen, just going into high school." He shook his head. "We went round and round. I wasn't about to be bested by some slip of a girl, though."

"I'm sure you weren't," Tim murmured.

"I adopted her, you see. I had the letter from her mother. I got a copy of her birth certificate. I insisted she come live with me."

"Did she?"

"Hell, no. We finally compromised. I convinced her the only way she could be truly independent in this world was to get the best education money could buy. And I had the money to pay for it. Finally we agreed that she would go back East to private schools, with her keeping a record of every damn dime I spent so she could pay me back." He chuckled. "Damn if she didn't do that very thing!"

Tim sat forward, startled. "How could she do that?"

"Out of sheer, unadulterated bullheadedness. She worked part time when she got a little older, and began to write on the side. Soon she started selling her work, and found a ready market."

"What does she write?"

"Damned if I know. She seldom shows me anything. I've seen a few articles in magazines, a couple of short stories."

"They must have paid well."

"Actually, I think she sold a book once, some historical journal or treatise. Hell, I don't know. But she managed to get a nice advance. Wouldn't keep a damned dime of it, of course. Wrote me out a check while she was still in school." He shook his head, his eyes lit with pride and admiration.

"You love her very much."

"Better than I've ever loved anyone. One of the reasons I was willing to spend so many years in Washington was so I could be close to her. Used to visit her all the time. Never missed a chance to see her." He closed his eyes. "Yes, sir. We've had some real good times together." His eyes opened. "And some real shouting matches. Lord, that woman's stubborn."

"So how did you get her to move to Colorado?"

"You know, that's a funny thing. She'd already told me that she was content living back East. Had no desire to come to these parts. I had to accept that. Had no choice. I flew East one time after I retired to visit with her. We'd gone out for dinner, like always. I guess I didn't have much to say. I'd really been missing her, even though it felt good to be home." He was quiet for several moments, as though reliving a memory. "Don't know what happened, really. I still feel foolish even thinking about it. I was sitting there listening to her, thinking about how beautiful she was, how proud of her I was, and damn if I didn't start leaking tears all over the place. Damned things kept trickling down my face like sweat on a hot summer day.''

He shook his head. ''Shocked the hell out of both of us, let me tell you. Elisabeth wanted to know what was wrong, and all I could say was, 'I miss you, girl. I miss you so much.'''

''Emotional blackmail,'' Tim said with a smile.

Charlie grinned. ''It worked. Damned if it didn't. She packed up and moved out here. Been with me ever since.''

''You're shameless, Charlie. Totally unscrupulous.''

''Well, I have to admit I like getting my own way,'' he pointed out in a modest tone of voice.

Tim began to laugh, then touched his head gingerly.

''Head still ache?''

''Some.'' He stood up. ''I need to go and you need to get some rest, Charlie.''

''Sit down, sit down. That's all I do is rest. Guess I got sidetracked a little, and there's still things you need to know.''

Reluctantly, Tim sank into the chair and folded his arms. He would keep the old man on track this time and try not to let him wander. Tim's head was beginning to gain his attention, and he knew he was far from recovered from the mysterious injury he'd received.

''Jason and Marcus are a couple of conniving jackals determined to get their hands on every bit of property they think should be theirs.''

''Such as your place in Colorado?''

"Everything. They resent Elisabeth's presence in my life. I had to do a great deal of cover-up work in order to convince them that their father was, in fact, married to her mother when I first found out about the alliance. Otherwise they would have made her life even more miserable."

"Does she know the truth?"

"Who knows? She's always insisted it never mattered to her one way or the other. She was still who she was and that had nothing to do with whether or not her parents were married."

"Good point."

"Anyway, Jason and Marcus inherited a great deal of money and property from Chuck and from their mother, Nancy, when she died a few years ago. Nancy's from an old, prestigious family with lots of clout in all the right circles. They fit right in." He muttered something under his breath about snobs.

"So you think they're going to give Elisabeth a bad time once you're gone?"

Charlie smiled a sharkish smile that reminded Tim of who he was talking to. "They're going to try." He shifted restlessly in the bed. "But I want her to have the homestead. It means something to her. It means nothing to them. Of course the only time I tried to broach the subject she refused to discuss it with me. Said she would just give it to Jason and Marcus if they wanted it, anyway."

"Will she?"

"Of course not. She loves this place. It's the only place she truly feels at home. She was raised on a ranch, loves horses, loves the outdoors. I've watched her blossom since she's been here."

"Being around you may have helped."

Charlie sobered. "I'd like to think so. She's given me so much. I'd like to think I've given some of that back."

Tim studied his friend for several moments in silence. "All right, Charlie, where do I come in with regard to all of this?"

When he saw the shark smile he knew he was in trouble.

"Well, at first I wasn't really sure. I wrote you because I needed to share with you some of my concerns about everything. I just needed to talk to somebody I could trust."

Tim felt a lump form in his throat and hoped he didn't disgrace himself with his own reaction to his friend's obvious sincerity.

"Thank you," Tim managed to say, "for your trust."

"Well, hell, man. If those big shots in the government trust you, why the hell shouldn't I?"

Tim smiled, shaking his head. There was only one Charlie Barringer. He was unique.

"I explained to you my concerns. At the moment Jason and Marcus are hovering like a pair of vultures, waiting to dive in and grab everything."

"Do they know you've left this property to Elisabeth?"

"Of course not."

"Are they going to contest the will?"

"They can damned well try, for all the good it'll do them. What's the point of having money if you can't pay for the best legal counsel around?"

"So there's really nothing you expect from me?" Tim felt as though a weight had been lifted from his shoulders at the thought.

"Well, at the time I wrote you the letter I was sort of hoping you'd be willing to look after Elisabeth, maybe. Give her somebody to lean on."

Tim smiled. "She doesn't appear to be a leaning kind of person."

"Don't let that damned pride of hers fool you. She's got a heart as big as the whole outdoors. Get past the prickly exterior and she's as soft and as sweet as a melting marshmallow."

Tim remembered the night before, waking up to find himself in her bed. My God, if Charlie had any idea that Tim had slept with Elisabeth, he'd permanently remove that portion of Tim's anatomy that could do possible injury to her. Tim broke out in a cold sweat at the thought.

"Maybe so, Charlie, but from everything I've observed since I woke up this morning, Elisabeth doesn't seem particularly enamored of me or my presence here."

"You don't understand, Tim. It came as quite a shock to Elisabeth to discover that you didn't recognize her."

"It was every bit as much a shock to me, let me tell you," Tim admitted.

"I'll never forget the day you first saw her," Charlie said in a reminiscent tone, as though it had been years ago rather than the few weeks that Tim knew it to be. "You seemed to almost be knocked to your knees when she walked in the door."

Tim nodded. "I can understand that. She's a beautiful woman."

"Yeah, she is, both inside and out. You looked like you were in shock. It was all I could do to keep from laughing."

Tim squirmed in his chair. "I'm glad I managed to keep you so amused."

"You had a lot of questions about her. Seemed to absorb every drop of information, much like you've done tonight, as a matter of fact."

Tim straightened. "Wait a minute, Charlie. I'm just trying to get to the bottom of all this, trying to find some explanations for what I'm doing here and why I can't remember anything."

Charlie sighed. "Well, as for the blow on your head, I'm afraid nobody seems to know much about that. You'd gone riding a few days ago, but you didn't bother telling anybody where you were going, not even Elisabeth." He grinned as though he found that amusing.

Why the hell would Charlie think Tim would tell Elisabeth if he decided to take a ride? Tim wondered.

"All I know is what I was told. Nobody wanted me upset, of course," Charlie's tone was filled with irony. "It seems your horse returned alone. Elisabeth had the presence of mind to get my hunting dogs out, gave them one of your shirts and went looking for you."

"Obviously they found me," Tim said stiffly, feeling like a fool not to remember any of this. It was as though he was listening to a story about someone else.

"Yes. You were still unconscious. No one knows what happened. There were trees in the area, and Elisabeth suggested you may have ridden under a limb and got knocked off."

Tim looked startled.

"I know," Charlie added with a grin. "I didn't bother to tell her that you've been riding since before she was born."

"Well, maybe not quite that long," Tim muttered.

"No, I decided that the less she had to worry about, the better." He frowned. "But I was really disappointed when she told me today that you had no memory of what could have happened."

"How long ago did this happen?"

"About three days ago."

"And I've been unconscious ever since? Why wasn't I taken to the hospital?"

"Oh, you regained consciousness enough to insist you were all right and didn't need to be hospitalized. Elisabeth agreed, although the doctor's been out to see you every day to make sure you were progressing normally. She wanted you there so she could look after you."

Elisabeth's concern puzzled him, unless it was because she understood the close friendship the two men shared. He would probably never understand her. As far as that went, there was no reason for him to try. Once he left here, there would be no reason for him to see her again. Tim was surprised to find the thought didn't particularly console him.

"You think I might have stumbled across something I wasn't supposed to?"

"There's that strong possibility."

"Hmm."

"Now you're beginning to see why I'm glad you decided to come see me in answer to my letter... then decided to stay."

Tim had been thinking about all they had discussed and looked up suddenly at Charlie's last remark. "Well, of course I'll stay for a while, Charlie. You know I wouldn't leave as long as you or Elisabeth might need me, although I don't see what I can do to help her. She may have to face some unpleasantness for a while after you're gone. But as far as I can see, that can't be helped."

"Yeah, that's the way I was looking at things when you first arrived, Tim. I couldn't see any way to protect Elisabeth from what the future might bring. That's why I was so damned pleased with your solution to the situation."

"My solution? What did I do?"

"Why, son, it's still hard for me to realize that you don't remember anything about it. You married her."

Chapter Three

Tim drove toward the Barringer homestead on auto-pilot, still in shock from Charlie's revelation. He was married? He couldn't seem to grasp all the implications.

Unfortunately, the more Charlie had revealed to Tim about his forgotten past, the more questions arose. Yet Tim knew he couldn't stay any longer. Elisabeth had been right to insist that Charlie rest. He didn't need to get excited.

As far as that was concerned, Tim hadn't needed it, either. His head pounded as though a fife and drum corps had taken over space inside his skull for interminable practice.

Elisabeth...my wife, he thought, tentatively returning to the subject of the shock he'd received. His mind kept returning to the idea much like a tongue returns to the site of a lost tooth... probing for pain or for sensation of some kind. At the moment all he could feel was bewilderment.

What the hell was he doing married? If Charlie was to be believed, it had been Tim's idea to marry. But then, could Charlie be believed? He was a devious old coot, as sly as they come. But Tim could think of no reason he would agree to such an arrangement, even if it had been Charlie's idea.

And what about Elisabeth? What were her thoughts on the subject? She could have told him this morning... could have explained. As a matter of fact, as soon as he got to Charlie's place he'd demand some—

Charlie's place: that sprawling countryside that was measured in miles rather than acres, that was already listed in many of the historical guidebooks of the area. Charlie's place until he died, whereupon it would become Elisabeth's property. Elisabeth, his wife.

What the hell had he gotten himself into? He was no rancher—or miner, either, come to that. Although he had his little ski cabin in southwest Colorado and a condo in Denver, Tim didn't consider himself a person with much in the way of property that needed managing. He was gone too much of the time. It was no accident that there was no one in his life who had any claims on him or his time. Greg and Brandi were the closest people to him, and they had learned years ago not to expect to hear from him regularly.

Greg and Brandi. What would they think of his sudden marriage? He could almost hear Greg laughing now. Brandi would probably be wanting to share recipes and baby clothes with Elisabeth.

His foot slipped off the accelerator at the sudden thought of baby clothes. He hadn't thought to ask Charlie how long he'd been married, but it couldn't have been more than a few weeks. Could it be possible that he might already be—

No. What was he thinking of? The marriage had to be a farce, something he and Elisabeth had agreed to do for Charlie's sake. Tim knew himself well enough to know that he would never—

Damn it! What a hell of a time to get a knock on his head and a memory lapse. Here he was in a personal crisis, not to mention the precarious state of Charlie's health. What a ridiculous time to lose track of a few rather vital weeks in his life.

By the time he turned in at the gate of the Barringer place, Tim was tired, hungry, in pain and more than a little angry that his mysterious dearly beloved had omitted to tell him a few basic facts earlier in the day.

She could have at least explained why they were sharing a bed. It might have eased his conscience somewhat when he'd had to face Charlie.

He followed the winding black-top road through the hills until the lights from the hulking mansion came into view. It was certainly ostentatious enough, Tim had to admit. He also knew that to Charlie, who had been born there, it was home. Perhaps Elisabeth felt the same way.

If that was the case, why would her brothers not want her to keep it? There were so many undercurrents in the situation, the nuances of which were still uncertain to him. He needed more information.

"Hang tough, Charlie," he said out loud. "Don't let us down now. We both need you."

He pulled into the parking space he generally used whenever he was visiting, near the multicar garage. As he got out of the car Tim could hear Charlie's dogs barking from their pen. Living this far out in the country might bother Elisabeth, now that she was alone.

But she isn't alone, he had to remind himself, walking up the steps to the front door. *She has you.* Why didn't he find the thought more comforting?

He no sooner closed the front door behind him than the foyer seemed to fill with people. Or maybe because of his head, everyone seemed to have a double. Mrs. Brodie appeared from the kitchen, and Elisabeth came down the stairway.

His eyes were drawn to the cool blond freshness of the woman who slowly descended to where he stood watching her. She had changed into a matching sweater and skirt of pale green. Her hair, still braided, was in a coil at the nape of her neck. He wondered if she had any idea how the hairstyle accentuated the purity of her facial bone structure.

Tim had never seen a picture of her father, Charlie's son, but if Elisabeth was any indication, he'd been a striking man.

"Oh, Mr. Walker, I'm so glad you're home. I was beginning to worry about you, what with your head and all. I was afraid this was too soon for you to be out of bed. What if you'd passed out or something trying to drive home? Elisabeth couldn't have taken too much more happening to her at the moment, I'm afraid.''

Although he heard Mrs. Brodie, Tim couldn't seem to bring his gaze away from Elisabeth as she paused on the bottom step, her eyes even with his.

"Were you worried?" he asked her in a low voice as though no one else was around.

Her eyes flickered to Mrs. Brodie hovering in the background, then she met his gaze. "I was a little concerned. You said you didn't plan to stay long with Granddad.''

He took her hand, feeling the slender coolness of her fingers. "That was my intention. However, he was so full of rather astounding information, I'm afraid I lost track of the time." He watched a faint wash of rosy color fill her cheeks.

"Are you ready to eat, Mr. Walker? Elisabeth suggested we wait for you.''

He turned and smiled at the woman standing nearby. "Yes, Mrs. Brodie. I'll just run upstairs and wash up." Still holding Elisabeth's hand, he squeezed it slightly and said, "Thank you for waiting for me." Feeling a strange reluctance to lose contact with her, Tim dropped Elisabeth's hand and stepped past her to go upstairs.

He had almost reached the top of the stairs when her voice stopped him.

"Tim?''

He turned and found her standing at the bottom of the stairway alone.

"Yes?''

"Did Granddad say... Did the two of you talk about—What I mean is—"

"We'll discuss it later, Elisabeth. I still have many questions. I hope you'll help me with some of the answers."

She nodded, looking almost unsure of herself for a moment. From everything he had learned about her today, it was no doubt a rare moment, and as such, should be savored.

They ate at a small table set into the alcove of the large dining area. As many times as Tim had visited Charlie he still hadn't gotten used to the sense of stepping back in time whenever he was there.

Since Mrs. Brodie continued to check on them periodically, Tim had no desire to start an intimate discussion with Elisabeth over dinner. Therefore he kept the conversation casual.

"I was surprised to find such an up-to-date medical facility in a town as small as Cripple Creek," he commented after a particularly long silence had stretched between them.

Elisabeth smiled. "Yes. Well, that's because Granddad donated most of the money for it. As a matter of fact, that was one of the arguments he used to convince me he'd be better off staying there than at home. Since he'd put so much money into it, he deserved to be their star patient."

Tim laughed. "That sounds just like him."

Elisabeth smiled her agreement, her eyes filled with sadness. "I don't want to lose him."

"I can understand that. He's really something."

"How long have you know him?"

"I'm not sure. Ten years, maybe. We met in Washington."

"He thinks a great deal of you."

Tim picked up his cup and sipped the steaming coffee before he answered her in a deliberate tone. "He must, to have allowed his adored granddaughter to marry me."

Elisabeth glanced toward the kitchen door before looking at him. "I suppose," was all she replied.

After they finished their meal, Elisabeth suggested they cross the hall to what at one time would have been called the parlor. A cheerful fire danced in the fireplace, giving the large room a cozy appearance.

"How's your head feeling?" Elisabeth asked after they sat in matching chairs across from each other.

"Better."

"Did you take the medication prescribed for you while you were upstairs?"

"No. I've switched to aspirin. Even though it doesn't take the pain away, it manages to dull it somewhat without knocking me out. We need to talk."

She glanced at her hands clasped in her lap but did not respond.

"Why didn't you tell me this morning that we were married?"

Elisabeth raised her head and looked at him, obviously surprised at the line of questioning. For reasons he didn't quite understand, Tim discovered their marriage was at the top of his list of needed answers.

"I wasn't deliberately hiding the information, you know. I just wasn't sure how to explain...how much you remembered about everything."

"It didn't occur to you that I might have been more than a little unnerved to discover that I was sleeping with Charles Barringer's granddaughter? With no memory of a ceremony I drew an erroneous, although perfectly natural, conclusion that was more than a little disconcerting."

She grinned, and he was surprised to see the mischievous light that appeared in her eyes. "Were you afraid that if Granddad knew about it, he would get out his shotgun?" she teased lightly.

"Knowing Charlie the way I do, I was more than a little afraid he'd use the shotgun on me rather than listen to any explanation I might offer. Given the fact that I couldn't remember a thing, I couldn't even come up with an explanation."

"You poor dear."

"Yes. You can understand my concern."

"Without a doubt. Granddad's temper is legendary."

"You don't seem to find it troublesome, though."

Her smile seemed to recall certain memories that Tim suddenly wished he shared. "Well, I've had considerable practice dealing with his temper."

"So he said. He's rather impressed with your temper, from what I gathered."

Her smile grew. "Nonsense. He just enjoys maligning my character, which doesn't surprise me in the least."

"Are the doctors giving him much more time?"

She shook her head. "They don't understand how he's hung on this long. They've given up cautioning him about his routine. He thrives on visitors, enjoys berating the nurses and gives the doctors fits. Yet all the tests show that his heart is worn out. He could go any time."

"He suggested that we marry, didn't he?"

Her gaze searched his face as though looking for something. He didn't know what it was. When she spoke her voice was lightly casual. "He's always worried about me and my welfare. It's a habit that he can't seem to break."

"What I don't understand is why you were willing to go through such a thing just to appease him."

"Don't you?" Her gaze wandered to the fire and she studied it for several moments in silence. "I would probably do anything I could to help him rest more and worry less."

That made sense to him. A lot of sense. Charlie might see her as an independent, modern female. Perhaps she was, in many ways. But her love had willingly placed her in emotional chains. The question was, for how long?

"I'd appreciate it if you would fill me in on our agreement."

Her green-eyed gaze turned slowly to meet his once more. "Our agreement about what?"

"The marriage. I'm sure I explained to you that with my work and general life-style, marriage doesn't really fit in to my plans." When she didn't comment, he went on. "I can understand that neither one of us wanted him upset. Now he can go, knowing that I'll be here for you." He thought about that for a moment. "And I intend to be, don't get me wrong. I know it isn't going to be easy for you to get through the next few months. He filled me in on Jason's and Marcus's probable reaction. You won't have to face them alone."

Her tone was level when she said, "I'm not afraid of Jason or Marcus."

"Well, that's good. Then you won't mind my admitting that although I'm not actually afraid of them, I'm not looking forward to making their acquaintance."

"Don't worry. I'll protect you, if need be."

She had spoken so quietly that for a moment he didn't believe he'd heard her correctly. She hadn't changed expression as she made her outrageous comment.

Tim couldn't help it. He began to laugh. Dear God, but she was adorable. This was the woman Charlie had thought needed protection? He almost felt sorry for her brothers. Almost, but not quite. She watched him, a slight smile appearing on her face.

"Thank you," he managed to say after a moment. "You don't know how much that relieves my mind. I know I'll be able to sleep better at night."

She chuckled but did not reply.

"Speaking of sleeping. I'm surprised that we're sharing a bedroom, under the circumstances. Since Charlie isn't here he wouldn't need to know our sleeping arrangements."

"He'd find out."

"From Mrs. Brodie, I suppose."

She shrugged. "Who knows how Granddad learns about things? For all I know he has this whole house wired for sound."

"That's a thought."

"Would you prefer the privacy of your own bedroom?" she asked.

"Not necessarily," Tim drawled. "I rather enjoyed waking up to find Sleeping Beauty in my bed this morning."

He was delighted to see that his remark caused her color to heighten. She wasn't nearly so bold nor so brave as she would like him to think.

"Can you give me some of the details of our marriage?"

She made a slight movement, almost as though she had flinched, but since her gaze remained calm and perfectly steady, Tim decided he must have imagined a reaction.

"What sort of details?"

"Oh, the usual. When... where... who was there. You know the sort of thing."

"We were married May second in a private ceremony in Granddad's room at the hospital. Because of the suddenness of the decision, two of the nurses witnessed it. The judge who married us is a long-time friend of Granddad's."

Tim found all this very disorienting. He also realized, with something like dismay, that he had no idea what day it was.

He rubbed his forehead, frowning.

"You're in pain, aren't you?" Her voice sounded soft and concerned.

"I'm more confused than anything. What's to-day's date?"

"It's Friday, May twentieth."

He'd been married for almost three weeks and had no memory of it. None whatsoever. He leaned his head against the back of the chair and closed his eyes.

"Why don't you get some rest, Tim? You've done too much today, you know."

He opened his eyes and met her gaze. Ignoring her comment, he asked, "Who found me?"

"Found you? What do you mean?"

"When I got my concussion."

"Oh! One of the ranch hands and I. We'd taken the dogs with us."

"Would you be able to find the spot again?"

She thought about that for a moment. "I suppose. If you think it's necessary. Sam guessed that your horse may have been spooked when you weren't pre-pared for it, and that you were thrown off."

"Sam's the ranch hand?"

"Actually, he's the foreman, I suppose."

"I don't know him?" That was a safe bet if Sam thought Tim could fall off his horse.

"No."

"Do your brothers know we're married?"

Elisabeth started to answer, then stopped for a mo-ment as though puzzled. "You know, I'm not sure. They haven't heard it from me, but I don't know if Granddad told them or not."

"Do they know he's in the hospital?"

"Yes. I called them."

"Have they been to see him?"

She nodded. "Jason flew out in his company's jet after Granddad's heart attack. Marcus was unavailable at the time, but I think he's called and talked with him."

"What do your brothers do?"

She grinned. "I've never known anyone with so many questions. I almost feel as though I'm on the witness stand. You leap from one subject to another without warning."

If she could only understand how he felt. For every question he verbalized, five more popped up in his head. It was as though he had walked into the middle of a movie with no idea of the plot or who the characters were. Worse than that, he felt as though he was supposed to be a part of the story and had no clue as to what his lines were.

When he didn't respond, she sighed. "Tim, please go to bed. I promise to answer more questions tomorrow. But you really need to rest."

"Will you come tuck me in and tell me a bedtime story?" He couldn't resist teasing her.

"Was that part of our agreement?"

"How the hell should I know? Our agreement, as you call it, could have been anything." He knew he sounded irritable, but it wasn't half what he was feeling at the moment.

She eyed him for a moment in silence, then got up. "All right. Here's what I'll do. Why don't you take a nice, hot shower and try to relax your neck and shoulder muscles a little. Afterward I'll give you a massage. That should help you sleep."

Slowly Tim came to his feet. "Why would you do that?"

She shrugged. "It wouldn't be the first time."

"You mean since my concussion."

Her color heightened slightly. "No. Before."

"You're in the habit of giving me massages?"

"I wouldn't call it a habit."

Why was she being evasive? Though he tried, Tim could not read anything in her expression.

What sort of relationship had evolved between the two of them during the two weeks after their wedding and before his injury? From the evidence it would seem that they shared the same room and bed.

Tim had trouble with that one. Perhaps he would agree to a sham marriage if he felt strongly enough about the reasons for it, but would he needlessly torture himself by spending night after night next to this warm, attractive, intelligent woman?

He felt that he knew himself fairly well and yet that appeared to be wholly out of character for him. Chivalrous? Perhaps. Martyr material? Not likely.

So what was the answer? He wasn't even sure of the question. And if he could formulate it, to whom would it be directed? Elisabeth didn't know him well. How could she possibly explain his motivation?

Elisabeth walked over to him and companionably linked her arm with his. "Come on. I'll walk you upstairs."

He had a hunch that she had used that particular form of cajoling with her grandfather with almost certain positive results. However, he wasn't her grandfather and his reaction to her soft breast pressing lightly against his forearm was anything but familial.

If he didn't know better, Tim decided, he'd swear he'd been out of his mind for much longer than a few days. How else could he explain his recent actions? Or perhaps the knock he'd gotten on his head wasn't the true cause of the amnesia. Blanking out his memories was probably the only way he knew to survive their current sleeping arrangements without a complete loss of sanity.

Now he was going to begin more memories. Tim had always considered himself to be a survivor.

Would he be able to survive his celibate role under these conditions?

Only time would tell.

Chapter Four

The sound of a phone ringing late at night was ominous to Tim, probably because good news never seemed to travel in such a manner. Only the urgency of bad news gave impetus to the need to arouse others from their sleep.

Elisabeth answered the phone on the first ring, turning on the lamp beside her. Tim raised himself on his elbow, running his other hand through his hair, while he tried to understand the message she was being given.

He already knew.

She had her back to him and was giving monosyllable replies as she continued to listen. The soft light highlighted the long waves of hair that fell across her shoulders and along her back.

He didn't remember her getting into bed with him. The last he recalled was the quiet strength of her warm hands kneading the muscles in his back and shoulders, relaxing him, soothing him, easing the pain that seemed to slowly recede in his head.

Tim glanced at his watch. It was almost four o'clock . . . the darkest hour . . . just before dawn.

Elisabeth murmured something, then carefully replaced the receiver, turned out the light and rolled onto her back, staring into the darkness.

"Charlie?" Tim felt a need to get her to talk to him.

"Yes."

"Who called?"

"Neil Swanson, Granddad's attorney." Her voice showed no emotion whatsoever. "Granddad had left strict instructions at the hospital. Whenever he went, he wanted Neil to be the first one notified. Neil knew what Granddad wanted done."

"Which is?"

She sighed. "He didn't want me having to call and tell anyone or having to worry about the details. Neil said he'd call back later and let me know the time set for the services." She sounded empty somehow.

"He was trying to take some of the burden off you."

"Yes."

They lay there in the dark, together and yet apart. Because of the size of the bed there was no reason for them to touch, and Tim hesitated to encroach on her space, but he had such a fierce need to comfort her, if only she would allow it.

Slowly he moved his hand until it brushed against her arm. He gave her the opportunity to withdraw, and when she didn't he took her hand, threading his fingers between hers.

"I'll never forget the first time I saw him," she said several minutes later. "My mother had died the week before. She'd been the ranch cook as far back as I could remember, and now that she was gone, the owner wasn't really sure what to do with me."

"Where were you living?"

"In Arizona. When my dad was alive they lived in Tucson. After his death she needed to find a place where she could look after me as well as work. Since she'd been raised on a ranch, it was what she knew best."

"Then Charlie showed up."

He could almost hear the smile in her voice. "Yes. Such a big man, with a booming voice and a no-nonsense manner. He was at the ranch house one afternoon when I got in from school. Said he'd just gotten word about my mother. Said he was my grandfather."

When she didn't say anything more Tim prodded her, knowing it would help her if she talked. "Were you surprised?"

"I told him I didn't know what he was talking about. My grandfather had been dead for years. That's when he said he was my dad's father, and nobody had ever accused him of being dead. Nobody had better try." Her voice caught at the words, and he knew she was trying to choke back a sob.

Tim moved toward her and pulled her into his arms. She gave no resistance, allowing herself to be turned like a limp rag doll.

"You know, I've known for some time that he was going." Her words were beginning to blur with the sound of tears. He tucked her face into his shoulder and began to stroke her back, molding her to his broad frame. "Losing my mom was such a shock because it was so sudden, with no warning. She woke up one morning not feeling well, and by night she was gone. I thought that was why it hit me so hard. Losing her was so unexpected. She was all I had."

She sniffed, and Tim rolled them both so that he could reach for a tissue from a box beside the bed. She lay partly sprawled across him, without awareness of the intimacy they shared.

He handed her the tissue.

"It doesn't really help, though, knowing you're going to lose them. No matter how prepared you are, you're never ready." The tears were coming fast.

Tim didn't say anything. He reached for more tissue and continued to hold her to him, lightly pressing her to him to remind her that she wasn't alone.

"Dear God. I loved him so much." The dam broke, and her sobs shook her. Her arms came around his neck, and she clutched him convulsively to her.

For the first time since he'd awakened the day before Tim recognized how important it was that he was there. She needed him, and somehow he had known that. Perhaps she maintained a show of pride and strength to the world around her—she was Charles Winston Barringer's granddaughter, after all—but at the moment she needed Tim, and he was thankful that he was there for her.

When the first storm of grief had passed somewhat, Tim stroked her hair away from her flushed face and said, "He loved you more than he ever loved anyone."

She caught her breath. "Did he say that?"

"Those were his exact words."

"But I was always arguing with him."

"What do you think kept him in such fine form? He thrived on arguments. You know that."

Her watery chuckle reassured him.

"He wanted you to be happy. I know he didn't want you to grieve over him."

"I heard that often enough!"

"He was tired, love. He was ready to go home."

"I know. I know it's selfish of me to wish for more. But he's all I have."

"You have me." Tim didn't know where the words came from, he only knew, when he heard them, that they were right. She had him for as long as she wanted him. She was important to him, her happiness was important to him. He never wanted her to feel that she was alone again.

He could feel her body stiffening and knew that she had just then become aware of how closely he held her to him. Despite the seriousness of the situation his body had readily responded to her. He had no control over his physical reaction to her. He could only hope that she knew he would not act upon it.

When she tried to pull away from him, he immediately loosened his hold on her. She scooted away. He didn't move but continued to lie on his back.

"I'm sorry. I didn't mean to try to drown you."

"That's just one of the functions of a husband, didn't you know?"

"You don't even remember being a husband."

Her voice sounded discouraged, almost defeated.

"Maybe not, but give me time. I'll get the hang of it."

"I doubt that you'll be around long enough."

He couldn't read anything into her comment and now that she was no longer within touching distance, he couldn't tell by touch whether she was relaxed or tense.

"Why should I leave?"

"Why should you stay? Charlie's gone now. He died happy, knowing I was being looked after."

"Maybe I like looking after you. I might want the job on a permanent basis."

He felt the bed move and knew that she had shifted. Her voice sounded closer. "Just a few hours ago you were enumerating all the reasons you weren't the marrying kind."

Damn. She was a hard woman to argue with. She could use his own words against him. "That was because I was still shocked to find out that I was married."

"I see. Now you're used to the idea."

He moved his hand until he brushed against her, then rubbed his palm against her cheek. "Let's just say that the idea has more and more appeal to me."

He heard her breath catch in the silence of the room.

"It would be different if you could remember," she finally said.

"Remember what?"

"Oh, nothing in particular, I suppose. I have such a sense of taking advantage of you. I could tell you anything and you would have to accept it."

"Is that what you're doing?"

"No! I wouldn't take advantage of you or the situation in that way."

"I never believed you would."

He moved his hand so he could feel the pulse in her neck, its rapid beat registering her agitation.

"Will you let me hold you? I promise not to take advantage of you, either. I just want you to know I'm here for you."

Almost childlike, Elisabeth returned to his arms, placing her head on his shoulder, resting her hand on his chest.

"Do you think you can get some rest?" he asked after a moment. "I have a hunch we're both going to need it today." She felt so good in his arms... as though she was where she belonged.

"I suppose. I need to start planning when I'm going to leave." She sounded drowsy, as though she were slowly drifting toward sleep.

"Leave? Leave where?"

"Leave here. I'm sure that Jason and Marcus will push to get me out of here as soon as possible."

"You think Charlie will leave this place to them?" He kept his voice carefully neutral.

"Of course. It's been in their family for a hundred years. It's their birthright."

"It's yours, too."

"No, not really. Except for the past couple of years, I've only spent summers and school holidays here."

"How much time have Jason and Marcus spent here?"

She sighed. "It doesn't matter. It belongs to them."

"Did Charlie know how you felt about the place?"

"Of course. We talked about it years ago. He was in one of his patriarch moods, determined to arrange everyone's lives to suit him. He said he wanted me to have this place, and I told him it wasn't worth fighting over."

"What did he say?"

"Say? That's too polite a word. He roared. Whenever he couldn't get his own way, Granddad roared."

She shifted, her hand idly playing in the curls on his chest. "I finally convinced him I'd be fine. I've never needed his money... well, maybe right at first. What I needed was his love and attention, and he was lavish with that."

"Well—" Tim turned slightly so she was tucked firmly against his body "—it doesn't matter to me where we live. I've got a condo in Denver. Or we could buy a place wherever you want."

She raised her head, and he knew she was trying to read his expression in the dark. "Tim, I thought we were agreed that the reason for our marriage no longer exists. I appreciate your being here for me. Granddad was right about that. But I'm a big girl now. I can look after myself. I don't need a keeper, despite what you two think.''

Tim thoroughly appreciated the feel of her body so warm against his. He closed his eyes. He was beginning to see what Charlie had been warning him about. Elisabeth had a great deal of pride and more than her share of independence. He was definitely going to need his rest at the moment because when she found out that Charlie had disregarded her wishes about the homestead, Tim had a hunch he was going to bear the brunt of her reaction.

"Let's get some sleep," he murmured, patting her shoulder then letting his hand slide along her ribs to her waist.

Strange how much he was looking forward to the coming skirmish. She was a worthy opponent. Charlie had raised her well.

Tim coaxed Elisabeth into going for a horseback ride that afternoon, hoping to get her out of the house for a while.

Tim had learned from Mrs. Brodie that Elisabeth had been spending all her days at the hospital. No wonder she looked so fragile.

He wondered if that was what they had quarreled about the day he'd gone riding alone.

Tim had awakened and realized he was beginning to have flashbacks. The relief that swept over him was tremendous. The ache in his head seemed to have almost completely dissipated, returning only when he was tired or under unusual strain.

Some of the flashes he got were in the form of silent movies. He couldn't remember what they were saying to each other, but he recalled Elisabeth's flushed face and vehement attitude. He remembered walking away from her, going outside, and later he'd gone to the barn, which was located, along with several other outbuildings, almost a mile from the house.

Charlie had warned him she was stubborn. Well, so was he.

This time, however, she had agreed to go riding. The day had turned out warm, but a fresh breeze kept it from being uncomfortable.

Elisabeth's mount was a palomino gelding, his mane and tail the same color as her silver-blond hair. They made a striking pair. The green cotton shirt she wore reflected the green of her eyes as she seemed to drink in the view of the mountains that surrounded them.

"There's no place anywhere on earth quite as beautiful, is there?" she finally said after they had ridden in silence for a time.

"I have to agree."

"Have you always lived in Colorado?" she asked as they allowed their horses to follow an almost indiscernible trail.

"Except for when I was in the military."

"What do you do now?"

He glanced at her from the corner of his eye. Was she testing him for some reason? "Why do you ask?"

"Because you've never said. When I asked Granddad he muttered something about government work."

"That's about it."

"But that could be anything from mail carrier to senator and all sorts in between."

"I'm a troubleshooter. I check out a situation, then return and report my findings and conclusions."

"Like an auditor?"

He grinned. "Something like that."

"You must work for the IRS."

He laughed. "Why do you say that?"

"Well, you keep hedging. I would imagine that most people would react negatively to the idea of having an IRS agent in their midst."

"Only if they have something to hide."

"Doesn't everyone?"

Tim stood up in the saddle, taking the weight off his rear end for a moment, knowing that he was out of shape for riding for any length of time.

"What do you have to hide?" he asked, watching her profile.

Elisabeth quickly turned her head toward him. "Why, nothing. What makes you ask?"

"Because you never talk about your profession."

"My profession!"

"Charlie told me you're a writer."

She glanced away from him, scanning the horizon. "Granddad always exaggerated everything."

"He said you sold a book once."

"Why would he tell you about that?"

"He was explaining how you wouldn't even let him pay for your education. Instead, you insisted on paying him back out of the money you received for a book."

Without looking at him, she said, "No wonder you were so long returning yesterday. He must have told you my life story."

"I was interested. Remember, as far as I was concerned I met you for the first time yesterday."

She was quiet, and Tim allowed the silence to spread between them. After a while Elisabeth spoke again, her voice musing. "I've always been interested in American history, particularly the Western United States. I enjoy reading about it, finding out little-known facts, then weaving stories about the people that lived in that time."

"Was that why you were willing to move to Colorado?"

She shook her head. "I moved back because Granddad needed me. He was too proud to admit it, but we both knew it. He was getting too old to travel. It really didn't matter where I lived. So I came home."

Tim glanced at the sun. "We'd better head back, don't you think?"

Elisabeth looked at her watch. "I didn't mean to stay out so long. Mrs. Brodie has so much to do, getting ready for everyone. And the phone was ringing off the wall."

"Why do you think I got you out of there? I suggested she call someone in to help her with the cooking and cleaning."

"I should have thought of that."

Tim tightened his hold on the reins, watching as she did the same thing. They turned and started back.

"How well do you know Jason and Marcus?"

"I've only seen them a couple of times. They attended one of Granddad's social gatherings in Washington when I met them for the first time."

"What do you think of them?"

Her voice went flat. "I have no opinion of them one way or the other."

"What do they think of you?"

She shrugged. "I'm sure you'll be able to ask them. According to Neil, they told him they'd fly in some time today."

"They'll stay at the homestead?"

She looked surprised. "Of course. It belongs to them now. Where else would they stay?"

Thanks a lot, Charlie, Tim thought.

Tim and Elisabeth entered the house through the kitchen. Two young women were working there, and the savory scents coming from the stove and oven promised ample nourishment to everyone. The women glanced up with shy smiles but quickly resumed what they were doing.

Mrs. Brodie came through the door from the hallway just as Tim and Elisabeth reached it.

"Oh! There you are. Jason and Marcus Barringer arrived a few minutes ago. They're having coffee in the library."

Elisabeth glanced down at her casual attire and made a face.

"Why don't you go upstairs and change? I'll go speak with them."

She was unable to mask her relief before she replied, "It doesn't matter. I'll have to see them sometime."

"They can wait a little longer. And you'll be more comfortable."

"That's true. If you're sure..."

Tim couldn't resist leaning over and placing a soft kiss on her mouth. Her lips tasted and felt as enticing as they looked. "I'm sure." *About a lot of things,* he added to himself.

Fully aware that he smelled of horses and outdoors, he crossed the foyer to the library and opened the door. As he entered the room, two men came to their feet and faced him.

They were obviously brothers—both tall, blond and tanned, both wearing dark business suits with vests and ties, both sizing him up as he was them. These men were nobody's fools. Elisabeth wasn't the only one who had inherited intelligence and charm.

The one on the left stepped forward with a dignified smile. Holding out his hand, he said, "I don't believe we've met. I'm Jason Winslow Barringer, and this my brother, Marcus Chandler Barringer. You must be the old man's foreman. I want you to know that you need have no concern about your position here. Our reports show that you have been doing a fine job managing the place." He glanced at his brother, who added a solemn nod of approbation.

Tim took Jason's hand and shook it firmly, then shook hands with Marcus. They were good. He had to give them that. The look, the tone of voice, the just-right grip of the hand. It was all there in the most subtle way imaginable, carefully putting him in his niche in their life.

He smiled. "I'm sure Sam's going to be immensely pleased to hear you approve of his efforts, gentlemen."

"Sam?"

"Charlie's foreman. As for me, well, I'm just part of the family...your brother-in-law, Tim Walker."

Neither man showed any reaction to his announcement other than to exchange a charged glance.

"Elisabeth's husband," he added helpfully.

"Ah. Elisabeth," Jason said smoothly. "Yes. The attorney mentioned that she was still here."

"Still?" Tim repeated softly.

"What my brother means to say," Marcus interjected, "is we weren't sure until we asked if she intended to remain here until after the funeral."

"Where did you think she would go?"

Once again the men exchanged a look.

"This is the first we knew that she had married," Jason offered.

"Yes, I got the impression that the three of you aren't particularly close."

Marcus coughed, and received a dirty look from his brother. He gave Tim a deprecating smile. "I know Charlie seemed to enjoy perpetuating the myth that Elisabeth was dad's daughter. We saw no reason to dispute the matter. She kept him entertained these last few years. That was the important thing."

"I see. Then you don't consider her your sister?"

Jason's chuckle was well-bred. "Definitely not, although I never ruled out the possibility that she was actually Charlie's bastard daughter. There is a certain family resemblance. I wouldn't put it past Charlie to cover his own peccadilloes with a story that makes him look like a benevolent patriarch rather than a scandalous old goat."

"So what you are saying is that Elisabeth could very well be your aunt?" Tim walked over to the empty fireplace and leaned against the mantle, his arms crossed.

"What difference does it make?" Marcus asked, clearly irritated with the whole subject. "The old man's gone now. I'm sure he's been generous enough with her. No doubt he's made some provision for her in the will. We have no argument with that."

Tim nodded. "Very generous of you both, I'm sure."

There was a tap on the door, and Tim noticed that it was Jason who responded, already taking over as master of the household.

"Come in."

Mrs. Brodie stuck her head around the door. "Would you gentlemen care for more coffee?"

Before either brother could respond, Tim smiled and said, "Thank you, Mrs. Brodie. I'd appreciate some fresh coffee about now."

Both men looked at him sharply, then returned to the comfortable leather chairs that were grouped around the fireplace.

"What do you do, Tim?" Jason inquired politely, crossing his legs without disturbing the sharp crease in his trousers.

"About what, Jason?"

"He's asking about your employment," Marcus prodded.

"Oh! Well, I'm what could be considered a private consultant."

"A consultant on what subject?"

"Oh, this and that."

Mrs. Brodie entered the room carrying a full tray. In a few strides Tim was by her side relieving her of her burden. She smiled her thanks, picked up the smaller tray and left the room.

Tim set the tray on the coffee table and sat on the sofa. He poured himself some coffee and leaned back, savoring the aroma as though he were alone in the room.

Marcus stood, walked to the table and poured two cups of coffee, giving one to Jason.

Jason took the cup and saucer and asked Tim. "Where's Elisabeth?"

"Upstairs changing. She wasn't aware we had company until we got back from riding." He took a sip of the coffee and gave a nod of approval. "Are you two married?"

Jason replied. "I am. Marcus is divorced. Why do you ask?"

Tim shrugged. "Just wondered. Great idea, marriage. Helps to keep your back warm at night, your belly full—" He smiled at the two men before he continued. "I'd say it manages to take care of all a man's needs."

"Is that what you'd say?" Jason repeated softly, barely veiling the contempt in his voice. "Just how long have you and Elisabeth been married?"

Tim shrugged. "Not long. It was love at first sight. Ya know what I mean? I took one look at her... she took one look at me... and there we were. We were married by the end of the week."

"Were you, indeed?" Jason murmured. "How interesting. What did Charlie think about that?"

"Don't know that I ever heard him say, now that you mention it. Of course he was in the hospital when we met."

"Of course."

"But Elisabeth doesn't have to worry about being alone now. She has me."

Marcus carefully placed his cup and saucer on the table beside his chair and came to his feet. He walked to one of the long, narrow windows and gazed outside. "Are you under the impression that Elisabeth is going to inherit this place?"

"It's her home, isn't it?" Tim asked.

Jason leaned forward, placing his elbows on his knees. "Not necessarily, no. She has been living here as a companion for Charlie. We saw no reason to disturb the arrangement. He needed someone. She was available."

"I understood that you two lived back East somewhere?"

"What does that have to do with anything?"

Tim shrugged. "I can't see any reason you'd want this place."

Jason nodded. "I'm sure you can't."

"I got the impression you both have more money than you'd ever be able to spend in several lifetimes."

A flash of distaste rippled across Jason's features. "There are other things in life besides money."

"Such as?"

"This place represents our heritage. I doubt that you would understand."

Tim finished his coffee and stood. Stretching his arms above his head, he said, "You're probably right." He glanced at Marcus, who still had his back to the room. "I've enjoyed chatting with you, gentlemen. Guess I'd better go upstairs and get cleaned up for dinner. Something smelled awfully good in the kitchen when I came through. I suppose you're staying for dinner?"

Jason seemed to have a little trouble moving the stiff muscles in his face into the semblance of a smile. "Naturally."

Tim nodded. "Then we can chat over dinner. Get better acquainted."

He closed the door quietly behind him and started up the stairway, wishing that Charlie was there. He would be enjoying all this immensely. Damn, he was going to miss the man. Thank God he'd found Elisabeth.

Chapter Five

Charles Winston Barringer's last services were held in Colorado Springs. The church was filled to overflowing with Charlie's friends and business associates.

A public figure for most of his life, he had drawn many people to him. He had an uncanny ability to recognize potential and encourage others in their use of it.

Tim recognized many faces from Washington. Legislators, Cabinet members and others not as well known gathered to pay their last respects.

Tim was proud of Elisabeth. She had handled the meeting with Jason and Marcus with quiet dignity the night before. Today, with equal decorum, she accepted the condolences of those who knew her grandfather. How could anyone not love this woman, Tim found himself thinking, then blinked. Where had that thought come from?

They were leaving the church after the service, preparing to go to the cemetery, when Tim felt a firm pressure on his arm in the crush of people moving toward the door.

"Why don't you answer any of your phone messages?"

He recognized the voice, just as he had recognized the face earlier. "I've been busy," he murmured without turning his head, his arm still around Elisabeth's waist.

"Yes, I can see that."

"Is it urgent?"

"Call when you can."

"When are you returning?"

"Immediately."

The crowd began to thin in front of them. "I'll call tonight." He never looked around, but continued to the waiting limousine.

As soon as they were settled inside, Elisabeth asked, "Who was that man?"

"My employer."

"He doesn't look like anyone's employer."

Tim smiled. "He would consider that remark a compliment."

"What did he want?"

Tim shook his head. "I'm afraid to guess. He may want me to go to work."

"Oh."

"Then again, he may want to congratulate me on marrying you."

Without looking at him, she took his hand, which had been resting on his thigh. "Granddad was right. You've been such a help. I don't know how I would have gotten through all this without you."

"You would have done just fine."

"I just wish—"

When she didn't go on he glanced at her, but she had turned her face away.

"What do you wish?"

"Nothing. I guess I'm still having trouble realizing that he's gone."

"Yes. I feel the same way."

She finally turned and looked at him. "I'm glad that you knew him so well. That you understood him. So few people really did."

"He was a very private man."

"So are you."

Tim frowned. "Why do you say that?"

"I don't know. You just seem different, depending on who is around. I don't think you are ever truly relaxed and just being yourself."

"And what do you consider being myself?"

"Warm . . . and teasing . . . like Granddad in many ways."

"I don't feel like your grandfather, Elisabeth."

She grinned. "That's not what I meant. He trusted you. That's very important to me." She looked at the passing countryside. "There aren't too many people Granddad trusted."

"With good reason."

"I know."

They were quiet the rest of the way to the cemetery.

Neil Swanson, the attorney, had suggested earlier in the day that he meet them at the homestead after the services to read the will. Marcus had made it clear they had no more time to waste, and had quickly agreed.

Tim had reason to be grateful that Charlie had prepared him for what was to come. The five of them assembled in the library, and Tim could see that Neil was not looking forward to what was coming. However, Tim was impressed with the way the attorney dealt with the matter.

"There are several minor bequests in Charlie's will that I won't go into at the moment, if you don't mind," Neil began. "Each of you will receive a copy of the will. The original has already been placed on file at the Teller County courthouse." He took his time looking at each of them. When his eyes met Tim's, Tim realized that Charlie must have told Neil that Tim knew what was coming.

Neil began to read Charlie's instructions regarding property in the East, stocks, bonds and other securities that were divided equally between Jason and Marcus. The amount was substantial. They took it as their due.

"I leave the remainder and residue of my estate, which shall include but not be limited to all cash on hand, CDs, automobiles and the real estate commonly known as the homestead located near Cripple Creek, Colorado and more particularly described in exhibit A attached hereto and made a part hereof, including all furniture and furnishings therein, to my granddaughter, Elisabeth Barringer, to be dealt with in whatever manner she shall choose and only at her sole discretion.''

The three Barringers appeared to be frozen in suspended animation. Tim and Neil exchanged a rueful glance.

''Why, that son of a—''

''I don't believe it! That old buzzard was crazy! He can't do that!''

Elisabeth was staring at Neil, her color nonexistent. Slowly she began to shake her head. ''I can't accept that—''

''Of course you can't!'' Jason agreed. ''That's preposterous! She has no right to any of this. She's just the bastard daughter of one of dad's or the old man's floozies. Who the hell does he think he is, anyway?''

''According to the documentation in my files, Charles Winston Barringer has sole and exclusive ownership of this property, and as the owner he can leave it to whomever he wishes.'' Without glancing up, Neil shuffled some papers before he continued. ''I also have here a copy of Elisabeth Barringer's birth certificate, which states her father's name as Charles Winston Barringer, Jr. In addition, I have copies in Spanish of the dissolution of marriage between Nancy Winslow Barringer and Charles Winston Barringer, Jr., and a certificate of marriage, also Spanish, between Catherine Ann Shelby and Charles Winston Barringer, Jr., dated eleven months prior to the birth certificate.''

Nice touch, Charlie. Tim made a mental salute to his friend. *You covered all the bases and dotted all the i*'s. Tim then winced at his use of the mixed metaphors.

Jason looked at Tim, his expression contemptuous. "And you knew about all this, didn't you? You moved right in on her, knowing that she was going to get her hands on this place. No wonder you rushed her into marriage." He got up and walked to the door, Marcus following him. "Well, don't start spending your money yet, you two. The man was senile. No question about it. I'll see you both in court."

The room was very quiet after the two men left. Tim watched Elisabeth closely, worried about her lack of color. She seemed not to have heard Jason's threats. When she finally spoke, she was looking at Neil.

"I don't want this place, Neil, or the money."

"Charlie wanted you to have it, Elisabeth."

"He knew how the others would react."

"Yes. He didn't care. He left me a letter to give to you." Neil smiled. "You know Charlie. He knew you would argue with him, but he had his reasons. At least let him share them with you."

Tears trickled down her cheeks, but her voice rang clear when she asked, "Where in the world did Granddad manage to come up with fake divorce and marriage papers?"

Neil looked startled, which reflected how Tim felt. She knew?

"I'm not sure I understand what you're talking about," Neil replied in a careful tone.

Elisabeth waved her hand as though brushing away his protest. "My parents were never married. My father never divorced his first wife. I can't remember how old I was when my mother explained all that to me. But they loved each other. That I know. That I truly believe. She kept all the letters he wrote to her whenever he had to be away from her. It didn't matter to either of them that another woman carried his name. My mother was in his heart. Her deepest grief was that he never had the chance to know about me and that I never had the chance to know him. His letters told me a great deal about him, though.''

She looked at Tim. ''My father was very much like his own father, ignored any of the rules that got in the way of what he wanted. If he had known about me I think he would have made other arrangements, but like Granddad, I think my father thought he was immortal.''

''Charlie knew better,'' Tim pointed out.

''Yes,'' she admitted sadly. ''I guess he did.''

''He wanted to protect you as much as he could. These papers will encourage your brothers to leave you alone.'' Neil tapped the file in front of him.

''But what am I going to do with this place? It's too big for one person.''

Neil smiled. ''Don't forget your husband, Elisabeth. You may decide to have a large family. And it isn't as though you'll have a hardship keeping it running smoothly. The one thing you'll never have to worry about is running out of money.''

Once again she made a brushing-away gesture. ''The money doesn't matter.''

''Charlie also said you would say that. He knew you very well.'' Neil stood, closing the file and placing it inside his briefcase. ''Here is the letter he left for you.

Read it, think about it, then let me know if I can assist you in any way.''

He came around the desk and held out his hand to Tim, who came to his feet and took it. Charlie had assured Tim that Neil was a good lawyer. Tim was impressed with his character.

Tim walked with him to the door and made sure it was locked behind him. Night had fallen while they had been in the library. When he turned to rejoin Elisabeth he noticed Mrs. Brodie hovering near the stairway.

''Are you and Elisabeth going to be the only ones for dinner?''

''Yes, Mrs. Brodie.''

''I can serve any time.''

''Please do that. We'll be in shortly.''

Tim walked into the library. Elisabeth had not moved, nor had she made any effort to read the letter Neil had handed to her.

''This makes it more real, somehow,'' she murmured without looking at him. ''More real than the funeral service. He's really gone.''

''Yes.'' Tim took her hand and pulled her gently to her feet, then slid his arms around her, holding her close.

''He always gets his own way,'' she muttered distractedly, and he grinned while he soothed her with his touch.

''He would be pleased to know you think so.''

''He's probably watching all this right now, having the time of his life laughing.''

''I wouldn't be at all surprised.''

''What am I going to do?'' She sounded so bewildered that his heart ached for her.

''Right now you're going to have dinner with your husband. Then I suggest a nice hot soaking bath, a soothing massage and a good night's sleep.''

Her arms slipped around his waist, and she held him for a long moment. Then she tilted her head and looked at him. ''I know I'm being weak, but I'm so glad you're here at the moment.''

''I'll always be here for you, Elisabeth.'' Tim knew at that moment that he was stating a profound truth.

She shook her head. ''No. You have your own life. I have mine. The play is over. The roles are done. But for tonight, I'm glad you're here.''

He knew that she was in no condition for an argument. It didn't really matter. More and more of the past few weeks had been coming to him today. His memory was returning. There were still blank patches, but he felt certain they would come to him in time.

Charlie's explanation had managed to jog earlier memories. He knew now why Charlie had wanted him there; knew that the situation was going to get more serious; knew that Elisabeth needed him more than ever; and he felt grateful that Charlie had entrusted her welfare to him.

He also knew that it had not been Charlie's idea for Tim to marry Elisabeth. It had not been necessary.

What he couldn't remember was if Elisabeth knew the truth about Tim's reasons for marrying her. Charlie had known. If she knew, she had given him no indication of it.

They ate in companionable silence. He could feel her exhaustion almost as if it were his own. As soon as he got her to bed and asleep, he had some phone calls to make.

It was time to plan for the next stages. Too bad Charlie couldn't be there. He would have been in his element.

"You don't have to do this," Elisabeth murmured into her pillow, more than half asleep.

Tim decided that he must have a streak of masochism inside him, because he was actually enjoying the form of refined torture he had chosen for himself.

Elisabeth was lying in bed after her bath with no more than a light sheet draped enticingly across her delectable derriere. He sat beside her, rhythmically moving his hands from her shoulders down to the base of her spine...over and over...back and forth, his fingers sliding along the slight indentation of her spine. Her skin felt like warm satin, without a blemish, and Tim felt as though he were going to explode any minute with desire.

Slowly moving his hands up from her waist, he allowed his fingers to slide to either side of her ribs so they brushed the soft plumpness of her breasts. She shifted slightly, the movement causing the sheet to slide an inch or two lower, so her rounded hips were bared to his gaze to create further torment.

"I want to do it," he admitted, his voice sounding more than a little hoarse. This time when his hands made their routine trek downward he allowed them to glide over her hips, kneading them softly, then slide over her legs. This time his thumbs lightly skimmed the tender flesh of her inner thighs.

She quivered.

"You . . . must be . . . getting . . . tired . . ."

"I'm enjoying it, believe me."

Once again he began his upward journey, lightly caressing each curve and hollow, lingering at her breasts before moving on to her shoulders.

"I'm glad." She sighed.

He allowed his mind to drift in an effort to release some of the tension created by touching Elisabeth so intimately.

Charlie had been right. The first sight he'd had of Elisabeth almost brought him to his knees, he recalled with a smile.

As soon as he had received Charlie's cryptic note, he had placed a call to him. When Charlie told him what he needed, Tim wasted no time leaving Denver and driving directly to the hospital.

Charlie had needed his advice about the situation, and Tim had spent some time discussing the matter in detail before Elisabeth had arrived. Only later did Tim discover that Charlie had sent her off on some trumped-up shopping expedition in Colorado Springs so he would have the opportunity to see Tim in private.

When she walked through the hospital door that first day, Tim felt as though he'd caught a hard left hook square in his solar plexus.

She had glowed with health and vitality. Her eyes sparkled, and the smile she wore for her grandfather had been so filled with love it took Tim's breath away.

The sides of her hair had been caught up and pulled into a knot at the back of her head. The rest had hung in waves across her shoulders and down her back. Her dress was some floaty material that swirled around her knees, revealing shapely legs that he longed to touch.

She had paused in endearing confusion when she saw him, and Tim had managed to get to his feet. He could almost feel his mouth hanging open.

"I didn't mean to interrupt," she managed to say, feeling for the door handle without turning around.

"Nonsense!" Charlie winked at Tim. "You aren't interrupting a thing. Did you manage to buy out the stores today?"

She grinned. "The dress shops were safe, but I went wild in the office-supply stores. They were having a half-price sale on paper and disks for the computer and—" She laughed. "I can't resist a sale. You know that."

"Elisabeth, I want you to meet a friend of mine, Tim Walker. Tim lives in Denver. Happened to be passing through and called the house, found out I was in the hospital and decided to see what the hell I was doing here."

Tim held out his hand, wanting more than anything to be able to touch the woman standing there. "I'm very glad to meet you, Elisabeth."

She placed her hand in his. It felt so small and delicate, as though it could be easily crushed. Her green-eyed gaze met his with an almost stunned expression. Was it possible she was feeling the same strong attraction that had shaken him? Tim had never reacted this way before to anyone. He felt as though the very air around them shimmered with the energy that pulsed between them.

He had no idea how long they stood there, staring at each other. Her gaze seemed to flit over each of his features, noting the dark red hair, the blue eyes, the way his clothes fit his body, the message in his eyes. There was no way he could hide his reaction to her, so he didn't bother trying. He just stood there, absorbing her, suddenly aware that this woman might have the ability to exert more power over him than any other human being in the world.

"Well, I'm glad to see that you two seem to like each other," Charlie said with a chuckle. "Why don't you sit down and get acquainted."

Elisabeth seemed to realize for the first time that they had been standing staring at each other for some time, her hand still firmly clasped in Tim's. Her face flooded with fiery color.

"I've invited Tim to stay with us for a few days, if that's all right with you, Elisabeth."

His comment seemed to add to her confusion. "Of course, Granddad. You know it doesn't matter to me who you have at the house."

"It's a little different now, though, what with me laid up here. I'm afraid it will be up to you to keep him entertained."

Tim turned to protest, only to meet Charlie's wink, which Elisabeth failed to catch.

"Oh!" She still sounded flustered. "Well, there's not much to do unless you enjoy horseback riding, that sort of thing."

Tim grinned. "I have a hunch I'll be quite easy for you to entertain." He might as well have come out and told her how much he wanted to make love to her.

Charlie's chuckle sounded pleased.

Tim had followed her home from the hospital in his car that evening. After dinner they had sat in front of the fire and talked for hours, as though they were old friends trying to catch up on each other's news.

They had talked about the things they enjoyed doing, places they had visited, music they liked, books they'd read, but neither one had talked about their work or about Charlie's health.

She had accepted his visit as a casual one. He'd implied he was on a vacation of sorts, which he was. He'd told her about his cabin in the Rockies and how Greg and Brandi had met each other there.

Elisabeth had expressed a desire to meet them, and he had assured her that she would.

As the hour had grown later, the firelight had grown lower, their voices had softened and their conversation had lessened. They had sat on the sofa sharing glances. He had been so exhilarated to have found her. Until now, he hadn't known he had been searching.

Their kiss had been as inevitable as the dawn. His whole body had ached with the need to hold her. She had responded with a naturalness that sent desire spiraling through him.

By the time they finally paused for breath, they were both gasping. His chest shook with the force of his heart pounding, and he could see from the quivering of her breast that she had been affected in the same way.

Tim wondered if he was under some kind of spell. Had some magic dust been sprinkled on him when she walked into the room that made him forget everything in his life? His job? His responsibilities?

They were no longer important to him. Nothing was as important to him as Elisabeth.

He told Charlie the next day while Elisabeth had stepped out of the room.

"Yeah, I kinda noticed your reaction yesterday when you first saw her."

Tim shook his head, feeling dazed. "I know it sounds crazy. How can I possibly explain it when I don't understand myself what's happened?"

"The question I have is, and you'll have to excuse an old man's concern, but what do you intend to do about it?"

"Well, it's a little too soon to be talking about marriage, wouldn't you say?"

Charlie nodded. "Under normal circumstances, I'd have to agree with you. But then, these aren't normal circumstances."

Tim recalled the earlier conversation. How could he have forgotten all that Charlie had told him? He felt like a fool. She would be in danger just as soon as Charlie was gone. And Charlie knew he didn't have much time left. Tim nodded, seeing Charlie's point. "As her husband I would be in a much better position to protect her."

"Maybe. At least being her husband it would only be natural that you'd be hanging around the place all the time, sort of watching what's going on."

"Would she agree to it?"

Charlie's eyes sparkled. He nodded to the door as it was pushed open. ''No time like the present to find out, is there?''

''Find out what, Granddad?'' she asked, walking over to the other side of the bed from where Tim stood and taking Charlie's hand in both of hers.

''I guess I never told you about how impetuous my old friend Tim is. Being filled with integrity, he thought maybe he should talk with me first, that's all.''

Her eyes sparkled as she looked across at Tim. Obviously she had gotten more sleep the night before than he had. When he'd finally forced himself to leave her at her bedroom door he'd spent the rest of the night imagining her in bed alone, imagining what it would be like if she weren't alone, and driving himself over the brink with his thoughts.

''I don't know, Granddad. Tim doesn't strike me as the impetuous type.''

The strange thing about it was that she was right. Tim was anything but impetuous. He'd learned to make lightning decisions at times, to rely on his instincts, but he'd never applied that skill in his personal life.

He hadn't had a personal life.

Until now.

''I told Charlie I wanted to marry you,'' he said, drawling the words slightly, deliberately lingering on each one.

''Why?'' she blurted out, then shook her head, embarrassed.

"The usual reasons, I guess. I have a sneaking hunch I'm not going to be able to get along without you in my life. The thing is, I don't particularly want to try. I was just discussing that when you walked in."

Charlie looked at Elisabeth. "You know my situation, darlin'. I haven't pulled any punches with you. Every day I'm here I consider a miracle. It would please me greatly to see you married to Tim before I'm gone."

"Granddad! You can't be serious! We just met."

Charlie nodded. "I know that. I'm the one who introduced you, don't you remember?" He shook his head. "I know it's unusual, and if you don't want to marry him, I don't want you to. What I want is for you to be happy. The thing is that I've known Tim for several years. You can't find yourself a better man, honey. You have no idea how unusual his reaction to you is. I've watched women around him before. He never notices them. He's told me time and time again that he didn't ever expect to marry anybody." He patted her hand. "He changed his mind as soon as he saw you. I think I knew it before he did."

Elisabeth's gaze found Tim's. "It's too soon."

Tim nodded. "Probably."

Charlie didn't say anything.

Elisabeth glanced at the man in the bed, then at Tim. "You really want me to marry him?" she whispered to her grandfather, her gaze caught up with Tim's.

"Only if that's what you want, honey."

She took a deep breath, then slowly released the air in her lungs. "All right."

As far as Tim could remember, Elisabeth had never said why she agreed to the marriage. Now as he watched her lying so relaxed on the bed beside him, asleep at last, he wished he could remember if they had discussed it later.

He recalled the simple ceremony, he recalled signing the marriage license and accepting the judge's congratulations, but he couldn't seem to bring into focus what had happened next.

There were still two weeks in his life that faded in and out. He remembered riding on the property, checking the area Charlie had told him about, the area Charlie was sure would draw others in their greed.

Charlie had been right. Like a novice, Tim had not protected his back. It wouldn't happen again.

His hands finally stopped moving across the silken expanse of his wife's uncovered body. More than ever he needed to understand his agreement with Elisabeth about the marriage. Had she insisted it would be a marriage in name only for the sake of her grandfather? She had certainly given him that impression since he'd been recovering from the blow to his head.

Were her explanations about their reason for sharing the same room and bed accurate? Would Charlie have cared, as long as they were legally wed? Tim thought not.

It was his wife's motives that he didn't understand, that he needed to know. Had he ever understood them? Ever known what they were?

He pulled the covers up, tucking them carefully around her. He needed to distance himself from her for a while or he would never sleep tonight. He could use the time to make some calls. Starting with one to Washington, to the man who didn't look as though he would be anybody's employer.

Chapter Six

The phone was answered on the first ring, despite the late hour.

"Hi, Max. It's me."

"You've created quite a stir, you know."

"How's that?"

"Don't give me that, Tim. Showing up at Charlie's funeral married to his granddaughter was bound to grab you some unneeded attention."

"It couldn't be helped."

"I understand your new in-laws are particularly curious about you."

Tim grinned. "They didn't waste much time. What have they found out?"

"Just what you knew they would. Despite all their strings, no one seems to have any information on you."

Tim began to laugh.

"Of course by now they're no doubt convinced you're operating under an alias."

"I'm sure they've also checked the legality of the marriage."

"So did I. When Charlie wants something done, he pulls in the big guns, doesn't he?"

"The judge happened to be available."

Max chuckled. "I'm going to really miss Charlie. He can never be replaced."

"True enough. Why were you looking for me?"

"Doesn't matter now. I had someone else handle it. What I need to know from you is what your status is now that you're married."

"I'm still working on that."

"Care to give me a few more details?"

Tim glanced around the library. He sat behind Charlie's massive desk, his feet propped up on the edge. The small desk lamp shed a pool of light on the green desk blotter. God, he was tired. He almost wished for the blessed oblivion of the pain pills.

"I'll try. You see, Charlie needed me to do some personal work for him. He knew what was going to happen when he died. There were a few matters he wanted taken care of, to make sure things went the way he wanted."

"Sounds like Charlie. The only man I know who would insist on his own way even from the grave."

"Yeah, well since it involved his granddaughter, I could see his point."

"Mmm."

That was one of the things he'd noticed, working with Max over the years. Max had the damnedest habit of making noncommittal sounds when he didn't want you to know what he was thinking.

"He knew that he was putting her in a certain amount of danger, but nothing I couldn't handle."

"So you sacrificed yourself on the altar of matrimony? Why, Tim, how altruistic of you."

"Go to hell."

He could hear Max's chuckle above the subtle hum of the long-distance line.

"So your work is now beginning."

"That's right."

"How long will it take?"

"From all indications, those he expects will give us some trouble will waste no time. The question is how they'll go about it. After meeting them I would hazard a guess that they won't play by any of the rules."

"Which is why Charlie called you in on it."

"Precisely."

"I take it we're discussing the Barringer brothers."

"What a sleuth you are."

"What do you intend to do?"

"No more than I have to. Neutralize them."

"They have no idea who you are, do they?"

"You've already gotten an accurate reading on them. They think I married Elisabeth to get my hands on this property. And they hate the fact that I'm already in possession. They aren't sure whether or not I know the true value of what we have."

"I take it you do, though."

"Charlie is very thorough in his briefing techniques."

Tim could almost hear Max thinking in the silence. Finally, Max muttered, "I just wish to hell he would have asked *me* if he could use you before pulling you in."

"You know as well as I do that you'd have agreed to it."

"Why didn't you let me know what you were up to?"

"Good question. As a matter of fact, I probably thought I had."

"What's that supposed to mean?"

"That I got a little careless a few days ago and got brained, which resulted in a little problem with my memory."

"What! Why didn't you let me know that sooner?"

"Why? So you could hold my hand? That's what my beautiful new wife is for."

"Are you saying you still haven't fully recovered?"

"Yeah, unfortunately. I think most of it's come back, but there's a few vague areas yet."

"Why haven't you asked for some help?"

Tim grinned. "My pride keeps getting in the way. But I've decided to call an old war buddy of mine to see if he'll play backup for me."

"Why don't I send someone?"

"I've already considered and rejected that idea. This is a delicate situation. I don't want Elisabeth any more upset than she is already. Losing Charlie has been rough on her. I figure if I have Greg come visit for a few days, she won't give it much thought."

"Gregory Duncan?"

"The same."

"Oh. Well, I couldn't find anyone better myself. I've always regretted the fact I couldn't recruit him."

"I don't know if he's available, but I intend to give him a call. I thought I might wait until things start heating up a little first so I can project a time frame."

"Isn't that a little risky, considering the tricks your mind's playing on you? If you thought you'd contacted me, there may be other things you thought you did but in fact have not done."

"I'm ninety percent certain I've remembered the important stuff. You just weren't that important in the overall scheme of things at the moment, boss."

"If you're hoping to get fired because of insults and insubordination, you're out of luck."

Tim laughed. "Well, would you consider an extended leave of absence, say for the next twenty to thirty years?"

Max paused before replying. "You're serious, aren't you?"

"It's something to consider. I don't like the idea of leaving Elisabeth for weeks at a time without contact."

"She wouldn't be without contact. You know we watch the families of our people when they aren't available. She would be safe."

"I meant direct contact between us. I'm ready to stay home, Max."

"There seems to be a rash of this sort of thing going around. I'm losing more good men this way."

Tim grinned. "You've gotten your pound of flesh over the years and you know it."

"I may use you on a consulting basis. I can't lose you altogether. You're too valuable."

"As a matter of fact, that's how I explained myself to my new brothers-in-law...as a consultant."

Max laughed. "One of these days that sense of humor of yours is going to get you in trouble."

"Well, all this girlish gossip is putting me to sleep, boss. Think I'll stumble upstairs to bed."

"Aren't you technically on your honeymoon these days?"

Don't I wish? "We've got time for all that later. First things first."

"My, I never suspected you of being the patient sort. Marriage has definitely changed you. You may end up downright civilized."

"Don't hold your breath. I'll check in when I need to. Otherwise you know how to get hold of me."

"Yes, but it doesn't do much good if you don't check your messages once in a while."

"I know. I'll do that right now."

"You can ignore mine. They're outdated."

"You're all heart."

"Sweet dreams, sweetheart."

Tim hung up, shaking his head. Then he retrieved the phone again and punched in the combination of numbers that hooked him into his answering machine. He listened, his smile growing as Max's early polite messages became more pointed and irascible, eventually coming close to abusive. He sobered, knowing that he'd made a bad slip not making sure Max knew where he was and why.

He could have been in trouble and needed help. Max's worried undertones had come across loud and clear. No doubt he'd been shocked to see Tim at the funeral.

It couldn't be helped.

Then he heard Brandi's voice.

"Hi, Tim. Since we haven't heard anything lately we assume you're out of the country on one of your hush-hush trips. In case you've forgotten, Cindy's got a birthday coming up in a few weeks—her first. Thought I'd give you a special invite to come help us celebrate. Anyway, give us a call when you get home. We'd love to see you. Greg sends his best."

There were several more calls on the machine, none of which were important enough to answer after this length of time.

Why hadn't he called in earlier? Had Elisabeth completely wiped everything out of his mind? He grinned at the thought. He wouldn't be at all surprised. From everything he could remember, she had mesmerized him completely. How else had she gotten him to agree to a platonic relationship when the very thought of her created all sorts of reactions within him?

He shook his head. He'd wanted to be close to her. At least he was with her at night. He wondered if he'd told her it was for her own safety? Probably not. He wouldn't want to alarm her. As far as that went, Charlie had secured this place with the most up-to-date surveillance equipment.

Tim wondered if the Barringer brothers were aware of Charlie's precautions. If not, they might have quite a surprise coming.

However, he wasn't going to underestimate them. They wouldn't be foolish enough to do anything personally. They would see that someone else took all the risks.

Sooner or later he would have to have a little brotherly talk with them. But he wanted to see what they planned to do first. In the meantime, he was going to spend as much time as possible convincing Elisabeth that their marriage would be as real and as permanent as he could make it.

The last thought he had as he settled his head on his pillow next to his sleeping bride was that he couldn't even remember the last time he'd kissed her!

Tim knew he was dreaming but he was enjoying himself too much to be concerned. He and Elisabeth were swimming in a lagoon filled with clear blue water surrounded on three sides by the gleaming white sand of a deserted beach. Palm trees swayed lazily in the breeze. Sunlight sparkled across the water and tinted her bare shoulders.

He reached for her, wanting to touch her, and she floated to him, her body nudging his. They were both as unadorned as the day they were born, but it didn't matter. They were in their own private paradise, having to share their tropical haven with no one but each other.

He tipped her chin slightly so he could kiss her, his mouth finding hers in a rush of pleasure. She seemed to melt against him, fitting her body to the contours of his. Her arms lifted to slide around his neck, which caused her breasts to nestle even closer... pressed seductively against his chest.

He could feel the tingling urgency of his body everywhere she touched him, and he quivered with need. Lifting his mouth from hers, he glanced into her face and saw the dreaming expression she wore. He knew he couldn't wait much longer to possess her. Lifting her high in his arms and holding her tightly against his chest, he waded through the water to shore, where he could place her on the soft grass in the shade of the palm trees and make delicious love to her.

He ran his hand lightly down her warm, bare body and felt her immediate response to his touch. Unerringly he bent his head and touched his tongue to the tip of her breast.

Perhaps it was her soft sigh that brought him out of his dream and caused Tim to realize that he was in fact making love to Elisabeth.

Faint moonlight flowed through the long windows, giving indistinct light to the bedroom. He could see her plainly. Her eyes were closed, but her arms were draped around his shoulders, her breasts only inches from his mouth.

He could feel his heart pounding in his chest at what was happening. When had this started, and how could he best handle it? Her lips were slightly parted, still moist from his kisses. Even while he watched her he allowed his hand to lightly slide across her abdomen down to the cluster of curls that protected her femininity.

She raised her hips to him in a coaxing movement that undid him. His fingers searched, then found what they were seeking, confirming that she wanted him, was more than ready for him.

Still more than half asleep himself, he allowed his feelings to overcome his thoughts. Once more he found her breast with his mouth and began to rhythmically tug while his fingers continued their own special brand of magic.

Elisabeth whimpered, kneading his shoulders like a kitten, lifting her hips to him in silent supplication.

With a swift movement Tim removed his briefs and moved over her. Blindly he found her mouth and possessed it in the same way he possessed her body—skillfully, tenderly and with a determination that could not be denied.

Elisabeth showed no signs of not wanting his possession. She clung to him fiercely, meeting his steady, rhythmic movements with ones of equal impatience as though she had been starved for his touch, denied of the pleasure they were finding in each other's arms.

As though they were two halves of a finely tuned whole they reached a climactic explosion together, each fiercely clinging to the other as their bodies trembled in the aftermath of their fiery ardor.

Tim felt almost boneless while he lay there. Because he had feared that his weight would be too much for her, he had rolled with her still in his arms until he lay flat on his back, with Elisabeth lying across his chest.

Neither of them had said a word to the other. It was as though both wanted to treat their tumultuous coming together as part of a moonlit dream sequence that might be shattered by a spoken word.

Tim couldn't seem to think. His body continued to pump the adrenaline and desire through him. As though disconnected from his brain, his hands yielded to the temptation of touching her soft skin, tracing from her shoulders to her hips in a yearning to memorize each curve and hollow, each texture that made her who she was.

He felt her shift slightly against him and reluctantly loosened his grasp. Lazily she touched her tongue to his neck, then delicately kissed him. Instead of pulling away, she allowed her hand to lightly flow across his chest, then down along the rigid stomach muscles, her hand gliding...soothing and yet arousing, despite their earlier fervor.

Tim turned his head slightly so his mouth rested against her forehead. He felt a fine sheen of moisture that he knew covered his body as well. He gently pressed a kiss there that began a tactile trail leading to her lips.

He felt the slight catch in her breath when he covered her mouth, leisurely exploring its depths, all the while fully aware of the sensuous pattern her fingers played across his torso.

They moved in silence and in slow motion, touching, tasting and tantalizing each other. No longer were they bound by fierce needs and unfulfilled longings. Now they had time to savor each sensation.

The tension built so slowly as to be almost nonexistent. It was as though at any time one expected to find the other had fallen asleep. Instead of sleep, however, their already sensitive bodies were feeling the increased tempo of a heartbeat, the soft exhalation of pleasure, the beginnings of urgency.

Still sprawled across him, Elisabeth slowly shifted, inch by inch, until she cradled his arousal. He lifted her slightly, just enough to enter and take possession of her once more.

Still in a dream state, they moved to an unconscious rhythm with slow thrusts and even slower withdrawals until, despite themselves, the surge of completion suddenly engulfed them, wrapping around them with a sudden greediness that insisted and persisted, casting them out of their sheltered lee into the full force of all the elements—wind, water, earth and fire.

By the time they were released from the elemental forces, both had succumbed to an even deeper sleep than that from which nature had previously aroused them. For a little while, at least, each had found a small measure of peace.

Tim woke up to bright sunlight and a sense that all was well in the best possible world. His head was clear, and he felt alert, rested and satiated. When he remembered why his eyes flew open.

He glanced at the bed. He was alone. Leaning on one elbow, he looked around the room, wondering where Elisabeth was and how long she had been gone. There were no clues. He ran his hand through his tousled hair and frowned.

Damn.

He needed to see her, preferably before they went downstairs to start their day. He needed to explain about last night, to—

Explain what? What was there to say, after all? They had needed each other, been drawn to each other, had clung to each other. Last night had been a culmination of all the stress and strain both of them had been under for weeks.

He got out of bed and started to the bathroom, wondering if she'd buy that.

The truth was that he had wanted her, had wanted her from the moment he had first laid eyes on her. He still couldn't comprehend how he had managed not to make love to her until now. But the fact was that he had, and that all the rules had been changed now.

Thank God.

They were married, and by damn they were going to stay married. He wasn't sure how he was going to convince Elisabeth of that at the moment, but he could be as stubborn as she was when he really wanted something. Now that he knew what he wanted he would be unswerving in pursuit of his goal.

She belonged to him now. She just didn't know it.

Tim was glad to have sorted all that out in his head by the time he reached the bathroom door, which opened in front of him and revealed his delectable-looking wife wearing a towel and a frown. He had a sudden compulsive need to remove both of them.

"Good morning," he said with a grin. "I was just coming to look for you."

Since he hadn't bothered covering himself Elisabeth was given an unadulterated view of her husband. She didn't appear to be overly impressed with the sight.

"Why?" After the first all-encompassing glance, her eyes remained on his. Her voice was as aloof as her gaze.

He ignored it. If anything, his grin widened. Miss Elisabeth might be able to use that cool, aloof gaze to good effect with others. In actual fact, she'd had results using it with him until now. Because now he knew the truth. Beneath that frosty facade lurked a warm and passionate woman he would never lose sight of, no matter how diligently she attempted to hide.

He leaned against the doorjamb and nonchalantly crossed one foot over the other, effectively blocking her exit from the small, steam-filled room.

"Why?" he repeated. "Because I wanted to suggest that it was much too early for us to be getting up. I'm sure you could use some more rest."

"I'm fine." Although her tone held steady, a tiny flush seemed to crawl across her cheekbones, and her gaze wavered for a moment. Just a moment, but it was enough. She wasn't nearly as composed as she would like him to believe.

"Honey, you are much more than fine. You are incomparable."

The soft color in her cheeks brightened to a crimson hue.

"Last night didn't mean a thing!"

After meeting her gaze for a moment he took a leisurely inventory of her, from the curls that were still pinned on top of her head to the wisps that had fallen around her neck and over her ears to the way the towel slightly flattened her breasts, causing them to swell above the rough material—reminding him of how they had felt the night before pressed against him—to her thighs, which were revealed by the towel wrapped around her, down the long line of her shapely legs, to her dainty ankles and feet. Without a doubt the woman was a true work of art. Tim had an urge to start at the bottom and kiss every inch of her body.

His thoughts must have been revealed on his face, he decided ruefully, as she uselessly tugged at her inadequate cover.

"Didn't it?" he murmured. "Are you sure?"

She stepped toward him as though expecting Tim to give way and allow her through the doorway. He did not live up to her expectations. She had made a tactical error in getting within arm's length of him. Never one to miss an opportunity, Tim snaked his arms around her waist and pulled her against him.

"You can't just—" was as far as Elisabeth managed to protest before his mouth found hers, effectively rebutting her statement. Obviously he could. And he did.

Tim took his time kissing her, enjoying the fact that she was determined not to give in to what was obviously between them and therefore held herself stiffly against him, her mouth primly closed. He used the time to nibble on her outthrust bottom lip, tasting it, testing its softness, letting his tongue stroke it until he was rewarded by her soft gasp as her mouth parted slightly and he gained entrance.

Somewhere in the ensuing moments, Elisabeth forgot about her towel and the necessity for keeping it firmly in place. At first her hands grasped his upper arms as though to prevent him from holding her any closer. Then, as though caught up in the play of muscles beneath her fingertips, she idly stroked the bare expanse of smooth skin stretched tautly over those same bunched muscles.

The towel shifted, slowly unfolding until her back was bare. Only the closeness between their bodies held the towel in place.

Tim didn't lift his head from hers, but continued to sip and savor her while he allowed his hands the freedom to roam across her back. She didn't seem to be aware of the moment when he lifted her in his arms and carried her into the bedroom and up the two steps to the bed. He lowered them both to the mattress.

He could not believe that anything could be more perfect than what they had shared the night before, but somehow the morning brightness seemed to enhance each movement as they clung to each other.

By the time he entered her they were both aching for completion and release, having deliberately teased and tormented and delayed their coming together until they were ready to explode.

When that internal explosion came it wiped out all memory of everything that might have come before, creating all new sensations of pleasure and release as though together they had been reborn.

Elisabeth was almost sobbing as she buried her head in Tim's shoulder, while he took long gulps of air to feed his oxygen-starved body. He couldn't begin to understand what kept happening between them. He just knew it was rare and needed to be carefully guarded, nurtured and, most important, appreciated.

They continued to lie there while he stroked her hair. He would never grow tired of touching her, holding her, expressing his need of her. He knew that. Did she?

When she finally lifted her head and looked at him he was dismayed to see tears in her eyes. The sheen made them sparkle like emeralds in the morning sunlight that filled the room.

"This doesn't change anything," she said fiercely.

"Doesn't it?" He kept his voice low and warily watched her.

"No. It just proves that we're normal, healthy human beings and that our present situation has thrown us into an intimacy that is not only understandable but expected." When he didn't comment she lifted her chin slightly and went on. "Once you're gone we'll forget everything that happened and just get on with our lives."

"Where am I going?" He asked the question with a show of interest that seemed to irritate her.

"Back to wherever you came from. Granddad is gone now. He died happy, knowing that his helpless little granddaughter was properly protected by the man of his choice."

"His choice?"

"Certainly. I knew he'd written you, even though he tried to make it seem that you just happened to be in the neighborhood. Neither one of you fooled me for a minute."

"I never tried to fool you. You were the one who told me about the letter, remember?"

"Oh, all right. Granddad tried, then."

"And you think that he wrote to ask me to rush over here and marry his helpless little granddaughter?" Tim couldn't control the laughter in his voice.

"I wouldn't put it past him."

"Could it be possible that I married you because I wanted to and for no other reason?"

"No, it couldn't."

"And why is that?"

"Because the more I've gotten to know you, the less likely it is that you were swept off your feet."

"Is that why you insisted on our having a platonic relationship?"

She glanced down, saw how closely entwined the two of them were and frowned. "We agreed," she muttered.

"But I don't remember the agreement."

Her eyes met his. "What do you remember?"

Why did he get the feeling his answer was important to her? He shrugged. "Oh, various things, some more clearly than others."

"If you remember anything at all, you will recall that you promised to leave once Granddad was gone and buried."

He wondered why she was lying. A promise of that nature would have been the last thing he would have consented to under the circumstances.

"Is that what you want?"

Her gaze shifted, and she attempted to move away. He tightened his hold on her just enough to dissuade her from her planned withdrawal.

"If we're going to argue I much prefer to do so in a horizontal position with you in my arms without any clothes on."

"We aren't going to argue. We're just going to each get on with our lives. I appreciate your being here with me these past few weeks, Tim. You and Granddad were right. But I see no reason to prolong the situation. It will only make it harder to get used to being on my own after you leave."

"You have no desire to make this a permanent relationship?"

She shook her head. "There was never any question of that. Never."

He couldn't deny that, since he didn't remember all the details. Just because he had decided he liked being married didn't mean she had reached the same conclusion.

Obviously she had no intention of continuing the relationship. Without her cooperation, what could he do about it?

Tim released her and climbed out of bed without saying a word. He walked into the bathroom and closed the door.

So much for trying to convince her that she couldn't live without him. He reached into the shower and turned on the water, then stepped under the hot spray. So much for the lonesome Lothario approach. He had to admit he didn't have any background or experience in how to convince a woman he loved her and wanted to spend the rest of his life with her.

He had a hunch he wouldn't be given a great deal of time to try to perfect his technique.

Chapter Seven

When Tim walked into the dining room he saw that Elisabeth was not alone. She was seated at the small table where Mrs. Brodie served the two of them their meals talking to a tall, lean man past his first youth. The man was dressed in expensive though battered boots, well-worn jeans and a work shirt that had seen multiple washings. He was twisting a Stetson around by the brim. Tim decided the man must be Sam, the ranch foreman.

He soon found that his guess had been correct.

"Tim, Sam's just told me that several head of cattle disappeared last night. The men found tracks that looked as though they were hauled out by a large tractor-trailer rig."

Tim motioned to a third chair as he sat. "Sit down, Sam, and have some coffee so I can enjoy mine. My brain works considerably quicker after I've had a cup or two.''

Sam seemed more at ease once Tim joined them, and Tim recognized him to be one of a certain breed of man who isn't comfortable around women, particularly if the woman happens to be his new boss.

Tim listened as Elisabeth plied Sam with a multitude of questions, some of which Sam could only answer with a guess.

Elisabeth immediately caught the implications. ''It's because Charlie is gone, isn't it? Somebody's letting me know I can't just expect things to go on as they were.''

''Maybe not, ma'am. There's always a certain amount of rustling that goes on in cattle country. We've probably gotten a little lax around here lately because there hasn't been much sign of it in these parts for several months. That's my fault. I'll do everything I can to see that the cattle are recovered.''

''You've notified the sheriff?'' Tim asked quietly.

Sam nodded. ''First thing this morning. He said he'd be out as soon as he could to see what he could pick up.''

Mrs. Brodie brought in their breakfast. Sam refused anything to eat and promised to let them know if there was any more information, then left.

''What do you think?'' Elisabeth said after Tim had allowed the silence to continue between them.

''About what?''

She just stared at him until he grinned. Something in his eyes caused her to drop her gaze and fiddle with the handle of her cup.

"You're right," she said in a low voice. "It's really none of your business what happens around here. I know that."

He shook his head. "Anything that concerns you will always be my business, Elisabeth, regardless of whether I continue to stay here or accept your edict and leave. I can't argue with you about our reasons for getting married or any agreements the two of us made when Charlie wasn't around. All I have to go by is my own feelings. And I feel committed to you. After last night I feel even more committed."

"That's what I was afraid of!" she cried. "That's why I didn't want us to make love. I didn't want anything to trigger that macho condition in you that would make you feel obligated to me."

"I don't feel obligated. I'm here because I want to be."

"Nonsense. You're here because Charlie got his own way again."

Tim grinned. "The man wasn't God, you know. He couldn't control everything."

"He did a great imitation of thinking he could, though."

Tim reached over and placed his hand on hers and felt her quiver at his touch. "Everything's going to be all right, Elisabeth. Let's just give it some time, all right?"

They sat there looking into each other's eyes. Tim could see the uncertainty and the pain in hers. He hoped she could see the concern and caring in his. ·

"What are your plans for today?" he finally asked.

She moved her hands to her lap. "I thought I would try to do a little writing."

"Anything in particular?"

He could almost see her withdrawing into herself. "Oh, just the usual scribbling I always do to entertain myself, as Granddad always used to say."

"Do you find it helps to write?"

"Yes," she responded coolly. "I often find that I like the people I write about a great deal more than the ones I'm around."

"Ouch." He leaned back in his chair and studied her. The warm, vibrant woman he had known was gone. In her place was the lady filled with pride who was fiercely independent. Well, he would allow her that pride and independence because he knew he could do nothing to change it. He understood both traits, having an abundant amount of his own.

If she didn't want him, he would accept her decision. He didn't have to like it, he just had to accept it. He also had to keep his promise to Charlie.

Rising, he nodded to her and said, "If you'll excuse me, I have some calls to make."

"Aren't you leaving this morning?"

"I know how eager you are to get rid of me, but there are a few details that Charlie asked me to take care of. I'll try to complete them as quickly as possible and get out of your hair." He left the room quickly, closing his mind to their situation.

He still had a job to do. He'd deal with how he felt later.

The first call he made was to Greg's office. Tim was relieved to learn that Greg was in.

Greg answered his phone by saying, "Is this really the Tim Walker I used to know, the one I haven't heard from in so long I've forgotten what he looks like?"

"Don't get smart."

"It certainly sounds like my old buddy, Timothy. How've you been?"

"Busy. Is it too late to celebrate Cindy's birthday?"

"Certainly not. Her first one has come and gone, of course. You know how time flies. But she's graduating from college now and we're going to throw a big bash that you're welcome to attend."

"Cute, Duncan. Really cute. How does Brandi put up with you?"

"She has a much better sense of humor than you do, I suppose. Where'd you misplace yours?"

Tim sighed and ran his hand through his hair. "Good question."

Greg's voice sobered. "Problems?"

"You could say that."

"Anything I can do to help?"

"Do you have any idea how relieved I am to hear you offer? Yeah, I could use some help."

"Name it."

"Is there a chance you could come to Colorado for a few days?"

"When?"

"As soon as you can get away."

"Alone?"

"Yeah."

"Denver or the cabin?"

"Neither. Cripple Creek."

There was a long silence. "Cripple Creek?" drawled Greg.

"I'm staying at Charlie Barringer's place. Have you been here?"

"No, but I suppose I could find it. Didn't I just read somewhere that he'd passed away?"

"The funeral was yesterday. He left a few things he wanted to have cleared up. I'd feel a hell of a lot better if I had you around to guard my back."

"Hold on. Let me check my calendar."

Tim doodled on the writing pad that had been placed on the desk, drawing squares, rectangles, circles with arrows pointing from one to the other.

"I think I can rearrange things so I could leave early tomorrow morning. That should put me there by dark."

"Thanks." Tim gave Greg directions, then said, "I suppose I'd better explain something before you get here. I'm, uh, married to Elisabeth Barringer, Charlie's granddaughter."

An explosive silence greeted him.

"Married?" Greg finally whispered as though the breath had been knocked out of him.

"At least temporarily," Tim added grudgingly. "I'll try to explain when you get here. It's all a little confusing at the moment."

"Do you want Brandi to know? She's going to be devastated that you didn't tell us sooner."

"I'd thought of that. If you don't mind, I'd rather you didn't. As soon as I get this matter cleared up, there may be nothing to tell her."

"We'll talk," Greg said quietly. "It sounds like you need to. I've never known you to do anything so out of character as to jump into a marriage with someone you don't know." He paused. "Or am I assuming wrong about your just having met her?"

"Your assumption is correct."

"Hang in there. I'm on my way."

Tim managed a grin. "The cavalry to the rescue. Just like old times, right?"

"I'll see you," Greg replied, ignoring the reference to the fact that Greg had once saved Tim's life when they'd been in the service. That was how they had met. Tim had never forgotten, and Greg always refused to discuss it.

After he hung up, Tim sat for a few moments, then decided to find Sam and wait for the sheriff. He had to do something, keep his mind occupied, keep the thought of Elisabeth at bay. That was the only way he knew to survive.

Tim spent the following hours riding with Sam in his Jeep, going over possible places to enter the ranch that were isolated enough for rustlers to risk coming on the property.

They agreed to hire extra help to spell the regular hands during off-duty hours. While they were checking the area, Sam obligingly pointed out the spot where Tim had been found a few days before.

Tim acknowledged to himself that he hadn't really believed Charlie's concerns were valid until he'd been attacked. He would not be careless again. He and Sam got out and walked the area, looking for signs that others had been there recently. The signs weren't hard to spot, as though the men who had made them hadn't been concerned with early detection.

Tim explained to Sam what he thought was happening and why, and accepted his offer of help when the time came. Now, more than ever, Tim knew that Charlie had accurately judged Jason and Marcus.

He found it strange how money and power affected some people. For some there was never enough. Since Charlie had been so concerned, Tim had assumed that he was leaving most of his estate to Elisabeth, which would naturally create an aggressive fight. Neil, his attorney, had pointed out that Charlie had known better. By evenly disbursing his estate, Charlie knew that no judge would consider throwing out the will when the only reason for contesting it was spite. In monetary value, Elisabeth had only received her due.

Tim's job was to make sure that she was allowed to live in peace.

He thought of her questions about his job and how she had suggested that he might be an IRS agent. Perhaps it was an idea he could utilize. There was more than one way to get a person's attention, after all.

Tim made a note to call Max when he returned to the house.

Elisabeth sat at the computer in the room she had converted into an office and stared out the window. She had used a need to write as an excuse to closet herself away from everyone. Mrs. Brodie knew not to disturb her until she decided to come out. Even her grandfather had always respected her need to be left alone.

Her grandfather.

She sighed, restlessly getting up. He seemed to be the basis of everything that was happening to her. At least her strong feelings for him seemed to control her behavior.

How had she allowed herself to be caught up in such a situation?

As far back as she could remember, Elisabeth had been taught by her mother that a woman had to be strong, that she had only herself to rely on, that sometimes emotions could betray a woman, causing her to make foolish choices.

Invariably her mother used herself as an example. She had been in her early twenties, living in Tucson, earning an adequate living working in an office, when she'd met Elisabeth's father. He'd had an appointment to see Cathy's boss regarding some real estate. She had been flattered by his attention and accepted his invitation to dinner that night.

Cathy had never been able to explain to Elisabeth how she could have known so quickly that Chuck Barringer was the man she wanted to have in her life. Since meeting Tim, Elisabeth could better understand her mother's reaction. Elisabeth had discovered the lack of control she had over her own emotions the day she'd walked into her grandfather's hospital room and seen Tim for the first time. Even now she couldn't begin to understand the thunderbolt experience it had been. Was it because of some hereditary flaw she and her mother carried that all their logical thinking processes disappeared when a certain type of male appeared in their lives?

Her mother had only been able to shake her head, unable to find the words to explain what had happened. Elisabeth could only accept that from their first evening together, Cathy and Chuck had known that something momentous had happened between them and that it was too important to ignore.

Chuck had been honest about his situation. He and his wife were separated. Because of his wife's family, background and concern for social standing, she would not consider divorce.

None of that had mattered to Cathy. They had discussed the implications of a possible pregnancy. As much as Chuck had wanted to father a child of Cathy's, they had known it was impractical and unfair and had taken precautions to ensure that she would not become pregnant.

Because of the papers he carried, she had been one of the first people to be notified of his unexpected death. Even now Elisabeth could see her mother's face whenever she talked about that time in her life. Death was the only eventuality neither of them had planned for.

Cathy had quit her job so she could travel with Chuck. She had planned to go with him when he went to Europe, but at the last minute she became ill, and Chuck had had to go without her. Had she been with him, she might have died as well. Elisabeth had a hunch that Cathy might have wished for such a fate.

But then her mother's face would light up as she told the next part of her story. How the illness that had prevented her from traveling with Chuck had not gotten better. That the news of his death had seemed to worsen her physical condition. That finally, knowing she had to get some help to get back on her feet, she went to the doctor, and he had told her she was pregnant.

She wouldn't believe it. They had used birth control. How had it happened? The doctor had explained that nothing was one hundred percent foolproof. The fact remained that despite everything, she was going to have a part of Chuck after all. Elisabeth became Cathy's miracle baby.

Elisabeth smiled at the memory. She had many happy memories of her mother. Cathy had wasted no time finding a place where she could have a child and raise it. She had devoted her life to raising Elisabeth.

Cathy had loved her little daughter. She'd laughed when no one believed Elisabeth belonged to her because she looked just like her father. Cathy's hair had been dark, her eyes gray, and she had been petite. Elisabeth knew from a picture she'd seen of him that she looked like her father. She really hadn't cared, as long as her mother didn't mind.

Elisabeth always listened to Cathy's stories about her love for Chuck, the choices she had made and the joy of having Elisabeth in her life. But in Elisabeth's mind she had perceived the problem Cathy would never point out: You can't count on love. You can only count on yourself. Things happen. People leave you, sometimes not because they want to, but because life works that way.

Cathy had proven Elisabeth's theory to her by dying when Elisabeth was still so young.

At fourteen, Elisabeth had known that she was capable of looking after herself and had been determined to prove it. That was when Charles Barringer
barged into her life and demanded the right to look
after her.

She smiled at the memory. Granddad was a great
one for demanding. He'd wanted to take her home
with him, wrap her up in tissue and soft cotton and
have her do nothing for the rest of her life, protected
from the world.

He had been too late to change who she was and
how she dealt with life. Most surprising of all, he had
accepted her. Oh, he had enjoyed battling with her,
more for the fun of the argument than that he had any
desire to win. He'd enjoyed crossing swords with her,
but had always fought fair.

Until now.

Bringing Tim Walker into her life when she was at
her most vulnerable had been a sneaky, underhanded
thing to do to her. And he had known it. How, she
didn't know, but her grandfather had known. She'd
seen the look of delight on his face at her reaction to
Tim.

How could he have done this to her? All her careful plans, her sensible views about life and herself, her
ability to think logically and practically had immediately dissipated like puffs of smoke in a sudden wind.

Would it have made any difference to her if Tim had
been a stranger to her grandfather as well as to her?
Probably not, she decided honestly. After that first
few hours together, when it seemed as though they had

always known each other, she was ready to place her heart in his hands.

She had done just that. She knew that Tim now believed she had only married him to please her grandfather. She was eager to grasp at that particular straw in an effort to give herself time to evaluate what was happening to her.

After he was hurt, she had been determined to distance herself from him. During his memory loss he had made it clear that marriage wasn't a part of his life-style.

She had known and understood that. Hadn't she felt the same way? Until she met Tim, of course.

Elisabeth understood herself a little better. It wasn't that she didn't love Tim or that she didn't need Tim; she didn't want to need him. She wanted to stay invulnerable to hurt.

Losing her grandfather had been a reminder, if she had needed one, about the pain of loving, then losing, someone.

Turning back to her manuscript, Elisabeth felt relief that at least she had her make-believe world she could escape to whenever life became too consuming for her. Thank God she had gained some level of professional security in her chosen field.

Thinking of her career reminded her of the argument she and Tim had had the day he had been hurt. He had come looking for her, too impatient to wait for her to surface. He had seen the letter from her editor, as well as the royalty statements that had arrived, which she had neglected to put away. Elisabeth hadn't expected anyone to come into her office and had grown careless.

She had gotten angry at Tim's questions, angrier still that he should criticize her decision not to share her success with her grandfather. She had reacted by becoming defensive, until they were both shouting. It had been a silly argument in some ways, but it pointed to the heart of her dilemma. She had spent too many years keeping people at a distance. Her reasons for not sharing her professional success with her grandfather had been based on the knowledge that he would not really appreciate what she was doing, and she didn't want him to ridicule her efforts.

Perhaps she'd had something of the same feelings about Tim finding out. As it happened, she never learned his reaction. By the time she was able to talk to him again, he had no memory of discovering her secret.

Elisabeth realized she was hoping he would leave before all his memories returned. Making love with him had been a mistake. It had merely served to strengthen her resolve about the relationship. She was weak around him, without willpower. She couldn't take much more.

The sooner he left the better. Eventually she would be able to get on with her life alone. She didn't want to consider the fact that it might be too late. The damage had been done.

Chapter Eight

Dinner that night was strained, although each of them took pains to be polite. Elisabeth's thoughts kept returning to the time when they would go upstairs and once again share a bed. Why had she thought they could sleep together and not be drawn to each other? But she had wanted to be near him, particularly once he'd been injured. After the doctor explained that there was little that could be done except to allow him time to heal, she had insisted he be kept at the house.

She had cherished those hours with him. She had spent the time sitting beside him, watching him, studying him and, when he murmured disjointedly, discovering how her calm voice and soothing touch seemed to comfort him.

She had also wanted to let him know that she had finally agreed with him about her work. The next time she'd been to see her grandfather, she'd told him the truth about her career. He hadn't been as surprised as she expected. He was very proud of her for showing the initiative and stubbornness to stick with it.

When Tim had awakened not recognizing her she had been shocked, unsure of how to handle the situation. She and her grandfather had disagreed about what she should do, but then they had disagreed about most things.

Sometimes she was convinced her grandfather argued just for the sake of being contrary.

Elisabeth glanced across the table at the silent man who filled her thoughts. She wondered what he was thinking but didn't feel she had a right to ask.

Tim's thoughts kept returning to Greg's upcoming visit. He reviewed his plans. He thought he had covered all the bases, but only time would tell. Now if Jason and Marcus would only step into the carefully baited trap, the matter would be taken care of shortly.

Then what? What more could he say to Elisabeth? He supposed he wasn't being fair to her. After all, she agreed to the marriage as a temporary measure. Did he have any right to demand that the rules be changed?

Was it her fault he had fallen so hard for her that he didn't want to think about a future she wasn't a part of?

"Will there be anything else?"

Tim and Elisabeth were startled by the sound of Mrs. Brodie's voice breaking into the silence that surrounded them.

Elisabeth was first to respond. "No, thank you, Mrs. Brodie. Everything was delicious."

Mrs. Brodie looked at their plates, then at the two people sitting there. "How would you know? Doesn't look like either one of you bothered to eat a thing."

For the first time since they'd sat down, each became aware of the other's mood and lack of conversation. They put their own interpretation on it.

Tim decided that Elisabeth was still upset with him for not having left. Elisabeth assumed Tim was irritated that she was still insisting that he leave. Since each felt justified in their position, there was nothing to be said.

When Elisabeth stood, Tim also got up. "If you will excuse me, I have some things to take care of."

She nodded. He disappeared into the library, and she slowly went upstairs, feeling drained. Perhaps she would go to bed early and try to get some rest. Tonight she would use some common sense and wear her gown to bed.

The memory of going to sleep the night before with his hands stroking and smoothing the muscles of her back and shoulders popped into her mind. She hadn't intended to fall asleep and was, in fact, surprised she did under the circumstances. But she had been under a great deal of strain, and his touch had been so gentle and soothing.

Later she had come awake to find him touching her in a new and more urgent way. She could no more have resisted him than she could have admitted to him how much she loved him. Her longing for him had worked against her.

She couldn't allow herself that weakness again.

* * *

Tim called Max and explained his idea about the brothers Barringer. In the long run, he felt his idea would work even better than bringing formal charges against them. Once he made them aware that he knew what they were up to, he needed a permanent lever to make sure they didn't harass Elisabeth.

Max laughed at his idea, but agreed that it would probably work.

Then Tim sat in the big overstuffed chair and thought about Elisabeth upstairs. Glancing at his watch, he was surprised to see how late it was. Maybe he'd be able to sleep. He hoped so. And he hoped to hell he wouldn't dream!

Tim heard Greg's car pull in the driveway the next evening and was outside by the time his friend got out of the car.

"You made good time," he said, greeting Greg with a warm handshake.

"I got an early start." Greg glanced around and gave a low whistle. "Quite a place."

"I know. It takes some getting used to."

"It looks more like a movie set than a working ranch."

"The ranching part is to utilize the land, not to make the place a paying concern."

Greg removed his suitcase from the trunk of the car and followed Tim to the front door.

"I guess you know you've been more than a little mysterious, my friend. Care to fill me in on what's been going on in your life?"

"I have every intention of doing so after dinner and once we're alone."

"Is your wife here?"

Tim held the door open for Greg. When Greg walked inside his question was answered. He saw the blond, green-eyed beauty standing in the foyer, a hesitant smile on her lips.

"You must be Greg," she said softly. "Tim has told me so much about you."

"And you're Elisabeth," he replied with a grin. Setting down his suitcase, he quickly covered the distance between the two of them and clasped her outstretched hand in both of his. "I'm sorry to say that Tim hasn't told me nearly enough about you, which is an omission I'm not sure I'm ready to forgive him for."

The man standing before her was several inches taller than Tim and not as broad. His blond hair was touched with gray and gave him a distinguished appearance that made her immediately feel comfortable with him.

"You must be tired if you made that drive today. Why don't we have coffee? Dinner should be ready in fifteen minutes or so."

Tim picked up the suitcase. "I'll take this upstairs. Your room is the first one at the top of the stairs. You shouldn't have any trouble finding it."

Greg took in the sumptuous foyer, the polished mahogany railing of the stairway, the gleaming marble floor, and shook his head.

Elisabeth grinned at his expression. "I know. It's really too much, isn't it? I feel as though I should be wearing full skirts with a multitude of petticoats and other unmentionables every time I come down the stairs.''

She led him into the front room and motioned for him to have a seat. Mrs. Brodie appeared in the doorway and Elisabeth asked for coffee, then sank onto the sofa across from Greg.

''I'm sure this place has some stories it could tell. How old is it?''

''My grandfather said that his father built it just before the turn of the century. He was one of the fortunate ones who discovered gold in the area, and he wanted a home befitting his new station in life.''

''Yes, I remember hearing once that the Cripple Creek area had one of the last big gold rushes in the United States.''

Elisabeth nodded. ''In the 1890s Cripple Creek was a flourishing metropolis. Now there's just a small community left. The principal source of income is tourism.'' She glanced around the room, then at Greg. ''I find the history of that era fascinating.''

Greg watched the woman seated across from him and tried to come to terms with the fact that she was Tim's wife. Somehow he had thought that Tim would never marry. Of course he had thought the same thing about himself a few years ago, and look at him now.

''How long have you and Tim been married?'' Only when he heard his question did Greg realize he'd voiced his thoughts. He was embarrassed with his bluntness. Fortunately Tim walked into the room and rescued him. Greg hoped he hadn't sounded to

Elisabeth as though he were interrogating a helpless witness.

"Almost a month ago, although I only recall the last few days," Tim replied. He sat beside Elisabeth and casually took her hand. Greg wondered about the tension he sensed between the two of them. His curiosity grew by the minute.

"Yes, you mentioned something about getting a blow to your head. How are you feeling?"

"Much better. The pain's almost gone, and my memory is returning—" he glanced at Elisabeth as he drawled the rest of his statement "—slowly but surely."

Greg could see her stiffen slightly. Glancing at Tim, he asked, "Did you find out how it happened?"

"It was just a careless accident on my part," Tim replied, with a slight shake of his head. "I haven't been on horseback in years."

Greg lifted a brow, but felt it safer not to comment. He was relieved when Mrs. Brodie came in to tell them that dinner was ready to be served.

Having Greg at the evening meal livened up the conversation and eased the tension for everyone. He shared hilarious stories about his children, and he and Tim regaled Elisabeth with stories about Brandi, as she was now as a wife and mother and years before, when she was growing up.

At one point Elisabeth said, "I'm so sorry she wasn't able to come with you to visit us." Greg threw Tim a questioning glance, which Tim returned without expression.

"Yes, she was, too," Greg responded in a bland tone. "Maybe next time," then wondered why Tim and Elisabeth would not look at each other.

By the time Elisabeth excused herself for the evening Greg was ready to throttle Tim if necessary to get some answers.

"I wish to hell I understood what was going on around here," he said once the two men were alone.

Tim poured them both a drink, then sat down across from his friend. "I appreciate the delicacy with which you handled the matter. Now you can see why I didn't dare have Brandi come with you."

Greg grinned, acknowledging the accuracy of Tim's hit. "Brandi has never been known for her tact and diplomacy. She would have been asking questions and demanding answers before we had gotten inside the house."

Tim leaned his head against the back of the chair and stretched his legs in front of him. "I hope Brandi wasn't too upset about not coming with you."

Greg took a sip of his drink and gave a brief sigh of pleasure. "Of course she wasn't. Brandi's mature and understanding." He glanced at Tim, his eyes sparkling. "And I didn't tell her that my unexpected business meeting was with you."

Tim began to laugh, and Greg joined him.

"You've learned a great deal about married life," Tim said after a moment. "I wonder if I'll be given that chance."

"Meaning?"

"Elisabeth is already asking when I plan to leave."

"I could think of many reasons she might want to send you packing. What is hers?"

Tim looked into his drink, then took a swallow. "Because, according to her, we agreed to marry as a temporary measure to please her grandfather."

"I had no idea you were so self-sacrificing. A beautiful, intelligent, wealthy young woman needs a spouse, and you quickly offer to help her out. How noble."

Tim toasted his friend. "I knew you would understand."

Greg slid down a few inches in his chair and propped his feet on the footstool in front of him, and Tim got up to freshen their drinks. After handing Greg his drink Tim began to fill Greg in on everything he could remember. When he finished, Greg shook his head.

"You are a source of constant amazement, my friend. How do you always manage to get in the thick of things?"

"Just my natural talent, I suppose," Tim offered modestly.

"So what's going on with Elisabeth's brothers now?"

"Half-brothers."

Greg waved his hand as though brushing away a pesky fly. "Whatever."

"According to Charlie, Jason visited him not long after Charlie was hospitalized to talk about the possibilities of reopening the gold mine located on the ranch."

Greg straightened slightly from his relaxed position and stared at Tim. "Elisabeth mentioned something earlier about a gold mine her great-grandfather owned."

"One and the same. Charlie said the mine was quite successful for years, but by the 1920s was barely breaking even, due to some problems with water seepage and a drop in gold prices. So his father closed it."

"Is it worth reopening?"

Tim thought over what he'd been told. "That's the big question at the moment. Geologists say that despite the millions of dollars worth of gold taken out of the area originally, there's an estimated eighty percent still to be recovered in the granite terrain." Leaning forward, he placed his elbows on his knees and held his glass between his fingers. "With new mining technology and the price of gold these days, reopening some of the existing mines has become an option to consider." He drained his glass and looked over at his friend. "I understand that a few of the mines around here have opened with varying degrees of success."

"I see."

Tim went to the bar and poured another drink. When he motioned with the bottle, Greg joined him, his thoughts caught up in the conversation.

"What Charlie realized when Jason visited him," Tim went on after they had reseated themselves, "was that Jason automatically assumed he and Marcus would inherit the ranch. They never gave Elisabeth a thought. What they wanted was Charlie's approval to go ahead and have the mine studied for its present mining potential. They were already looking toward the future when Charlie wouldn't be around.''

''But Charlie left the ranch to Elisabeth, I take it?''

''Yes. He'd had his will drawn up several years before and saw no reason to change it. Both men lived in the East and never came out here. He and Elisabeth considered this place home. However, he could see the potential for conflict once he was gone.''

Once more comfortably draped in his chair, Greg asked, ''How does Elisabeth feel about all this?''

''That's the hell of it. Elisabeth doesn't know about the new interest in the mine. Charlie didn't want her worried about it. Or worse, he didn't want her turning the place over to the brothers upon demand.''

''So that's where you come in, I take it.''

''Supposedly, yeah. In case they need some convincing to leave her alone.''

''I don't see any reason you had to marry her, though.''

Tim's smile was filled with self-mockery. ''My reasons for marrying her were much more basic than that. They were very territorial, in fact.'' He swirled the liquid in his glass. ''I wanted her to belong to me, so I used the situation for my own reasons.''

''How caveman of you. I've always known you lacked a certain amount of civility in your nature, but I must admit you've surprised me.''

''Unfortunately, Elisabeth isn't buying any of this.''

''Good for her.''

''Whose side are you on, anyway?''

Greg lifted his brows in mock astonishment. "Why, I'm always on the side of truth and justice, where else?"

Tim shook his head.

"Does she know how you feel about her?"

Tim thought about that question for a long time before he answered. "It's all so complicated. From what I remember about our first meeting and the subsequent marriage arrangements, I was sure she did." He stood and began to pace the floor. "The damnable part is that I only have vague recollections of the ceremony. Then things are hazy. I'm not sure what is a dream and what's real." He paused, his hands on his hips, and frowned at Greg. "Then, a few mornings ago, I woke up with what I thought was a monster hangover pounding in my head in a strange bed with a woman I could have sworn I'd never seen before."

Greg knew this was serious, but the picture Tim painted was too humorous not to laugh. Tim's reluctant grin acknowledged that he understood Greg's amusement.

"Just think how Elisabeth must have felt to have her new husband look at her one morning and say, 'My God, who are you?'"

"Yes, I know. Charlie pointed that out to me. Since then, she's been polite but kept her distance." *Most of the time,* he added silently.

He refused to feel guilty about what had happened between them the other night. She had been too responsive, too open to his advances for him to feel that he had taken advantage of her.

"So what are you going to do?"

"About Elisabeth? I don't know. As for the mine, some of the ranch hands are keeping an eye on the area. I think Jason's going to try something soon. There's been some activity already. If he thinks his efforts will go undetected, I suspect he'll see what's down there. If it's worth it to him, he may decide to convince Elisabeth not to keep the place." He explained about the missing cattle. "I think he could very well be behind that, hoping to discourage her."

"So you intend to discourage him from discouraging her, is that it?"

"Close enough."

"And where do I come in?"

"As a witness, for one thing. If you're willing, I would also like you to go with me to visit Jason at his office in New York."

"When?"

"Soon. Within the next couple of days, if I've figured Jason correctly."

Greg was quiet for a few minutes, and Tim relaxed once more in his chair. He needed some rest. He hadn't gotten much sleep the night before. He thought of Elisabeth in bed upstairs and wondered why he thought he'd be able to sleep any better tonight.

Greg stretched and looked at his friend. "Yes. I think I'd like to be dealt into this hand. It might be fun."

"I appreciate it."

Greg lifted his brow slightly. "Oh, you'll pay for it."

"How do you mean?"

"You're going to be given the pleasure of telling Brandi that you got married without telling her. After the fuss you made when she and I snuck off, she's not going to take your doing the same thing lightly.''

Tim rose and switched off the lamp by his elbow. The men turned toward the hallway. "If I had my say," Tim said as he checked the lock on the front door, "I'd be more than willing to have another ceremony that included you and Brandi. All we have to do is to convince Elisabeth."

"You can always explain that your friends insist. I'm sure she would understand."

They walked up the stairs together and paused in the doorway of Greg's room. Tim rested his hand on Greg's shoulder. "I'll do what I can. But I can't promise anything."

"Nonsense. I've never known you to give up on something you wanted in your life, Tim. You aren't about to give up now."

Tim grinned. "You know me well." He started down the hallway to join his wife for what was left of the night.

Chapter Nine

Tim silently opened the bedroom door and slipped inside. Elisabeth had left a small nightlight on in the bathroom, and it gave off enough light for him to see the shadowy shape of furniture and her still form lying asleep in the mammoth bed they shared.

Without haste he removed his clothes and quietly joined her. He smiled when he saw the demure gown she wore. He wondered if she thought he found her less enticing dressed in her soft cotton. How little she understood that it was her, who she was, that created such a riot of feeling within him at times that he felt almost choked with its intensity.

Her very independence, her need to be self-reliant, her refusal to cave in when the odds were against her, were all qualities Tim found endearing. He loved her strength of character and her integrity. He loved all the qualities that made up the package so delectably and attractively known as Elisabeth Barringer Walker.

Unable to resist being close to her, he moved until his body was only inches away from hers. She lay on her side, facing him. With trembling fingers he smoothed a strand of hair away from her cheek.

She stirred, murmuring something that sounded like, "Tim?"

"I'm sorry. I didn't intend to wake you," he whispered.

She shifted her leg, grazing him, and her lashes fluttered. "What time is it?"

At least that's what he assumed she mumbled. He smiled, drawing her closer against him and nuzzling her neck.

"Late. Very late."

"Mmm," she replied, burrowing deeper into his embrace. "You okay?" she said after a moment. He heard the concern in her voice, something she wouldn't allow herself when she was fully awake. Now she was operating on instinct, without her guard in place.

He followed the curve of her back and hips with his hand, pressing her body more intimately against his. "Now I am." He nibbled at her ear. "I've missed you."

"Mmm." She sleepily pressed her lips against his cheek in response.

"Do you have any idea how much I love you?" he whispered, trailing kisses across her jaw and down her neck.

She touched the back of his head with her hand and slowly caressed the thick hair there, but made no response.

"I want to marry you, Elisabeth. I want you to know how much I want you in my life. I don't want there ever to be any mistake about that." He raised his head and kissed her on the lips, and she responded by wrapping her arms tighter around him.

"Will you marry me?"

He felt her body jolt as though she'd just received a shock, as though she was finally awake for the first time since he'd come to bed. She stiffened and pulled away so she could see his face. Touching his cheek worriedly, she asked, "Tim, are you all right?"

He smiled. "I'm fine. Why?"

"Has your memory gone again?"

"No."

"Why would you ask me to marry you?" she asked, concerned.

"Because you seem in such a hurry to end our present relationship. I wanted to make it clear that I still want to be a part of your life."

He could feel her relax against him once more as though she found his words reassuring on some deep level. Tim slid his hand under her knee and pulled it over his thigh.

"Tim?"

"Yes, love."

"What are you doing?"

He smiled at the lack of concern in her voice. She was still more than half asleep. "Making love to you."

"I don't think that's a very good idea."

He kissed her, then said, "I think it's an excellent idea. I think it's the best idea I've had in hours... possibly days."

"Tim?"

"Hmm?"

"Have you been drinking?"

"A little brandy, that's all."

He kissed her again. She responded, which encouraged him immensely.

"I don't want to love you, you know," she said, her voice as soft as a young child's.

Since she was running her hands across his shoulders and back, her body pressed provocatively against him and was returning his kisses, he wasn't unduly alarmed by her comment.

"Why not?" he asked lazily, shifting so that he could open the front of her gown and caress her breasts with his mouth and tongue.

"I'm afraid," she admitted softly.

"Of me?"

"Of being hurt, of being alone, of caring too much to survive without you."

He straightened and kissed her again—slowly and with gentle thoroughness. "You don't have to be alone, sweetheart. Don't you know that yet? I'm here. I'll be here for as long as you want me." Tim lay propped above her, resting on his forearms, which he placed on either side of her head.

The light caught the glitter of her eyes, and he leaned over her and kissed each eyelid softly, reverently. "I love you, Elisabeth," he whispered.

"Oh, Tim, please don't say that. I can't bear it. Not now. It's too soon."

"Too soon to know or too soon to admit it?"

She shook her head, and moisture slid from beneath her closed eyelids. He kissed each tear away.

"Don't be afraid, love. Don't let fear rule your life. Don't push me away."

There were no more words between them. He showed her his love in physical form, reverently expressing all that he was feeling. At one point she sat up and helped him remove her gown, then turned toward him once again.

It was almost dawn before they fell asleep, exhausted, in each other's arms. Even as his eyes closed Tim realized that Elisabeth had never given him the answer he wanted from her.

Tim felt as though he'd only been asleep for a few minutes when the phone rang. This time he was closest to it. Fumbling for the receiver he snagged it with two fingers and brought it to his ear.

"H'lo?"

"Mr. Walker, this is Sam. We've got company."

"Thanks. I'll be right there."

He was out of bed by the time he'd returned the phone to its resting place.

"Who was that?" Elisabeth murmured.

"Sam. I asked him to call me early this morning. I'd forgotten when I came to bed last night."

She raised her head and looked at him. "Why?"

"I wanted to get an early start. There are some things I wanted to check out that can only be done in the early hours."

"Oh."

"Go back to sleep, love."

"You didn't get much sleep, either," she pointed out.

He grinned. "It was worth it. Believe me." He leaned over and gave her a hard, swift kiss, then backed away before he lost his will to resist.

This was the signal he'd been waiting for, gearing up for. Now things would begin to move, and he could get on with his efforts to woo Elisabeth to his way of thinking.

A few minutes later he tapped on Greg's door and opened it. "We've got company, Greg. I knew they'd show up."

Greg sat up and stretched. "They picked a hell of an hour to come visiting," he grumbled, coming to his feet.

Tim laughed. He could feel the adrenaline moving through him. "I don't think they intended to disturb us."

Greg was already dressing, his movements economical. "Thoughtful of them."

"Without a doubt. Also very considerate. I hope they'll have the information that would have taken us several months to obtain."

He went out the door with Greg close on his heels. Tim turned on a pocket flashlight so Greg could see the stairs, but kept it on only long enough for them to make it down the stairs before switching it off. He didn't want to alert anyone who might be watching the house that people were stirring.

The sky was still black and filled with stars when they stepped outside. Because of the altitude and the early hour they could see their breath when they breathed.

Tim saw a movement in the shadows, then Sam stepped away from his Jeep. The men joined him without a word. They rode for several minutes in silence before Tim asked, "Did you see how many there were?"

"Jess counted four before he sent one of the men to get me up. Jess knows not to let himself be known to them unless they try to leave before we get there."

They parked the Jeep a fair distance from the entrance of the mine, making allowances for the way the night air carried sounds. They moved swiftly and silently through the night, all three men trained in stalking. When they were within shouting distance of the mine, Jess stepped out from behind a group of boulders to meet them.

Only then did Tim realize that he could see the surrounding area. The sky had begun to lighten in the east. It wouldn't be long before dawn.

"They haven't made any real effort to be quiet, Sam," Jess pointed out. "They brought in a couple of trucks and some kind of equipment and disappeared into the mine."

Sam looked at Tim, waiting for instructions.

"How many men do you have here with you, Jess?" Tim asked.

"Six."

"Armed?"

He nodded. "Rifles."

"Fine. Have them stay out of sight of the mine entrance, but make sure it's surrounded. When I give the signal I want all of them to show themselves. There won't be any shooting, if I've read the situation correctly. These are engineers, hired to do a job. I'm just using you guys to impress on them and the man who hired them that I mean business."

Sam and Jess nodded and melted into the shadows around them.

"Now what?" Greg placed his hands at his waist and leaned back, stretching. He sounded as though he could fall asleep. Obviously he wasn't being affected by an adrenaline high, Tim thought with a smile. Either that, or he wasn't going to admit it.

"We wait. You can always go curl up in the Jeep if you want to get some more sleep."

The brief flash of a smile answered him. "Oh, I think I can manage to stay awake if you can."

Thinking back over the past few hours, Tim acknowledged that he probably hadn't had much more than an hour's sleep. But it had been worth the lack of sleep to find Elisabeth so responsive in his arms. Her feelings ran deep, he knew, much deeper than she was willing to admit. But surely after last night she could no longer ignore the intangible tie that bound them so strongly together.

Tim lost track of time as they waited. Neither man spoke but were content to share the early morning view of the mountains. They watched a doe with her fawns tiptoe through the meadow nearby on their way to an unseen stream that could be heard in the stillness. Other wildlife went on with their morning routines, ignorant of the human eyes watching them.

The sound of men's voices and boots scrambling over rocks was an unwelcome intrusion in the pastoral quiet. Tim moved closer to the entrance, waiting in the shadows of the sentinel-like pines that stood nearby.

Several men walked along in single file, talking and making notes. None of them had looked up. When Tim spoke they glanced around, startled.

"Good morning, gentlemen. Looks like the weather's holding nicely, wouldn't you say?"

"What the—?"

"Who the hell—?"

"Say, what's—"

"Perhaps you aren't aware of it, but you're trespassing on private property. Some people get a little touchy about their gold mines even when the mines aren't operational."

One of the men stepped forward, pulling his hard hat off his head. "There's obviously some mistake here. We have written instructions from the owner giving us permission to be here. We've been in and out of here several times in the past few weeks. Nobody's said anything."

"And just who gave you this permission?"

The man flipped open a metal-bound notebook and shuffled through the papers. He lifted one, squinting at the signature. "Jason Barringer," he read.

"Mr. Barringer has never owned this property and has no authority to give anyone permission to be here."

"Now wait a minute. I don't know what's going on here but I have my instructions." The man glanced at the others and they moved over so they stood in a V. "I don't know who you are, mister, but you aren't going to start handing out any orders around here."

Tim turned his head slightly, his gaze resting on Sam, who stood out of sight of the other men. Tim nodded. The small group standing in front of the mine looked astonished as several men carrying rifles materialized around them.

Pleasantly, Tim said, "I'm sure the sheriff would like to have the opportunity to meet with all of you and have a little chat. He's been having some problems in the area lately with unauthorized entry, stolen cattle, that sort of thing. No doubt he'd be interested in discussing the matter with you."

The men with the hard hats looked at each other, then at their spokesman and, without waiting for instructions, headed toward their trucks.

"Look, I don't want any trouble," the man began.

"Neither do we. If you'll come with us, I think we can get this matter settled to the satisfaction of all concerned."

Sam pulled up at that moment in the Jeep. Tim motioned for the man to get in next to Sam. Then Tim and Greg got in behind him.

They began the trek to town. "I don't understand what's going on," the engineer said, shaking his head in bewilderment.

Tim replied, "That's all right. You will soon enough."

Elisabeth came awake with a sudden jerk, then realized she had only been dreaming. The bedroom was filled with bright morning sunshine, and she knew she must have overslept.

She rolled over and stared at the place where Tim had been earlier, remembering what had happened the night before. She groaned and buried her head in the pillow. That man had the power to turn her brain into mush by doing no more than holding her. Every time he kissed her, her body turned to gelatin.

Her first mistake had been to think she could continue to sleep beside him after lying to him about the nature of their marriage. Just because he didn't remember those two weeks didn't mean that she could ignore what had taken place between them. But when the unexpected chance to gain some control over the situation had come her way, she grabbed it. What she hadn't taken into account was that she would betray herself.

Elisabeth crawled out of bed and padded into the shower. How could she possibly hope to think clearly as long as she was in his presence daily and shared his bed every night? Why was she so weak that she couldn't find the self-discipline to move her things into another room, insist that the marriage had served its purpose and get on with her life?

Her love for her husband had captured her as surely as if he'd wrapped her in thick bonds that could not be loosened.

After she dressed, Elisabeth wandered down to the kitchen and made some toast, poured a cup of coffee and stood there munching on her breakfast while daydreaming about Tim.

She would never forget their wedding day.

Her grandfather had been so pleased. Tim had been laughing, teasing the nurses, thanking the judge, and she had stood there watching the scene, convinced she was out of her mind.

Ever since she'd first seen Tim, she had been acting out of character. When had she ever been so biddable, so agreeable . . . so enamored?

Because they hadn't wanted to be gone far from the hospital, Tim suggested they take a ride, maybe find a decent-looking restaurant and have something to eat, then go back to the homestead.

Once again she had allowed him to take control of the situation. He'd acted so relaxed, as though getting married was nothing new to him.

Elisabeth glanced around the kitchen, disoriented for a moment because she'd been so caught up in her memories. Rinsing her cup, she decided to go upstairs to write in hopes of getting her mind off Tim.

She no sooner sat down in her chair when her memories resumed . . .

"I suppose we should tell Mrs. Brodie," Tim had said as he held the car door open for her to step out. "Otherwise, she might have an attack of some sort when I follow you into your bedroom tonight."

Elisabeth could feel herself blushing and hated the ridiculous betrayal of nerves. His grin became a chuckle when he saw the look on her face.

"Uh, look, Tim. We should think about this before doing anything hasty."

"Well, you know her heart better than I do. If you think she can handle the shock..." He left the sentence hanging, took her hand and began to draw her to the front steps.

"No, about sleeping in my bedroom," she blurted out.

He stopped in his tracks. Turning her to face him, he said, "There's surely no question about that, is there?"

She stood looking at him, unable to respond.

"Wait a minute. Are you under some kind of crazy impression that I married you because of Charlie?"

"It's just that we don't know each other very well and—"

"Exactly. But we have the rest of our lives to get acquainted, and I want to do it sleeping next to you every night."

Why was she protesting, she wondered. Who did she think she was kidding? She hadn't been able to sleep the night before, just knowing that he was down the hallway from her. The kiss they had shared that first evening had awakened something inside her that refused to go back to sleep.

He had never given any intimation that he would treat the marriage as one without conjugal rights.

Whether to tell Mrs. Brodie or not was not tested because she wasn't in evidence when they went in. Tim quietly followed Elisabeth into her room. He looked around with an interested gaze, then walked over to the bed that took up almost one entire wall of the room.

"My God. What's this?"

She laughed. She couldn't help it. "My grandfather found that somewhere and carried it home to surprise me one year right after I went away to school. The original hangings were rotten so he had new ones made with matching covers. He said it's several hundred years old and was brought to America from somewhere in Europe." She walked over and touched one of the drapes. "He's convinced some king slept in it."

Tim walked around it, eyeing the platform on which it stood. There were steps on either side to get up to it.

"It's big enough to hold a dozen kings. Don't you get lost in it?"

She smiled. "I've grown used to it. He had a mattress custom made. It's very comfortable." She leaned against one of the four posters and watched as he wandered around the room, picking up ornaments and studying them, then replacing them. It suddenly occurred to her that he was nervous. Perhaps as nervous as she was. Not that that was possible. No doubt he had shared a bed before, while she had always slept alone.

Elisabeth wished she had more experience. She had always been aloof from boys her own age, wary of becoming too friendly. Her mother had cautioned her about encouraging someone if she weren't careful. So she had been very careful. She would scarcely exchange a word with a boy.

Her classmates would laugh to see her now. She had been the young woman in college who never dated, who spent all her time studying or writing, who knew so little about men. And she had married a man she had just met.

Abruptly Elisabeth turned and went into the bathroom and closed the door. She was trembling so hard she thought her knees were going to buckle. Glancing into the mirror, a white-faced woman stared back at her with large, shadowed eyes.

How ridiculous. She was acting like one of the wimpy virgin heroines in one of her historical novels. What was she expecting him to do, attack her? She smiled, trying to picture Tim in a scene from one of her books.

No doubt her editor would be amazed to discover that all those sensuous love scenes had been taken completely from Elisabeth's fertile imagination. Since she'd been an apt student she fully understood human anatomy and related subjects. But none of that knowledge helped her to deal with her emotions at the moment.

She felt as though she had to walk into a classroom for a final exam without having studied for it. She had no idea what would happen to her if she were to flunk. Take the course over? What if she couldn't learn? Had no aptitude?

What a silly twit she was being. With jerky movements she pulled her clothes off and got into the shower. The soothing spray caused her to relax somewhat, and by the time she stepped out, she was able to see her situation in a lighter vein.

All she had to do was to explain to Tim that— Well, she could just say that she had never— Then again, she could keep her mouth shut and let him find out on his own.

The coward's way, perhaps, but better than stammering her way through a ridiculous confession. Elisabeth reached for her gown, which hung on the back of the door, and slipped it over her head.

She eyed her reflection in the mirror. The hot spray had warmed her, given her cheeks more color and caused her hair to form wispy curls around her face. She shook her head. She couldn't hide in here all night, she decided firmly. Lifting her chin slightly and filled with conscious resolve, she opened the door and strode into the other room . . . only to find Tim lying across the bed asleep.

Elisabeth almost burst out laughing at the difference between her imaginings and reality. He had probably gotten tired of waiting for her and had stretched out to become more comfortable. He'd removed his suit jacket, his socks and shoes, and unbuttoned his shirt.

Moving carefully so she wouldn't disturb him, she crept up on the bed and scooted over, giving him plenty of room. She'd left the bathroom light on for him and now wasn't sure whether she should turn it off or leave it. Since turning it off would mean that she had to get up again, she chose the easier course.

She slowly stretched out on the bed, determined to allow him to rest, and bit her lip to keep from laughing. Her eager bridegroom must not have gotten any more sleep the night before than she did.

Elisabeth didn't remember going to sleep, but she definitely remembered waking up. Tim was kissing her, touching her, murmuring to her, and she felt as though her skin was on fire everywhere he touched her.

"So sweet," he murmured, "so lusciously scented and sweet."

Sometime in the night he had obviously come awake enough to get undressed. There was no doubt in Elisabeth's mind that he had not bothered with pajamas.

He tugged at her gown, sliding the thin straps off her shoulders and shimmying it down her body until she was as bare as he.

Elisabeth would never forget that beautiful night when Tim had initiated her into the rites of love-making with all the painstaking skill at his disposal. How had he known that she had been frightened and had needed some time? By allowing her a chance to relax and fall asleep Tim had insured that she never regained her stiff uncertainty, which might have contributed to her discomfort. His tender caresses gently led her from one plateau of arousal to the next. When she hesitantly imitated his caresses he gave her whispered encouragements in his passion-roughened voice.

By the time he took her she was as eager as he to move to this next joyous step of sharing. How could she have known what beauty there was to be given in such a manner?

He taught her about her own body and its secret responses. During the following days they had spent their time with her grandfather, their nights in each other's arms.

Until the day they quarreled...the day he was hurt.

Chapter Ten

Looking back, Elisabeth knew the quarrel had been silly, but it had been further evidence that she was losing control over her life...all parts of her life, even her professional one.

She had gone into her office looking for something without a thought as to how revealing it would be to Tim, a man who obviously missed very little.

He'd walked in without her hearing him until he spoke. "Who is Lisa Barry?"

She froze in her task of looking through her top desk drawer, then slowly turned around. He was holding an award that had come in the mail a few days before. She had opened it, glanced at it then tossed it aside. Lisa Barry was not on her list of priorities at the time.

He was reading the certificate. Lisa Barry had won the nomination for best historical writer of the year, an award given by a prestigious national publishing magazine.

"I am," she said evenly, despite the fact that her heart was pounding in her chest like cannons going off for a twenty-one-gun salute.

He glanced around then, taking in the reference books, the computer, several shelves that included her books. He walked over and touched each one.

"You've written eight novels."

She nodded.

"Charlie thought you'd only sold one."

"I know."

He tapped his finger against the shelves. "Does he know about these?"

She shook her head.

"Why not?"

She couldn't answer the question. Was it because she had been afraid Charlie would make fun of her? Because she had enjoyed not sharing her secret life, not even with her grandfather? Because—

"I saw no reason to tell him."

Tim turned and looked at her, and the expression in his eyes caught her off guard. She had never seen him look that way. A frisson of fear ran up and down her arms.

"So you have kept the information that you are a published, award-winning author from not only me, your husband, but your grandfather, the person you reputedly love more than anyone in the world? What other secrets do you keep locked inside that private little head, I wonder?''

"I don't see that it's anyone's business whether I'm published or not. Granddad knows I write. He wouldn't care about the kinds of things I write about."

Tim leaned against the doorjamb and studied her as though he'd never seen her before, as though he wasn't too sure he liked what he saw.

"No doubt you've had a good reason for building the walls you carry around with you. Perhaps they've helped you to survive this far. But to keep your grandfather in the dark about something like this is the height of selfishness. The man is so damned proud of you that he glows at the mention of your name. He would have enjoyed every single moment of each book, from manuscript to publication, but you're so damned afraid to let anyone see you're human, that you struggle and worry, that you have moments of doubt and despair, you've bottled up everything that makes you a real person. All any of us are left with are the careful reflections of who you want us to see."

He straightened. "I feel sorry for you, Elisabeth. You're hurting yourself much more than you've hurt Charlie." He took a step back so he was in the hallway. "Forgive me for trespassing in your private domain. You may be sure I won't do it again."

He strode away, leaving her standing there staring at him.

Hours later she found out that he had gone riding. Then his horse had returned without him.

A light tap on her office door brought Elisabeth out of her reverie. Since Mrs. Brodie never bothered her in the office, she knew who had tapped. She quickly moved to the door and opened it. Before she could say anything, Tim spoke.

"I'm sorry for bothering you when you're writing. I just wanted to let you know that Greg and I are leaving for Denver. I'm not sure how long I'll be gone. It may be a few days."

She could only stare at him in shock, her mind still caught up in the whirling memories of the last few weeks. "You're leaving?" she finally repeated.

He leaned down and gave her a brief but thorough kiss. "Yes. But I'll be back. We have to talk."

With that he spun on his heel and strode away, disappearing down the stairway at the front of the house. She stood there as though paralyzed. Where was he going and why? She hadn't said goodbye to Greg but maybe he, too, would be back.

Yes. They had to talk. Somehow she had to come to terms with her feelings and her fears. She had used Tim's memory lapse to try to run away, at least emotionally, from what they shared, but her continued responses to his lovemaking made a mockery of her efforts.

As much as she loved him, did she have the courage to remove her walls and allow herself to be vulnerable? Could she survive?

The question had now become: could she survive without him? Elisabeth had a strong hunch that she didn't want to test herself. Not now.

Tim and Greg drove to Denver, stopping at Tim's place long enough for him to pack a few items of clothing he had not taken to Cripple Creek with him. Then they drove to the airport and caught an evening flight to New York.

After landing at La Guardia, they directed the cab driver to the hotel where Tim had made reservations. Since both of them knew the plan, there had been little conversation during their travels.

Crawling into bed that night Tim had a fleeting thought that he would be sleeping alone for the first time in almost a month. He had already grown accustomed to finding Elisabeth next to him. He lay there, staring into the dark, going over the surge of memories that had been flooding his mind during the day.

She had lied to him about their relationship. He realized that now. He remembered with great clarity their first night together and how nervous she had been. Their long drive had done little to relax her, and by the time they had reached her bedroom she had been trembling with anxiety. He had known then that he couldn't force her into a relationship she wasn't ready for.

He had waited for her to come out of the bathroom to tell her, reminding himself to have the patience to take it one step at a time. Eventually he stretched out across the bed. At least they were married, he remembered thinking. No longer did he have to sleep down the hallway from her. The important thing was that they were together.

Tim had felt like a fool when he woke up and discovered that he had drifted off to sleep. She was asleep. He had gotten up and taken a shower, then crawled into bed beside her. Thinking to give her a soft kiss good night he had moved closer to her. His kiss lingered, and his hand lightly brushed against her.

She had turned toward him, relaxed and at ease. Would he ever forget that night or the nights that followed?

Why had she lied about those days and nights spent loving each other, growing increasingly close?

Had she still been angry because he had found out her closely guarded secret, the existence of Lisa Barry? Yes, he'd been upset with her attitude and he had let her know it. His impatience had gotten the better of him. Why did she have to be so guarded with everyone, including the people who loved her?

Hadn't she understood why he'd been so upset? If she was still keeping her grandfather at a distance after all these years, where did that leave her new husband?

He had several questions for her, but first he wanted to deal with Jason Barringer. Whatever happened between him and Elisabeth, Tim wanted to know that she would be left in peace by the other members of the family. This trip to New York should take care of Charlie's wishes. After that, Tim intended to deal with his own.

He shifted in bed, turning on his side. Tim realized that he was looking forward to the meeting tomorrow. He smiled and drifted off to sleep.

The next morning Tim and Greg stepped out of the taxi that had brought them to the Wall Street address from their mid-town Manhattan hotel. The imposing edifice standing before them towered high above them, its marble walls attesting to several generations of

money that had married and intermingled to produce
the man they had flown halfway across the continent
to see.

Tim looked at Greg and they exchanged a smile that
boded ill to someone, then walked to the entrance.

After being questioned at several different levels, the
two men were finally ushered into the executive offices, Jason's lair, high above the clouds. From the size
of the waiting area that greeted them as they stepped
off the elevators, and from the ornate furnishings,
Tim recognized the subtle intimidation inherent in
everything they came across.

At long last they were directed to Jason's adminis-
trative assistant. The man rose from behind his desk
and came around to greet them. Tim knew what the
assistant saw—two men in expensive, conservative
suits with an air of quiet power and determination.

"May I be of some assistance to you, gentlemen?"
the young man asked with a smile.

Since Tim knew that the man had already been notified of their presence in the building and their desire
to see Jason Barringer, the question was prompted by
curiosity more than politeness.

"We'd like to see Mr. Barringer."

The young man's head was nodding before Tim
finished speaking. "Yes, sir. That's what I understand. However, it seems that you neglected to call
first for an appointment. Had you called, I could have
explained that Mr. Barringer is tied up in meetings and
won't be available all day." He turned and looked at
an appointment calendar on his desk. "Perhaps you
could return—"

"Oh, that won't be necessary." Tim opened his briefcase and pulled out a large manila envelope and handed it to the man. "Just tell him that his brother-in-law brought these for him."

For a moment the man looked startled, then he quickly resumed his blank expression.

Tim gestured to the comfortable-looking chairs opposite the large desk. "We'll be right here should he change his mind about seeing us."

Tim and Greg sat while the young man warily watched them. Glancing at the double doors on the other side of the desk, the man must have made up his mind to follow Tim's instructions rather than take a chance on misunderstanding the situation. He nodded and disappeared behind the doors.

Tim and Greg refused to meet each other's gaze. Instead, they reached for a couple of magazines in unison and began to flip through them.

The man soon reappeared.

"Mr. Barringer can see you now."

Tim nodded. He and Greg walked through the door the young man held open, then paused inside the room until the door closed behind them.

The room appeared to be large enough to hold a basketball court. Light flooded through the eastern wall that was made entirely of glass, as was the south wall. The desk could have been used for a game of table tennis.

As they walked toward the desk, the man seated behind it watched them without rising. They did not stop until they reached the edge of the desk. Then they stood waiting.

Jason took in Tim's apparel, then turned his gaze to Greg. He glanced at the manila folder in front of him and flicked his finger against it.

"Care to tell me what this is all about?"

"You wanted to know about the potential of the gold mine on the homestead property. I decided if you were so willing to spend your own money to find out, the least I could do was see that you got the information as quickly as I did."

"What's the meaning of the statement signed by the engineer?"

"Oh, that. Well, the sheriff wanted to get all the facts clear on what was going on. The engineer was very obliging, as you can see."

Once more Jason looked at Greg. "I don't believe we've met."

Tim spoke up. "This is Gregory Duncan, my attorney."

Jason's brows went up. "What happened to Neil?"

"He's Charlie's attorney."

"I see." Jason made a steeple of his fingers. "What do you want from me?"

"I want you to leave Elisabeth alone. You have your empire, you and Marcus. You've never shown any interest in the Colorado property before. It was never yours. It belongs to her now because Charlie wanted her to have it."

"According to these reports, the mine looks promising."

"Yes, it does. I intend to tell Elisabeth that you and Marcus had the preliminary work done as a wedding gift for us.'' He smiled. ''For which we thank you very much. It was a very generous gesture on your part.''

''I don't need to ask what's in this for you.''

Tim met his gaze with a level one of his own. ''Given your perspective about life, I'm sure you think you have all the answers. There is one thing I feel I should mention, though.''

''And that is?''

''For some reason Charlie didn't like you, Jason, grandson or not. Perhaps it had something to do with the dossier he kept on both you and Marcus over the years, a detailed account of your business practices, many of which would prove to be interesting reading material to the IRS.''

Jason straightened in his chair and leaned forward, but he didn't say a word.

''Charlie felt that once he was gone you and Marcus might try some of your tactics to convince Elisabeth to leave the ranch. He knew how much you enjoy intimidating people. If there's one thing you enjoy more than money, it's power. Charlie understood that very well.''

''You can't prove a thing. Our business practices are perfectly legal.''

''Of course they are. But you know how it is. Once the IRS starts nosing around a company they tend to watch it a great deal more closely, scrutinizing, auditing. So many decisions are left to their discretion—interpretation of the statutes, that sort of thing. They can stick with you closer than a cocklebur and can be just as hard to get away from.''

''Are you threatening me?''

"Why should I do that? We understand each other, just as Charlie understood you and me. He passed me those dossiers in case they were needed. I promised to guard them carefully."

"You son of a—"

"Ah, ah. Name calling is so juvenile, don't you agree? We're grown men...relatives, actually. No reason we can't get along."

Tim nodded toward the papers. "Those are your copies to keep. We have the originals. If we should have any reason to think you or Marcus are behind any problems that might occur around the mine or the ranch, Mr. Duncan will be in touch with you."

Jason stood. "Now, wait a minute. We can't be blamed for everything that might happen out there, for God's sake."

"Of course you can't. Just as we certainly can't be held responsible if the IRS suddenly begins to take an intense interest in your many businesses." Tim spread his hands. "Things happen. All part of life."

He and Greg walked out of the room, into the lobby, into the elevator, through the echoing marble lobby on the ground floor and out to the street.

Tim took a deep breath and sighed. "Ah, smell that fresh diesel and soot-filled air. A welcome relief to the rather closed atmosphere we just left, wouldn't you say?"

Greg lifted his brow. "I got a distinct scent of fear upstairs."

"Not surprising."

"So that takes care of Mr. Barringer."

"I think so, and so did Charlie. I think Jason will take into consideration the possible consequences of going after Elisabeth, and decide that it isn't worth the risk."

"I don't think the man knew what hit him."

"That's the point. Nothing's hit him, yet. Charlie wanted to give him fair warning. If the man behaves himself, he'll be home free."

"If he gets vindictive, he'll—"

"Find out a little more about the uses of power."

A cab pulled up and they got in and headed uptown.

Greg dropped Tim off at the homestead but refused his offer to spend the night. He wanted to put in a few hours on the road to Missouri so he would be home by the next day.

Tim didn't insist. He had other things on his mind. He let himself into the house and looked around.

This house would always remind Tim of Charlie. He could almost hear Charlie's voice from the other room, smell the scent of the cigars he'd smoked until the doctors had insisted he give them up. He would miss the old man. He just hoped he had carried out his instructions in a way that would have pleased him.

Carrying his bag, Tim started up the stairs. He decided to shower and change before dinner. He was tired. He'd done a great deal of traveling in the past couple of days. Plus he had a feeling of letdown, which was not unusual. He generally experienced the feeling whenever he finished an assignment.

The water felt good beating down on his shoulders. He stood there for a long time, allowing his mind to stay blank. He didn't want to think about the next few hours and how important they would be to his future.

When he walked into the bedroom he glanced at the bed. Never had it seemed so inviting to him. Slowly he walked over to it. Climbing the stairs, he decided to relax for a few minutes. He still had plenty of time before dinner. He'd just stretch out for a while, then get dressed and go find Elisabeth.

Those were his last thoughts before he fell sound asleep.

Chapter Eleven

Tim was awakened by a lingering kiss. He opened his eyes and saw a green-eyed young woman with moonlight-tipped blond hair staring at him. Her hair fell around them like a silken veil, enclosing them in a scented haven.

"I've invented a new fairy tale," she whispered with a smile. "The sleeping prince, found in all his natural splendor, adorned only by the soft shadows of early evening, awaiting the touch of one special person to arouse him from his slumber."

Tim slipped his arms around her, making sure he wasn't still asleep. She felt very real in his arms. "You'd better kiss me again. I may still be dreaming."

Elisabeth searched for and found his mouth once more. This time Tim took control, threading his hand through her hair, his fingers splayed against the back of her head. With possessive insistence he explored her mouth with his tongue, delicately probing. She met his thrust with a dainty, duel-like rhythm of her own.

When the kiss ended they were both breathless.

"If I'd known I was going to be greeted with such an enthusiastic welcome I might have considered leaving before now." Tim began to stroke her back, wishing she wasn't wearing so many clothes.

"You've missed the point," she said with an impish grin, running her finger along his jawline.

"Which is?"

"I'm trying to bewitch you so you won't ever want to leave me again."

Tim's hand stilled at the words. "You are?"

She nodded her head emphatically.

With an unexpected move he rolled until she was lying beneath him. He propped himself up on his elbows and stared at her. She gazed at him with a serene air he wasn't sure he'd ever seen before.

"You mean all those hours of careful preparation I've spent listing the reasons we should stay together were unnecessary? All my arguments, my most persuasive manner, my unassailable charm aren't going to be called upon to convince you?"

"You sound disappointed," she pointed out dryly.

He laughed. "Not on your life. I'm relieved, even if I don't understand."

"Don't you? Then you underestimate your own charm."

"None of my friends would agree with you, believe me."

Elisabeth placed her hand along his jawline. "I love you, Tim."

Her words jolted him as though he'd received an electric shock. He could feel his heart racing so fast he wondered if it was going to spin out of control.

"When did you discover that?"

She cocked her head, as though in deep thought. "Oh, a few hours after I walked into Granddad's room and saw you standing there for the first time."

"That soon?"

"That soon. We were sitting together on the sofa in front of the fireplace. You were talking and I was watching you and I realized that now I understood why my mother had chosen to spend her life with my father, despite everything that stood between them."

"So when I suggested that we marry, you agreed because..."

"Because I had no other choice, feeling the way I did."

He rewarded her for her honesty by giving her a very thorough kiss. When he raised his head he was frowning slightly. "Then why did you lie?"

"About what?"

"When I had my memory lapse. Why did you want me to believe that ours was just a pretend marriage?"

Her cheeks pinkened. "You remember differently?"

"Yes. I remember everything that happened between the two of us. No wonder I found myself making love to you in my sleep. No wonder it felt so natural. We had already been together so often. So why lie?"

"I think that at some deep level I don't fully understand, I was trying to protect myself from being hurt. Before I met you, my life had been carefully controlled and choreographed. I was in charge. I knew what I wanted in life, or thought I did—a sense of safety, a haven, a place where I'd be without pain."

"Cemeteries offer such a place, you know."

She reached up and nipped his ear. "Meeting you put me in a tailspin. You didn't give me time to think, to gain control, before we were married and caught up in the whirlwind of our desire for each other."

"And you didn't like that?"

"I was afraid of it. Your losing your memory gave me an opportunity to regroup, to try to regain my sense of self, to come to terms with everything that had happened and to apply some logic to the situation." She ran her fingers along his collarbone, then made a trail across his chest. "Besides, I wanted to give you an out."

"Me? What are you talking about?"

"You were so shocked to see me when you woke up that morning, don't you remember? As though you couldn't conceive of a reason you would wake up in my bed. I felt as though I was seeing the real Tim Walker for the first time, not the man I'd married and been living with. I was getting a true reaction from you because you no longer remembered any promises you might have made to Charlie."

He groaned. "I never made any promises to Charlie where you were concerned."

"You told him you would protect me. That you would take care of me."

"Of course I did. You were my wife when I told him that. I suppose I assumed that you would also protect and take care of me, as well." He touched the back of his head where he'd been hit. "Which you did."

"I just didn't want you to feel obligated to me, that's all. Particularly if you couldn't even remember who I was. I thought if your memory didn't return you would feel free to leave without any complication."

He cupped her breast and gently massaged it. "Do you consider yourself a complication?"

"I didn't want to be." She shifted slightly, moving her legs so he lay between them. "Granddad told me that you never stayed in one place too long and that I would be taking advantage of you if I tied you down and took away your freedom."

"Oh, he did, did he?"

She nodded.

"Maybe I'm ready to be tied down, as you call it. Freedom isn't all it's cracked up to be. I know what it's like to be somewhere and realize that nobody knows... or cares... where you are. There's your ultimate freedom. It's a cold and lonely place, and frankly I'm tired of it. I can think of nothing nicer than to discover that my whereabouts are important to somebody, that there's someone somewhere who is thinking about me, concerned about me, maybe even a little worried if they haven't heard from me."

"Does that mean you're going to stay here with me and not go running off without any explanation like you just did?"

He grinned. "Well, you have to give me a little time to adjust to my new status in life. I'm not going to be able to change overnight."

"Are you going to tell me where you've been?"

He leaned down until his lips were only a fraction of an inch away from hers. "I might be persuaded to talk if I were given the proper incentive."

She raised her head to kiss him, then with a sudden lunge pushed him off balance so he fell back while she scrambled off the bed.

"What was that for?" he asked in an aggrieved tone.

She glanced over her shoulder at him. "You're much too eager to be coaxed, my friend. Besides, our dinner is getting cold."

"How can you think about food at a time like this?" He sat up, pushing his hand through his hair. He was thoroughly aroused, and since he was as bare as the day he was born, his condition could not be overlooked.

Elisabeth was thinking the same thing, but she had scarcely eaten since he'd been gone, and she had to eat now. Besides, Mrs. Brodie would be pulling her hair, trying to keep their meal edible.

She picked up a pair of his jeans and tossed them to him with a grin. "I'll see you downstairs."

Elisabeth waited until halfway through their meal before she brought up the argument they'd had about her career the day he was hurt.

"You mean the discussion we had about your alter ego, Lisa Barry?" he asked.

"Yes. I felt guilty about your being hurt, as though somehow I was at fault because we had argued earlier—" He shook his head at her fractured logic, but she continued. "I also felt a little guilty about telling you our marriage was just pretence—"

"Now that was a totally justified guilt."

"Before Granddad died I finally told him about Lisa Barry and asked his forgiveness for not sharing her with him."

He took her hand. "I'm glad. He deserved to know."

"Yes. I felt very ashamed of myself because he was so pleased for me...surprised, of course...but his pride was apparent. I'm glad you goaded me into telling him before it was too late."

"I am, too."

She studied the man across from her for a moment before she said, "Having you come into my life blasted so many of my ideas and beliefs about myself. It was as though I was really looking at myself for the first time, and not really liking what I saw."

Tim glanced at her plate. "Are you through eating?"

She looked down, surprised to see that her plate was clean. "Why, yes, I suppose I am."

"Good." He pushed away from the table, took her hand and led her out of the dining room. Instead of crossing the foyer to the front room for coffee, he turned toward the stairway.

"Tim, it's not even eight o'clock yet."

"I don't care. I have this very sudden urge to get horizontal. I can't quite remember why. Maybe my memory's slipping again. Perhaps you'd better come with me and make sure I'm all right.''

She shook her head and with a chuckle followed him up the stairway.

Come to think of it, she realized, he had never told her where he and Greg had gone, or why. Maybe she would test her persuasive powers and see how potent they were.

Elisabeth smiled. Perhaps she had found a new career. Being married to Tim would certainly be entertaining and educational. With a protective movement across her stomach she mentally added, *And probably broadening.*

Epilogue

From her vantage point atop a small rise, Elisabeth viewed the never-ending beauty of the mountains that surrounded her home. This little knoll had always been a favorite place for her to come whenever she wanted to be alone with her thoughts for a while.

Today was one of those days.

Bright wildflowers splashed brilliant color across the meadow, and the green of the aspen and birch trees added richness to the scenic panorama spread before her.

She glanced at the envelope she held in her hand. Elisabeth had lost count of the number of times she had read the letter it contained, her last message from her grandfather. Today, the first anniversary of his death, seemed an appropriate time to bring it out once more, as though in some way she could share the serenity and the beauty of the place with him.

The stationery crackled as she removed the expensive sheets of paper from the envelope and stared at the distinctive handwriting that belied his years. He had written it on her wedding day, but had waited until he was gone to have it given to her.

She began to read.

My darling Elisabeth,

Words cannot begin to express the joy I felt today as I gave you in marriage to such a fine young man as Tim Walker. In the years that I have known him, he has impressed me with his quiet integrity, his determination and plain common sense. I had hoped that someday you would find a man worthy of all you have to offer. It is my belief that you have found him. Thank God he immediately recognized and appreciated you for who and what you are...a very special person.

I can rest easy now, knowing that Tim will always be there for you. I know what you told me about not wanting the ranch given to you, so I know you are going to be upset with me when Neil reads the will. Please hear me out before you make any decisions.

Despite all that I have ever accumulated in this life, the homestead has always been where my heart resides. I was born there, all my roots are there, and I would like to think that you and your children will continue to live there down through the years. I have made the necessary arrangements to see that you are given no trouble over this inheritance, and I trust Tim to take care of any unpleasantness that might occur. I know I can count on him to keep both of you safe and secure.

I have always felt that God understood my loneliness, so He sent you to me to add meaning to my life. I always regretted that your father never knew you, and if there's anything to what the churches say about an afterlife, I know that he was pleased I managed to find you and bring you home where you belong.

The only request that I leave with you is to be happy in your newfound love. Give of yourself, for if you do, you will discover as I did that no matter how much you give, you seem to receive double and triple the amount in return. Never be afraid of loving, no matter what happens. Love is what makes everything else in your life worthwhile.

Your loving grandfather

There was a slight sound from somewhere behind her, a rustling of the thick blades of tall grass. She hastily wiped the moisture from her eyes before glancing around. Her eyes lit and she watched Tim striding up the hillside toward her, a baby tucked comfortably into the curve of his arm.

His smile became a laughing grin when he saw her face turned toward him. "Hello, darling. I wouldn't have disturbed you except your daughter can't tell time. I've been trying to explain that she couldn't be hungry yet, that she only ate a short while ago. But she's as stubborn as her mother and refuses to listen to reason.''

He leaned over and carefully placed the baby in Elisabeth's arms before sprawling alongside her in the grass.

Young Jessica left no doubt in anyone's mind what she expected, no, insisted, on having, and Elisabeth unbuttoned her blouse and brought the tiny infant to her breast. Jessica's fretful cry was cut off in midsound, and she began to noisily enjoy her meal.

"What a little pig," Elisabeth muttered with a sigh. "I have trouble picturing us ever making a lady out of her. She wants what she wants when she wants it."

Tim cupped her other breast. "I don't see anything wrong with that philosophy. It's always worked very well for me."

She leaned toward him and gave him a brief kiss, which he returned with enthusiasm. When their lips parted Tim leaned back so Elisabeth could lean against him.

"What a beautiful spot. No wonder you enjoy coming up here."

"Yes. Granddad and I used to come up here and have picnics during the summers I was home. He said he always felt like a king sitting here, the master of all he surveyed."

Tim glanced down and saw the letter lying beside her. He recognized it as the one Neil had given her the day of her grandfather's funeral. She had waited until Jessica's birth to give it to him to read. He had been touched by the sensitivity she had shown in giving it to him then, at a time when he'd felt so inadequate to be all the things Jessica needed in a father.

Charlie had believed in him and Charlie had been an excellent judge of character. He had seen something in Tim that Tim himself wasn't sure existed. All Tim knew was that he would do the best he could to provide the safety and security Elisabeth and Jessica, and any other children they might have, deserved.

He watched his young daughter greedily clutch her mother's breast and smiled, understanding and appreciating her greed.

Elisabeth was his love, even when he hadn't remembered all that they had shared. Somewhere deep inside he had known and recognized her importance in his life and her place in his heart, a love never to be forgotten.

*   *   *   *   *